Cover art and illustrations (copyright © 2011) by Ryan Jones
Author photo by Jillian Saltmarsh

Step One and Step Two *are reprinted from Twelve Steps and Twelve Traditions, page 21 and page 25 respectively, with permission of A.A. World Services, Inc.*

Come away, o human child. With a faery hand in hand. For the world's more full of weeping than you can understand. Quoted from William Butler Yeats, "The Stolen Child", written in 1886.

ISBN: 146355821X
ISBN-13: 9781463558215

To Megan,

L.A. ICE

a novel

With Love & Light,

Kathy

For my mom, Carolyn Moore Ready, who shared with me her love of books and inadvertently turned me into a story-teller. As magical as words are they could never adequately express my love and appreciation—

Kathleen

I didn't set out to be a meth addict. I had dreams, potential, plans…like everyone else

~~*Michael James*

PROLOGUE:
THE CIRCLE OPENS

*L*ast night's dream was still squirming around beneath her skin. She'd seen him again, the same man she had dreamed of recurrently when she was a little girl. His dark eyes were as familiar to Stevie as any she'd seen in flesh and blood, but the rest of him was hard to recall once her conscious mind took over and the dream's details faded into the unknown recesses of her mind. Her angel, that's what she used to call him when she told her mother about him. Each time he led her back home from the lost place her dream had taken her to, the hot sands of the Sahara that scorched the skin of her tiny feet or a dirty city on the other side of the world where people spoke with a mystifying tongue.

She was thirteen when she told her best friend about it, and her friend had said it was like a wedding cake dream, where a slice of cake placed under a pillow gives the dreamer an image of her husband to be. Stevie didn't say so at the time, but she hoped that wasn't the case, not because of the man, but because of the lost feeling she had until he appeared and the separation from him that inevitably occurred. Every time he let go of her hand she immediately awakened with grief squeezing her heart like a python. Until the night before seven years had passed since she last dreamed of him. She was twenty now.

"Stevie," she heard her mother call. Her voice was strained, exhausted.

The sun had just risen and the driveway of her parents' magnificent oceanfront home was still glittering with gold as if tiny pieces of the sun had been left behind to mark her path. She was leaving home. One hand was on the door handle of her little red jeep and the other was in its usual place, clutching a quart bottle of Absolut, the one thing on Earth she could not live without. "Tell Daddy I said..." She flipped her middle finger at her mother, standing desolately in the doorway and her mind took a picture. The photograph she captured was of her mother looking as old and worn as her robe and slippers, peering painfully at her through eyes remarkably similar to her own.

Stevie knew exactly how to file that image so that she wouldn't have to think about it. She brought the bottle to her mouth and swallowed a hot gulp of vodka, then climbed into the jeep. She didn't look back to see if her mother was crying or not as she drove away. Today she had more important things to think about. She was leaving Massachusetts to spend the summer with her cousin in Atlanta. And after that, well, who knew what might happen? Maybe she'd meet a nice southern boy. Her future stretched out in front of her like a motion picture on a wide screen television. A new life— that was what she needed, something so different from her old life that she'd never have to look back, never have to think about all the things that were making her run away.

She took a long drink from the vodka bottle that was snuggled between her thighs like a lover and slid on her Rock & Republic aviators to block the early morning sun. In less than an hour she'd be at the airport in Boston where she would ditch her car and buy an airplane ticket with her father's credit card. She was headed south, not knowing she was about to get exactly what she asked for: A new life and a new love; a new everything.

CHAPTER ONE:
MICHAEL

Through the haze of the remainder of last night's high, he could hear the footsteps of his roommate coming closer. He forced himself to sit up on the couch where he had crashed the night before and combed his fingers through his long dark hair. His eyes fell first on the familiar objects of the apartment: several guitars, a Hendrix poster, his surfboard leaning against a wall, and a half-empty square bottle of Jack Daniels on the coffee table in front of him. He rubbed at his nostrils with his thumb to search for dried blood, and when it came back clean, he allowed his eyes to fall upon the fresh track marks running up the milky whiteness of his left forearm.

Michael James looked younger than he really was which was remarkable given his lifestyle. Maybe it was his big brown eyes that peered suspiciously out at the world through thick black eyelashes or the dimples he revealed on those rare occasions that he smiled wide enough to show them. He would be twenty-two in October, a true-to-his sign beautiful Libra, but he could have passed for a high school student. Even his build was youthful, with a thin waistline and a muscular chest that was branded by the indigo ink of a tattoo—the name of his band— above his left nipple.

"You're late for sound check, man," his roommate, Rob, said upon entering from a back bedroom. "Maybe this'll help." He tossed a small package, not much bigger than a postage stamp, onto the table. Rob's pace never faltered. He exited the apartment without waiting for a response. Had he looked back, he would have seen Michael with one hand barely supporting his head and the other shaking so severely that it could hardly hold onto the hypodermic needle it was clutching.

"All right," Michael said to himself. "All right then."

He tapped his jittery fingers rhythmically on the table, reached for the whiskey bottle and brought it to his mouth. His Adam's apple bobbed erratically as he swallowed the amber liquid and sloshed some of it down his chin and onto his bare chest and belly. He found a t-shirt on the floor and wiped the whiskey off his body before he turned his attention back to the needle. His hands were still shaking too much. He narrowed his eyes in frustration and tossed the needle before opening the tiny package. A small grunt escaped him when he saw the white powder. Instinctively he started to sniff and rub at his nose as he dumped it onto a small mirror and carefully cut it with a razor blade into four exactly symmetrical lines.

He was a different person entirely when he was onstage performing with the methamphetamine coursing like oxygen through his veins. Not a person in the audience could have guessed that without it, he would not have been there. Michael felt like a fraud every time that thought crossed his mind. Still, there was nothing to be done to change it. He had invited the beast into his life and there it remained. There was a time when he was cool and confident on his own, without the speed to amp him, but that was four years ago, back before he started feeding the beast.

A Goth dude in the crowd wearing black eyeliner was offering him a shot. Michael bent at the waist and took it from his hand. The crowd

cheered maniacally as Michael downed it in a gulp. He perceived that
per usual he could gain the crowd's affection quicker by drinking than
by singing or playing his guitar and wondered if they had any idea how
insulting that was. The rule, he figured, went something like this: to
be respected, a musician doesn't have to be great at his instrument as
long as he knows how to *party*. It's the getting wasted that matters.
That's what the crowd can relate to. *Do it* was the chant of the ever-
mindless throng. Michael slapped his hand and now the Goth guy was
the hero, receiving praise from his friends. It was like that—nothing
more than a meaningless chain that went on and on.

The band had a strong rhythm section to back up their front man.
The drummer, a/k/a drug dealer, Rob, never missed a beat. His playing
was flawless for two reasons; he had been playing since he was five years
old and he never got trashed until he stepped off the stage. He was a
Jack Daniels man who knew better than to dabble in the meth he sold
to his friends. He'd seen it all before. Once it went up the nose, it was
only a matter of time before either the pipe or the needle started to look
attractive. And there was no money in that. It was the old adage in a
new skin: never, never mix business with pleasure.

The throb of electric bass started again as the band pummeled into
a new song. Michael grasped the microphone, anticipating the opening lyric, turned and smiled uneasily at the bass player, the only guy
on stage with hair less than an inch long. Matt. He didn't smile back,
but his eyes implored of Michael *are you all right?* Michael, his shirtless body shiny with sweat, threw his head back and spun, breaking eye
contact with Matt, and once again faced the crowd. To the rhythm of
Matt's instrument, he shook his head, his sweat spraying his followers.

Under Matt's father-like gaze, Michael danced deliriously around
the stage and sang into the microphone. When he was high, there was
nowhere else he'd rather be. It was almost like flying into space and

looking back at the planet Earth—maybe what it felt like to die—who knew? People in the crowd looked like faces in a magazine. They weren't real, only people who adored him for what they thought he was, not the real Michael, the one who was shaking too much a little while ago to manipulate a needle into his vein. A bleached blonde up front shrieked and threw onto the stage what looked like a letter with his name on it. Second rule in rock music: if you're a front man, you're *hot*, no matter what you look like, no matter how you behave, and no matter who you really are. Sometimes he'd smile at the women who threw themselves at him, but it never went farther than that. That would shatter the whole illusion. Besides, he had room in his life for only one love now, the one whose name was branded on his chest, close to his heart.

The more he swiped at his nose, the more blood sprayed out of it and stained the couch and carpet. "What, whatizzz this shit?" Michael slurred, staggering barefoot and shirtless around the room like a car in a crash-up derby. His hip made contact with a CD holder that teetered and finally landed, throwing dozens of CDs askew, the sound partially absorbed by the soft carpet.

"Sit down, Michael," Matt said firmly. "I'll get you something for it."

He fell obediently onto the couch as though this was a play they had rehearsed many times before. Matt brought a hand towel from the kitchen and pressed it against his nose.

"You have to stop this shit, you know," he scolded.

Michael grunted and rolled over so he was facing the back of the couch. He pushed Matt's hand away, but the blood was dripping down his cheek now and pooling in his ear. Matt sighed and tried again. This time Michael didn't fight him, not even when he wet the towel in the kitchen with warm water and cleaned his face with it. Afterward, he looked like a little boy with his damp ringlets falling around his face that was pink from Matt scrubbing it. It was a familiar sight to Matt. They'd known each other since they were two years old.

Matt waited until Michael was passed out cold and the blood was stopped before he picked up the phone. He had promised Michael's mother that he would let her know when he was unconscious so that he could be carried to the car without a fight. Matt's head was resting in his hands, dead weight, when the knock startled him. He didn't realize he'd fallen asleep while he was waiting. It had been a long day; first the full time day job, then the gig. "Hang on," he said in a whispered tone, as if his voice full volume might wake up Michael.

In five businesslike steps he was at the door and Mr. James was inside. Matt could not remember a time when he didn't know Mr. James, but even if they had never met there would be no mistaking that he was Michael's dad. Robert James had the same dark brown curls, the same soulful eyes and the same winsome grin. He was a glimpse of Michael in twenty-five years, if Michael somehow miraculously survived. Although it seemed that every physical characteristic was acquired from his father, it was his mother that Michael resembled on the inside. His curiosity, intensity of mind and Matt's favorite—his habit of laughing like a twelve year old with no ability to control it—all came from Mrs. James. But it had been awhile since Michael had laughed like that.

"How'd it go tonight?" Mr. James asked.

Matt shrugged. Same as always.

"Did he give you a hard time?"

"Michael? No. He never gives me a hard time."

"He must save that for us," Mr. James mused and stepped closer to the couch where his son was curled up in the fetal position, sweating and shivering at the same time.

"I'll get him a sweatshirt," Matt offered, then disappeared into a back bedroom to find one. When he returned, Mr. James was on his knees next to the couch, his hand on Michael's head. Matt turned his eyes away. This was always the hardest part for him.

"Michael," his dad said hopefully. Then a little louder, "Michael, can you hear me?" He spent what seemed to Matt like an inordinate amount of time waiting for a response. Matt was tempted to tell him that a bomb could have gone off in the room and Michael wouldn't have heard it, that in fact a fire alarm in the hallway the prior week didn't disturb him. Instead he handed him the sweatshirt and watched him thread Michael's lifeless arms into the sleeves like he was dressing a newborn baby.

When he slid his hands underneath Michael to lift him into his arms, Matt intervened. To watch Michael's dad carry him like that would be more than he could take. "I got him," he said and crouched down to maneuver Michael onto his shoulder. He was lighter than last time, Matt noticed as he straightened into a standing position. Maybe a hundred and forty now, his capable mind quickly calculated. In the past four years, he'd lost close to thirty pounds. Mr. James patted Matt's back. "It'll be all right," he softly suggested.

"Yeah," Matt replied, but he'd never been good at bullshitting. His baby blue eyes were transparent and at the moment were filled with fear and doubt. He quickly turned them away, started walking and didn't break stride all the way down the three flights of apartment stairs and into the parking lot where Mrs. James was waiting outside the family Volvo. She opened the back door and Matt carefully placed Michael in the back seat before he greeted Mrs. James with a familiar embrace. He started to reassure her, but thought twice about offering words of false hope and silently got in the back seat next to his best friend.

They had been traveling for a couple of hours and had almost made it to the drug and alcohol rehabilitation center in Georgia without a hitch. It wasn't too far over the state line from Florida, where they lived. The sound of his teeth grinding against each other should have served as a warning that Michael was about to come to, but Matt was fast asleep and missed the cue. The melodic rhythm of the highway passing under them had lulled him into a dream. They were twelve again, on their dirt bikes. Michael's helmet was off and he was grinning at Matt over his shoulder, his bike five feet from the edge of a deep ravine. "Want me to jump it?" he asked. His words were slow and pronounced.

"No!" Matt yelled, but the hum of Michael's dirt bike kept getting louder and louder. He couldn't scream loud enough for Michael to hear him. Michael turned his back to him and revved the throttle, his feet lifting off the ground. "No, Michael!" Matt shrieked. But he was too late. The exhaust from Michael's dirt bike slapped him in the face as he sped toward the edge. The cold wind licked at Matt's cheeks—but why was the exhaust so cold? Michael was airborne over the ravine, his eyes gazing upward at the sky. He had released the handles and his arms were spread like Jesus Christ on the cross.

Matt awoke with a start. The car door on Michael's side was open—he was trying to escape. The cool early morning air was being sucked into the car like a vacuum and Michael was leaning into it as if it were inviting him to. Mr. James saw it in the rear view mirror and swerved into the breakdown lane. In the second before Michael tumbled out of the car and under its wheels, Matt caught hold of the hood on his sweatshirt. For a frozen moment Michael hovered over the pavement flashing by underneath, almost like he was flying, his arms outstretched, before Matt yanked him back into the car.

But it wasn't over.

He swung his fist at Matt, and clipped him hard under his chin. Matt got a hold of both wrists and gained control over his arms, but his legs were still free. He kicked at Matt with both feet and tried to push his own body closer to the open door. The car came to a stop. Mr. James scrambled quickly out of the driver's seat and into the back.

"Don't let go of him, Matt!" he cried out.

"I won't," Matt answered, determined. He stared straight into Michael's glassy brown eyes that were wild now with the torment of imprisonment. "I won't let go," he repeated forcefully. Michael stared back every bit as fiercely. *I hate you* was in his eyes. *You betrayed me.* Mr. James somehow managed to get on top of Michael and hold his legs motionless while Matt kept his upper body powerless. Then he pulled the door shut behind him. Mrs. James was in the driver's seat now, crying, but waiting for instruction.

"Hit the lock, Elizabeth, and drive." She did. The Volvo screamed down the highway feeling more speed than it ever had in its short life. Michael continued to struggle. His thin body had more strength left in it than either Matt or Mr. James had anticipated. But two strong and healthy men against one sick and nearly emaciated one was no real fight. The car was speeding, trying to navigate onto the exit and the tires screeched.

"Elizabeth, slow down. Get the rehab on the phone. Tell them we need help in the parking lot."

They arrived to find a female nurse and two large men waiting for them. Michael went berserk when he spotted them. As the car slowed to a stop, one hand managed to briefly escape Matt's powerful grasp. Like a wild animal in a trap, his only thought was freedom—he reached for the door handle. Miraculously, the door opened before his hand made contact. A gigantic man stood in the doorway between Michael and freedom, peering in at him through Coke bottle glasses. "Take it easy," the behemoth said with his voice unexpectedly soft. "We won't hurt you." Then he turned his eyes to Mrs. James. "Do you have the paperwork?"

"The judge gave us sixty days," Mr. James interjected. "Papers are on the front seat."

Michael caught a glimpse of his mother, sobbing helplessly and trying to gather the forms. He attacked the only way he knew how. "Don't do this. Don't do this, Mom. Please. Please, don't. I'm asking you to please just, please take me home. Mom, take me home." Mrs. James hung her head. She couldn't look at him, her baby begging for help. How could she look in his eyes and turn her back on him?

"Mrs. James," the big man intervened. "If you take him home, he won't have a chance. Let us see if we can give him one." Mrs. James nodded her weepy head and handed him the papers. "I'm John," he continued. "I'll be Michael's counselor." John quickly perused the papers for the judge's signature and tucked them in his shirt pocket before he hand motioned the nurse with the hypodermic needle to come closer. He held Michael securely, and with the assistance of Matt and Mr. James, managed to flip him onto his belly and pull his jeans down in the back.

"I won't forgive you Matt!" Michael shouted as the nurse jabbed the needle into his buttocks. "Do you hear me? I won't forgive you." And then he was unconscious again.

CHAPTER TWO:
STEVIE

Sleep had fallen like a dark cloak around her last night once things quieted down. And now her eyelids were stuck together like they'd been super glued, sleep still beckoning to her like a deep, silent forest she could hide in. But someone was singing in a throaty female voice, *Amazing Grace how sweet the sound*, amidst the clang of dishes and silver ware. Stevie groaned. It was her first day in rehab. The air didn't smell like urine and vomit like she'd thought it would, but she hadn't expected the Jesus songs either. She managed to ply one eyelid open. An overweight woman with skin as smooth and brown as milk chocolate and a voice like church bells was preparing a small table with her breakfast. The food looked so appealing it was worth the effort to open her other eye.

She sat up in the hospital bed and tried to drag her fingers through the tangled mess that was her hair.

"Good morning, Stephanie," the woman said. "I'm Louisa May. My friends call me Louise." She didn't seem to mind that Stevie didn't respond. She gave her a smile as sweet as the maple syrup Stevie could smell coming from the table and went back to her song, humming it this time. It sounded just as pretty without the words.

Stevie assessed her surroundings. There was no door to her room, only a doorway so it could remain eternally open. Same for the windows that looked out into the hallway—there were no shades or curtains so she could be watched like a lab rat. Making sure she didn't hang herself, she guessed. A nurse's station was within view and an old woman was walking around it steadily as if someone was making her propel by remote control. Her matted hair and skin that was badly scarred by broken blood vessels made her look like a street person. The only saving grace was the new furry robe and flannel slippers she was clothed in. Someone somewhere loved her. Someone must have loved her enough to buy her new clothes. She didn't look capable of buying them for herself.

Sixty days. For sixty days she had to stay here. Who ever heard of going sixty days without a drink? Not even normal people did that. But she had to stay here now. Her parents wouldn't let her come back home after her stint in the Atlanta hospital for alcohol poisoning. The familiar combination of nausea and shame rose inside her like water over a sinking ship every time she thought about that day, when she'd awakened in a drunken fog with her bare feet dirty and bloody as if she'd been walking on broken glass, and an intravenous needle stuck in her arm. The Phenobarbital, they had told her, was keeping her from having an alcoholic seizure. But it wasn't the sickness or the battle wounds that hurt the most. It was her parents' refusal to help her. *Not this time* they'd said. They had relayed the message to her through the recovering alcoholic doctor at the hospital, Dr. Tom. He was the guy who took care of her for three days, had cared for her in a way that her own father never had, even though she was a stranger to him. Her father was too busy being pissed off because she had once again tainted the precious family name.

How convenient that she was a thousand miles away. No one had to know.

It was a conundrum to her. Did her parents actually think that she *wanted* to be an alcoholic, that she was deliberately choosing drunkenness over social drinking just to scorn them? Maybe they thought that if they shamed her into feeling bad enough about herself she would change, like alcoholism was something that could be degraded out of her body, like when people used to use sticks to beat mental illnesses out of patients.

Drunk, druggie, boozer, lush, burnout, freak. Whore.

She wasn't even old enough to drink legally and already she had been called more names than she could remember by the people who had come and gone in her life (but mostly gone). Why couldn't anyone see what was so clear to her, that nothing could change her into anything other than what she was? It was like trying to change a television channel with a defective remote control. She was the station...stuck. No matter how many times the button got pushed, there she would be, the same old Stevie. Same old screw up.

Louise was removing the silver covers from all the plates of food and the old lady was still circling the nurse's station like a robot: no smile, no frown, no indication anyone was residing inside her body; only a blank stare and the monotonous step after step after step after step. "That lady walking the track out there, is she the one that was screaming last night?" Stevie inquired.

Louise breathed out a compassionate sigh. "That's Barbara. She's a little confused."

"You think? She scared the crap out of me. I just got to sleep when she started wailing like someone was slitting her throat."

"I'm sure it wasn't that bad," Louise replied. "Would you like coffee?"

Stevie nodded at the coffee question. "Regular," she instructed. Louise looked up. "With cream and sugar." Down south they didn't seem to use that term, "regular". Maybe they were lightweights when it came to coffee, but they weren't lightweights when it came to Jack

15

Daniels or cocaine. She'd found that out the hard way. She'd rather have God strike her dead than party with those good ol' Atlanta boys again. "It *was* that bad," she argued. "It was like trying to sleep in an insane asylum. And that nurse, Julie, kept coming in to take my blood pressure."

Louise handed Stevie her coffee. She was a wise soul who knew only to fill it half way or Stevie's shaky hands would spill it. That was the kind of wisdom that came from working detox. "Give it time, you'll be good friends," she suggested.

Stevie snorted condescendingly like the spoiled brat that she was. "With Julie? I don't think so. I don't need friends here, anyway. I only need sixty days to pass so I can go home."

"Mm hm," Louise hummed right into the song still pouring from her.

Stevie sighed. She wanted to eat breakfast. Her stomach was growling like a watchdog, and even the bowl of white mush, whatever it was, looked appetizing. There was a fat wad of butter melting into it. She had almost forgotten what it felt like not to be hung over in the morning and to have an appetite. The problem was she had to go to the bathroom first. "Do you have to watch me pee?" she asked with her head resting childishly on one hand. The night before when she was admitted Julie had stayed in the bathroom with her so she wouldn't mix water with the urine. No tampering with the drug testing. It was humiliating, and it took her about half an hour to get the pee out with Julie standing right there staring at her and the plastic cup squeezed between her legs.

Louise boomed out a great big grandmother-like laugh. "Not to-day, darlin'," she answered with her face shiny and cheerful, shaking her head side to side. She was nice, and maybe funny. Stevie didn't want to like her. She didn't want to like anyone in the place, but she couldn't help it. She liked Louise enough to light a cigarette in front of her. And that said a lot. It was a struggle now because of her hands. Her body was rebelling against the absence of alcohol. Even with the Phenobarbital they were still feeding her to counteract it, her hands shook like a washing machine on spin cycle.

She could get the cigarette to her lips; the hard part was keeping the lighter on the end of it long enough for it to catch. This time it did without too much trouble. She took a deep drag, breathing in the soothing nicotine. "Who's that guy?" she asked and nodded her head toward a man standing outside her door. He was in his mid-thirties and was wearing jeans and sneakers, but had a stethoscope around his neck. He seemed to be watching her with his peripheral vision while talking to a nurse at the same time.

"That gentleman right there?" Louise asked and turned her lovely teardrop-shaped eyes onto Stevie. They reminded her of cow's eyes, all peace and tranquility and not a trace of aggression. Stevie nodded once, barely, like she could hardly be bothered. "You haven't met Dr. Jim?"

"Haven't had the pleasure," Stevie answered snidely and blew smoke out her nostrils. She didn't even mean to cop an attitude. Sometimes derisive comments shot out of her mouth like a rattlesnake, without even warning *her* they were coming.

Louise's formerly gentle cow eyes were now the enraged eyes of a bull. Her glare was almost scarier than the concept of being locked up without alcohol or drugs for sixty days. Stevie tensed up so much she actually bit the cigarette. "Dr. Jim is a good man," Louise said slowly, terrifyingly. "You understand?"

"Yeah," Stevie grumbled with her tomboyish voice. Holy shit. Talk about saying the wrong thing. She started to add *sorry*, but was too scared to open her mouth.

"He saved my life, Dr. Jim," Louise added and her voice was all sticky like she was about to cry, but then she started humming the church song again. The bull eyes were going away, weirdly morphing back into cow eyes. By now all the silver covers were off the plates of food. "You better get moving. Your first twelve-step meeting is in half an hour. You'll get to meet John." An insider's chuckle gurgled from her throat.

Stevie narrowed her eyes. What exactly was Louise implying with that mad scientist cackle? She started to ask, but decided not to run the risk of offending her again. With her luck, she'd say John saved her life too. "What do people wear to twelve-step meetings?" she asked instead.

"Anything they want," Louise replied and gave her a smile as warm as the butter melting on her breakfast plate, as if she were never really angry at all. "I'll see you at lunch, Stephanie," she added, and headed out the door.

"Wait," Stevie said urgently.

"What's the matter? You need help picking out your clothes, a big girl like you?"

"Very funny," Stevie huffed and rolled her eyes arrogantly at the woman who was at the moment her only friend on the planet. "I just wanted to know what that white stuff is…in the bowl." She pointed a long slender finger toward the tray of food.

Louise laughed like it was the funniest thing she'd ever heard, bent over and slapped her chubby knees even. "That's grits, honey, don't you know that?" Stevie started to answer that she'd never had the pleasure but quickly bit her tongue. The next line Louise sang as if it was the last line of the gospel song bubbling out of her. "It's going to be an interestin' two months." Then she left, still singing… and laughing.

What had she gotten herself into? Georgia was like a different universe. *Two months?* She'd never make it. She slid her legs over the side of the bed and touched her feet deftly on the floor. She knew better than to rise quickly. She tried that once when she was still in the hospital and landed on her face. That Phenobarbital was tricky stuff. It occurred to her that she probably looked like the old lady lap walker the way her feet moved so slowly and carefully into the bathroom.

When she closed the door behind her, she was confronted by something she hadn't anticipated, her own reflection in the mirror that did not remotely resemble the fresh young face that used to belong to her. It hadn't changed overnight, of course, but that's one of the things about getting sober. You start to see things the way they really are, not the way you've imagined them to be.

"What the fuck?" she said to the face in the mirror. "What the fuck happened to you?" She stared into her own intelligent green eyes, the only part of her that she recognized. Her face was swollen like a melon and her skin that used to be fair and flawless was covered in angry red blotches. Even her mouth looked distorted. It was like a Picasso portrait; nothing added up. She didn't have any tears to cry. She wished she did so she could weep over her own self-annihilation, but that faculty had been lost somehow. It went away with her ability to feel.

Stevie allowed the cigarette to fall from her lips into the toilet. It hit the water with a hiss that sounded more alive than she felt. She promised herself that she would not look in a mirror again for quite some time. It was too devastating to her psyche.

She had a pair of True Religion jeans that she had pretty much lived in for the last three weeks since she left Massachusetts. Now they felt like home, so she slid them on her long legs and threw on a vintage concert t-shirt, Van Halen tour 1981. Her hair she couldn't cover up as easily as her body so she pulled it into a ponytail without using a brush or looking in the mirror. Pieces stuck out like barbed wire. This was as close to being ready as she was going to get. She had all the essentials: a pair of worn black flip-flops, a full pack of Marlboros and a lighter. On second thought, she picked up a hot pink notebook off the small table that held the remains of her breakfast. She had devoured almost all of it, even the grits that felt like rabbit pellets on her tongue.

Don't hesitate, she told herself when she reached the small lounge in the detox unit. She walked straight in without making eye contact with the five or six patients eating their breakfasts and claimed a seat at an empty table. The room smelled like coffee and freshly baked blueberry muffins and looked like a hospital waiting room, but cozier. There was upholstered furniture and framed paintings on the walls. Stevie opened the pink notebook that Dr. Tom at the hospital had given her and scribbled the date: June 29, 2008. He had suggested that it might help her to keep a journal. She liked the idea. And she could use it to write her poetry. Besides, she was hoping it would make the other patients nervous enough to stay away from her...like a hot pink wall.

So much for that theory; the chair across from her screeched across the floor as a guy in his early twenties fell into it and then stared at her until she looked up. A pair of interesting eyes, one deep brown and the other a placid blue, confronted her. She had never seen eyes like that on a human being. In fact, she'd only seen eyes like that once in her entire life, on a dog that lived down the street when she was a little girl. That was the same dog that bit her brother Scott and caused her father to threaten yet another lawsuit.

"I'm David," the guy said gruffly and didn't wait for her to introduce herself before he got to his real reason for talking to her. "Are you an alcoholic or a drug addict?"

Good question. If it weren't multiple choice and she could make up her own word, it would be "chemist". She was very good at using exactly the right amount of speed or cocaine to counteract the overdose of alcohol that was used to counteract the anxiety that came from too much speed or cocaine. And so on. "Alcoholic," she tried to say, but it was like the word had legs of its own and it tripped and fell off her tongue. It sounded something like *alcoooooholic-c-c*. Jesus freaking Christ. Why did she have to talk to anyone at all? She would have holed up in her room if she knew how to get to the step meeting. Her plan was to follow the other patients from a distance, like a stalker.

David blasted out a laugh. It wasn't an affectionate, empathetic laugh. It was the guy on the playground who pointed at the kid who fell and bloodied his knee—that laugh; the kind that made your face turn red before you could stop it. "Yeah, me too," he finally said and nodded his head enthusiastically like he was proud of it. "Since you're not coming off drugs, they'll probably only keep you here a few days."

"Yeah, and then what?" she asked.

"Then you go over to the rehab side. It's supposed to be good over there. We get our own rooms with a bathroom and a queen-sized bed. And there's a game room."

"Hm," she muttered, processing it. "Why don't we go over right away?"

"There are doctors and nurses here in detox all the time in case one of us has a seizure or something. And they don't want to move us until we don't need the meds anymore. It's a waiting place, I guess." He shrugged.

"Like Purgatory," she said quietly.

He grunted a full-blown pig snort. "Yeah, like Purgatory. We've got to get to the step meeting. Want me to show you where it is?"

Stevie fabricated a receptive expression on her face and nodded. (Alcoholism breeds great actors.) Even though David had perhaps the most beautiful eyes she had ever seen and a crop of thick black hair that made his eyes stand out so much that they were impossible not to stare at, she hated him. *I won't tell him anything,* she told herself.

"How'd you wind up here, anyway?"

She clenched her jaw tight, unflinching. *I went out drinking with some good ol' boys and my cousin found me passed out on the sidewalk in Atlanta* passed silently through her mind. *And apparently I was raped—again— because my clothes were torn.* She blinked her emerald green eyes, pushing the thoughts back down deep, deep into the abscessed pool of her mind that held all the rest of the crud she never wanted to think about again.

David got tired of waiting for her response. "So, what's your name then?" he asked.

"Stevie Gates." *And no, my mother wasn't a Fleetwood Mac fan,* she thought but didn't have to voice. David, unlike most people, didn't ask.

"I never heard that name before, not for a girl."

"It's short for Stephanie."

"Stevie," he spit out like a dirty word. "We better get going. Trust me you don't want to be late for one of John's step meetings." He abruptly walked off and she followed him like a lost lamb, too scared to ask why.

CHAPTER THREE:
PURGATORY

The chairs with built-in desktops had been placed in the shape of a circle, about forty in total, and the same hardcover sky blue book was resting on each one. From where she stood in the doorway, Stevie couldn't quite make out the title that was depicted in white letters, but she didn't waste much time on it. She was too intrigued by the cluster of people already seated. It was the oddest conglomeration of human beings she had ever seen in one room. They ranged in age from pre-teen to elderly, and if not for the different skin colors, they might have passed for family members, so comfortable they appeared in each other's presence. Most of them were chatting and carrying on as if it were the most normal thing on Earth to be sitting in a classroom filled with alcoholics and drug addicts.

David didn't hesitate at the door like Stevie did. He walked right in and claimed a seat without another glance in her direction. Where should she sit? Her heart felt like it was pumping erratically and she was starting to sweat. A slight tap on her shoulder made her jump. The petite teenage girl responsible for it giggled at her response.

"You're new, right?" the girl asked. Her pixie haircut, fawn-like eyes and tiny frame combined to create the impression of a fairy. Stevie liked her immediately. "You can sit with me if you want," she offered when Stevie finally nodded, "I'm Allison."

Stevie followed her to the only two seats left side by side. She was relieved to have someone to sit with, but was so nervous she couldn't think of anything to say. A cigarette would fill the awkward space. She pulled one from the red pack, trying not to let the plastic covering make a sound that would attract attention to her. When it was secure between her lips, she tried to light it, but the God damned thing kept jerking out of the flame before it could ignite. What was she thinking trying to light a cigarette in front of a room full of people? She imagined they were all staring at her, panicked and the cigarette fell like a traitor from her mouth. She stared down at it, afraid to look up.

With her peripheral vision she saw Allison's little hand venture toward her desk. She took the cigarette and lit it, then handed it back and shrugged casually. *No big deal* she seemed to imply. Stevie gave her as much of a smile as she could muster and took a deep drag. Now she could try to relax. A step meeting, what the hell was a step meeting?

A hush fell over the room. An enormous man, resembling a professional linebacker, stood in the doorway. In his charge was a guy about Stevie's age with hair and eyes the color of fresh brewed coffee, but skin as fair as hers. He looked like he just fell out of bed, his hair a nest of messy curls and his eyes only half open. A lit cigarette dangled recklessly from his beautiful mouth. Stevie realized she was staring at him and looked down. She had forgotten about her cigarette and the ashes were spilling onto the book on her desk. The words *Twelve Steps and Twelve Traditions* were now smudged with gray.

"Find a seat, Michael," the linebacker ordered.

The guy looked like he was too tired to put up a fight. He ran a hand languidly through his long hair while his big brown eyes moved defiantly around the circle of faces. When they fell on Stevie, his eyes narrowed and they stayed there for a prolonged moment like he was opening up a window and looking inside her. Then something astonishing happened—he grinned at her and unleashed dimples that made him look like an entirely different person, softer and sweeter. Stevie didn't smile back. She was too stunned. She couldn't imagine why a guy like that was smiling at her. Allison elbowed her, but it was too late. He turned away and took fluid-like steps across the circle.

She shared an infatuated glance with Allison. "Oh my God," Allison mouthed and Stevie very nearly burst into nervous giggles that she was sure would have resonated as hysteria. Her heart was pounding so hard she felt like the rest of the people in the room could hear it or at least see it thumping through her shirt. *Michael. Michael*, she thought as she watched him drop into the seat next to David. She had always liked that name.

Michael's keeper took the last empty seat in the circle and rapped his knuckles on the desk as if he needed to do so to get the group's attention. "My name is John and I'm an addict," he announced. "Today we'll discuss Step One in the program of Alcoholics Anonymous: *We admitted we were powerless over alcohol, that our lives had become unmanageable.* Some of you might think this doesn't apply to you. If you listen long enough, you'll find out it does."

Michael smashed his cigarette out, laid his head down on the desktop and closed his eyes. A giggle gurgled out of the prepubescent kid with big round blue eyes sitting on the other side of him. John glared at him for a tense moment. The kid straightened up in his seat and put on an innocent face as quickly as if he had pulled a mask from a drawer.

"Jake. You with me?"

Jake wriggled uneasily in his seat and with a jerk of his head shook his unruly golden hair off his face. To Stevie, he looked more like he belonged on a surfboard than in a drug rehab, a California boy. But he was nothing close to that. He was a ward of the state of Georgia, a foster kid in between homes. "Uh huh," he answered.

Still John didn't take his eyes off of him. "Excuse me?" he said sternly.

"I'm with you John," Jake offered with a soft southern drawl. Even Stevie exhaled relief when John finally turned his eyes away from him and continued his lecture.

"If you're anything like I was when I was a patient here, you might be sitting there wondering if you're really an alcoholic. Maybe you think being here is all a big mistake or someone else's fault. Well, folks, I'm here to tell you this: If you're in this room, it's because you've earned your seat. No one ends up in rehab by mistake. Now, if you want to learn how to stop using and stay stopped, keep your ears open and your mouth shut until it's your turn to speak. We'll read this chapter out loud a paragraph at a time then go around the room again until everyone has had a turn to talk about it."

Okay, so now she understood what a step meeting was. And now she had to think of a way to escape. The grainy grits in her stomach stirred threateningly at the thought of speaking in front of the group. She quickly formulated a plan—she'd go to the ladies' room and take her sweet time getting back. Someone beat her to the punch and raised her hand. It was the elderly woman who was walking laps around the nurse's station earlier, still wearing her robe and slippers. She told John she had a headache and asked for permission to go to her room. He shot her down and told her to read the first paragraph.

Apparently it wasn't her first step meeting because she knew exactly what to do. She introduced herself as "Barbara, alcoholic," then held the book to her puffy face and read out loud, one eye twitching like she was having a stroke. It was too much to think about—the possibility of the old lady having a stroke and the unintelligible words she was muttering. Only five days had passed since Stevie arrived in the hospital emergency room with alcohol poisoning, and the drug fog in her brain still hadn't lifted. But at least now she could remember the last time she showered and brushed her teeth. She had even changed her clothes every day, but sometimes the nurses had to remind her. For the past six months or so, hygiene had dropped on her priority list to somewhere below preventing DTs and alcoholic seizures. It was degrading having to learn all over again how to take care of herself. She ventured a glance at the dark-haired guy, asleep now. If he knew how messed up she was, he never would have smiled at her.

Barbara stopped reading, but that over-enthusiastic eye of hers kept moving as if it had a will of its own. The guy sitting next to her picked up the ball. He was about thirty years old with sunburn-red skin, a mustache like the Marlboro man and a thick accent. Stevie imagined him arriving at the rehab on a horse, and it made her grin, even more so when she noticed his boots, carved out along the sides with fancy swirls. Only the spurs were missing. After a few sentences, John interrupted him and addressed the group.

"If you're a drug addict, don't feel left out. Everything in this book applies to you, too. We don't discriminate. Alcohol is just another drug, like cocaine or heroin. And for all of you who got here from drinking, don't be thinking that once you've done your time here you can go home and get away with smoking weed or taking pills. How many of you have thought about that?"

Through thick glasses that made his eyes look frighteningly tiny, he peered around the circle. More than a few people were smirking. "Yeah, I thought so," he added. "Go off the booze and you'll be fine, right? *Wrong.* A drug is a drug is a drug. It's all the same thing. Addiction is about doing whatever we can to change the way we feel. The first step is putting down the substances. Then it gets really tricky. Then we have to learn how to live in our own skin without picking them back up."

Stevie looked down to avoid his penetrating eyes. She was trans-
lucent, she was sure, and John, the gargantuan, was talking to her.
Somehow he knew she had been thinking that she could smoke weed
when she got out. It was alcohol she had trouble with. She couldn't
seem to stop herself from pouring drink after drink into her body, even
after she was totally smashed. That's how she ended up with alcohol
poisoning, and it wasn't the first time. But why not weed? She'd never
been wasted on that, only sort of...mellow.

John was still seeing through her and answered her question. "Any
substance you put in your body will eventually lead you back to your
drug of choice," he said, then nodded at the Marlboro man to prompt
him to read. Holy shit; it was creepy the way he did that.

The little boy, Jake, was reading now, struggling with almost every
word like he was in first grade. His finger pointed to each word before
he said it out loud. Stevie wanted to take the book out of his hand
and read it for him. When he finished, it was Michael's turn, but John
skipped right over him to David. She noticed that no one else seemed
surprised by that, not even David who was already reading. John didn't
strike her as the kind of guy who would let anyone off the hook. When
it was her turn, she stammered at first, but quickly grounded herself.
She was the only person so far who was able to read every word without sounding them out. Attending the best high school in an upper
middle class Massachusetts town saw to that. It was the first time she
was actually aware of it, the contrast between her privileged life and the
not-so-privileged life of others.

A strange thing happened when time ran out and the meeting ended.
Everyone in the room stood up and held hands. When Michael didn't
voluntarily join in, John lifted him out of his seat by the back of his
worn jean jacket. He didn't seem embarrassed or self-conscious about
it. He just stood up straight without making eye contact with anyone

and held his hands out, waiting for someone to hold them. Then he closed his sleepy brown eyes again. It allowed Stevie the opportunity to look at him without him knowing it. He was tall, about six feet, and had a slender body, but a broad chest and shoulders. His dark brown curls fell loosely around his face and halfway down his neck. And he had the thickest black eyelashes, like little boys sometimes have but inexplicably seem to lose before they're grown men. Beautiful. That's how he looked to her, beautiful and sad.

When the circle was fully connected, everyone chanted the Lord's Prayer together. The words felt bigger and more powerful because of the numerous voices and their variations, almost like church but without the fear. Stevie knew the words. They were hammered into her as a child, but time had made them foreign to her, like something she had observed at a primitive ritual in a past life or heard in a dream. It felt like the rhythm of voices was under her feet, making the floor vibrate. She was the only one with her eyes open. Stevie looked around and noticed something: She was one of the pieces. She was part of the chain. For some reason it strengthened her to know that, even if she was only connected momentarily. Her eyes closed and for the first time in longer than she could remember, she bowed her head and prayed.

That night she ate dinner with Allison, David and a patient named Liz, a woman in her early thirties who looked anemic with mousy hair that fell halfway down her back, ashen skin and black circles underneath her dishwater gray eyes. Stevie conjectured that she looked sickly because she didn't eat anything of substance. She was picking at a salad with no dressing and a side plate of sliced apples. Stevie had a friend in junior high who fed the exact same food to her giant iguana. Its pallor wasn't that different from Liz's.

Now her watery gray eyes were focused on David. "Who was the guy you were sitting with at the step meeting?" she asked and bit into an apple slice.

"I wasn't sitting with anyone," he snapped without taking his attention away from his meatloaf and potatoes. One arm circled around his plate like he was guarding it, much like a dog with its dish. Stevie wondered if he'd growl if she moved a hand closer to it.

"The guy John brought in," she ventured. "He sat right next to you."

"The one with the dimples," Allison added as she pushed her plate out of the way and opened a bottle of bright pink nail polish.

"They let us use nail polish?" Liz asked her.

"Yeah, but not nail polish *remover*." She shrugged. "We could drink it."

David's beguiling eyes focused intensely on Allison. "You mean the guy you and Stevie were staring at?"

"I wasn't staring at him," Stevie asserted.

"You were staring at him," David repeated as if there was no room for argument and put his fork down. "He's drug scum. Trust me; you don't want to know him."

"He doesn't look like…that," Stevie weakly rebutted.

"More like an angel," Allison crooned and blew gently on her wet nails.

David snickered. "That guy's no angel. He's into ice."

Allison and Stevie exchanged a questioning glance, but Julie, the nurse, entered the room and approached the group with her infamous blood pressure cuff before David could respond. He held his arm out so she could attach it to him without bothering to greet her, and shot his mouth off again. "You know methamphetamine?"

"A speed freak," Allison said to Stevie with the air of someone three times her age.

"Yeah," David agreed. "That's what they call it: ice or L.A. ice. Last rehab I was in, my roommate was a meth addict, a violent bastard. He grabbed someone by the throat."

"So you're assuming the guy at the step meeting's like that?" Liz asked with no inflection in her voice whatsoever, like the talking dead, or an interviewer on talk radio.

"They're *all* like that."

Pfffff the blood pressure cuff sighed as it released air and Julie detached it from his arm. "Are you talking about Michael?" she interjected. David made a sound that was remarkably similar to the blood pressure cuff exhaling. Acting annoyed was one of the things he did best, Stevie had noticed.

"The *meth head*. The guy that was strapped in his bed until today."

Stevie gasped then covered her mouth with her hand a second too late to masquerade her reaction. The expression in Julie's eyes seemed like a mirror of her own feelings. With his reckless words David had conjured images of psychiatric patients, like the ones in *The Bell Jar* and *One Flew Over the Cuckoo's Nest*.

"Maybe get to know him before you say things like that," Julie suggested. "Michael's a good guy."

"A good guy? You're kidding, right?" David scoffed. "He's a filthy meth addict."

Stevie racked her brain. What did she know about meth? She had snorted it a few times in high school. The guy she bought it from called it crystal meth. He said it was no big deal, like diet pills. It did feel that way, like uppers—only faster—and she could drink all night on it without passing out. It served her purpose well, like the cocaine did; it kept her from losing control or passing out. But it was hard to come by where she lived. Had it been readily available, by now she might be a "meth head" herself.

She watched Julie attach the cuff to Liz and vigorously squeeze the pump. She could tell by her terse movements that she was angry at David's comments. "He's no different from you," she finally said.

David laughed at her preposterous suggestion. With the collar flipped up on his Abercrombie polo shirt, he reminded Stevie of a student council president slamming the "dirtballs" of the school into the ground. And he wasn't finished.

"I guess nothing else matters because you like his face—"

"And his body," Allison quickly threw in. "Did you see the way he walks?"

Liz burst out laughing at Allison's observation and at how animated her face was when she said it, like Michael's walk was the eighth wonder of the world. It was a strange sight, Liz suddenly coming to life like that, similar to watching a magician's scarf transform into a bird. Julie grinned a little, too, before she moved the cuff over to Allison's tiny arm.

"He is awfully cute," she agreed.

"I'm not judging him because he's into meth...or ice or whatever," Stevie said to David. For some unidentifiable reason, she felt the need to defend this stranger, the one who made her forget to breathe every time she thought about him. "I've done it."

"What'd you do snort it, rich girl?" David snarled. "Because there wasn't any coke around? The meth head boots it. He's got tracks up and down his arms. But who gives a fuck if he's a street junkie, right? As long as he looks like an angel."

CHAPTER FOUR:

POWERLESS

The sign on the door read *But for the Grace of God*. Stevie's hand lingered momentarily on the door handle. It seemed like a perverted joke to her that those particular words adorned a meeting room where sick women convened to talk about their addictions. Her eyes scanned the small circle of women inside the door. Out of the people she knew, there was Barbara, the lap-walking elderly woman who looked like a bag lady with broken blood vessels spreading like tree roots on her nose from so many years of alcohol infesting her body, and Liz who had tried dozens of times to get sober so that she could be what was expected of her, a normal wife and mother. Every time Stevie looked into Liz's dull, lifeless eyes she got the impression that alcohol had eaten her from the inside out so that only a husk was left. Her closest friend in the circle was Allison who at seventeen had already lived on the streets.

What grace of God?

Today there was a new patient in the small group of female detox patients. She was dressed like a punk with magenta hair and body piercings, three on her face alone, and was wearing what appeared to Stevie to be an exorbitant amount of black liquid eyeliner. Her black t-shirt bearing the blood-red word *Rancid* was cut short enough to allow her soft white belly to hang out of it. She was trying to look fierce, glaring at anyone who dared to glance in her direction. It seemed to her that of all the women in the group, the punk girl's defenses were the most obvious. She was so terrified that she had built walls painted magenta and black to hide behind. It might have worked out in the real world, but not in a drug rehab. Every woman in the place was an expert at constructing fortresses. They just disguised theirs differently, like Barbara in her robe and slippers. (Maybe if she looked like a typical grandmother/housewife, everyone would treat her like one.)

"Take a seat, Stephanie," the bulldoggish counselor, Ellen, ordered. "And be on time from now on." Stevie plopped down between Liz and Allison and avoided her eyes.

Ellen was her counselor, an addict too, but clean for something like a million years. For this reason, Stevie found she could get little past her. "You can't bullshit a bull shitter," Ellen said every time she tried. At only 5'4" with yellow hair out of a box and too much makeup, she was tougher than she looked. She was the first person in Stevie's life that stopped her from getting what she wanted, and already she resented her for it.

The deal on women's group was that patients could voluntarily share whatever was on their minds. Only nobody really wanted to share, at least not while they were still on the detox wing. It was all most of them could do to communicate with each other one on one, especially with all the Phenobarbital swimming through their blood streams. Every day it was the same gig. They all avoided Ellen's eyes until someone finally broke down. Today it was the punk girl who couldn't stand the pressure—so much for the unbreakable facade. She raised a milky white hand. The black polish made her nails look like claws.

"I'm Melanie, an addict. I got here last night."

"You've been here before, though?" Ellen's French manicured nails tapped the desk.

"Yeah. Last time you said I should open my mouth to save my ass. So, that's what I'm doing." Ellen nodded, but didn't comment.

Melanie looked like she had no intention of saying anything else, but Ellen's hand gestured *keep going*.

"Uh, my dad dumped me here 'cause I came home high and I was s'posed to baby sit my little sister." When Ellen still didn't turn away, Melanie flipped her hand over with the palm facing the ceiling like a waitress without a tray and snorted disgust through her nostrils instead of responding with words. This was a *telepathic* punk.

Ellen paid no heed to her theatrics. "What's your drug of choice?" she asked.

Melanie thought it over and only came up with a shrug. "I like 'em all," she admitted.

The entire group burst out laughing. It was an honest response they could all identify with on some level. Melanie's Snow White-like cheeks turned bright pink and she laid her head down on the desk. Apparently she thought they were laughing *at* her.

Allison raised her hand. It was the first time Stevie had seen her do so. It took Ellen about twenty seconds to let go of her visual grip on Melanie and hone in on Allison. "I'm Allison and I'm *not* an addict—" And all of two seconds to cut her off.

"Then maybe we should hear from someone who is," she said. Allison's mouth dropped as Ellen's attention turned to Stevie. "How about you, Stephanie, why are you here?" Melanie lifted her head to watch. She must have sensed the looming execution.

"It's Stevie." She cleared her throat. "Because I…drink too much?" The lilting question mark at the end of her statement no doubt cued Ellen in on her lack of intent to say anything real, anything honest.

"So, are you an alcoholic?" Way too slowly; way too nice.

Stevie budged one shoulder. Of course she was an alcoholic. She couldn't remember a time when there was even a question of it in her own mind. She'd known since she was fourteen or fifteen and was the only girl in her group who thought it was a good idea to get a good buzz on before school on a regular basis. It wasn't denial that was keeping her from admitting it. It was a way of blocking Ellen from digging any deeper below the surface, a monkey wrench.

"You started detoxing at a hospital. So, it's been more than a week, right?"

"I guess."

"You guess. You've been taking Phenobarbital all that time, is that right?"

Stevie barely nodded her head and narrowed her vibrantly green eyes that were preternaturally alert now, like an animal's when it's being hunted. Ellen had cornered her before, but never in front of the group. Stevie was capable of being articulate—that comes naturally to daughters of lawyers—but she wasn't sure she was strong enough or vigilant enough to hold Ellen off, to protect herself.

"Do you think that would be necessary if you weren't an alcoholic?"

Of all the eloquent words available to her, *fuck you* passed through her mind. "I'm not a doctor," spit from her mouth.

"I'm not sure you need to be a doctor to answer the question. Let me ask it this way: Do you know what would have happened to you if you hadn't taken the Phenobarbital?"

In the vile stillness that seemed to be suffocating her, choking every last bit of clean air out of her lungs, Stevie looked down at her jittery hands with the still broken and grimy fingernails. She hated Ellen for exposing her and she hated the women in the circle for hearing it. "I could have had a seizure," she surrendered.

"An *alcoholic* seizure," Ellen quickly corrected her. "Do you understand that you can die from an alcoholic seizure, Stephanie?"

Stevie stared her down, the strength coming from some unknown reserve. "Stevie," she hissed.

Ellen wasn't swayed. "Last week a guy not much older than you, *Stevie*, died right out there in the hallway from an alcoholic seizure. Twenty-four years old. He didn't get here soon enough." Ellen's eyes stayed fixed on her for a long moment as if she was trying to use them to bore peepholes into her skull before she turned them to Liz who was enthusiastically waving an arm around, trying to lure the lion from its prey.

"I'm Liz, and I know I'm an alcoholic," she announced. "I made it eleven months this time. That's the longest I've ever gone."

"So, what happened?" Ellen asked. Now her attention was fully on Liz.

Stevie exhaled.

"I had wine with my husband on our anniversary—only one glass, though. I wasn't really worried because I thought I could control it. I'd been sober for almost a year." Liz looked around like she was expecting reassurance from someone. A few of the women laughed outright at her naiveté. But they weren't kidding anyone. Stevie knew they'd all been in the same position. The alcoholic brain is a particularly strange and cunning breed. Over and over and over again it convinces the sick person that there's a reprieve in the deadly game, as if a child's voice has yelled out the words *olly olly oxen free* and everyone, even the most desperate of drunks, can magically be safe again.

What's more illogical, she wondered, the fact that the brain continues to give the same false message or the fact that the alcoholic continues to believe it?

"A couple days later I bought a bottle of vodka like I used to," Liz continued. "My husband came home from work and found me passed out on the kitchen floor. I was cooking dinner and the stove was on. My baby's only three." Liz's eyes pleaded with Ellen to say something to save her, a few simple syllables to somehow carry her quickly and effortlessly back to sobriety. She reminded Stevie of a lost dog, the way it's willing to cozy up to anyone, even the meanest person on the sidewalk for the slight possibility of a finding a way home. *Pathetic disillusionment*, she thought and closed her eyes. Addiction seemed like a prison door to her. There's only a key to *get in*, not out.

Ellen must have thought she was falling asleep because she started talking at the top of her vocal cords' capacity. "I hope you're all listening!" she bellowed.

How could anyone not? Stevie pondered. Her voice was as loud and annoying as the late bell in high school that used to splinter through her hung over brain.

"This is one of the ways the program works," Ellen continued, "by hearing what other people have gone through because of their addictions. You should all be thankful to Liz. She went through all that pain so you don't have to."

Stevie huffed. So much for that bridge back Liz was searching for.

"*Listen*," Ellen scolded and Stevie could have sworn she was speaking directly into her eardrum with a megaphone. "None of you are safe putting alcohol, in any amount, into your bodies. The smallest trace of it can set off a compulsion to drink. That is the nature of the disease. Even mouthwash and cold medications are dangerous because they contain alcohol. Remember, you are al-co-hol-ics." The way she pronounced the word slowly and with an inappropriate cheerfulness caused her to bear a remarkable resemblance to a flight attendant happily urging passengers to remember how to attach an oxygen mask on route to a fiery death.

"Medically speaking, that means you have an allergy to alcohol. Now, I want you to think about that for a minute. If you were allergic to anything else, wouldn't you avoid it? Say, for instance, you broke out every time you ate strawberries, you wouldn't eat them, would you?

Yet we do it over and over again when it comes to alcohol, some of us every single day. That, ladies, is what makes us alcoholics."

Ellen smiled at Liz as if they were sharing an inside joke. Liz didn't smile back. Stevie didn't feel much like smiling either. Her alcoholism scared her, made her feel completely out of control. She had a picture in her mind's eye of herself and her disease battling against each other. It looked like two rabid dogs tearing each other to pieces.

Getting sober is like breaking up with a life-long lover. The grief comes in stages: shock, anxiety, anger, despondency and depression. In the early days acceptance is way, way, way off the radar screen for even the most optimistic of drunks—and there aren't many of those. By the time most people arrive for treatment, their emotions have been thoroughly anesthetized, and all enthusiastic thoughts have been sufficiently drowned. For Stevie there was a gaping hole, a feeling like something vitally important to her existence had been torn away, but no one could teach her how to grieve the loss of her most precious loved one, the bottle. It was something she'd have to stumble through on her own, like any other kind of grief.

She was somewhere between shock and anxiety as she lay on her bed trying to figure out what the fuck to do with her hands when Allison burst into the room dressed in her pajamas and toting a brand new pack of Marlboros. *Perfect timing* she thought as Allison tossed it to her. "I don't think I'll stay sober," she admitted as she lit one and let the smoke do its magic, chasing the anxiety straight out of her chest.

"What are you talking about? You didn't even say anything about my hair," Allison fussed, looking very much like a wood nymph in a Renaissance painting with her short-cropped peroxide blonde hair and her tiny lower lip pouting.

"I'm sorry. It looks good. How'd you get away with it?"

"Julie helped me. Do you really like it?"

"Yeah. I wish I had enough balls to go blonde."

"*Platinum* blonde. We could cut yours."

"What do you think the odds are of them trusting us with scissors?"

"Yeah I know, but Julie can do it."

Stevie's chestnut brown hair was long and wild. She never took time to care for it the way she knew other girls did. It was all she could do to remember to wash it. If it was in her way, it went into a ponytail, nothing more complicated than that. It didn't look stylish or even pretty, but still it was hers. It was familiar. "I don't think so," she said. "I'm moving over to the rehab side tomorrow. I'm self-conscious enough."

"Why do you think you get to go over already? I've been here longer than you."

Stevie didn't feel like recounting the story again about starting detox before her arrival or about how it came to pass that she was in the hospital in the first place. Pieces of the night had started to flash back: a man's fingers gripping her arm and dragging her out of the bar, her feet stumbling underneath her...the red flash of the ambulance light... the homeless guys shouting profanities...She closed her eyes tightly and shrugged. *No idea.*

"Can I French braid it?"

"Sure," Stevie agreed and turned her back to Allison. They had become fast friends, something that had rarely happened in Stevie's life. In rehab bonds are formed quickly. When everyone and everything familiar is taken away: friends, family members, cell phones and computers—even the drink or drug that has taken precedence over all those things—the playing field is leveled. Stevie felt like she was stripped naked in the midst of a large and unfamiliar crowd...defenseless. But she wasn't alone. All the patients felt like that. Allison's tiny fingers worked like a spider weaving a web. When she was done, Stevie looked in the mirror over her dresser and blinked. She really did look better.

"Let's try some eye liner. I've never seen eyes that green." For a seventeen-year-old kid, Allison had an undeniable talent for knowing what to say. Stevie felt her spirits rise immediately. Some alien emotion fluttered around in her chest—hope maybe? Sitting cross-legged on the bed, she rolled her eyes toward the ceiling while Allison penciled a line under them. When she checked her reflection again, her eyes stood out like precious gems against the rest of her face that seemed a little less bloated than a few days before.

"Do you really think it's possible to get better?" she threw out. Her reflection had bolstered her confidence. Before today she couldn't look in a mirror without thinking it was a street person staring back at her, that somehow her pretty young face had been transformed into a homeless creature that nobody wanted anymore. She stole a second glimpse—she seemed to be changing before her own eyes, like a butterfly pushing off its cocoon.

"You know how it works, right?" Allison asked with a chipper little voice.

"They scare the crap out of us by telling us all the things that could happen?" Like in Health class when they show videos of all the kids who have died. She wasn't convinced the people who made the videos weren't lying, anyway. The stories were so unrealistic: girl number one smokes pot for *the very first time*, wanders into the road and is struck dead by a car; girl number two does four shots of whisky *for the very first time* and dies of cardiac arrest. The only real kid she'd ever heard of who died the very first time he did anything was from using inhalants. And she knew a lot of drug users.

Allison shook her towhead lightheartedly. "It's not about fear. It's about God."

"Yeah right." Stevie opened the new pack and lit a butt. Wasn't that a contradiction of terms, anyway? The equation she'd been raised with was God=fear.

"No, really. No one told you that? There's no cure. Doctors don't know how to fix addiction. The only way to get better is to ask God."

"You mean here in the south that's what they believe because of the Bible belt? Up north people probably do it different."

"No, everywhere. You'll get it more when we read the rest of the steps."

Stevie fell onto her back on the bed and grunted like an old man. The God topic was a daunting one for her. When she was growing up she prayed every night before bed until she was old enough to understand the words. Then she figured out that God was someone to be afraid of unless she was a person who did everything right, and she didn't. She started drinking when she was still a little girl, in the summer before sixth grade, and with the alcohol came all the behaviors that would throw her out of favor with the Catholic God. The priest at her church said she had to confess her sins to be clean in God's eyes. But when you're fourteen years old, how do you tell a grown man in a robe that you've sinned by having premarital sex, or that you've horded lunch money like a miser to buy drugs instead of food? (Was that even a sin? And if so, which one?) As far as she could tell, the only commandment she hadn't broken yet was *Though Shall Not Kill*. Why would God help her?

"What are you so worried about?" Allison asked.

"God doesn't like me that much. I think I better chance it with the doctors."

"That's stupid."

Stevie shrugged. Was it? How about all the lies she told to her parents so she could pull all nighters, the bottles of vodka she stole from them or the time she slept with her best friend's boyfriend? Images of people she had met so far at rehab floated through her mind—surely they had done things, too. If God knew all of that, wouldn't he turn his back on all of them? She pictured them getting down on their knees to pray—John, the giant, and Ellen, the bitch. Did they talk to God? And what about David, or the bewitching brown-haired boy, Michael? "So, do you do that, pray I mean?"

"Well, no, but if I were an addict I'd do it. You know if I wanted to quit, because it works for other people, like Julie. She's a drunk—she told me."

It took a minute for Allison's words to penetrate. She really didn't believe she was an addict. Stevie had known her for just a few short days but *she* knew Allison was an addict. Why else would she have had sex with a stranger for cocaine? She told the story like it was a high school prank, but it stopped everyone who heard it cold in their tracks. Liz and Stevie had shared a concerned look while Allison giggled about it. Stevie let the complexities of the disease wash over her. Maybe that's why God was so important, she concluded, because no one on Earth was smart enough to figure it out.

Perhaps she could apologize to God without the priest, and promise that she'd try to do better. Hell, if she stayed off the alcohol there was no way she couldn't do better. After all, it's not an easy thing to crawl into bed with someone else's boyfriend when you're sober, but it's a very easy and even reasonable thing to do when you're drunk.

Allison interrupted her musings. "I'm going to bed," she announced, already on her way out the door, "but I'll see you in the morning before you go over to rehab. Just think; you'll get to meet *him*."

Stevie rolled her eyes at the comment and sighed, sure the *him* Allison referred to would have not the slightest interest in meeting her. That smile must have been a fluke. Maybe he thought she was someone else?

44

Stevie glanced over at the clock. It was 1:21 in the morning. Being in rehab was like visiting a different time zone. No one but the speed freaks (who needed to catch up on sleep) went to bed before midnight. Still, in another six hours Louise would be dragging her sorry ass out of bed for breakfast. She looked out into the hallway through her bedroom door and saw people passing by, nurses, aids and patients who couldn't sleep or who had recently arrived and were disoriented. In Purgatory there was no such thing as privacy. Self-consciousness tried to stop her from getting down on her knees, but she didn't let it. The only prayer that danced through her mind like a childhood chant was *now I lay me down to sleep* and that seemed grossly inappropriate.

Finally a few stray syllables found their way to her lips. She sent them out into the universe: "God, whoever you are, I'm lost."

CHAPTER FIVE:
THE WOLF PACK

Next to the women's hallway in the rehab wing there was a small but comfortable hang out room the patients referred to as "the den" with a couple of couches and numerous over-stuffed chairs. It also contained one framed art print, *The Scream*, chosen, Stevie conjectured, by someone with either a sadistic nature or a good sense of humor.

At the moment the den was empty except for the Marlboro man, whom she almost didn't recognize because he'd shaved off his shaggy moustache. Louise was unpacking her clothes in her new room and Stevie planned to write in her journal until she was done. Then she could hide out in there—and actually shut the door—until it was time for the morning meeting. She figured she could pass the guy unnoticed on the way to a lounge chair, but no such luck. He stood up and offered her his hand.

"How ya doin'? I'm Brian," he said.

Brian? She would have figured him for more of a Jed or a Billy Joe. Stevie took his hand and forced the corners of her mouth to curl upward. It probably looked like a snarl, but she meant it as a smile. The muscles in her face were stiff from not using them, like they'd been stabbed with Botox. "Stevie," she managed to get out.

"Come on, sit with me," Brian suggested. She took a close look at the man addressing her. His weathered complexion matched his hands that looked like they worked hard for a living, so different from her father's that were almost seamless and blanched as if he'd been locked in a closet (or law office) for his entire life. The premature laugh lines on Brian's face and his twinkling blue eyes hinted at a kind nature. Sometime in recent history her instincts had developed a sensitive fight or flight response when meeting men for the first time, but right now her instincts were as still as pond water. He cleared a newspaper off the couch, and she sat down beside him, clutching her journal. She noticed his eyes fall on the pink notebook, but he didn't comment on it.

"You just come over from—"

"Purgatory."

"Purgatory? That what you call the detox?"

"It's a pet name," Stevie ventured.

"Oh. So, is that why you're wearing the Nirvana shirt, 'cause now you've arrived?"

Stevie glanced down at Kurt Cobain's alluring face gazing like a fallen angel from her time worn t-shirt and reflected on Brian's observation. He seemed like he'd be fun to banter with. "I don't know, you tell me," she said and the corners of her lips actually curled up on their own without her directing them to. "You're the one that lives here."

"Well, you know, I don't actually *live* here," he rallied. "I'm just staying here for—let's see—seven more weeks and one more day. I haven't got it down to the minutes yet. It's not a bad place, but I'd sure as hell not call it Nirvana." The southern accent was over the top, but in a good way. It made her insides giggle. "When I'm not getting sober, I live with my family about thirty miles from here."

"You married and everything?" she asked.

"Mm hm, for now anyway."

It was an odd comment. Should she or shouldn't she? Ah, what the hell. "Don't you love your wife?" she asked him.

"Oh yeah, I love her. It's not that. It's just, well, stuff happened, stuff I hope she'll forgive me for, that's all. But you're how old?"

"Twenty," she answered and waited for the *you're not even old enough to drink* line.

Brian smirked. "Twenty. Wow. Might be hard for you to understand what I'm talkin' 'bout at twenty. Prob'ly haven't even had a real boyfriend yet."

Yeah right. Who did he think he was talking to, some Midwestern Christian girl who spent every summer in Jesus Camp? It didn't take that much gray matter to figure out he was talking about infidelity, and at twenty she was an expert on that subject. Sleeping with her best friend's boyfriend—that was one side of the equation, but she'd been on the other side, too, with the one boy she thought she loved in high school. Then there was the time she found out her father wasn't the perfect husband he made everyone believe he was. That nauseating moment had been an unremitting source of reflection: What was worse, seeing her father kiss another woman on the mouth or dealing with her mother's refusal to believe it? It had been a battle to look either of them in the eye ever since.

"Don't do that, all right?" she stated simply, quietly. It wasn't really a question.

"What? Don't do what?"

"Talk to me like I'm five. My father does that. And don't assume I'm like every other twenty-year old girl you've ever met, because I'm not."

Brian sat back in his chair and the mirth ran out of his eyes. Even their shade of blue appeared paler. He crossed his hands behind his head while he seemed to search the walls that were painted a calming celadon green for the right thing to say. Stevie watched and wondered what he'd come up with. He picked up his cigarette pack, lit two and handed one to her. It was a good move, very smooth. "Sorry," he offered in a soothing voice as she took it from him. "Where you from? You've got an accent."

"Actually, farm boy, I think you're the one with the accent."

Brian laughed loudly, hooted almost, and shook his head at her in disbelief. "Hot damn, girl!" he hurled. "I'm not a farm boy just because I'm from the south."

"And I'm not sheltered and inexperienced just because I'm twenty."

"Okay, point taken...seriously. So, can we drop it now?"

Stevie nodded. She was enjoying this. Now she couldn't stop herself from smiling if she had to. "I'm from Massachusetts, south of Boston on the coast."

"Nice up there?"

"Except in the winter...too cold."

"Yeah, but now it's summer. So what are you doing way down here in Georgia?"

There it was again, the inquiry. She gave him her standard response, the one meant to make a clean break from the topic. "That's a story you don't have time for."

"Who says?" he shot back and her eyes measured him. Even through the cloud of smoke encircling him like an aura she could see that his mouth was set in an affable grin.

Just then Louise returned from the women's hallway. "You're all set, my darlin' girl," she informed her as she approached with her arms wide open. Stevie stood up and rested her head on Louise's well-padded shoulder, allowing herself to be completely enfolded in her embrace. Louise was her favorite person in the whole place. Whenever she was nearby, it felt like home. "Your friend David's coming over later today," she told Stevie.

My *friend* David? she thought. "He is?" she asked. "He didn't say anything."

"Maybe he didn't know."

"Maybe he didn't tell me because he didn't care if I knew," Stevie grumbled. "I'm not sure he likes me." With a perfectly sculpted face and those intriguing eyes, David was what Liz liked to call "Hollywood Handsome" (behind his back, of course). He was, but damn, the guy was hard to get close to.

Louise laughed and it was like gospel music, deep and soulful. It made Stevie hold on to her a little tighter. "He got up with you this morning, didn't he?"

If Louise had announced that aliens landed their spaceship in the detox Stevie couldn't have been more astonished. It was true that David was in the small lounge when she woke up that morning and he even hugged her before she left. "But he didn't tell me that was why he woke up so early," Stevie answered and grinned again despite herself.

"He's good at pushing people away. You ought not to let him," Louise advised.

It was an insightful comment. David's façade certainly screamed out *Get the fuck away from me!* But maybe not complying with this silent order was the first step to becoming his friend. Maybe, Stevie thought, it was his way of weeding people out. He was undeniably antagonistic, but there was more to him than that. She'd had a couple of late night conversations with him where he had come clean about his alcohol abuse and she had realized he was a deeper character than he usually let on. Like her, his disease was advanced for his age. That's what happens when you start drinking when you're still a little kid. He had nearly killed someone with his car, he'd disclosed. When he admitted that to her, she wondered why he trusted her with it.

She didn't know why, but she knew he did because he waited until after Liz and Allison went to bed to say it.

His story wasn't as shocking to Stevie as David might have thought. She had been around drunks her whole life, in fact had been raised by them. Her one and only sibling, Scott, didn't break the chain either. At one time he had been her best friend and drinking buddy until one day before school he walked in on her snorting lines in her room. Since then he sat across from her at the Sunday dinner table, but that was about it. (Scott and David had that in common, a loathing disregard for drug users.) Regardless, there was no denying that Scott was a drunk, just like her. And car accidents and drunks go hand in hand. Even the great litigator himself, her father, had totaled a couple of BMWs.

"I'll stop by to see you time to time," Louise whispered before she pulled away from Stevie's childlike embrace. Stevie lingered awkwardly, watching her walk away, a four year old on the first day of preschool.

"So, you were about to tell me your story," Brian interjected. It occurred to Stevie that she could excuse herself and stick to the plan, but she decided against it. She didn't know that Brian would soon become one of her closest friends on the planet, but so far he was the only person she knew in rehab. And he really did seem like a nice guy.

She sat back down and started talking, and before she knew it she had told him everything. Well, not *everything*, but a lot. She told him about how she had been getting drunk since she was eleven years old and how her parents didn't even pick up on it until she was fifteen and got arrested because they were too drunk themselves to notice their inebriated little girl. She told him about how her father was a dickhead lawyer who ran everyone into the ground, including her, and how he expected her to go to law school and be just like him. She confessed to Brian how she really wanted to be a writer and that she stayed out all night before the SAT and took it with a buzz on because she didn't want to go to Boston College, even though that had been the plan since she could walk.

When all that went over without a flinch—he was actually *listening*, like he cared— Stevie told him about the drugs she started using to keep herself from passing out and about how she still couldn't stop the blackouts no matter how many pills she took or lines she snorted. She admitted for the first time that drinking was the real reason she got kicked out of college. She even told him a little bit about that last night in Atlanta that landed her in the emergency room. But she didn't tell him about the rapes. She never had and never would tell anyone about that. Dr. Tom at the hospital had known, but not because she had told him. She knew it when he softly voiced the one point that had convinced her to go into residential treatment: *No one can hurt you there, Stevie.*

She told Brian as much as she could bear to say about herself. If he was going to judge her, let him do it now and get it over with. He didn't. "I'm a falling down drunk, too," is all he said, and with those words they were friends. She decided then and there to never again call him the Marlboro Man and never to let on that she even thought it. Now that she was getting to know him, he didn't seem like such a Redneck. "Hey, you know how you said you want to be a writer?" he posed. "I got a friend here that writes. You ought to meet him. He's smart like you, prob'ly the smartest guy I ever met."

With all the garbage out, she barely thought about the words that came from her as she sparked up a cigarette and breathed in the comforting drug. "What's his name?" she asked nonchalantly. She wasn't remotely prepared for what spilled from Brian's mouth.

"Michael," he said. "Michael James."

It was unquestionably the most electric moment of her short life, standing outside the dining room with her hand in Michael's and her breath stuck somewhere between her lungs and her throat. She could actually feel the energy pouring from his hand into hers. Maybe that was what was clogging up her ability to speak. Brian had just introduced them and, like a normal person, he had offered her his name. "Michael," he had said, "I'm Michael." As if she didn't already know.

Brian thoughtfully broke the silence and spoke her name for her. He even recounted for Michael why she was called Stevie—because as a six-year-old she won a fight against a kid in the neighborhood who later complained that her name should be Steven, not Stephanie and the boys had christened her. "Stevie" was born out of her mother's refusal to accept the masculine name and her own refusal to answer to anything but. To this day the nickname was a thorn in her mother's side. Michael seemed to get a kick out of the story and slipped on that little boy grin that knocked her and Allison out the first time he did it, a shy smile where he showed his dimples but not his teeth. *That* might take some time to get used to, she told herself.

"Come on," Michael prompted and she followed him to a table where the little boy, Jake, was eating lunch with a roguish-looking character whose greasy hair, tattooed neck, missing teeth and black eye caused Stevie to take a step backward. Her eyes shifted to Jake. He was a beautiful kid with features so soft he could have been a cherub on the ceiling of the Sistine Chapel. It was hard to believe he was a drug addict.

"Stevie, this is Marcus, a good friend of mine," Michael told her, gesturing to the guy with a tattoo of a snake coiled around his neck. Its forked tongue seemed to be pointing at her. Stevie recognized him from step meetings as a hardcore drug user who earlier that day had told an amusing story about how his wife packed heroin in his lunch box every morning before work. "And this here is Jake. Hey, Jake move over so Stevie can sit down, all right?"

Jake immediately scrambled out of his seat and into one on the other side of the table. It was a formal dining room with chandeliers and cloth napkins, but with Jake gnawing on a peanut butter and marshmallow sandwich Stevie couldn't help feeling like she was in a junior high school cafeteria.

"Your hands are as bad as Michael's," Marcus stated matter-of-factly, his voice as hoarse and raspy as she imagined the snake's voice would be if it could talk.

Stevie recoiled and dropped her cigarette. It rolled under the table and then—as if that weren't bad enough—Michael dropped to his knees and crawled under the table to retrieve it. She stood paralyzed, feeling every flash of pale pink to bright red that crossed her mortified face. Not even her eyes dared to move until Michael was on his feet again, handing her the still lit cigarette.

"You a meth addict, too?" Marcus asked.

"Leave her alone, Marcus," Michael said but his voice was so tranquil that it didn't sound at all like an order. It was more like a civilized suggestion. And Marcus nodded his head agreeably as if he was willing to swallow it.

"No. Alcoholic," Stevie spoke out and with an even shakier hand brought the cigarette to her tremulous lips. She thought about dropping it and stepping on it to take the attention off her hands, but that didn't seem right, not in the formal dining room, and especially after Michael chased it under the table.

Jake momentarily shifted his big round eyes from the crust he was tearing off his sandwich onto Stevie, who despite his move to the other side of the table, had still not taken the seat. "Don't feel bad," he offered. "All of us're fucked up."

The words sounded depraved coming from his little boy mouth that had marshmallow jammed into its corners. Stevie suddenly realized that although Brian had already sat down and started eating, Michael was still standing because *she* was and quickly claimed the seat. He sat right beside her and immediately grasped the coffee decanter as if he had been waiting for the opportunity. "Want some?" he asked her. She shook her head. His hand was so jittery it couldn't control the decanter and coffee poured not only into his cup but onto the saucer, then overflowed and seeped into the white linen tablecloth.

"You'd think by now they'd know to use those plastic table cloths," Brian remarked. Stevie stiffened. She thought he was being insensitive until she realized everyone except for her was laughing, even Michael. His tongue shot out from behind his teeth and the little lines around his eyes got squinty before laughter gurgled out of him. "You can walk around the room and know exactly what tables Michael sat at this week," Brian added.

"The ones with the big ol' brown coffee stains!" Jake shouted and then burst out laughing again.

"We think Michael shakes because he drinks coffee all day, but John says it's from the meth," Marcus told Stevie.

"I have to drink coffee. I can't stay awake without it," Michael explained, leaning in close to the table and drinking from the coffee cup without picking it up. The image brought back Stevie's days in the hospital, when she wasn't able to drink from a cup without someone helping her. She could still hear Dr. Tom's voice telling her, "I'll discharge you from the hospital when you can eat peas with a fork." Those words had terrified her. She had imagined being stuck in that hospital forever.

"'Cause he ain't got speed—that's how come," Jake explained. "Says coffee's the next best thing."

The comment took Michael's smile away and suddenly he was a different person.

"It is," he said quietly, "for now anyway." He scrunched his eyebrows together and Stevie noticed there was already a wrinkle between his eyes from doing it habitually. It was his masculine eyebrows and strong nose that saved his face from being feminine. He wasn't a prettyboy, but with his long eyelashes and angelically shaped mouth, he was close. The shift in his energy made Stevie wish she was a painter so she could capture the darkness she saw in his expression when he made the last remark like she had seen the light in it at the step meeting when he smiled at her. Like Monet's cathedral at dawn and then again at sunset, it was all beauty, just different sides of it.

By now Michael was cutting his food methodically into evenly sized pieces. When he was finished, he used his fork and knife to divide the pieces into separate camps: chicken in one pile, roasted potatoes in another. He had even cut the green beans so they resembled the lengths of the rest of the food and took special care to assure they didn't touch the potatoes or the chicken. He looked up expectantly and Brian handed him the salt and pepper. This was obviously a routine. Stevie noticed that unlike the other guys, Michael had placed his napkin on his lap.

She took the napkin from the plate in front of her and spread it on her lap, the way she'd been raised to. Her parents were alcoholics, but they had mastered the necessary skills of social elitism and passed each and every one on to her. She mustered her courage and scooped a spoonful of pasta onto her plate, but didn't dare go for the red marinara sauce. She stabbed a piece with the fork (that's the trick—using the fork as a spear not a forklift) and raised it off the plate. She was moving it flawlessly toward her mouth when suddenly, for no apparent reason, the fork plummeted from her hand and onto her plate with an abrasive clang. Michael nearly leaped off his seat from the sound and she could hear Jake trying to suppress his laughter.

"Holy shit," Marcus chortled. "You scared the crap out of me."

With that Jake could no longer hold it in. "D'you see Michael jump?" he snorted, his mouth wide open and loaded with chewed up peanut butter and bread. Stevie stared down at her plate. Out of the corner of her eye she could see the piece of penne that had flown off her fork on Michael's plate wedged between the potato camp and the green bean camp. What would he do, make a joke out of it or push his plate away in disgust?

"So, Stevie, you're from Boston Brian said?" It was Michael, not laughing, only talking to her as if she hadn't done something stupid, again. He actually stabbed a potato and ate it.

"A small town south of there," she answered and briefly met his eyes. He smiled encouragingly. Then he picked up the breadbasket and held it out to her as an offering. *It's easier when you can use your hands* he seemed to be intimating without saying it out loud for everyone else to hear. She selected a warm roll, grasped onto it like a hawk and nibbled it. It was almost effortless without utensils.

"Thanks," she said softly and he smiled again. There was something about Michael James that made her feel like she'd known him forever. And his eyes were oh-so-familiar, as if she'd seen her own image reflected in them many times before.

"I was supposed to go to Boston once," he told her with a confidential air like he was sharing a secret. "Didn't work out, though."

"Really? Why were you going there?"

He hesitated. "It's a long story. Maybe I'll tell you some day."

Jake's curiosity got the best of him. He stopped rolling around on his chair in hilarity like a possessed elf. "How come you were goin' there? You never told us 'bout that."

"Never will, either," Michael said and winked playfully. "Hey, you want to be my Addictionary partner tonight?" he threw at Stevie.

"Your what partner?" she sputtered.

"Addictionary. After the night meeting, we usually play."

"Or poker," Marcus interjected.

Jake narrowed his eyes. "He's only askin' you 'cause Brian says you're smart."

"No, Jake. You got it all wrong, bro."

"I don't know how to play," Stevie argued.

Michael dismissed her concern with a wave of his hand. "Don't worry about it. I'll teach you."

CHAPTER SIX:
AN UNEXPECTED JUNKIE

The game was set up in the recreation room, a huge living-room like space that provided lots of chairs, round tables, a large screen television and cozying up spots for the patients to hang out together, as well as pool and ping pong tables. Jake was sitting next to Stevie at a table with a cigarette tucked behind his ear. Soon after the game started, he moved his chair closer to hers, leaned in against her and snaked his arm around her back.

"Jake," Michael said softly from across the table and shook his head. Stevie tilted her head quizzically, not understanding why he intervened. Jake was only thirteen. It wasn't like he was hitting on her. But then Jake pushed his chair away from the table and held his hands up like he was caught. Michael watched him with one eyebrow raised.

"Got to bust a piss, anyway," Jake announced and shuffled lethargically away. Even after he left the room his obnoxious laughter could be heard.

Stevie was six years old again in that moment, playing the fool to one of Scott's practical jokes. Why was she always so naïve when everyone else, even thirteen year old Jake, was so worldly? Earlier that day he had approached her with a pathetic expression on his baby face, his eyes watery and wistful. She had kissed his forehead and given him a big hug. And Jake had held on for a long time, his face resting on her breasts.

"It's all right, Stevie," Michael said. "He just...doesn't know." She nodded at him like she understood, but she didn't. Maybe he intuited that because he continued. "Jake's a foster kid. His mom died when he was a baby and his dad's in prison. It's hard to know what's okay and what's not when there's no one to tell you." The statement hit her like a slap. She was raised in dysfunction, but she'd never had to fend for herself.

Michael was wearing a red t-shirt with the sleeves cut off that showed Jimmy Paige bent into the ecstatic position of a musician at one with his instrument. The color of the shirt made Michael's features stand out dramatically: his fair skin, perfectly arched eyebrows and deep red mouth. Stevie looked into his brown eyes and for the first time noticed how much emotion was reflected in them. She lingered in the moment, wondering who was really inside there until it occurred to her that she might not be ready to look any deeper into Michael James, and turned away.

Marcus coughed like an emphysemic old man, drawing the group's attention before he pushed the conversation forward. "Last night Jake was in my room pawin' through my stuff. He said he was lookin' to get high, but I think he was lookin' for som'in else."

"You're a homophobe," Brian chuckled and gave Stevie a nudge with his elbow.

"Jake's not gay," Michael stated quietly, his eyes on the lit cigarette he was twirling between his index finger and thumb, not on Stevie's perplexed face.

"A couple days back a guy got thrown out of here for doing stuff with Jake," Brian explained. Doing stuff...doing stuff...with Jake? Her brain tried to absorb it.

"Imagine having to tell your girl you got kicked out of rehab for getting a blowjob?" Marcus suddenly threw out and Stevie's stomach nearly heaved out the dinner roll.

"From a guy," Brian added. "I heard Jake got a pack of cigarettes out of it."

"He's not even a guy," Michael argued, his melodic voice rapidly increasing in volume. "He's a kid. That piece of crap should be in jail for what he did to Jake."

Marcus' sweeping grin revealed every missing tooth. "Kid's like a midget," he taunted, "an adult in a kid's body. No jokin', you ever talk to him 'bout somin' serious? If your eyes were closed, you'd think he was twenty one."

"Didn't they teach you in prison to stay away from thirteen-year-old boys?" Michael snapped. All the while his eyes were focused keenly on Marcus.

"Come on now," Brian interceded. "Marcus might be a freaking mess, but he's not a pedophile."

Marcus choked on his mucous. "What the fuck?" he growled.

Michael laughed out loud at Marcus' reaction. "Sorry, man," he conceded.

Stevie was still struggling to keep up with the conversation. Of course Marcus looked like a prisoner, but in her wildest dreams she hadn't imagined that he actually was one. What would her parents think if they could see her now playing Addictionary with a nearly toothless former prison inmate with a poisonous appearing snake inked permanently into the skin of his neck? Now *that* was an entry for her journal.

"We're up," Michael said and grinned sweetly at her. Damn. She'd play Addictionary with Jimmy Hoffa as long as she could sit across the table from that smile.

The game was like charades, but the subjects were contained to "alcohol", "drugs" and "gambling". Michael chose a card from the "drug" stack, most likely because of his familiarity with the subject. "This one's too easy for us," he said and pretended to take something small from his back pocket and unwrap it. Then he carefully dumped it on the table and chopped it with an invisible blade. His nose was agitated by his hands' expert actions. He started to sniff. In her mind's eye Stevie could see the powder sculpted into perfect lines. Michael's blood seemed to be pumping faster now. She should have stopped him before he brought the imaginary straw to his nose, but she didn't. As a result, that image would forever repeat in her memory like an MTV video.

"Meth," she said flatly.

Michael roared his approval and raised his hands in victory. Then he threw the card down as evidence, like he was spiking a football after a touchdown, but Stevie didn't feel like celebrating. She didn't even feel like playing the game anymore. Watching Michael act out his addiction was a chilling experience. Little goose bumps were all over her arms. And now he was rubbing his nose with his thumb and sniffing like he was trying to keep the meth from dripping out, as if it had really happened.

"Now that's horseshit," Marcus said accusingly. "Anyone would've said cocaine."

"What are you talking about?" Michael reeled.

"I'm talking about the girl getting it right the first guess. Why'd you say that?"

Stevie's head snapped in Marcus' direction. The answer was so obviously meth—Michael's drug of choice. How could he not have noticed how obsessive Michael was about it? She started to say so until she noticed the snake eyes on his neck staring her down. She looked over at Michael for support. He was still high from the imaginary speed, beaming across the table from her. He could barely keep his feet and hands still and his eyes had a whole new intensity. "Oh, stop being a prick and lose gracefully, Marcus," he spit out. "She knew because she's intuitive." *He is so enjoying this* she realized and grinned despite her apprehension over Marcus' aggressive comments.

"Here's what I think," Brian offered sedately, leaning in like the mediator between the two of them. "How about we switch partners?"

"No. No, we're not doing that," Michael shot back. "You two are the biggest babies. Christ, Jake's more of a man than you." Jake, arriving back at the table, lifted his head proudly at the comment. "All right, here's what we do," Michael continued. "We keep the same partners, but play a different game. Cool?"

Marcus and Brian exchanged suspicious looks. "Cards?" Marcus ventured.

"No, I know," Brian answered confidently. "Trivia."

"Trivial Pursuit? All right. You guys can have Jake." Marcus scoffed at the suggestion, but Jake didn't seem to mind. He was excited just to be included. "He's got more brain cells left than the rest of us," Michael added.

"Hey, that's true," Marcus agreed. "And he might know stuff from school. What grade you in Jake?"

Jake hesitated like it was an answer that needed a lot of concentration. "Sixth," he finally said.

It was nearly 2:00 a.m. when the game finished and Michael walked Stevie back to the beginning of the women's wing, but not all the way to her room because men weren't allowed for any reason in the women's hallway. To her complete captivation, the Trivial Pursuit game had revealed Michael to be some sort of intellectual and she hadn't been expecting that. Although he was obviously bright, she had figured him to fall more in the street-smart category. "How did you know all those answers tonight, like the one about Fitzgerald's first novel?" she asked him.

"My mom's an English professor," he told her. "I grew up with Fitzgerald."

"Really?" she practically gasped. There was nothing she loved more than books. Maybe she had finally met someone she could talk to about them. That was a rare find in the drinking and drugging world. Even when she was still in high school the only people she knew who cared about fiction were the super straight kids in her honors English class, and they didn't seem to love reading the way she did, for the pure beauty of the words. Books were more like a puzzle to them—another formula to untangle, like calculus.

"Who's your favorite writer?" she tossed at him.

"John Irving," he answered without hesitation.

The excitement bubbled up her air pipe and out of her mouth in a laugh so loud the nurse behind the desk next to the women's hallway looked up and frowned at them. Obviously Stevie loved John Irving, too. "Sorry," she whispered to the crabby nurse who looked like she'd sell her soul to be home in bed and turned her beaming face back to Michael. "Which one? I mean, which Irving novel is your favorite?"

His eyes smiled. "At the risk of making you hysterical, I think I'd have to say *Setting Free the Bears*."

Her mind quickly absorbed the information. *Setting Free the Bears* was Irving's first novel. She loved first novels, too. They were usually unrefined and honest. She started to ask if he read poetry, but there was something more pressing she needed to ask and the nurse was glaring at them now as if she were trying to push them with her eyes toward their respective rooms…like telekinesis. Stevie stepped closer and spoke in a hushed tone. "What do you think about Marcus?" she asked. "Do you think he's all right?"

"What do you mean 'all right'?"

"Like…to hang out with?" As soon as she saw his eyebrows pinched together, she knew she shouldn't have asked and tried to back paddle. "It's just that I've never met anyone like him," she murmured. Earlier, after lunch, Brian told her that Michael and Marcus had been tight since they experienced some "horrors" together in detox, but he didn't elaborate. Maybe they knew the guy who died of a seizure in the hallway, she conjectured. But during the game they were practically quarrelling so she thought that Brian might have overestimated the relationship.

"Or like me?" Michael asked, and now his eyes weren't smiling at all, as if the light had been snuffed out. And his bottom lip looked a little fuller than it did a second before.

"Well, no. You're nothing like Marcus."

"Yeah, I am," he countered. "Only I'm a couple of steps behind him." It was impossible to fathom what he was talking about. He read John Irving, for Christ's sake. How could he be like Marcus? "There's a lot you don't know about me," he stated so quietly it was almost a whisper. His voice didn't sound angry. It was as warm and buttery as melted chocolate.

But she was in defense mode. "There's a lot you don't know about *me*," she shot back and immediately regretted it. The hostility in her tone sounded like her father, like broken glass. And she'd thrown it at him as if it was normal every day behavior to go straight for the jugular. Michael sort of moved his head like he at least acknowledged her comment as he combed his fingers through his long dark hair. Her eyes absorbed his hands that were large with long graceful fingers, like an artist's hands, and his nails were trimmed and clean. They didn't look like the hands of a junkie.

Michael with an elastic tied on his arm...breaking his milky white skin with the silver point of a hypodermic needle...pushing the melted rock into the deep blue stream that was his vein. She closed her eyes and forced the image from her brain. She was an expert at such magic tricks. She could blind her third eye by barely trying. He was the son of an English professor, a reader of Fitzgerald, a defender of thirteen-year-old boys. Eyes like a poet. Voice like an instrument. Hands like an artist. Not a junkie. *Not a junkie.*

"Listen," Michael finally said, "today's been good."

"Yeah," she agreed. She didn't even smile, but on the inside she laughed at the understatement of his comment. Until the last sixty seconds, today was probably the best day of her life so far. She didn't know exactly why, but being in the same room with Michael made her feel euphoric, weightless almost, like if she lifted her feet too high off the ground she might float away like a helium balloon. For the first time in memory she felt as if life wasn't a total nightmare. "I'll see you tomorrow," she announced without revealing any of this and walked down the women's hallway toward her room.

"Hey, Stevie," she heard him say right as she reached her room and turned back one last time to look at him. His hands were in his pockets and he was shuffling his feet nervously, like a little boy at a school bus stop. She wondered if he really was nervous, if behind that confident façade he was as scared as her. "Want to meet for breakfast?" he asked. She nodded and he actually looked relieved, as if she might have said no.

"Sweet dreams," he offered and walked away.

CHAPTER SEVEN:
UNATTAINABLE

*S*tevie's jeans were rolled up to keep them clean, but she had given up on her flip-flops that were coated in gooey mud. She was stooped down next to the duck pond trying to liberate a white lily from its underwater stalk with Michael close by tossing bread to the ducks. "Did you know there are water lilies six feet wide in the Amazon?" he asked.

She looked up at him to read his face. The sun was shining behind his head like a halo. "You're making that up," she said and tugged hard on the roots. Not a budge.

"No, I'm not. The fish eat them. I think we need something sharp to cut the stems."

"I doubt they'd let us out of their sight with razor blades or steak knives."

"We could be like Bonny and Clyde and bust out." Michael's eyes lit up at his own suggestion and infectious laughter rolled out of him, starting in his belly and making its way upward until it was floating through the air like soap bubbles. "What do you think?"

"I think you've got a big imagination," she answered, but couldn't resist smiling back at him, the wild restless boy who looked like an angel even without the sunshine halo. Out of the corner of her eye, she saw Allison running toward her. She dropped the lily back into its watery bed and could have sworn she heard it sigh relief when her fingers finally let it go. It was beautiful and perfect, but its roots were far too stubborn.

"I'll get it," Michael proposed and stepped closer to the tenacious flower.

"No, don't. You'll ruin your sneakers," Stevie said and stood just in time to receive Allison's embrace. Her small frame felt even more diminutive than she remembered. Three days had passed since Stevie's move from detox, but it felt more like three weeks.

"I can't believe I'm outside!" Allison exclaimed. "I feel so free." She threw her arms out and spun like a tiny ballerina on top of a jewelry box. Michael caught Stevie's eye and they shared an intimate smile. Allison suddenly stopped twirling as if that very second she had become aware of his presence.

"This is my friend Michael," Stevie said and he extended a hand to shake Allison's.

"You're Allison, right? I heard about you."

"Really?" Allison asked, wide-eyed. "From Stevie?"

"Mm hm," Michael replied and bent down to gather some stones. When he turned his back to skip one across the pond's tranquil surface, Allison lifted an eyebrow at Stevie and mouthed *what the hell?* Stevie shrugged her shoulders innocently.

"What room are you in?" Allison asked, still not taking her eyes off of Michael.

"Fourth on the right."

Allison gasped excitedly. "I'm right across the hall from you, fourth on the left! I missed you so much. Did you miss me?"

"Of course," Stevie answered a little too quickly.

Allison folded her arms in front of her and narrowed her eyes. "I bet," she said. "Hey, I can make coffee now. Want to stop on the way to women's group?"

"Sure," Stevie agreed. The coffee bar in the den was a privilege of graduating detox. Caffeine and sugar quickly became the chemicals of choice for most patients. Alcoholics tended to crave ice cream and soda because of the abrupt removal of sugar from their bodies. Coffee, because of its "up" effect, was popular with the cocaine abusers and speed freaks, like Michael, to rally the "down" effect of coming off their true drugs of choice.

"We should go then," Allison suggested.

"Right now?"

"I don't want to be late. Ellen will hold it against me. I swear that's why I was the last one to leave Purgatory, and it sucked."

Stevie giggled at Allison's use of her pet name for the detox. "Yeah, okay, you're right," she agreed. In detox the two of them were late to enough meetings to draw negative attention from Ellen, and now Stevie had other issues with Ellen without throwing tardiness into the mix. "Michael, want to head back?" she asked.

"I'll stay awhile," he answered. "My meeting's not 'til 10:15. John's running late."

Stevie hesitated. It was silly, she knew, but she always hated parting from him. Maybe if she turned her back on him one too many times he'd no longer be there, as if she had imagined him into being and without her energy focused in his direction he would disappear like fog in the sun. In a mere three days he had filled that empty spot inside of her so perfectly that it was as if he had been there all her life and the gaping hole had never existed. How could he be real?

"I'll make you coffee," she offered. "It'll be in the pot on the left."

He gave her an appreciative grin. "I've got a lunch meeting with John after men's group then a men's step. I should be done by 3:30."

"I'm meeting Ellen at 3:00 for who knows how long," she said. "Sorry."

"Dinner then, I guess," Michael answered. "Sucks how they take the whole day. I'll see you guys." Then he turned his attention back to the group of ducks who, empowered by numbers, were swimming together toward him and his bag of bread. He was tossing pieces in front of him and talking softly to them when the girls walked away.

Allison lasted about two minutes into the walk back before she burst. "Oh my God, you have to tell me the whole story!"

"What story?"

"About Michael—what else?"

Embarrassed at the thought of him overhearing them, Stevie tried to shush her, but realizing it was beyond her power to control Allison's buoyant enthusiasm, she started walking faster to create more distance between them.

"What's he like? Is he nice? Are you seeing him?" poured from Allison all at once. Every time Stevie started to answer, another question came spurting out.

She stopped walking and looked back at Michael stooped down next to the pond with the ducks closing in on him. He looked so sweet and innocent with his curls spilling out the back of his baseball cap and one knee showing through a hole in his jeans that she wished she had her cell phone so she could take a picture. "One question at a time," she suggested. No sooner had she said it than she brooded over how to explain Michael to Allison. She hadn't figured it out for herself yet what their relationship was even though they had spent virtually all their time together for the past three days.

They walked outside whenever they were allowed to. It was the closest thing to privacy that existed at the rehab, even though the nurses watched them through the windows—for what Stevie wasn't sure. Michael would bring bread for the ducks and they'd sit next to each other on the grass. That was where they'd had their first conversation about the depth of his meth addiction.

Allison intruded on her thoughts that were pushing her into a dark mood, anyway. "Okay, first question," she threw out. "Is he nice?"

"Yeah," Stevie sighed and a light-hearted laugh escaped with her breath. That was an easy one. He's *so* nice, she wanted to say, but held it in, and *so* smart and *so* funny...

"But is he as nice as he is cute?" Allison asked. Stevie nodded confidently and Allison beamed in response. "Do you like him?"

"Well yeah, I mean, who wouldn't?"

"Really, is he that great?"

"Yeah, he's that great," Stevie replied and finally tore her eyes off him. They slowly pushed their momentum back into walk mode.

"Wow. So then, what's wrong with him?"

"Nothing. He's...perfect," Stevie told her and laughed at her own assessment of Michael. Well, to her he was perfect. She'd certainly never met anyone like him. He could talk about art and novels as easily as he could talk about rock music. And he'd read Yeats. *Seriously*, she pondered, *how many twenty-one year old guys have read Yeats?* She doubted that would matter much to Allison, but it mattered a great deal to her.

"Then why is he here?" Allison inquired, and Stevie plunged back down to Earth.

"Oh. Meth."

"Oh shit, you mean."

Stevie stepped ahead. How dare Allison slam Michael like that when she didn't know anything about him? Allison had to move her legs about three times as fast as Stevie to catch up to her long strides. "So, David was right about him, I guess," she said as she caught up. Stevie stopped walking and laid the death stare on her.

"No, David wasn't right. Why would you say that? You don't even know Michael."

"But you know how bad it is right, meth?" Allison spewed.

"What're you an expert on it now?"

Allison flinched. "Not really, no. But he doesn't shoot up does he, like David said?"

Like David said. Looking back on that night in detox when they all talked about him over dinner, Michael seemed like a different person than the one David had described as strapped in his bed. What a horrible visual that was, but it couldn't be true. David was probably only trashing him to discourage the girls' attraction to him. Still, Allison's question was easy enough to answer. Yes, he did, he absolutely did shoot up—she had seen the track marks on his arm. She had seen them and she had even run her fingertips over them once when he rolled up his sleeves. His dark eyes had met hers when she touched them, and that had started the conversation, the one she could barely think about now without cringing. Okay, so the truth was Michael was a junkie, but he was still Michael and that was all that mattered to her. And she was a repulsive drunk, but he'd stuck around no matter how much she told him about it. And she had told him a lot.

"What do you think you are, Allison?" Stevie spat out like poison from her tongue and watched the confusion spread on her friend's impish face. She had learned this trick from her father who always said the best defense is a good offense. "So what if he used needles? You're an addict, too. You're an addict just like us, whether you admit it or not. So get over it." Stevie turned away and walked into the building, leaving Allison alone outside. It was the meanest thing she'd ever done, but she didn't feel bad about it. Anger was raging through her chest like a forest fire threatening to consume her. Allison had focused on only one part of Michael out of context with the rest of him. It wasn't fair and she wouldn't stand for it. In the course of the argument, one thing had become absolutely clear. Her loyalties had shifted. She'd defend Michael against anyone.

CHAPTER EIGHT:

HOME

Most of her nights started out the same way, lying on the wooden floor of the open-air veranda opposite the dining room with Michael's denim jacket jammed under her head like a pillow, and him by her side, watching the Georgia sky turn from sapphire to ink black. On nights when the sky was dark enough she could have sworn the stars were within reach, floating like protective spirits right above their heads.

Michael noticed things like that, the way the sky changed constantly, like a movie screen revealing a dynamic landscape. Before Stevie met him, she used to acknowledge the stars on the nights they shone the brightest, usually when there were no clouds and the moon was only a small slice of the whole, but other than that she was pretty much oblivious. He told her once that he used to get home late at night and be too amped on speed to sleep so he'd sit outside and watch the horizon change colors. It was miraculous, he'd said, how the pink ran right up to the blue without bleeding into it, like someone had deliberately painted it that way. It was the reason he believed in God. The beauty he saw in nature was too precise for it to have been randomly created.

It seemed like Michael paid attention to everything: the different shades of green, gold and brown in the grasses near the pond; the titter of one bird compared to the squawk of another; the soft vulnerable feeling of a frog's belly (Once he caught one and made her touch it, too.); gradations of color from one person's blue eyes to another; a hue of purple that he'd never seen before tucked inside a flower's petals; the half-inch scar on her left elbow from the time she experimented with Scott's skateboard, and the holes in her ears that she never bothered to fill with earrings. His observations had an effect on her. They made her notice how magnificent the world was and how much she'd been missing.

On this particular night it was the 4th of July and the rest of the group, their "wolf pack" as John called it, was on the veranda, too, waiting for darkness to descend so they could watch the fireworks in the field behind the building. Michael rolled onto his side, with his head resting on his hand, and leaned in toward Stevie. His voice was almost a whisper, the way it always was when he wanted to be alone with her, as if he believed he could force out the rest of the world by not acknowledging it. "I was just thinking," he said, "When I'm back on the beach at home, I'll be looking up at the same sky and feeling like you're right beside me, but you'll be a thousand miles away."

A dagger tore through her chest and into her gut. It happened every time she thought about being separated from him. Michael lived in Jacksonville, Florida. Once she returned to Massachusetts, the entire east coast would stand between them. Massachusetts. The sheer loneliness of going back there and trying to pretend—again—that she was something she wasn't made her wish she never had to. Finally she'd found a place that she fit in, not as someone's daughter, or the smart kid in school, or the rebellious and out of control kid, but just her—her without the money or the parties or the alcohol. This place was a refuge like no other. It was *home*.

Feeling Michael's dark eyes moving over her face, she rolled onto her side to face him and noticed the flutter of his black eyelashes as his eyes shifted to the curve of her hip and her waist. There was a rule at the rehab that prohibited physical contact between patients. That line in the sand was getting painfully old.

"Check out the meth head, talking like Stevie's his girlfriend," David snickered. "You don't really think you'd have a chance with someone like her, do you?"

"What's that mean, 'someone like me'?" Stevie asked David, but she wasn't looking at him. She was watching Michael. He was unpredictable in a way that she hadn't quite figured out yet. When they were alone, there was a steadfastness to his personality that she could depend on. He was quieter sometimes than others but always the same thoughtful and soft-spoken Michael. When other people were around, however, he could become agitated, for good reason or for no reason at all. Dr. Jim had prescribed a small dose of antidepressant to counter the removal of methamphetamine from his body, and Stevie figured that was playing a role in his fluctuating moods. Agitation was growing inside him now, preparing to strike out like the snake on Marcus' neck. She could see it in the black flash of his eyes and in the way his lips sucked so hard on his cigarette that the burning tip became long and orange.

"Shut up, David," Brian warned, "before he beats the crap out of you."

"I don't know about the rest of yous, but that's what I been waiting for," Marcus commented, which caused Jake to burst out laughing.

David sneered. He had already made it clear that to him Marcus, like Michael, was a waste of space and not even worth responding to. He was oh so sure that all drug addicts were the same, a vile life form polluting his otherwise perfect world. Brian looked over at Stevie and rolled his eyes. He was David's friend, like Stevie was, because when David wasn't on his druggie rampage, he was a nice guy, but he was completely infuriating when he was. A "blind spot", Stevie called it, David's blind spot.

She could see that Jake was itching to jump into the conversation but it was taking him a minute to find the right words. He didn't like David from the get go and he took it as a personal slap every time he tried to trash Michael. Jake was an expert at character assessment. He could read a person's facial expressions and body language as well as any child psychiatrist or fortune teller at an amusement park. Decades of life experience had been squeezed into thirteen years. When it came to pain and suffering, he was like a hound dog; he could smell it and sometimes even know the cause of it without understanding why. Truth be told it was intuition carved out of his own tortured past.

"Ain't no talkin' to Budweiser man," he finally said. "He knows it all."

"I'll teach you to talk to me like that, baby freak," David threatened.

"That won't be happening," Michael breathed. He'd remained quiet for so long the sound of his voice came as a surprise. He swiftly moved into an upright position, but not sitting like most human beings would do it. Instead he curled his body underneath him with his weight leaning on his haunches, like he was a cat ready to launch from his feet.

"So what's the story then?" David said boldly, but his attitude didn't hide the tremble in his voice. "Is that what you think, that she's your girl? Huh, meth head?"

What was it in David, Stevie wondered, that motivated him to practically beg someone to kick the life out of him? Something must have happened to him that he couldn't bear to live with. Maybe he thought whatever it was could be beaten out of him. Her heart raced for poor David who was about to be slaughtered because of his own stupidly big mouth. But still Michael remained as motionless as a gargoyle. He tilted his head to one side and stared silently at David with his intense eyes as if David were an exhibit in a museum. The cigarette fell from his lips and Stevie saw his mouth soften. That was the moment she knew Michael wasn't going to hit him.

"No man, that's not what I think," he finally answered and brought his body into a standing position. His hand momentarily rested on Jake's head as he passed him on way to the glass door that led inside the building. "You're not a freak," he said softly.

Marcus shook his head at David. "You must be as stupid as you look," he barked. "The guy took on John. What do you think he'd do to you?"

Took on John? "Wait," Stevie called to Michael, "I'm coming with you." He turned to face her and lingered in the doorway. His eyebrows knitted together betrayed the anger he was trying not to show.

"Me, too," Allison said as she quickly scurried to her feet and followed Stevie.

When the girls caught up, the three of them walked in silence down the hallway toward the door that led to the field where the fireworks were going to be. Stevie couldn't process what had happened on the veranda fast enough. When Michael answered David's question, did he mean he didn't think of her as a girlfriend? Or did he mean he thought she wouldn't think of him that way? She was scared to find out, but she had to. She thought she might be falling in love with him. *Breathe* she told herself and reached for his hand. Her heart plummeted to her feet. He was so surprised by the gesture that he stopped walking. So she stopped and Allison, walking ahead, stopped, too.

"Awww," Allison crooned when she turned around and saw them holding hands.

Michael threw his head back and unexpected laughter poured out of him. Then to Stevie's complete enchantment, he brought her hand to his beautiful mouth and kissed it.

The night air felt like a warm humid blanket draped across her bare shoulders. If she closed her eyes and focused on the feeling, it reminded her of the hot air breathed out of a horse's nostrils on a fall New England day. When she was ten or eleven she used to visit a horse named Molasses who lived within walking distance from her house. With her eyes closed, she could almost hear his loud exhalations. She was sitting on a blanket with Michael and Allison that she had dragged from her room to watch the fireworks. Other small groups were gathered on blankets nearby, including Julie and two other nurses.

"I wish I could stay with you guys forever," Allison was saying. She had spent the afternoon in individual counseling with Ellen trying to determine where she would live after her release. She wanted to return home so she could be close to her friends, but Ellen disagreed. At home was Allison's alcoholic mother who was too absorbed in her own disease to notice when she was in trouble, not to mention Allison's friends who were still actively using substances. Ellen had suggested she move into a women's sober house for six months to a year, a structured, nontoxic environment that could serve as a transitional step before returning home. There was one nearby, in Valdosta, where Ellen could frequently check on her. Of course that was the last thing Allison wanted. In her mind, Ellen was the enemy. She wanted as many miles as possible between them.

"Guess that would be the blind leading the blind," Michael remarked.

"What do you mean?" Allison asked him innocently.

"If one of us picked up, it'd be like dominos."

Like dominoes, Stevie mused.

"Do you miss doing meth?" Allison asked him and Stevie cringed. She and Allison had shared a few heart-to-hearts on the subject. Although she didn't judge Michael harshly anymore the way David did, Allison still had a lot of curiosity about the subject. And Stevie, well, she sensed that Michael didn't want to talk about it, so she rarely brought it up, and never in front of other people.

True to character, Michael thought about it for a long time before he answered her. He even lit a cigarette in the silence and blew smoke rings that floated toward the sky until they became part of it. "It's not that I miss it," he explained. "It's just that I know it's not there, you know? I wake up in the morning and say 'oh yeah, it's this life, not the other one', and I can go back to sleep because I don't have to worry about it, not today."

"But if you were at home you'd be worried about it?"

Michael smiled at Allison's inquiry and reflected again before each word carefully came from him like they were creating a piece of fine art, a sculpture constructed of words instead of clay. "It's like this video game Matt and I used to play in junior high. We'd race to see who could get to the castle first without the dragon burning us to crisps. But sometimes the dragon would be sleeping and we'd get to play without being scared of being killed. It's like that. The dragon's not dead, but it's sleeping."

The dragon's not dead, but it's sleeping. Michael was an amateur fiction writer so it wasn't that unusual that he utilized metaphors in his speech, but the one he had just used was disturbing. It made shiver bumps crawl up Stevie's spine like an inchworm.

"Who's Matt?" Allison asked.

Michael sucked more smoke into his lungs as Stevie watched intently for his reaction to Allison's question. He misinterpreted and passed her the cigarette. She took the opportunity to smile at him reassuringly and check his expression for uncertainty. He was okay. Maybe he could talk about it. She took a drag and handed it back.

When their fingers made contact her heart *b-bumped* in her chest as if it had been electrically resuscitated, and he met her eyes as if he had felt it, too.

"He used to be my brother—well, not really but we always used to say that we were," Michael explained. "We grew up next door to each other and were best friends our whole lives. His parents got divorced and his mom, I don't know she was just a really fucked up person. I used to call her Dexi because she lived on Dexatrim and vodka—probably still does…" When his voice trailed off, he used his middle finger to angrily flick his cigarette away.

Stevie's body tightened with apprehension. "What?" Allison pushed.

He took a nervous breath and held it for a minute like he was trying to decide whether or not to say it out loud. "She tried to blow me once when I was fifteen."

Out in the real world a disclosure of that magnitude would have drawn breaths of shock and *oh my God* responses, but in rehab, most people have been there in one form or another. Addiction breeds all kinds of sick behaviors that are nearly impossible to avoid. What happened to Michael was fairly close to some of Stevie's own experiences. Still, she didn't know what to say. She let her head fall back and looked up at the stars. It was easier than seeing the pain on his face.

"What'd you do?" Allison asked.

"Nothing. I got up and went home. Anyway," he said sharply as if the divergence in the conversation was completely meaningless.

"Soon after that she met some guy and moved to Miami. Matt didn't want to go so my parents let him live with us. They didn't adopt him or anything, but they treated him like a son."

By now Stevie had spent countless hours with Michael. He had told her all about his parents and their expectations of him, how his father was an architectural engineer and his mother was a college professor and they both wanted to see him conquer the world, but not even once had he mentioned Matt or the traumas they went through together. And the phrase *used to be my brother* gave her the impression that Matt might have died, but she knew by the way he was avoiding eye contact and sucking on his bottom lip that he'd disclosed as much as he was capable of for one night.

"It's a perfect night for fireworks, isn't it?" she threw out and reached behind her head to remove the elastic band that was holding her hair in a messy ponytail. Michael's eyes took her in as she shook her wild hair onto her shoulders. "Look, they're starting!" she exclaimed and pointed excitedly at the sky, but Michael didn't turn away.

"Your hair looks good like that," Allison observed. "You should stop pulling it back."

"It's like a mane," Michael added.

"A horse's mane?" she asked him playfully.

"No, a lion's," he answered and it made her laugh.

"Yours is more like a horse's, Michael," Allison suggested.

"Mine?" he asked, amused. "I have hair like a horse?" He shook his head like one.

"A mustang," Stevie voiced, "a wild mustang." His hair was just as dark and glossy.

"A mustaaang," Michael repeated and broke into a dimple-bearing grin. "That's funny, isn't it? The words mean the same thing, but mustang sounds a whole lot better." Stevie smiled right back at him,

83

barely able to contain it. Michael always made comments about words. He told her once that he liked them not only for how they sounded, but for how they felt on his tongue. It made her want to crawl inside him.

"Were you like this when you were little, all excited at the fire-works?" he asked her.

"I don't remember," she replied. "This is the first 4ᵗʰ of July I've been sober since I was ten." Michael looked so stricken by her response that she wished she hadn't said it. He had a way of brooding when she talked about drinking as a little kid. Once he even got tears in his eyes when she told him she used to hide bottles in her toy box. For Michael it was different. His parents didn't drink at all (because his grandfather was a roaring drunk he said) and although he described it as "love at first gulp", he didn't start drinking until he was a junior in high school. "But I'm happy now," she added with a nervous titter. It must have been contagious because affectionate laughter rolled out of Michael and then Allison. Stevie laughed along with them at the ridiculousness of it all—all the fourth of Julys she spent wasted and thinking she was having a good time. She let it all spill out, not because it was funny, but because it felt good to get rid of it.

"I can't remember the last time I wasn't high on a holiday," Allison admitted, "but it is fun, isn't it?"

Michael fell onto his back on the blanket and watched the fire-works. "Yeah. Yeah it is. Who knew, huh?"

He reached for Stevie's hand and brought it close to his face, examining it. Anxiety stirred like a brew in the pit of her stomach. She'd cut her broken nails, but she still hadn't painted them. Maybe he thought she had hands like a guy. They weren't tiny and feminine with perfectly sculpted nails like Allison's.

"Check this out," he said, scrutinizing her fingers.

"What?" she asked defensively, certain she didn't want to hear his answer.

"They're beautiful. You could be a musician with these fingers." She sighed relief and giggled all at once. Michael smiled that knock the breath right out of her smile and slid his fingers through hers so they were woven together. "Come here," he whispered and pulled her onto the blanket beside him.

Excruciating, that was the word. It was excruciating to be lying that close to him. They weren't touching each other, except for their hands, but the intimacy was almost unbearable. His fingers wrapped around hers sent waves of shock through her. Every nerve ending in her body seemed to be vibrating. Maybe that's what making love is supposed to feel like, she thought. For her it had never been that way, but maybe because she'd never done it sober, or with someone she was truly in love with. She wanted to meet his eyes, but was suddenly too shy as if the slightest glance could reveal what she was thinking. So instead she looked up at the sky and let her fingertips explore his hand. The muscle under his thumb was strong and there were calluses on his fingertips. *From what?* she wondered.

"Can I still be here?" Allison suddenly blurted out.

Stevie pulled her arm until she lay down beside them on the blanket. They were all silent as they watched the explosion of colors light up the night sky. *A celebration of freedom*, Stevie thought. It couldn't be more fitting.

CHAPTER NINE:

TANGLED

The hum of voices hit her ears like a swarm of monster mosquitoes as soon as Stevie opened her bedroom door. It was coming from the den at the end of the women's hallway where a group of women from the local sober house were preparing to host a meeting. Extra chairs had been brought in and most of the rehab patients were gathered already, including Michael who was reclining in a lounge chair. As soon as he spotted her, he caught her eye and patted the front of the seat where his long legs were stretched out, telling her he was saving it for her. Her heart skipped a beat at the invitation.

"I'll get us coffee," she offered when she reached him and tousled his hair. Since the night of the fireworks, she couldn't seem to keep her hands off of him. It was embarrassing almost, like that first rush of hormones in junior high. Even in her sleep she was touching him, dreaming of his eyes and his mouth, his strong chest and slender belly. And his hands, the way they melted her. In her dreams she knew exactly what it would feel like to be with him. And she awoke with all kinds of physical sensations, as if she had been.

Michael took his cup from her, the one without the cream in it and exactly three teaspoons of sugar, and moved his legs aside so Stevie could sit between them. Brian and Liz were sitting on a couch nearby and she greeted them while handing Michael some chocolate chip cookies and biting into one of hers. Stevie had noticed that Liz, like herself, appeared to be resurrecting. A new light had replaced the strange hollowness in her eyes. The four of them spent a lot of time together—like couples, but not. Liz and Brian were both married and even had children at home, and she and Michael, well, they weren't officially a couple, even though it felt like they were. The staff at the rehab prohibited relationships between patients. Three times already she had been dragged into Ellen's office for the sole purpose of discussing her "friendship" with Michael.

Her mouth was full of cookies when Michael leaned in close to talk to her privately. "Hey, there's a full moon tonight," he said in her ear.

"Oh yeah?" she tried to say without spraying cookie crumbs out with her response. She had learned something about herself during her rehab stint, that she had a bad habit of shoving too much food in her mouth, but only when there was chocolate involved. And Michael was the one who'd noticed it. He called it her "chocolate monster" as if it were some kind of playful being who lived inside her with a will of its own. Apparently the abrupt removal of alcohol from her body had given birth to it.

Now he laughed at the jumbled up word that made its way past the cookies and out of her mouth. "Yeah," he said. "We ought to check it out." This time she had the good sense to nod. "It's called the thunder moon," he continued and his fingers brushed her hair off her face only to reveal her cheek packed with cookies, like a squirrel carrying acorns. It made him crack up laughing again. When he got over it, he finished his point. "In July the full moon is the thunder moon. That's what the Native Americans called it."

"Hm," she mumbled with her mouth closed as tight as a vault. Where did he come up with this stuff? Phases of the moon? Apparently while she was out partying into the wee hours of the morning he was high on meth but devouring textbooks.

"So, it's a date?"

She almost choked. It took too long to respond, like she was thinking it over. "Yeah, sure," she sputtered and turned her attention to the women who were about to host the meeting so he wouldn't notice her face changing colors.

A podium was set up and behind it were five chairs where women from the sober house were seated. The way they laughed and chatted together so easily caught Stevie's attention. If she were one of them waiting to speak, either her head would be between her knees by now or she'd have vomited on the floor. She'd never been able to speak in front of a crowd. Technically, it was her demise from the upper crust college that her father had bought her way into after she was turned down by Boston College. After showing up drunk to her debate class and staggering to the podium, she was escorted by security out of the school…forever. Since that infamous day her father had probably spoken to her all of a half dozen times, and that was over six months ago. Apparently he saved all his valuable words for his son who was skilled enough at hiding his alcoholism to make it into Harvard Law School where he would be starting in August.

A willowy young woman with straightened black hair stepped up to the podium and introduced herself as Lee Ann. At AA meetings like this one, the people hosting the meeting took turns sharing their stories, sometimes referred to as "drunkalogs" with the audience. Right from the start, Lee Ann's story was so close to Stevie's own that the hairs on her arms stood up. She talked about drinking as a child and about how she never went anywhere or did anything throughout high school without alcohol. By the time she started college, she had to drink to get out of bed in the morning and to stop her hands from shaking. She talked about how humiliating it was for people to smell alcohol on her, but how she could never quite kill the stench. It seemed to ooze from her pores. She drank because she had to, she said. Her body needed it.

Stevie identified so strongly with the drunkalog that it felt like Lee Ann was telling *her* story, not her own. She looked over her shoulder at Michael, needing the comfort of his eyes. It was right there waiting, just like she knew it would be. When she turned her own eyes back to Lee Ann, his hand stroked her back for a minute. Without a word, he understood. He got it.

Then something unexpected happened. Lee Ann looked straight at her and gave her a message—at least it seemed like it was directed to her. "It doesn't have to be that way," she stated. "You can live your life free from alcohol, like I am. That's what I learned when I was a patient here, that I had a choice. And today I choose not to drink. They say a sober alcoholic is a miracle, and that's me—that's us. Thanks to AA and this place, Ellen and John and all the people here who help us, we're all walking miracles."

As Lee Ann stepped away from the podium, everyone in the room clapped loudly, except for Stevie who was still stunned by her words, as if they had been offered up to her alone. Maybe there really was a way out of the hellhole called alcoholism. *A way out*. It was almost unfathomable. She wiggled her body closer to Michael's so she could whisper close to his ear. "That's how I want to be someday," she told him.

"What do you mean?" he asked, sitting up and reaching over the side of the chair to place his empty coffee cup on the floor.

"Strong...like her."

As Michael brought his arm back up he wrapped it around her waist. She felt his hand resting on her hip and the scruff of his whiskers on her cheek as his face brushed against hers. "You're already strong," he said quietly. "You just don't know it yet."

When he let go and sat back in the chair, her blood seemed to be rushing recklessly through her veins, like a tidal wave that could wash all the bones out of her body. She didn't debate it in her head before she leaned back against him, only followed the impulse. He did the same and wrapped his arms around her waist, and it was the happiest she could ever remember being, with Michael's warm breath in her ear and his strong arms holding onto her securely. Someday, looking back, that moment would be one that she would have lived over and over again if she could have. She'd have hit the rewind button again and again.

The perfect moment didn't last long. Ellen permeated it with her powerful glare. Stevie felt it and quickly sat up. It wasn't good enough. Ellen stormed over, grabbed her by the arm and jerked her off the chair. The entire group watched (even the new speaker stopped talking momentarily) as she dragged Stevie into the women's hallway. "How many times do we have to go through this?" she demanded.

Stevie jumped instantaneously into defense mode. "Why do we have to go through it at all? It's not like we were getting high. We were listening to the meeting."

"Relationships are *not* allowed. It's dangerous for your sobriety—"

"You don't know us. So how could you possibly know what's right for us?"

Ellen's face turned bright red. Even her glasses looked a little steamed up. She reminded Stevie of one of those cartoon bulls with steam snorting from their noses. "Stevie, that's enough," she said fairly calmly. She was probably silently counting to ten, Stevie conjectured, like they teach in those anger management classes. "If you want to talk about this during one of our sessions—"

"I don't," Stevie snapped and turned to walk back toward the meeting. It was the moment she realized the entire group was listening to the argument. Liz made eye contact with Stevie and shook her head disapprovingly at her like her mother sometimes did when she was arguing with her dad. She was chastising her with her eyes.

Ellen stepped up behind her. "Listen," she said, her voice controlled, but not soft enough that Stevie's friends couldn't hear, "You need to keep the focus on yourself. So, you either create some distance between you and Michael James or I'll do it for you."

Like the water lilies, Stevie contemplated, *our roots are now tangled*. And it seemed unfathomable to *un*tangle them on demand. She stepped away from Ellen back into the midst of the group. Michael slid onto the floor to give her the chair. She tried to meet his eyes, but felt tears choking up in her throat and had to look away. This time her eyes fell on John, who was watching the exchange with interest. He didn't appear angry, though, like Ellen who looked like her head would blow right off her shoulders any minute her face was so red. He almost looked sad, like he felt sorry for them. But surely that wasn't the truth. He was probably insensitive and judgmental, exactly like Ellen.

"How long you think it takes to be a recover*ed* addict?" Stevie asked the group later that night when they were playing cards in the recreation room.

All the veterans—Marcus, Brian and Liz—laughed. "No such animal," Brian stated flatly.

"I've heard people say that," Stevie argued. "That they were recovered."

"Haven't you figured it out yet, Stevie—that most people are full of shit?" Marcus flung out. "The only recovered addict is a dead addict."

"Oh now that's comforting," Michael commented, and rubbed his nose with his thumb. Stevie had noticed that he either rubbed his nose or sniffed compulsively whenever they talked about using. "Where'd you get that, Marcus?"

"What do you mean, where'd I get that? I been in and out of detoxes since I was twenty-two."

"How old're you now?" Jake asked.

"Thirty-nine since May."

Jake's eyes grew big and round as silver dollars, as if Marcus had said *ninety*-nine.

"Once an addict, always an addict," Liz chimed in, and Brian, her perpetual back up, nodded his head vigorously.

Stevie rolled her eyes and snickered. "What'd Ellen tell you that?" she asked.

"No, actually. You were wrong about her earlier, you know. She's an alcoholic."

"No shit. Believe me she made a big point of telling me that the first day I got here. She thinks she can use that as a way to get close to me, but I'm not telling her anything."

"The more you dump while you're here, the easier it'll be to stay sober," Brian advised.

"I've dumped plenty," Stevie replied and glanced over at Michael, sitting beside her like a partner in crime. "What, you think because she's an alcoholic that means she understands what we're going through, Liz?"

Liz laid her cards down on the table. "What I think is that you don't know anything about her life."

"Oh, and you do?"

"Yeah, I do. We live in the same town. I know her family. She's married and has two little kids. You've made her out to be a monster, Stevie, but she's not. She wants to help you."

"No, she doesn't—maybe you, but not me. She doesn't even like me."

"That's because of me, though, because she hates me," Michael threw in.

John had entered the room and was now standing by their table waving around a hand full of mail. He tossed an envelope to Liz (the one with a flower drawn on it in orange crayon) and another to Marcus. Jake was watching with excitement in his eyes, as if it was possible that some long lost relative might come to his rescue, or at least write him a letter. "Who hates you?" John asked Michael.

"Stevie's counselor."

John let loose an enormous laugh. It conjured up images of the jolly green giant. "I hope you don't actually believe that, Mr. James. Here you go. I brought you three letters from home. How do you like that?"

"You can keep 'em. That's how I like that."

John moved his oversized head slowly like he was thinking it over. "One of these days you ought to break down and open one of them. This one's got a CD in it."

"Yeah and how do you know that?" Michael asked.

"Because I'm the one who screened it."

"Isn't that nice?" Michael sneered. "There's trust all over the place, from the ones who write 'em to the ones who read 'em."

"I didn't read it," John said. "I had to open it. Believe it or not, some people mail drugs in here. I can't let that be happening."

"Why not?" Marcus joked.

"Yeah, we were planning a party, John. What'll we do without the cocaine?" Brian added, chuckling raucously as if it was the funniest thing anyone had ever said.

"You guys can figure that one out," John replied with a big, bear-like yawn, his arms stretching half a mile. "I've got to get home. I'm starting to feel like I live here."

"You mean you don't?" Allison asked innocently.

John chuckled and started to leave, but turned back. "Hey, Michael, are you sure about this? It's Linkin Park *Meteora*." He waved the envelope around enticingly.

"Can I have it?" Jake asked. "I love Linkin Park."

"It's all yours, man," Michael said without hesitation. "Toss the letter in the trash."

Jake couldn't contain his excitement, as if he'd finally received mail. "Who's it from?" he asked.

"Matt," Michael answered. "But I don't want to talk about him."

"He your brother?" Jake asked.

"What'd the man say, Jake?" Marcus scolded and Jake sunk a little deeper into his seat. "Hey let's watch *Pirates*, huh?" Marcus suggested.

"Again?" Allison complained. "I know every line in that movie."

"Now I know I'm going home," John mumbled. He handed the envelope to Jake and walked off, but stopped briefly to yell back to Michael. "Are we meeting one on one in the morning?"

Michael shook his head. "Got to see Dr. Jim at 10:00."

"Oh yeah," John answered. "Men's group first, though, at 8:30. Be on time. Good night y'all," he said to everyone else without looking back again.

CHAPTER TEN:

FINALLY

Of course he wasn't on time to men's group like John had warned the night before. He never was. The guys were all outside already and sitting in a circle on the grass when Michael showed up toting a huge cup of coffee, his cigarette pack tucked neatly in his t-shirt pocket. It was only 8:40 a.m., but already the Georgia sun was living up to its reputation. The guys were sweaty and red-faced, except for Michael, who was fresh from the shower, his wet hair combed back slick and cool off his face.

"Whatta you know, meth head decided to show up," David grumbled. Michael froze in his tracks, his body stiff with tension.

"Take a seat," John ordered, but Michael didn't. He stood like a statue staring with his eyes that were almost black from fury focused on David, who in turn wriggled around uncomfortably. "All right, I'm game for this," John said. "Are we getting it over with?" Michael turned only his eyes to John and nodded slightly. "So, what's the deal, David?" John asked. "What's your problem with Michael, my friend?"

"My problem with the meth head? You mean, other than that he's a freak?"

Michael's muscles visibly tensed. He clenched a fist and bent down to put his coffee cup on the grass. Marcus and Jake stiffened, too, and leaned forward like they were ready to attack. Michael shook his head at them. After a moment, Marcus slowly sat back and Jake followed suit. It was John that pushed the momentum forward.

"I'm tired of this, David," he said in almost a yawn. "It's getting in the way of my time and I don't appreciate that. So, say your piece and get it over with. But know that I'm not backing you up. You're on your own."

David shot John and the rest of the group a disgusted look, as if he couldn't believe they weren't all on his side. He scowled at Michael. "The shit you're pulling with Stevie," he hurled. "You're tryin' to get something from her."

"Oh man," Brian muttered. "You're wrong. You're wrong, David."

"Better shut it, mother fucker," Marcus warned.

But conviction was in Michael's eyes. His hair practically bristled. He was ready. Just one more hit. "Say it," he said softly. "What you're thinking right now, say it."

David actually had the nerve to laugh. "All right, you asked for it." He smiled at John, who sighed at his complete inability to see what was coming and took his glasses off to put in a safe place. "Okay, meth head, here it is," David said almost gleefully. "The only reason you're with her all the time is because you think you'll get laid."

The movement was so quick that he barely finished the sentence before Michael lifted him off the ground by his Abercrombie collar. David didn't stand a chance. He wasn't strong enough or fast enough to compete with Michael's fist that hit his face as fast and steady as a piston. John pulled Michael off and managed to hold one arm back but his other hand still had David by the shirt. "That's enough, Michael!" he shouted.

"Got AIDS, junkie?" David spat out along with the blood from his mouth that splattered on Michael's face and clean white t-shirt. "Don't give a shit if you infect her?"

"I'll fucking kill you!" Michael screamed in his face and shook him like a dog with a chew toy with the one hand John wasn't holding back.

"I said that's enough. Now let go," John scolded. Michael flung him onto the ground and paced like a wild animal, his breath coming in short, violent spurts. Still David didn't stop egging him on, his mouth his only weapon.

"Didn't I tell you the meth head's dangerous?" he pleaded to John, wiping a streak of blood from his now misshapen nose onto the back of his hand.

Michael lunged toward him, but John held him back again and this time Brian helped.

"You could kill him," Brian hissed. "You have to stop."

It took a minute or so, but the words sunk in and Michael started to calm down. Everyone else was completely silent, waiting to see what would come next. Michael took a measured step toward David and no one tried to stop him this time. "Name's Michael," he growled. "You got that? Not meth head. *Michael*. You say anything or do anything else that hurts her, next time I won't let go." David shrunk back when Michael's hand, blood streaming from its split knuckles, reached for his coffee cup, but he didn't need to be afraid. It was over. Michael walked back to the building without another word.

"Good thing Dr. Jim's doing exams this morning," John stated simply. "You're first in line, David. Hopefully he can straighten out that broken nose."

Stevie nearly fell off the couch when she saw Michael with the blood spattered on him. He entered the building and took urgent strides toward where she was waiting with Liz and Allison in the den to be called into the exam room for her physical. "I'm sorry," he called out to her once he was within earshot.

Sorry...Sorry for what? The first thing that crossed her mind was that he'd somehow got his hands on meth and snorted it. She knew about the nosebleeds. He had told her that he'd starting using needles because his nose was "blown apart". But blood was all over him, like a cloud dropped blood drops on him instead of rain.

Michael interpreted the horror on her face. "It's not my blood," he said into her ear. She had jumped to her feet and was clinging onto his neck, holding him so close the deep red stains on his shirt were smudging onto her baby blue Foo Fighters t-shirt.

"Oh my God, Michael, what happened to you?" she sputtered. Her hands quickly brushed his curls off his face to search for the source of bleeding.

"It's not my blood," he repeated and his mouth looked slack and sad, but uninjured.

Just then John entered, dragging David by the arm. "Get off him, Stevie," he said, but she didn't respond. Her mental faculties were absorbed by David's mangled face and trying to fathom what had happened. His nose was oddly misshapen, one eye was swollen shut and his lip was split in more than one place with blood spewing out. "I said get off him!" John shouted and she let go. "In my office, Michael, now." He walked away as John pulled David over to the door that led to the exam room and knocked on it.

Dr. Jim didn't look that surprised when he opened it and saw what was left of David's face. "Bring him on in," he said to John in his usual carefree manner and John did. Dr. Jim was dressed like he was on route to a basketball game, not about to fix someone's broken nose, which wasn't unusual. He rarely dressed like a physician and that worked to his advantage. The patients respected him because he didn't act like he was better than them. "I'm just another addict," he always said. "Wash it off with soap and water, Stephanie," he said now before he closed the door behind David and himself.

The women stared at each other in stunned silence. Stevie looked down at her blood smeared shirt and hands. "Finally," Liz said with a soft voice. "I'm so glad that's over."

"Me too!" Allison agreed. "All that tension was fucking with my head."

"They'll send him home, won't they?" Stevie asked Liz.

She shook her head confidently. "I don't think so. You need to go clean up."

"But why not? They told us that—that fighting would get us kicked out."

"They might have told you that, Stevie." Liz made eye contact with Allison.

"So what? Why would it be different for Michael?"

"Because it is different for Michael. Don't you know?"

Stevie's eyes scrutinized Liz and Allison. Why would they know something about Michael that she didn't? "Say it," boiled out of her. "Why do you think that?"

"Because they don't want him to go home—ask him about it," Liz suggested.

Louise came barrel-assing around the corner, wagging a finger at Stevie. "Have you lost your mind touching that boy's blood?" she chided. "The good Lord gave you better sense than that. Now you get in your room this instant and get that shirt off." She turned her worried eyes to Liz and Allison. "If there's blood on the floor, don't you touch it." Liz calmly nodded her understanding and that set Louise in motion down the women's hallway toward Stevie's room, fussing about bad boys getting into fights and what was wrong with them? And so on.

Stevie followed like a walking corpse in a horror movie, her eyes blank and her hands and chest tainted with blood. She was in over her head, *way* over her head. Even though she knew that Michael was okay she couldn't get rid of the feeling that something terribly wrong had happened to him and she couldn't have stopped it. Even if she had been there, she couldn't have stopped it. David was hurt and he was her friend, but still almost all her anxiety was focused on Michael and the thought that she might never see him again.

She tugged the Foo Fighters t-shirt over her head in her bathroom and left it in the sink. Louise had said something about using bleach. That would probably ruin it. On the countertop was the white water lily from the duck pond. She had given up on it, had written it off as something too beautiful and perfect to be obtainable—like Michael— but he had proven her wrong. That morning it had been waiting for her in a bottle of water at the beginning of the women's hallway. When she saw it, her heart leapt into her throat. She didn't need to see her name scratched onto the label with a pen or even recognize Michael's handwriting. She knew the second she saw it that he had gone to the pond without her and done battle with the roots. And she hadn't even thanked him for it yet.

Her fingers touched the bright yellow stamen. It left a residue on her fingertips that looked like fairy dust. What would Michael call that color? Marigold or canary, maybe. Plain old yellow would never quite suffice in Michael's clever mind.

By the time she returned to the den with her journal in hand, he was sitting in her seat. He had changed his shirt, too. At a glance, there was nothing left of his appearance to suggest he'd been in a fight. But a closer look revealed open cuts on the knuckles of his right hand, probably from David's teeth, she surmised. Allison scooted over so she could sit beside him, but she remained standing.

"Are you leaving?" Stevie asked him, lifting her chin defiantly. He shook his head. "Why not?"

"Because…it's a long story," he said and looked around as if he were uncomfortable answering publicly. Liz and Allison picked up the vibe and moved to the other side of the room. Stevie fell onto the couch beside him.

"You want to tell me that story?"

"Yeah. Yeah, I do, but not now. I'm going in soon."

He meant he was going in to be examined by Dr. Jim. "Okay," she replied and opened her journal. She was staring at it, trying to think of something to write. Some time had passed since her last entry. Her last notation was the first draft of a poem about him (*"You move like liquid uncontained…"*). She had put the journal away shortly after meeting Michael because she didn't need the crutch anymore, now that she had someone to talk to that she trusted. But today's events had caused her to take a few steps back—not so much the fight, but what was revealed afterward, that Liz and maybe even Allison (and who knew who else?) knew things about Michael that she didn't.

"What are you writing?" he asked.

She shrugged her shoulders, still staring at the blank page. "Nothing." From her peripheral vision, he appeared to be completely composed, like a normal guy waiting to see the doctor, not someone who had just beaten the living shit out of someone.

"Yeah, I know how that goes."

"Mm hm." *I still can't look at you.* She probably looked totally idiotic staring at the blank page, but it was better than looking at him and having to deal with all the emotions that would come with it. She scribbled…nothing, only ink.

"I started a song yesterday," Michael offered.

101

A song? He'd never told her he wrote lyrics. He'd said he wrote short stories and she'd told him about her poetry and her ambition to be a novelist. The revelation was far too compelling not to look up. She met his eyes. "For any particular reason?" she asked, trying her hardest to sound like she didn't really care but was trying to be polite.

He inhaled smoke from his cigarette, the reflex of his introspection.

"I have a band," he finally disclosed. It was enough to make her close the notebook. "I play guitar and I sing. That's…what I do." So much was rushing through her head: how he didn't want to talk about his work and how he didn't go to college even though he was super ridiculously smart, and the calluses on his fingertips. She wanted to say *who the fuck are you?* Instead she lit a cigarette and fought the urge.

"I thought…" His head fell back on the couch as his words trailed off, but his big brown eyes were wide open. His notoriously thick black eyelashes couldn't hide the fact that he was thinking and analyzing, and growing agitated. His fingers tapped nervously on his knee. "…that you'd judge me by it."

"By what?" she asked.

Before he could answer her, Dr. Jim, standing in the doorway with a fat medical file, called his name. Julie, the nurse, was beside him. Michael smashed his cigarette out and walked away without another word. Stevie watched him shake hands with Dr. Jim like an old friend and pass through the door with Dr. Jim's arm around his shoulders. Her chest filled up with pain, as if she were having a heart attack. If she could go to her room and bawl her eyes out maybe the pain would leak out of her, leak out all over the bedspread like a big blot of ink. But Julie was hand motioning to her.

She followed Julie's cue; somewhere between the couch and the door the tears gained more momentum than she could fight. They were spilling out of her eyes now, streaming down her face and onto the shirt she'd just changed into. She'd told Dr. Tom when she was at the hospital that she didn't think she could cry anymore. She was flat-line, emotionless and had been for over six months. He explained that she had suffered some kind of an emotional breakdown. The word *breakdown* had come as a shock. It was the kind of word that in the wrong hands could get her permanently extricated from her family. But maybe Dr. Tom was wrong; maybe she was just saving all those tears for this very moment. Who knew so many could be contained in one human body?

"Are you all right?" Julie asked. She looked a little scared, Stevie noticed.

"I don't know," she confessed. *Maybe I'm having another breakdown*, she wanted to say, but didn't dare. They might transfer her to a psychiatric hospital.

"It's been a hard morning. I'll get Ellen. She's on the detox wing—"

"No. No, I won't talk to her," Stevie insisted.

Julie looked like she wanted to debate the issue, but Stevie had answered so emphatically that it must have thrown off her game plan. She approached Stevie and embraced her. Stevie sobbed onto her shoulder, feeling like she was a child again and it was still okay to let every emotion pour out of her like water from a garden hose, silent but relentless. "You know, David's going to be okay," Julie offered.

"Is he?" She lifted her face off of Julie's shoulder.

"You'd be surprised—he looks better already. Dr. Jim fixed his nose. Of course tomorrow when the bruises set in…"

"What about Michael?"

"I don't think David got a punch in."

"Yeah, I know but…"

"But it's not really the black eyes and broken noses we have to worry about, right?" Stevie nodded her head that seemed ridiculously heavy at the moment (maybe because it was full of tears?) and cried some more. "It's what going on inside of us that makes them happen. That's the real danger."

"Yeah," Stevie agreed.

"All addicts have a lot to work through," Julie answered. "All the junk we pushed to the bottom of the heap when we were using because we didn't want to deal with it is right there waiting for us when we get sober. Meth addicts are especially volatile. You know, that's why the counselors discourage relationships—"

"Ellen told you that...about Michael and me?"

Julie shook her head. "She hasn't said anything. But you don't think I'm blind, do you? I've seen you together."

"Oh," Stevie said and hung her head. She felt like a fool. Why did she always have to wear her emotions so outwardly, like a huge letter A, her own personal scarlet letter?

"I can understand the attraction. If Michael were clean, it would be different."

"But he is. He is clean now," Stevie argued.

Julie was quick to correct her. "No, Stevie. He's *getting* clean. He has a long way to go. Don't expect too much from him too soon. Let him get a handle on things. Methamphetamine addiction is very difficult to break."

"You mean harder than alcoholism?"

"Completely different monster."

Her words brought to mind Michael's words, *the dragon's not dead, but it's sleeping.*

"I don't know how much Michael's told you," Julie continued, "but he has a good family. They've been through a lot trying to save him."

Save him. Save him. The words sounded so ominous, so...threatening. "Really? Do you know about Matt?"

"I met him in the parking lot the night Michael was admitted. But I think that's enough about Michael James. I'm sure you've been told by now that relationships aren't allowed because patients need to focus on themselves. So, let's talk about you."

"What about me?"

"Well, to start you told me when you got here that you hadn't menstruated for a few months. Have you got your period yet?" Stevie shook her head. "Hm," Julie added.

"I'm not pregnant," Stevie quickly informed her. "I wasn't having s—" She started to say "sex", but realized at the last second she was wrong. She wasn't having voluntary sex, but rape was still sex. How many times that thought had crept into her mind and she had shoved it back out like a dangerous intruder. She wouldn't allow herself to even entertain the idea that she could be pregnant—by a stranger she couldn't remember penetrating her. But someone had. Someone undoubtedly had. She couldn't argue against the torn panties and the stickiness on her thighs when she came to in the hospital. What would Michael think of her if he knew that?

"We'll have to do a pregnancy test."

"No, please Julie, don't," Stevie protested. "I can't handle it."

Julie sat down next to her on the exam table and placed her warm hand on top of Stevie's. "Listen," she said, "lots of women stop menstruating from drinking too much. The same thing happened to me. That's probably all it is. But if it's more than that, it's better to know so we can deal with it. I'll help you."

"You won't tell anyone?"

"No. Except for Dr. Jim, but I promise he won't tell anyone either."

"He, he doesn't know."

"Michael?"

Stevie nodded her head and avoided Julie's kind eyes. "I promise," Julie assured her.

"Okay." Stevie watched Julie retrieve the pregnancy test from a cabinet and thought about the last time Julie made her pee in a cup, on the night she was admitted. She'd hated Julie for it. So much had changed. Back then she thought Julie was the enemy, and she didn't even know there was a Michael James in the world.

"When you're done, leave the urine sample next to the sink, and then you can go back and sit with your friends. You don't need to see Dr. Jim today unless it comes back positive. I'll call you in to tell you privately either way, okay?"

Stevie nodded and took the plastic cup from Julie's hand. When she slid off the exam table, Julie stopped her.

"One more thing," she intimated. "Remember I said that alcoholic women sometimes stop having their periods? That's because alcohol interferes with ovulation, but your body will correct itself as long as you don't drink. You might have been careless about birth control in the past and gotten away with it, but you can't afford to be now. So even if the test comes back negative, you'll need to use precautions from now on. Got it?"

"Yeah, I got it," Stevie told her, wondering if she was referring to Michael and her. Julie didn't actually think they were having sex, did she? How could they? They were monitored practically twenty-four hours a day. Even after Ellen and John and the rest of the staff went home for the day, the nurses were still there. And of course there were the night supervisors who sat in the back corner of the lounge watching them during games and movies. To even be alone with Michael seemed an impossible feat, but something in Julie's words of caution told her that it wasn't.

CHAPTER ELEVEN:
THE BAD DOG

Michael never showed up for lunch. Earlier in the day, Marcus told Stevie he saw him walking out to the parking lot with Dr. Jim, which raised all kinds of ridiculous imaginings in her mind. When he didn't arrive on time for the afternoon step meeting, she went from concerned to outright scared. John closed the door behind the last patient, and she felt her chest tighten. No one missed step meetings, not for any reason. David was there sitting next to John even though he was beaten to a pulp, but Michael wasn't. Why would he have left with Dr. Jim? She made nervous eye contact with Brian: *where is he? Don't know* he shrugged.

She kept glancing out the window to the courtyard he would need to cut through if he were going to show up. Finally, more than halfway through the meeting, he appeared. It was a blistering hot afternoon and Michael's hair was damp with sweat, making it look glossy black and the hot breeze was blowing it off his face—like a mustang's mane. Her eyes stayed on him as he approached, oblivious of her. Something was wrong. His pace was a little too quick, his brow was furrowed and his mouth was set in a pout.

She lost sight of him for a moment when he entered the building. Then she heard the door open abruptly with no care being given to the interruption it was creating. The sound made her jump. Michael was a polite guy always, unless he was really pissed. When his eyes fell on her, she smiled nervously at him. He held her gaze like he was trying to communicate with his eyes, but he didn't smile back. Then he followed Marcus' cue and sat down in a vacant seat between him and Jake.

"We're on Step Two," John told him. *"Came to believe that a Power greater than ourselves could restore us to sanity."*

"I know what step two is," Michael snapped. "We've been through it a few thousand times."

"And apparently that wasn't enough," John coolly replied. "When you interrupted us we were talking about trust."

"No shit? That's ironic, isn't it?"

Stevie noticed that Michael was making a funny sound, like he was grinding his teeth.

"You'll get your turn." With that John turned away, but Michael didn't. His stare remained fixed on John, hatred in his eyes. The energy was tangible. A confrontation was about to happen, a bad one. *Jesus Christ, Michael*, Stevie mentally pleaded, *let it go. Whatever it is, please let it go.* The day had already presented her with more than she could cope with. If she was anywhere else, she would have stood up and walked out so she could be alone in her room and not have to watch whatever was about to happen. But walking out of a step meeting would not be tolerated.

The entire group waited restlessly while a new patient, not yet among the living, tried to talk. It was a fifty-something year old guy with a reddish purple nose wearing pajama bottoms and dirty slippers. Ashes from chain smoking polluted his desk and tattooed his forearms with gray smudges. He was white knuckling the edge of the desktop, as if he were scared of falling out of his chair. Stevie thought he was wise to hold on for dear life. His face was already pockmarked with bruises and he even had a bandage over one eyebrow. Apparently fall-ing would be nothing new to him.

It was painful to watch. The effects of the medication were making it nearly impossible for the poor guy to speak. Most of his words were unidentifiable and he was slobbering drool onto his chin that hung like an icicle between his face and the desk. Stevie wondered why they both-ered sending new patients to step meetings. The guy clearly didn't know where he was. He was talking only because everyone was looking at him as if they expected him to. He just mumbled on and on until John told him to stop. Then he laid his pathetic head down in the ashes and spit and fell asleep. Liz, sitting next to him, reached over and removed the still burning cigarette from between his fingers.

Jake was next, then Michael. "What do you have to say, Jake?" John asked him.

Jake cracked a smile. A cigarette was protruding from between his teeth, not lit, just hanging there to taunt John. He wasn't allowed to smoke because of his age, at least not overtly. He was always cupping a lit one in his hand or hiding it under the table in the recreation room during games. A cigarette was always tucked behind his ear so that he could take it out and play with it at meetings. Everyone knew it was more about rebellion than anything else. It was Jake's *fuck you* to John and everyone else on the planet.

"I'm Jake," he drew out slowly, "an addict". It always killed Stevie to hear him say it out loud. His strong southern drawl accen-tuated the fact that he was just a kid. Jake never paid attention to what step the group was on. He talked about whatever he wanted to. David told Stevie once that he thought Jake did that because he didn't have any parents to teach him boundaries. It made perfect sense to her. Maybe that's why he thought it was okay to inappropri-ately touch the female patients. Michael was the only one who drew lines for Jake. He took it literally when Michael called him *brother* or *bro*, and, therefore, he let him tell him what to do. But no one else had the privilege.

Jake went on a rant about the high that granted him his admission this time. He took three hits of the psychedelic drug mescaline at a rave and when he somehow arrived home, his foster parents found him crawling around in the street in front of their house, barking like a dog. He was transported to the hospital by ambulance and afterward was sent to the rehab. And another set of foster parents pulled out of the deal. Another bridge burned. Jake didn't remember any of it, he said, but his whole face lit up when he talked about it, like it was a war story and he was proud of it.

When he was done, John finally responded to Michael's glare. "Do you want to open this up to the group or would you rather take it up with me after the meeting?" he asked.

"I want to take it up with you now, in front of the group," Michael growled.

"Okay then, what's the problem?"

"I just got off the phone with my parents." The words that seemed to boil up from the depths of Michael's body and spill out his pores were captivating to the group. No one was allowed to call home. "They moved my stuff back home, said you told them to."

"Oh," John said flatly and the resulting silence was painful. The entire group seemed tense, except for John. He repeated himself with no apology, "So, what's the problem?" Stevie stiffened. She thought that any second Michael might spring from his chair and grab John by the throat. She didn't want to watch anymore, but was too fascinated not to. It was like driving by a car accident and not being able to resist the demented urge to gawk. Apparently the whole room felt the same way. They were all staring dumbly.

"The problem is that you're a fucking liar," Michael pushed out like he was spitting the words at John. "Every time we talked, I told you I was going back to *my* life when I left here, back to *my* apartment. And every fucking time you listened and didn't say anything. They said you told them the first day I got here to move my stuff out of my place and back home. Did you?"

"You were on your ass," John flatly pointed out. "What appears to be eluding you is just how quickly you can *fall back down.*"

The last three emphasized words circled Stevie's brain like children around the mulberry bush and brought to mind the childhood chant: *Ring a-round the roses, pocket full of posies. Ashes! Ashes! We all fall down!* She had read once that the seemingly innocuous nursery rhyme was actually about the Black Plague, the red mark on the skin with a ring around it signified its arrival in the human body and the last two lines were a prophecy that all were going to perish. The fact that John's words called the frightening song from her brain felt insidious and premonitory. She forced it from her mind.

"Are you going to answer me?" Michael demanded. John glanced at his watch. "Just tell me this. Why is it we're supposed to be honest about everything? We're supposed to trust you and tell you everything, but you don't have to be honest with us?"

"You weren't ready to hear it," John answered, still with no emotion in his voice.

"Who the fuck are you?" Michael yelled. "This is *my* life. Who the fuck are you to make that decision without asking me?"

"When you arrived here, Mr. James, you were in no condition to make any decisions about *your* life. If you think otherwise, you're living in a fantasy world."

In one fluid motion, Michael stood up and flipped over the desk he was sitting at. His arms must have used more power than he realized because for a slow motion second a startled expression was on his face as the desk became airborne, and then crashed down in the middle of the circle. John jumped up from his seat defensively, but Michael wasn't heading toward him. He was in the hallway already, but having to open the door had slowed him down.

John caught up and grabbed his t-shirt. "You're not going any-where," he shouted.

"Get the fuck off me!" Michael screamed back at him as he turned and threw a punch that clipped John's jaw before he could intercept it.

John shoved Michael into the wall and Stevie squeezed her eyes shut. John was twice as big as Michael, but Michael was twice as fast. With her eyes closed she couldn't see the fight. She could hear it, though, Michael trying to escape and John's breathless groan when some part of Michael's body hit his stomach. John must have gained control and dragged him off because their voices sounded farther and farther away until they were out of earshot. More than thirty people were in the classroom, but it was completely silent until the sound of restrained giggling slowly broke the silence.

"That was fuck'gin hilarious," Jake giggled out and most of the patients burst out laughing.

"Think we can leave?" Liz asked.

Stevie scurried out of her seat and Liz and Allison followed close behind until they were all in her room. They had barely sat down on the bed when there was a quick knock and the door opened. Ellen stood in the doorway.

"*Really?*" Stevie whined.

"What?" Ellen asked innocently. "I only want to tell you that I brought some movies from Blockbuster. We'll have a short women's group after dinner from seven to eight, then you'll be free for the rest of the night. I thought you'd want to know."

"Wow, thanks, Ellen," Allison responded with childlike appreciation.

"No problem. I heard you guys had a tough day." No one responded except for Stevie who only rolled her eyes at the understatement. "Are you okay?" Ellen asked her.

"What do you think?" Stevie snapped. She didn't bother to look at her. Her eyes stared down at the bed and her hands spread on it like starfish to hold herself steady.

Ellen looked like she'd been slapped. She stood in the doorway for an awkward moment. "See you at dinner," she finally said and pulled the door closed behind her.

"What was *that*?" Allison asked, raising a perfectly plucked eyebrow.

"I told you she's not a monster," Liz answered.

Stevie lifted her face. It reflected her frazzled emotions; her eyes flashed intensely and her lips trembled. "Know what would be perfect right now? A bottle of Absolut."

"You shouldn't kid about that," Liz scolded. "It's not funny."

Allison came to her rescue. "Yeah, it is... 'cause she doesn't really mean it."

Stevie grumbled. The truth was if she had the chance she would have sucked on the bottle until she couldn't swallow anymore, until the hot vodka had washed the anguish out of her chest. If the day got any worse, she might have to go looking for one.

It was Brian that saved her from her own self-will. When she had insisted on being alone and banished Liz and Allison from her room, they had ventured into the den where they found Brian. And he had asked them to fetch Stevie so that he could talk to her.

"Hey, darlin'," he said when he saw her approaching, her face twisted into a spoiled temper tantrum-ish scowl. He offered her that sweet southern boy smile, and it made her feel the *tiniest bit* better until he opened his mouth again. "Let's take a walk," he suggested. "We need to talk."

Her heart landed in her stomach like an egg flung off a skyscraper. "Michael's gone?" she gasped.

"No, no. He's still here," Brian said gently. "He's in John's office." He placed his hand on her back and nudged her into walk mode toward the dining room, where she could see Ellen drinking iced tea with Julie. The luscious aromas of what would soon be dinner assaulted Stevie's nostrils and made her tummy growl. Biscuits and gravy...

Brian was always a gentleman; he never passed anyone by without at least a "hello". Now he approached the women and after exchanging pleasantries, asked Ellen if it would be all right for them to sit outside on the veranda. It was rare that anyone went out during the day because of the sweltering heat, but at night they were allowed to be there without permission as long as someone was in the dining room situated right across the hall to keep an eye on them through the glass door, which was pretty much always the case.

"Sure," Ellen answered cheerfully. Maybe her face was cheerful, too, but Stevie couldn't see that. She had turned her back on them without greeting and was waiting for Brian by the glass door. Ellen was probably congratulating herself right about now, Stevie figured, for being right about Michael. *See? I told you he was trouble.*

It was 5000 degrees outside—at least it felt that way. God *damn*, this would have to be a quick conversation. "Do you know anything?" she immediately asked.

"No. Sorry. But I think it'll be okay."

Stevie grunted. She didn't think so. Why would they let Michael stay after he beat up David and then fought John? She lay down on her usual spot of floorboards that was in the shade of the building, but still significantly warmer than her body.

"You know, Michael's probably my closest friend in this place," Brian confided as he sat down beside her. "Maybe anywhere."

Stevie looked over at him. He was sitting cross-legged and his blue eyes were squinting at the desert-like sun. *The Marlboro Man.* Her lips grinned at her own joke, but her insides didn't. Her body felt under siege. Some alien emotion was at the stern.

"My point is, Michael's a good person," Brian said with his gracious southern drawl.

"I know that, Brian," she snapped…again. "He's *my* closest friend, too."

A monstrous greenhead fly was zzzzzooming in on Stevie's face and neck. Brian waved it away gently, as if it were smoke. "I know you know. I'm just reminding you, that's all. We all make mistakes. Michael could tell you about a few of mine."

"He hasn't," Stevie responded with some attitude. "In case you were wondering."

"I wasn't," he said so softly that she almost didn't hear it. Then he broke down and told her about the woman he'd had sex with a month or so before and about how he felt like killing himself the next day when he woke up and realized what he had done. He had never been with a woman other than his wife, he said. They'd been together since high school. It was a stupid thing that happened after he downed about five too many Captain Morgan and Cokes. He came clean with his wife right away. She didn't throw him out as he'd expected. Instead she'd given him an ultimatum: stop drinking, starting with a residential treatment program, hence, his arrival in Purgatory. "You probably think I'm a lowlife now that you know that about me," he concluded.

Stevie sat up and pulled her sweat-damp hair off her face. "I already knew, Brian," she told him. "Not because Michael told me. I figured out what you were insinuating the first time we met. And no, I don't think you're a lowlife. I think you're fucking awesome." A laugh burst out of her when she saw his eyes pop open in shock.

"I'm a good Baptist boy, you know," Brian teased. "I never heard a lady talk like that in my life." (It sounded like myyy liiife.)

It made her giggle some more. "Do you really go to church?" she asked him.

They shared an amiable smile. "Just 'bout every week. My wife, she likes to sing."

"So that's why you go to church, so your wife can sing?"

Brian chuckled. "Well, mostly I guess that's why. 'Cause it makes her feel good."

It was a nice reason Stevie thought in the comfortable silence that followed, nicer than going for fear of burning in Hell.

"We been together since ninth grade, but for Michael this is all new. I'm thinking maybe you could give him a little time to catch up. He doesn't mean to upset you."

"But he has no idea how much it does. I'll think about it, though, what you said. Now let's get back inside before I melt. I don't have southern blood like you, you know." Brian laughed and she did, too. And the craving for Absolut? Gone.

They were almost halfway through dinner when Michael finally showed his precious face. He entered the dining room with a burst of energy, a smile sweeping his lips and revealing his dimples through his whiskers. Until that moment, no one had known his fate. Stevie tried not to reveal the relief that was swimming like baby fish through her stress-ridden body, but actually heard herself exhale as the apprehension left her chest.

"D'you miss me?" Michael asked of no one in particular, sliding into the last empty seat between Stevie and Liz.

"Where were you today?" Liz asked with a stern tone. Stevie loved it when Liz pulled out her mother voice. She would let Liz grill him about the day and would stay out of the conversation. That way she could find out what happened, but still keep her cool and no one would see how freaked out she was. It was a pointless plan. They all knew, anyway.

"Hospital," he responded casually, sticking his fork into a pile of mashed potatoes smothered in gravy. His response startled Stevie enough to change her game plan.

"Why?" she asked, with absolutely no resistance.

"Dr. Jim brought me to have a CT scan of my head," he answered a moment later, once a gulp of milk had washed the potatoes down his throat.

"But I thought Dr. Jim was checking your heart," Stevie countered.

"He was, because of the arrhythmia, but when I told him my nose still bleeds, he wanted a CT scan."

"What's a rhythmia?" Marcus inquired, his mouth stuffed with food.

"It means my heart beats out of rhythm…a battle scar from the meth."

Brian's brow wrinkled with worry. "So what happened with the CT scan?" he asked.

"Guess I've got a hole in my nose from snorting drugs." Michael shrugged like it was no big deal. Or maybe, Stevie figured, it was because he wasn't all that surprised.

"Perforated nasal septum," Liz stated. She was the group's medical expert, having made it through almost two years of a nursing program before dropping out. She had just mentioned to Stevie that evening on the way to the dining room that she still had thoughts about going back. Maybe if she could stay sober this time, she'd said.

"Yeah, that's it," Michael agreed. "They think there's something in deeper, too. The whole thing probably sounds worse than it is."

Stevie wasn't so sure. It sounded bad to her. "So, what are they going to do about it?" she asked him.

While Michael buttered and then quickly devoured a biscuit, he told the story. Dr. Jim and the radiologist both thought he needed to be evaluated by a surgeon. So Dr. Jim contacted a friend of his from medical school that was now a surgeon in Savannah and John was driving Michael to see him the next day. He told the group the diagnosis and the need to temporarily remove him from the premises had met the criteria for breaking the no contact rule. Dr. Jim had insisted that he call his parents, and it was the phone call that incited the blowout with John. "It's been one hell of a day," he concluded.

Stevie's lips became so taut they resembled a cartoon mouth, a horizontal line like Charlie Brown's. She hated when that happened, but she couldn't control it. Every time she got really mad her nerves got so tense that it felt like someone was pulling her skin from both sides of her face. It had been one hell of a day all right. Did he even realize what he'd put her through?

She pushed her chair away from the table, refusing to meet Brian's eyes that she was sure would be pleading with her to sit her ass back down. "See you guys," she said tightly.

"Wait a minute," Michael stammered. He dropped his fork into his mashed potatoes and followed her. She didn't wait and instead quickened her step. "Hold up, Stevie," he called after her and caught her hand before she reached the hallway. "Can't we talk?"

If they were anywhere else those soulful eyes of his would be seducing her out of her anger by now, but Stevie could see both Ellen and John watching them with her peripheral vision. Maybe Michael was somehow immune to being tossed out, but she certainly wasn't. And unlike Michael who received droves of letters (and promptly refused to read any of them), she had yet to receive a letter from home. Clearly, her parents were embarrassed by her, not because she behaved like an alcoholic—Hell, the whole family did that. The problem was that she was caught and now institutionalized for being an alcoholic, and (God forbid) the secret was leaked out to the family thanks to Stevie's cousin/ former friend. If she got kicked out, she had no idea where she would go.

"Later," she whispered and pulled her hand away from his.

CHAPTER TWELVE:
CAME TO BELIEVE

*L*ater didn't come until almost midnight when everyone else decided to watch the scary movie Ellen rented from Blockbuster and finally left them alone on the veranda. "It's about black holes," Jake told them as they stood up to leave.

Melanie was by Jake's side, but her hair was brown now, not pink. Stevie noticed they'd been spending a lot of time together lately. It turned out the ferocious punk girl was only fifteen years old. Although it somehow wasn't as obvious when her hair was still magenta, Melanie was the kind of shy that could make every person in the room feel uncomfortable just by being there. She rarely opened her mouth to talk, except at meetings when she was obligated to and she never smiled, but Stevie had often noticed her huddling together with Jake, whispering. It made her wonder what they were up to, like they were formulating some kind of juvenile revolution to overthrow the rehab.

"What's a black hole?" Allison asked.

"Don't know," Jake admitted. "Guess we'll find out when we watch it."

"Do you want me to explain it to you?" Michael asked.

"Do you know?"

"Yeah, I know." So Michael, lying flat on his back on the wood floor and staring out into the universe, began to explain the concept of black holes and Stevie again noticed how much he knew about the world for someone who never attended college.

"Where'd you learn all that shit?" Marcus asked, interrupting him.

"High school, I guess," Michael answered. He was grinding his teeth again. Undoubtedly that's what he was doing. Stevie made a mental note to ask him about it.

"I didn't learn that in high school," Brian argued. "Did you go to college?"

"No," Michael softly protested.

"Where'd you learn it then?" Marcus pushed.

"Dude, I don't know. Maybe I read it in a book. I used to read a lot."

"I still don't get it," Allison said. "Let's watch the movie. Stevie, you guys coming?"

"No. We'll catch up with you later."

Michael sat up and Marcus slapped the back of his head as he walked past him. "Don't be a dog out here," he warned. "Frank'll turn you in." Frank was a greasy-looking night supervisor with little pig-like black eyes that stared out at the patients through black rimmed glasses like Clark Kent always wore. He was one of the "night narcs" whose job it was to keep an eye on them, but he rarely wandered from the recreation room where he set up camp with his junk food, newspapers and comic books.

"'kay, man," Michael replied and moved over to Stevie's side. She slid a hand onto his leg and he held it in his. "I missed you today," he offered when the group left.

"I hated today," she admitted. "I felt like I didn't know you."

"You sure you still want to?"

She wasn't sure if he was kidding or not, but she nodded her head in case he was. "So, what's the name of your band?" she inquired. Of the dozens of questions today had bred, that seemed the most benign. Michael threw his head back dramatically, the way he always did when he was blown away by something. "Just tell me," she pushed. His shirt was unbuttoned and underneath it he had on a white beater t-shirt. His fingers tugged the neckline of the t-shirt down, exposing his left nipple and the letters tattooed above it in deep blue ink. "Oh my God, Michael," she gasped. *"L.A. ICE* is the name of your band? You— named your band after meth?"

"Yeah," he grumbled and closed his eyes. "Want to keep going?"

"Did you think I'd judge you by that, too?" she asked. She wasn't sure if his surprised expression was caused by the question or by her fingers that reached for the tattoo and traced the letters. The skin of his chest was unexpectedly soft, like flower petals. It made her wish she could trace it with her tongue instead of her fingers.

"Let's sit down here," Michael suggested and slid off the bench onto the patio floor. Two nurses and a nurse's aide—it was Louise Stevie noticed—were having a break in the dining room and could easily see them on the bench. Stevie moved down beside him and he slid an arm around her waist. It was so warm and comfortable sitting close to him in the dark, snuggled inside his arm that it didn't matter so much anymore that they discuss everything that had happened. She was happy just to be there, holding his free hand in both of hers, playing with the silver ring on his finger, with no one gawking at her.

"I'm sorry about today," he said so close to her ear that his lips actually touched it. In the night air his breath was the whoosh of bird's wings on her skin, warm and hushed.

"I'm not mad at you, Michael. It's not that."

"I know. I get it," he said and licked nervously at his lips. "You want me to tell you…? What should I tell you first why I didn't get thrown out?" He took a drag off his cigarette and exhaled his words with the smoke, his eyes hidden by the cover of his eyelashes. "Because I didn't come here voluntarily, that's why. I didn't want to get clean." He waited a minute for it to sink in. She was watching his face, studying him. When he opened his mouth, she noticed one of his front teeth was a little bit shorter than the other one like it was worn down, probably from grinding it. Maybe that was why he hid them all the time. He was always smiling, but he rarely parted his lips. "My parents had me committed because they're scared the meth will kill me."

"Oh," was all she could muster.

"That's why I didn't tell you, because you'd think there's something wrong with me."

She shrugged. "But there's something wrong with all of us," she argued. "There's a lot wrong with me, things you don't know."

He shook his head adamantly. "No, Stevie. You don't understand. You can still get better. You can have a normal life."

"What and you can't?" She thought he was playing in some kind of morose way until he abruptly stood up and started pacing. Within seconds, she missed the warmth of his body. "Please sit with me," she pleaded, but he kept pacing as if she'd never said it. His mind appeared to be racing behind his flickering eyes.

"I didn't set out to be a meth addict," he muttered. "I had dreams, potential, plans...like everyone else. But I got caught in it and now...now I don't know if I can stop using. Honestly, I don't think I can."

It was the single most frightening statement she'd ever heard in her life. "Michael—" She'd started to argue against the validity of it, but he cut her off. What was going on below Michael's confident surface was finally sinking in. He'd been in treatment more than a month and all this time he had no expectation of staying clean. He was only going through the motions because he had to. She finally understood David's comment about him being strapped in his bed. They were trying to contain him so he wouldn't take off.

"Before I got here—before I knew you—I never thought I'd stop. I thought I'd use meth until my heart exploded, like everyone said it would. But that was because I thought my life was over, you know?" He was absolutely frantic, moving intensely like a wild cat in the jungle, words pouring out of him like liquid. "Now I don't want it to be, but I've done things I can't take back."

"Like what?"

"Like everything, like doing meth for four years. I can't undo that."

"No one's asking you to," she said quietly. She caught his hand mid motion and pulled him back by her side.

"There's more," he breathed onto her neck. She was holding him now, as close as she could, trying to calm him down. His body was shaking in her arms. She stroked his back, the way he always did for her when she was upset. There were things she needed to confess, too—like the pregnancy test—but it was all too overwhelming.

"I know Michael," she said as comfortingly as she could. "There's a lot more, but you don't have to tell me everything at once. It's okay. Whatever it—whatever you're carrying around won't matter. It won't change how I feel about you. Don't you know that?" He didn't answer her, but he tightened his grip around her waist.

"I want to tell you something else," he suddenly said. She gave him a squeeze before she let go of him and braced herself for whatever was about to come out of his mouth. Maybe he had a girlfriend or maybe even something worse. But what, what could possibly be worse than that? "When I was a senior in high school I got accepted to M.I.T.," he blurted out as if he were confessing a sin.

"What? What'd you just say?" she stammered.

"It's hard to believe, huh?"

"No, wait. You misunderstood. I thought you were going to say something bad."

"I told you that once, remember—that when I was a kid I wanted to be an engineer like my dad?"

"I remember, but how did you get into M.I.T.?"

"My SAT scores, I guess, and my dad went there." A smile crept onto her lips and she couldn't get rid of it, even though Michael was still completely somber. It was an astounding image—Michael with a backpack walking around the streets of Boston, Michael, the adorable boy from Jacksonville, Florida actually attending college forty minutes from her house. She could have passed him on the street or bumped into him on the train. What would have happened? Would she have fallen for him like she did here in that one fleeting moment? Or would she have been too drunk or high to notice? Her smile faded at the thought. "What?" he asked, "you didn't think I was smart enough?"

"That's ridiculous. I know how smart you are. It's just that M.I.T. is in Cambridge—that's Boston."

"That's the first thing I thought of when we met. Remember I told you I was supposed to go to Boston? Now I think that maybe we were supposed to meet, either there or here in Georgia. Do you ever think that?"

Only you swam through her brain. *Only you could say something so beautiful.* She wrapped her arms around his waist, settled her head on his chest and listened to his heart. It *sounded* in rhythm. "You mean like John said, everything happens for a reason?"

"Yeah. Remember he said there's no such thing as a coincidence? Maybe he's right—maybe everything that happens in the universe is by design."

By design. She closed her eyes to think about it. His chin was snuggled against her head and his chest was gently lifting her face with each rise and fall of his breath.

"The night we met I went to bed and stayed awake thinking about how weird it was to be meeting you here. I kept thinking *why now, after everything that's happened, why now?* But I think it was on purpose—you were supposed to be here now...and so was I."

How could she respond? Sitting in the dark with Michael under the black Georgia sky, his arms snug around her and the sound of his heart beating in her ear was beyond anything she'd ever dreamed. For women like her, she'd imagined, men like Michael were as unreachable as the water lily growing alluringly in the duck pond but held fast by an invisible grasp. Even the smell of his skin was intoxicating. She breathed him in.

"When I was younger I always used to think that someday I'd meet someone, you know?" he threw out lightly. "Someone like you that I could talk to. I guess I finally gave up. My last girlfriend was a whore. That was two years ago."

"What do you mean?" Stevie asked, fighting back the sudden urge to vomit.

"I mean she was a whore. She slept with everyone in the band, except Matt. He was the only one smart enough to stay away from her. But I didn't know. I—I thought she was my girlfriend."

Stevie leaned forward with her elbows on her knees. She couldn't take it—the two things happening at once, his calming, melodious heartbeat and his excruciatingly painful words. He stroked her back and then played with her hair and she was content again. Her untamed hair that had always been a curse felt like silk in Michael's hands. It made her think of King Midas with his golden touch, but the magic in

Michael's hands was even more miraculous. It made her feel like she was more than she really was.

A cigarette was dangling loosely between his lips James Dean style and he was squinting his big brown eyes at her when he asked, "You ever slept with anyone and regretted it later?"

The question made her want to cry. *Your body is a precious thing. Save it for the right person*, her ninth grade health teacher had said, and Stevie had thought it was a lie she was using to manipulate the students, to turn them into drones. There was no *right* person, only some men who might care enough to ask before taking. Who would have believed that her health teacher was telling the truth? There really was a right person. His hands were in her hair and she had blown it. "Yeah," she whimpered.

"It shouldn't be that way. It's because we're messed up. We would have known better if we weren't, like Matt did. That girl, she didn't care about me. She was only into me because I was the singer in the band." So that's why he didn't tell her about the band, Stevie realized. He thought she'd judge him by it, he'd said, but it was the opposite of what she'd imagined. It wasn't that he thought she'd disrespect him for it. He wanted to know that she cared about him as a person, not in a superficial guitar god idolatry kind of way. "I didn't love her, though. I don't want you to think I did. I never loved her."

"So what happened to M.I.T.?" she asked to change the subject. She couldn't bear the thought of him with someone else, talking to her like this, with his voice soft and sacred and turning her into something beyond her own imagination with his magical hands.

"I didn't show up. For six months I told my parents I couldn't do it. They weren't listening. They kept saying 'you'll be fine once you get there. You're just nervous'.

So I took off. I got in my car and ran away from the whole thing."

127

"With Matt?"

"No. Not with Matt. He was one of the people looking for me. I went to Daytona with a drummer I know—you know Rob, my room-mate that I told you about. He turned me on to meth one night when I was wasted on tequila, and I took to it right away. I woke up sick the next day and all I could think about was doing it again...so I did and it took the sickness away. We were gone for two weeks and I was flying on speed the entire time. When I left home, I was a scared kid. By the time I got back, I was a meth addict. I was seventeen. My parents were so disappointed I couldn't even look at them."

"They were worried," Stevie suggested.

"They were disappointed," he repeated. "I wasn't what they wanted me to be." There was so much in his last statement that she could relate to that it made her chest throb. That's exactly how she felt when she got kicked out of school. A "laughing stock", that's what her father had called her. "But Matt, he is. He's the son they always wanted." He laid his head against the bench and shifted his gaze toward the waning moon overhead.

"Oh my God, Michael," she finally breathed, "you don't really believe that?"

"It's the truth. If you met Matt, you'd know what I mean."

Stevie pondered the complexities of Michael's relationship with Matt. It sounded like sibling rivalry, even though they weren't really brothers. "So, he's not into meth I take it?" she asked.

Michael laughed out loud at the suggestion. "Matt," he declared, "is terminally straight. Don't get me wrong. He's got good reasons for it."

At least now he was smiling again. "He's not in the band then?" she asked him.

"Oh yeah, he is. He's the bass player—I talked him into learning it."

"A terminally straight bass player? That must suck for him."

"Not really," Michael responded a little defensively. "The lead guitarist doesn't use. I mean, he drinks his fair share...but no drugs. And Matt's a good player. People like how he plays. It's kind of like his personality, really solid and not too flashy."

"You and Rob are the only ones into meth?"

There was a fat pause before he replied. It was something Michael didn't even like to think about never mind say out loud, Rob and his imaginary meth relationship. "Except for the first time in Daytona, I've never seen Rob use," he finally said. "And honestly I was so trashed that night, I'm not sure if I'm remembering it right. He says he does it when we're not playing, but we're roommates and I've never seen it. I don't believe it anymore. I used to, but I don't now." Stevie's mouth dropped open a bit like she was about to ask a question and Michael quickly interrupted her. "He does it for the cash."

Her eyes dropped away from his. She understood it must have been painful coming to terms with the fact that someone who was supposed to be his friend was lining his pockets by feeding his illness. "Tell me more about Matt," she suggested.

"Well, he manages the band," he offered. "He books all the gigs and everything. He almost got us signed once with a record label. Of course I screwed that up, too."

She met his eyes, but didn't ask him to explain. Instead she played with the ring on his finger and waited. "After I blew the M.I.T. thing, getting the band signed meant everything to me. Matt got the A&R guy to show up one night at a gig, but I was too fucked up and paranoid to go on stage."

"You wouldn't do that now," she offered.

"Honestly, I don't know if I could do it now either. I've never fronted the band without being high. You're the only person I've ever told that to. It's pathetic, huh?"

She shook her head. "No. Nothing about you is pathetic." He looked over at her with that little boy grin that always made her stop breathing, his sleepy eyes closer to shut than open. "Want to go to bed?" she threw out.

"Sure," he answered playfully, as if she had meant it as an invitation, and finally allowed a little bit of laughter to flow out of him, like plucking a string on a guitar.

"You can always go back," Stevie suggested, "to school, or M.I.T. even."

Michael laughed at first like she'd meant it as a joke. When she didn't laugh along with him, his expression gradually became pensive. "Do you think that?" he asked. "I mean, really, do you think that?"

"Well yeah. Why not?"

One hand reached for her face and held it carefully before he touched her mouth with his. And she was sinking, sinking, sinking; falling so fast she couldn't keep her balance. Her arms moved around his broad shoulders and held on. When he stopped kissing her, she had become mute; there were no words important enough. She could only stare at his beautiful crimson mouth that she had loved since the first time she saw him and wait for him to do it again. His thumb moved across her bottom lip before he kissed her again, this time with more urgency.

She pulled away and his dark eyes became a question mark, the worry line etched in his brow. She touched his face with her fingertips. "Thank you for the water lily," she whispered and felt his dimple with her thumb when his lips broke into a grin.

He pressed his mouth against hers a little harder, the tip of his tongue just barely touching hers. One hand ventured to the nape of his neck, then into his hair and she wrapped her fingers around his soft curls. She was melting into him dizzily, her heart no longer beating, but moving in a long whir, like a bird's. *You taste like sunshine and the beach and honeysuckle and summer rainstorms, like everything I have ever loved,* she thought, *and I have never ever felt like this before.*

They could have been kissing for five minutes or forty-five minutes when Julie opened the glass door and walked from the hallway out onto the veranda. They were both lost in the moment and were startled by her voice.

"You need to go inside, guys," she said.

Stevie felt Michael's whiskers brush across her chin and heard him say "okay" before she was able to process what was happening. "We were just leaving," he added.

"Yeah, I could see that."

Michael bit his bottom lip. "Really, we were. But we got... sidetracked." The last word forced a nervous grin to his lips. That was all it took for Julie to fold.

"I won't say anything, but go inside now so I don't have to."

"That's cool, Julie, thanks," Michael said sincerely, pulling Stevie to her feet.

"Be glad I wasn't Frank," Julie answered as she walked away.

CHAPTER THIRTEEN:
THE GOOD DOG

And just like that, life changed...again.

By eight thirty the next morning Stevie and Allison were already up and sitting across from each other at the coffee bar. Stevie hadn't slept much the night before because of the rush of adrenalin surging like electricity through her bloodstream, and Allison hadn't slept at all because of the scary movie. Since six thirty she had been in Stevie's room and was now telling her all the details of the movie as they sipped coffee, although it seemed based on Allison's comments that she still didn't understand the part about the black holes. Her gaping "Oh my God" suddenly interrupted the flow of conversation.

Stevie spun on her barstool to follow Allison's gaze down the men's hallway. It was Michael she was staring at, Michael, but almost unrecognizable. He was dressed in a pale blue button down shirt with a pair of freshly pressed khakis and clean white sneakers. He was clean-shaven and had gel in his hair that was keeping his curls back from his face. He looked like a prep school student. The only sign of his edgy personality was the red pack of cigarettes protruding from his front shirt pocket. He approached Stevie and Allison with confident strides, smiling proudly.

"Morning," he said. His hand pressed against Stevie's back as he passed her on his way to the cupboard and she felt the now familiar warmth tiptoeing up her spine.

"You look... *unbelievable,*" Allison spewed, still gawking. She spun her bar stool so she didn't have to take her eyes off of him.

"Thanks," Michael replied without looking over at them. "I have that doctor's appointment." His hand was searching through the cupboard for a travel mug. "What are you two up to?" He found the mug and began filling it.

"Talking about last night," Allison answered innocently and Stevie choked on her coffee. She hadn't told Allison anything about what happened between her and Michael, but by Allison's comment he probably thought she had spilled out all the details.

Michael turned to face her. "You all right?" he asked. Stevie nodded her hideously red face in response and shot daggers at Allison as soon as Michael turned his attention back to precisely measuring the sugar for his coffee. When the lid was securely on the cup, he headed back toward the men's hallway, slowing down only long enough to kiss the top of Stevie's head. "See you when I get back," he said over his shoulder.

"What?" Allison demanded of her friend, who was glaring ominously at her.

"Of all the things you could have said," she fumed.

"All I said was—wait, did I miss something? What happened last night?"

"Nothing happened...just...drop it."

"Oh my God, you slept with him!" Allison exclaimed.

Okay, that was the second person in twenty-four hours who had made a similar accusation. What'd she have the word *slut* tattooed on her forehead? "No, I did not sleep with him. How could I have?"

"Well, what happened to him then? That's not the same guy that flipped the desk over in the step meeting yesterday. I mean, right?"

Right; she was right but Stevie wasn't about to tell her so. At least Stevie thought she knew what had happened, but she didn't dare say it out loud in case she was wrong. Michael had made a decision to stay clean. He was planning to reclaim his life. What was it he said when he walked her to the women's hallway last night? That they had a lot to work on together. *Together.* That was the word that crashed through her brain like a tsunami and kept her awake half the night. And he was smiling when he said it like it was a good thing. She shrugged her shoulders at Allison: *No clue*, but her whole face was lit up thinking about it... again. She probably slept last night with a smile on her face. A tap on her shoulder brought her back to reality. "Oh, no," she spurted before she even swiveled in her seat to identify who the finger belonged to.

"So happy to see me?" Ellen asked.

"Hi Ellen," Allison chirped. Since the Blockbuster gesture, Allison seemed less resistant to her. Yesterday after dinner she'd also given Allison permission to make a five-minute phone call home. Maybe Ellen actually does know what she's doing, Stevie thought. Maybe it's all about bribery. But hm, that wouldn't quite work for her, would it? If she called home, no one would pick up the phone.

"Ready to do some work?" she asked Stevie.

Maybe it was the phrase Ellen chose because Michael's words rang through Stevie's ears, *we have a lot to work on together.* "Yeah, I am," she answered sincerely and stood up. "Okay if I bring my coffee?"

Ellen searched her face in the stunned silence (for sarcasm perhaps?). "Absolutely," she replied and gestured grandiosely toward her office with her arm. It was all going smoothly—they actually chitchatted for the very first time the whole way to her office—until Ellen brought up the Blockbuster movies right as they sat down.

"I made it through the romantic comedy, but not the horror flick," Stevie told her.

"Yeah, I know. Frank said your group watched the second movie late last night, but you and Michael weren't there."

Shit. Shit, shit, shit, Stevie's brain reverberated in near panic. It was only a few days prior that Ellen warned her to create some distance from Michael—and she had, well, during the day at least. But night, she presumed, was off limits. Ellen went home to her husband and kids and Stevie spent every single second with Michael. It didn't occur to her that Ellen might have people reporting back to her. Again, *shit.*

"But you weren't in your room, either."

"Why do you say that?"

Ellen rocked back and forth in her chair and fingered the rim of her coffee cup while Stevie turned a dozen shades of pink. Maybe Julie told her that she walked in on them. Stevie was always so good at lying to her parents. She had it down to an absolute art. Why couldn't she manage to think of a good lie to use now? And to think at this very moment Michael was in John's car, probably being served the same interrogation. *Coincidence?* She thought not.

"Because Louise looked in your room."

"Why?" Stevie finally sputtered. She wasn't sure she wanted to hear the answer, but her curiosity was piqued. Nurses and nurse's aides never came into her room during the night, not since she'd been transferred to the rehab wing. They checked her vital signs only twice a day now, during normal hours.

"Your brother called. The rule got stretched some yesterday so I thought I'd let you talk to him, but no one could find you."

"You were looking for me last night?"

"I wasn't looking for you. I was at home on my cell phone with Louise. She was looking for you, and she was worried."

"We were just talking," Stevie blurted out. "On the veranda—we weren't doing anything."

"It's okay, I know. Julie called me back after she found you."

"Oh. Well, what else did she say?"

"Is there more?" Ellen asked, grinning like the Cheshire Cat.

"No. No, a lot of stuff happened yesterday, that's all. We had a lot to talk about."

"That's for sure. So, I heard your boy Michael—"

"He's not *my boy*, Ellen."

"Okay. So, I heard *Michael* apologized to John this morning for what happened yesterday." That was the biggest surprise of the conversation so far, and more evidence of what Stevie already suspected, that Michael was making a turn around. Stevie smiled at Ellen—sincerely even. She was so proud of Michael for apologizing that she couldn't even try to hide it. "Whatever you guys talked about last night—I guess it helped."

That was an acknowledgement, wasn't it? Maybe it wasn't quite an admission that she was wrong about Stevie's relationship with Michael, but it was at least an acknowledgement that she had underestimated it. "You know Ellen," she ventured, "The stuff we talk about together, not only Michael and me, but all of us, helps a lot."

"Oh, I know," Ellen agreed without even a blink. "I remember. I came through here, too, six years ago. My friends from here are a big part of the reason I'm still sober."

"Really? You're still friends with them?"

"Not the way you might think. I'll always think of them as my friends, but I don't know if I'll ever see them again. I'm the only one who stayed sober."

Stevie took a long drink of her coffee and let the words sink in. What if her friends all picked up? What if she did or Michael? They were the best friends she'd ever had, but surely not all of them were going to stay clean and sober.

"Stevie, if you think I'm hard on you, it's for good reason. Do you know what the odds are of maintaining sobriety? Statistics say one out of every forty people stay clean and sober, and that's only the first year."

Her lips went numb, tingling like bees were underneath her skin trying to get out. There were about forty patients between the detox and rehab units combined. Could it be possible that only one of them would make it? Now her arms were crawling with the invisible insects and that electric blue adrenalin-induced mood was quickly turning gray. "Is that true, Ellen? Or are you saying that to scare me away from Michael?"

"For what reason, Stevie? What reason would I have to keep you away from him other than that it's dangerous to your sobriety? If you two stay together when you leave here and one of you picks up, you'll both go down."

Like dominoes.

"I'm not only trying to protect you. I'm protecting Michael. If he uses meth again, he could die."

Ashes! Ashes! We all fall down! Stevie's brain taunted. She sat forward on her chair. Sure, that risk existed for all of them, she knew that, John constantly reminded them at step meetings, but Ellen's words seemed to imply more. She felt a chill climb up her vertebrae as her conversation with Michael the night before pushed to the front of her conscious mind. "What do you mean?" she tentatively asked.

"He has health issues, but I'm sure you know that. What you might not know is that when he arrived here, his blood pressure was so high, we were afraid he'd have a heart attack or a stroke. Dr. Jim stayed with him around the clock for three days. He's the best friend

Michael's got right now. And John's his second best friend. Don't underestimate that relationship, Stevie. It could keep him alive."

Somewhere around the blood pressure comment, Stevie had forgotten to keep breathing. She suddenly realized she was shorting out on oxygen and loudly gulped in air. She wanted to argue that Michael was too young to have a heart attack or a stroke—it was ridiculous to even think of it, to accuse Ellen of fabricating the whole story to scare her. But there was one problem: she'd always had an innate ability to recognize truth when she heard it. The only way she could deny Ellen's statement was to lie to herself. And Michael's own words—what did he say? That he'd thought he'd use meth until his heart exploded *like everyone said it would*. She dropped her head into her hands and tugged at her hair with her fingers. How could he be so young and be so sick? But it was exactly like her, wasn't it? Dr. Tom at the hospital had spoken almost identical words to her. *You're disease is so advanced, if you keep drinking you might not see twenty-one.* "I don't want to go back to it, Ellen," burst out of her. She lifted her head to face her and realized tears were streaming from her eyes. "I don't want to drink anymore."

"Good," Ellen said. "Make the right decisions and you won't have to. You can make it, you know. I can see it in you."

Stevie dabbed at her eyes with her t-shirt. "What do you mean? What do you see? Because I can't see anything."

"My sponsor calls it an 'indefinable spark'. I don't know how to explain it, but I know it's there."

Her sponsor? It was weird to think that even Ellen the bulldog needed help. "Thanks. Thanks for saying that," Stevie mustered.

"No problem. Imagine the life you can have, Stevie? You've got a good mind. Without your disease holding you back, you could do anything."

Like Michael. His parents wanted him to conquer the world, he'd said, and after last night's talk, she understood why. It was because they knew he could. If he hadn't picked up meth, Michael would have graduated from M.I.T. by now. Stevie wanted to thank Ellen again because she so badly needed the encouragement after all the demeaning comments her father had made, but she was slobbering too much to articulate it.

"I think that's probably enough for today, don't you?" she advised and Stevie silently nodded. "Tomorrow I want to talk about living arrangements when you leave here. I'm thinking a sober house, either here in Georgia or back in Massachusetts." Stevie lifted her head. Given her family situation, she should have seen this coming, but she didn't. "Think about it," Ellen suggested, and she—the biggest surprise yet—agreed.

Michael still looked like he walked off the cover of GQ magazine when he finally returned from Savannah and joined the group in the dining room right in time for dinner. "Hey, y'all," he said playfully, claiming his regular seat next to Stevie. Bearing their boundaries in mind, she reached for his hand under the table.

"I brought you something," he told her and gave her hand a squeeze before he dug into his shirt pocket and pulled out a clear plastic package filled with chocolates. "They're chocolate covered pecans."

"Pecans?" Brian teased. "What're you tryin' to turn her into a southerner?"

"What about it?" Michael challenged, but his eyes were shiny and smiling.

"Thanks," Stevie whispered and kissed his cheek before she thought twice about it. His skin was smooth and soft, not like the whiskers last night. And he smelled good.

"So what'd you bring the rest of us?" Marcus goaded.

"Dude, you got any idea how long it took me to talk John into this?" Michael said and pushed his breath out in a huff before he started seasoning his food like a scientist—precisely the right amount of salt on the broccoli, and exactly the right amount of pepper on the baked macaroni and cheese. Stevie noticed how badly his hands still trembled...like hers. She opened the bag and popped a couple of chocolates; they melted like Heaven on her tongue. She passed the bag around, but only Jake was interested. He looked as happy as she felt to be eating chocolate covered pecans instead of dinner. She stuffed five more in her mouth. Leave it to Michael to remember her chocolate monster.

"So what's up with the clothes and all?" Brian asked Michael. "You look like a counselor...John junior."

Michael put his fork down. "No," he stated emphatically. "I had to see the surgeon and I figured—"

Allison cut him off. "He looks amazing," she said unabashedly.

"Wait, what's that all about?" Marcus taunted. "You never say I look amazing."

"You look nice, Michael," Liz stated matter-of-factly, the mother's quiet viewpoint.

"I'm feeding the good dog, that's all," he ventured.

"What's that mean, feeding the good dog?" Allison asked.

Michael's face lit up like he had been hoping someone would ask. "It's an AA story John told me," he blurted out excitedly. "Okay, it goes something like this. There was this Native American kid that had some kind of personality problem—I'm not saying this exactly right, but you'll get the gist of it. Anyway, this kid's mom was worried about him so she went to see the medicine man of the tribe. She told him that her son had two distinct personalities, one was gentle and kind, thoughtful—all that good stuff. The other side was angry and vola-tile—did the wrong things all the time."

Michael stopped talking and took a few bites of macaroni. No one else said a word. And no one else was eating—they were all waiting for the rest of the story. "Soooo," he breathed dramatically, obviously enjoying the limelight, "the mom told the medicine man that she felt like her son had two dogs living inside him, a good dog and a bad dog. She wanted to know what to do about it." After the set up was com-plete, he allowed a nice long theatrical pause. Stevie stifled a giggle while he selected a roll and took his time buttering it. He had them all in the palm of his hand and was absolutely *loving* it.

"What'd the medicine man say?" Brian asked, taking the bait.

"He said, 'the one you feed will live'," Michael announced majesti-cally, and swept his arm in front of him like a royal storyteller from days of old. "So, I'm feeding the good dog." No one seemed to enjoy the story as much as Michael did, except Jake who snorted appreciatively at the theatrics, and Stevie who understood why John told him the story in the first place. It was the best description of Michael she had heard yet.

"Very entertaining," Brian remarked. "What'd the surgeon say?"

Michael sighed at the banality of the question. Ho hum, back to real-ity. "I've got to have surgery, but it's all right. It can wait until I get home." Stevie's eyebrows pinched together like Michael's usually did. "It's okay, Stevie," he added as soon as he noticed. "You know how I get those headaches? The surgeon said that's what it's from, and the surgery will fix it." He pointed to a platter of biscuits with his fork and Brian passed them to him. Michael buttered two of them and then doused them with gravy.

"Holy crap. N'wonder you're gaining weight," Marcus chuckled with his gravelly voice that was similar to a person with laryngitis, from years of chain smoking, Stevie figured. He always said if he had to choose he'd rather smoke than eat.

"Growing boy," Michael shot back lightheartedly. A big dollop of gravy fell off the biscuit on route to his mouth and landed in a light brown puddle on his baby blue shirt. He took it off and hung it over the back of his chair, and with a mischievous grin ran the fingers of both hands through his long hair, releasing the curls from the gel. And as quick as that, the prep school student was gone; From *GQ* to *Rolling Stone* in less than thirty seconds. Sitting there in his white beater t-shirt with his just-fell-out-of-bed messy hair, he was the front man of a rock band again. And Stevie couldn't take her eyes off of him. "What'd I miss today?" he asked.

"David sat with us at lunch," Jake spilled out quickly, as if he'd been waiting for the first opportunity to say it.

"Oh yeah?" Michael responded and turned his attention back to his plate of food.

"It wasn't my idea. And I didn't talk to him," Jake added, scowling fiercely at all the culprits who had.

Michael looked up at Jake. "That's all right, bro. You can talk to him. How was your session?" he asked Stevie. She nibbled on her lip. She was thinking about telling him what Ellen said about the sober house, but wasn't sure she wanted to talk about it with everyone else. "Did you give Ellen hell?" he added with a wink.

Stevie laughed. "Surprisingly, no," she answered.

Liz, picking at her customary plate full of fruits and vegetables had been waiting for her turn to speak. "Have you seen a cardiologist since you got here, Michael?"

He seemed to hesitate, Stevie noticed. He wasn't looking up, which was unlike him—not to make eye contact when someone spoke to him. Instead, he was playing with his food. "N—no," he finally said. "Maybe when I first got here, but I'm not sure about that." He took a bite of salad smothered in bleu cheese dressing and added, "Why?" A daub of white dressing stood out against his deep-hued mouth until his tongue found it.

"Because yesterday you said you have an arrhythmia. People with arrhythmias usually have them monitored by a cardiologist."

Her gaze shifted to Stevie, whose eyes were wide open with worry. The pause was Jake's chance to jump into the discussion. "Why y'always eat rabbit food, Liz?" he asked, missing the importance of the conversation he was interrupting.

"Because drinking destroyed my liver and now it can't process fat," Liz answered. "See what you've got to look forward to?"

"That's why I do drugs. They're better for you. Besides, I ain't goin' be a drunk like my ol' man."

"Funny, that's what I said," Liz answered quite seriously, but Jake laughed as if she were making a joke.

"Me, too," Stevie said. "Ellen says I can't live at home when I get out because of my parents' drinking."

Michael started to remark on Stevie's comment, but Marcus interrupted. "Yep, my father, too—least that's what they tell me. I never met the bastard."

"Shit knows I'm in," Brian added to the sound of Jake's wild background laughter. "Anybody here got a dad that's *not* a drunk?"

"It's my mom, not my dad," Allison said quietly.

"My dad never picked it up," Michael told them. "But his old man died of cirrhosis."

Jake's hilarity died away into a look of bewilderment. "You mean your grandpa's a drunk?" Maybe it was Jake's use of the word "grandpa" that made it seem like he was five years old and discovering for the first time that the world had a dangerous side to it, or maybe it was the fact that she had devoured the entire bag of chocolates, but Stevie's stomach suddenly felt sick. She exchanged a glance with Michael.

"Yeah, Jake," Michael said gently. "My grandpa was a drunk."

Jake licked jelly off the corners of his mouth, the biscuit in his hand oozing butter onto his fingers and streaking down his forearm. "Do you miss him?" he asked, licking the butter off his arm with his pink tongue but keeping his big round blue eyes on Michael.

"I never got to know him because he killed himself with alcohol." The table became hushed—familiar story. "Not me, though," Michael suddenly said, breaking the silence. "You don't have to live like that either Jake."

"Or die like that," Liz added, picking at a piece of raw broccoli with her fork. "So, Michael, what were you saying about the cardiologist?"

"I wasn't saying anything about the cardiologist," he answered tightly, his eyes intently on Liz now as if he was warning her not to travel any farther in that direction. When he finally broke eye contact, he gulped his milk like he was downing a beer.

"Dr. Jim takes care of that, right, your heart?" Stevie asked, sliding a hand onto his lap.

Michael softened his gaze before he turned it to her. "I don't want you to be scared about that," he said in a hushed tone, as if she was the only one at the table. "Dr. Jim does an EKG every week. When I get out I'm having an echocardiogram. There's nothing to worry about, okay?" he added, but his soulful eyes looked worried to her.

"Okay," she surrendered.

CHAPTER FOURTEEN:

BROTHERS

Once Michael started, it was hard to stop. That was true for everything in his life. Now it wasn't good enough to stay clean. He wanted the chance to be the person he could have been if he never started using drugs. His plan was to get an engineering degree and still get his band signed with a record label. He started spending a lot of time with John talking about how to accomplish that, and after they came up with an aftercare plan, he actually broke the boycott and wrote to his parents. With John's blessing, he told them about his plans and asked for a part time job as a clerk in his father's engineering firm.

He was lingering at the coffee bar with Stevie before they had to split up for their morning men/women's groups when he received their response. John entered in his towering, exuberant manner, grinning like a schoolboy. "I've got two things to tell you, Mr. James," he announced with his most official voice. "First, I just got off the phone with your dad. Your parents are still in shock over your letter."

"What—what'd my dad say?" Michael asked, immediately swiveling back and forth on the bar stool and tapping his fingers on his knee.

"He said yeah, he wants you to work for him. He's blown away that you want to. I talked to Elizabeth—I mean, your mom, too. She said she's counting down the days on the calendar. She can't wait to get you back home."

Michael smiled and couldn't stop that either. "Yeah?" he asked with trepidation.

"Yeah. Really," John assured him. "We talked about your aftercare plan. They're real excited about you going to college, but I told them you agreed not to start classes until you've got a year clean under your belt. That means *next* fall, right my friend?"

"Yeah, John, I told you that. I know what I've got to do."

"Including everything else we talked about?"

Michael turned his eyes away and lit a cigarette. He took a drag and handed it to Stevie, whose eyes were sharply on him. While breathing it in, she watched his face. It was clear to her that John had touched a nerve. Exactly which nerve she wasn't quite sure, but she could tell by his avoidance tactics that it was a sensitive one. "I don't know about that," he mumbled. "But I'll think about it."

"You've got eight days left here to think about it, maybe talk about it. So, that's number one. Here's number two." John took a letter from his shirt pocket. "It's from Matt," he said and handed it to Michael. "Now I want you to read it." Michael studied the perfectly formed, almost calligraphic letters on the envelope. The name Matthew Thompson was on the return address.

"You know how I write?" Michael inquired of Stevie. "Not like this at all, huh?"

"You're an artist," Stevie stated simply and sipped her French roast. "Everything about you is creative. Why would your handwriting be any different?"

John seemed amused by her analysis. "Talk to Stevie about the band, Michael," he suggested. "She knows you better than I do."

Michael squeezed her knee until it tickled so much she busted out in giggles. "And she still likes me. Imagine that?" *Try tripping over my heart in love with you*, Stevie thought. *I liked you the first time I saw you. I loved you every second after that.*

John glanced at his watch. "Seven minutes 'til group. Stevie, make sure he reads that letter. And Michael, enough bullshit; read the God damn thing." Then he left the room like a lumbering grizzly bear. Like always, it felt like a little bit of his presence stayed behind even after he was gone.

"Well?" Stevie challenged. "You've got seven whole minutes to read it."

He didn't need seven minutes. Matt had only written two words on the piece of yellow striped legal paper: Still friends? He didn't even sign it, only jotted down those two words with the question mark following it.

"Wow," Stevie vocalized, impressed by it. It was almost like something her father would do, whittle everything away until deep down at the core, he found the real issue.

"What do you think I ought to do?" Michael asked her.

By now they had spent hours talking about his friendship with Matt and Matt's "betrayal" by plotting with Michael's parents to have him court ordered into treatment. As much as Michael seemed to want to, he couldn't bring himself to forgive him. Matt had been living with him in his apartment and playing bass in his band. He knew Michael's schedule, when he was using and when he was likely to be passed out. After days on end using meth with little or no sleep, he always eventually crashed, even if he had to drink a fifth of something to make it happen. So Matt knew exactly when to strike. To Michael it was like Judas Iscariot leading the enemy to the inner sanctum. Without Matt, his parents could never have done what they did. And what they did to him was wrong. Wasn't it?

"I think you ought to write to him, that's what I think you ought to do." (She loved mimicking him when he used those southern boy phrases.) "And forgive him, Michael. If it weren't for Matt you wouldn't be clean."

"If it weren't for Matt, I wouldn't be alive," he answered as he folded the letter and tucked it in his pocket.

"I wish I had a friend like that," Stevie mused.

"You do, remember?" Michael replied before he took the letter back out of his pocket. An old coffee can on the counter was holding pens for just such an occasion. Michael chose one and crossed out the word "friends". Stevie's breath caught in her throat. Surely he wasn't going to continue the battle. Everything else in his life was getting back on track. Why not this, too? Underneath the crossed out word, Michael scribbled the word *brothers*. "Think that's lame?" he asked.

"It's not lame," she said, trying not to let her voice crack. "It's the right thing."

Michael nodded casually like it was no big deal, but Stevie knew it was a *huge* deal to him to let go of something that had caused him so much pain. Matt was the one person on Earth who he trusted above all the rest and through the distorted eyes of his disease, Matt had taken that trust and trampled on it. But through Stevie's eyes, Matt was the person who brought Michael to her. He had saved his life. Every night when she got down on her knees to thank God for her new sobriety, she thanked God for Michael's, too, and for Matt who had made it possible.

Michael had Jake by his side in the recreation room, teaching him how to play pool when David entered and eyed them. Jake looked like a miniature version of Michael with his hair gelled now, too, and wearing Michael's weathered Jimmy Eat World t-shirt even though it hung to his knees. He narrowed his eyes at David and elbowed Michael in case he didn't see him. "It's all right," Michael said quietly with his cigarette still dangling from his mouth and one long curl falling down over his eye. He moved the cue away from the ball and stood erect. "Hey man, you want to play?" he threw out casually.

David nodded his head slightly. "Sure," he finally answered and walked toward them.

Judging by Jake's face, he couldn't quite fathom what was happening. He had outwardly pledged that David was the enemy, the only person in the whole place that he hated because of the things he had said about Michael—the only person he'd ever met that he wanted to grow up and be like. Jake laid his stick against the table and turned to walk away, but Michael caught his arm. "Listen, brother," he said, "it's not worth it, all right? Trust me on this." David reached them before Jake could respond. Michael held his hand out so David could slap it and he did. It took Jake another moment to swallow it, but he eventually did the same and David slapped his hand, too.

They had barely started playing when John, wearing a Clemson jersey, entered and held up a football. It was Sunday afternoon and the patients had free time. Although it was supposed to be John's day off, he spent more Sundays with the patients than he did at home. But he always made it a point to be home on time for Sunday dinner at 4:00— that was his wife's rule and everyone in the place knew about it. "You guys in?" he asked.

"Fuck yeah!" Jake responded and Michael and David burst out laughing. Even though all the guys in the group had promised John they wouldn't let Jake talk like a "street punk", sometimes things came out of him that were too funny not to laugh at.

This time John let it go. "All right then, let's get going," he suggested. "I've only got a couple of hours." It was a good thing John knew as much as he did about football because Jake had never played before, and neither had Marcus, who in a rare moment of humility agreed to be taught. It took a good thirty minutes for John to explain to them what they needed to do. John suggested they all take time to practice throwing the football around. Marcus liked that idea for two reasons: he didn't have to worry about humiliating himself, and he didn't have to remove the cigarette from his lips. The guys didn't care if they got to a game or not. It was a whole new freedom for them to be outside for a while throwing a ball around like normal guys.

The women were hanging out on the sidelines until they realized they could play without being tackled and crushed, and joined in. Jake's friend Melanie was there, too, flirting with him. It was almost shocking behavior to witness in someone who had been so habitually reserved. At one point, she actually tackled him onto the ground and wouldn't have gotten off him if John hadn't told her to. She laughed and Stevie had to turn her head to verify that the sound had been emitted from Melanie's throat. A giggle sounded as alien coming from her as it would have coming from John.

"What the hell happens when I'm not here?" he asked Stevie when she was within earshot.

"Trust me, John. You don't want to know," she answered, teasing him, and winked at Michael, who was venturing closer.

"What are we talking about?" he asked.

"What we do at night when John goes home."

"Oh, *that*."

John looked back and forth between the two of them like he wasn't sure if they were kidding him or not. "Maybe I'll start spending some nights here," he mused.

"Oh Christ, please don't," Michael laughed. "Like ten hours a day isn't enough."

"Michael!" David yelled from across the field. "Are you playing or not?"

It took Stevie a second to realize why Michael faltered the way he did. David had used his real name...for the first time. The *meth head* days were over, finally.

Michael grinned boyishly. "Yeah, I'm playing," he responded, "throw me the ball." And David did.

Time went by quick as wind and before they all knew it John was racing to his car and screaming maniacally over his shoulder for them to go back inside immediately. They weren't allowed to be outside in a large group without a counselor. He was so scared of his wife's wrath (who reportedly was only 5'2") that he didn't take the time to herd them in. "Marcus," he yelled through his car window, "Make sure they go back inside." And with that he roared out of the parking lot in his old beat-up Chevy, leaving a puff of gray exhaust and the catcalls of the wolf pack behind. Marcus was pointing to his chest like he couldn't believe someone had made him responsible for something, especially *people*.

"Marcus is in charge of us?" Jake teased. "That's the balls."

"Watch your mouth," Marcus ordered. "And get inside."

The remarkable thing was that they all did. Just as they entered the building Jake ran up behind Michael and punched him in the back. Michael groaned dramatically. "Watch it, man," he complained, "you might hurt me." That was Jake's favorite thing—getting Michael to say that. It always put a swagger in his step. Maybe he thought playing football had toughened him up, made him a little bit closer to being a man. He stretched his spine out and walked as tall as he could, but he still only came up to Michael's shoulder. His face was red and his hair was wet through with sweat, but he was obviously content to be carrying the football under his arm like it belonged there.

"That was fun, huh?" he said.

"Yeah, it was," Michael agreed.

"So brother..." Jake began, mimicking Michael. "Can I talk to you 'bout som'in?"

Michael nodded his assent and Jake jerked his head toward the men's hallway, then led Michael to his room and closed the door behind them.

"What're you in trouble or something?" Michael asked in response to Jake's sketchy mannerisms. He lit a cigarette and tossed the pack to Jake.

"Nah, nothin' like that. I just wanted to ask you..." He lit a cigarette and started to fidget. He crossed one calf across his knee so he could inspect his worn out Converse sneaker then stuck his index finger in a hole and tugged on it. "It's 'bout sex."

"Oh, okay," Michael answered and for a split second the skin around his eyes got crinkly like he was about to laugh before he matched Jake's serious expression.

"I'm just wondering...where you do it. I mean, how you do it— no, shit no that's, that's not what I meant."

"Jesus, Jake. What the hell are you talking about? Just say it."

"How you get *away* with it."

"How I get away with it? You mean here?"

"Yeah, you and Stevie."

"Oh man," Michael sighed. "Is that what you think?" Jake resembled one of those bobble head puppies that peer through the rearview windows of cars, his head bobbing and his big innocent eyes watching Michael for any information that might magically emit from him. "It's not like that. And if it were, I wouldn't be talking to you about it."

"How come?"

"How come what, we're not doing it or I'm not talking to you about it?"

"Well, both I guess."

Michael laughed and fell back on the bed. Staring at the ceiling, he blew perfect circular smoke rings that floated like apparitions above him. "It's not that simple. Sex is complicated, Jake." He lifted a hand and destroyed the smoke circles with his fingers.

"I know." Jake's drawl drew out three syllables instead of two, and his face looked pained, like Michael had kicked him.

Michael sat up and put his cigarette out. "I know you know," he conceded. "And I know it's not really like you're thirteen because of everything you've been through. But that thing with Phil, it wasn't that long ago."

Jake's face turned bright red. "You think that's how I am?"

"No. No, Jake, that's not what I meant. I know you're not gay. That guy did something to you that he shouldn't have done. What he did was his fault, not yours. I just thought, you know, maybe you need time to get over it."

"Didn't help last time," Jake said. "I don't think there's gettin' over it, you know?"

"No, not really. Are you saying someone else did that to you?"

"My foster parents—not the last ones. Ones in Abilene. That's why I knew how."

"Jesus *fucking Christ*," escaped Michael in nearly a cry. With his hands behind his head, his fingers tugged compulsively at his curls, his engaging mouth contorted into a painful grimace. "What the fuck, bro?"

"People do that. Don't you know? And it don't just go away 'cause time goes by. Ask Stevie. She knows it." He turned his eyes to his thumbnail and gnawed on it.

"Wait, what do you mean by that, she knows it? What are you talking about?"

"You know, 'cause she been raped—"

"Okay, fuck. Stop, Jake. Stop talking." Michael sprung from the bed and started pacing like a cat again, all agility and speeding energy. His body moved manically around the room until his eyes fell on the red pack of Marlboros on the bed. He lit one and sucked on it until the end turned orange. "Did she tell you that?" he asked.

Jake searched for more fingernails to chew. "Nah," he sighed. "Didn't she tell you?"

Michael stared at Jake long and hard like he was trying to find information written on his adolescent face. "I got to go," he said abruptly and reached for the door handle.

"But wait. It's a girl, you know, a girl that I want to..."

"I know, Jake, I know. It's Melanie."

Jake's mouth became slack. He was thinking. "How you know?"

"Because I can see it, man. People can see it."

"Like I see it in Stevie?"

"Yeah, listen, I don't want to talk about that anymore, all right? Don't say that to anyone else, you understand, Jake? Because that's serious shit you're talking about."

"Yeah. I know."

Michael sighed at the weight of Jake's response and at the wise beyond his years expression on his face. Of all people, Jake knew just how serious that shit was. "All right, you want to know what I think about you and Melanie? I think you should think about it first because it's a big deal—it's not a game, and because you can get in a lot of trouble if you get caught. But if you do decide to do it, try to figure out a way to get condoms, a'ight? That's the best I got because I don't really know what's the right thing to say." He reached for the door handle again, shaking his head this time.

"Hang on. Don't open it yet." Jake's little boy mouth crept into a mischievous smirk. He walked to the dresser, pulled out a three-pack of condoms hidden under his socks and waved it around for effect. "Ought to take your own advice," he suggested, then tore one off and threw it to Michael.

Michael threw his head back and laughed at the gesture. "Holy shit, Jake," he said and pocketed the condom.

CHAPTER FIFTEEN:

SERENITY TO ACCEPT THE THINGS I CANNOT CHANGE...

The water lily was still floating innocently in a bowl of water in Stevie's bathroom, but it was wilting, the edges of the petals turning brown. Observing it now, free from its watery bed one would never guess that a short time before it had been hopelessly tangled, something invisible but insidious below the pond's surface holding it fast. Even though it was declining, Stevie still admired it and was doing so at the moment Allison stopped by to tell her that Michael was waiting for her in the den and seemed to be distraught.

"What did you mean" he demanded of her when she approached the den from the women's hallway, "when you said that men hurt you?" She was within reach now, but she withdrew a bit when she heard his words. He extended a hand to her hip and pulled her closer. "What did you mean by that?" Allison had said that he was upset, but what was coming from his mouth was completely unexpected.

"What—what are you talking about?" she stammered, knowing exactly what he was talking about, but trying to figure out how he knew.

He shook his head frantically like it wasn't a good enough answer. "I've got to talk to you," he insisted and ventured over to the nurse's station just a few feet away. "Can I sign us out?" he asked the overweight nurse sitting like an unhappy sentinel behind the desk with her bowl of peanut M&Ms. "We want to go to the duck pond."

The nurse frowned and checked her watch like it was hard work to do so. "For how long?" she griped.

Michael shrugged his shoulders. "How long will you give us?"

She looked at the ceiling and brought one hand up under her chin as if it required great concentration to calculate a response. "Thirty minutes," she finally said. "Stay in sight."

Michael signed their names in a notebook on the counter and entered the time, 5:08, then turned back to Stevie. She was still in the same spot, but her expression looked frozen to her face and there were tears in her eyes. "Oh shit," he mumbled and threw his head back. "I'm sorry." He took her hand in his and tugged her toward the exit. John had cut them slack on the handholding. On the trip back from Savannah, he had told Michael it was okay. *But nothing even remotely resembling sex*, he'd emphasized.

As soon as they were outside with the door shut behind them Michael embraced her. "Because of what I said, is that why you're shaking?" She dug her face into his neck and grasped onto his hair with both hands. "It's okay. It's okay," he whispered. "You don't have to tell me." Ten out of their thirty minutes passed right then and there with him holding onto her while she sobbed tears all over his shirt. "Come on, let's go to the pond," he finally suggested. They didn't murmur another word until they were sitting hip-to-hip on Michael's denim jacket, and a half dozen ducks swam closer.

"We should have brought bread," Stevie observed and Michael smiled at her.

"I could go get some," he proposed, his eyes squinty from the bright sunlight. She shook her head and then rested it on his shoulder.

"Give me time," Stevie pleaded. "There's a lot I need to tell you, but I can't do it all now. The first time—"

"Wait, you mean it happened more than once?"

Stevie looked at the grass instead of him. She pulled strands out and scattered them as she measured her words. "The first time I was thirteen." She glanced over at him and saw his jaw clench, but he didn't say anything so she kept going. "It was Scott's friends—three of them. They came home and found me passed out on the living room floor. My best friend had left me there after a party. It was the first time my parents went away for a weekend and left us alone."

Michael rose and walked closer to the water, his fair complexion flushed and his eyes black and shiny as molasses, before he returned and paused in front of her. "What'd Scott do to them? What'd he do, Stevie? Because I think I would have killed them."

She dropped her face into her hands and waited while he walked it off. She could hear his breath, strained and irregular. How could she tell him that Scott had done nothing, or that he didn't even know when it was happening because he was passed out, too? Of course she was unconscious, so the reality of it had come to her in bits and pieces the next morning when she woke up, her head throbbing like someone was hammering on it. Her panties and skirt were on the floor next to her. She was still wearing the new blouse she had bought to wear to the party, but it was torn and some of the buttons were missing. The telltale sign was the soreness between her legs and the stickiness that turned out to be a mixture of blood and semen. She had lost her virginity that night. They had stolen it.

When she couldn't hear Michael's erratic breathing anymore, she lifted her face. He was stooped down in front of her, his eyes wet with tears. "I can't even fucking fathom this," he vented. "How could something like that happen...to a thirteen year old?"

"You'd be surprised how easy. In every crowd, at every party, there's some guy—"

"Stop...please," he heaved and took a couple of minutes to catch his breath. "I'd never let that happen to you. Do you know that? I would never let anyone hurt you."

She scarcely nodded her head. "I'm sorry, Michael. I'm so sorry that I'm not what you thought. And there's still something, something else...that I have to, to t-tell you—"

"You don't have to tell me anything. And don't be sorry. You *are* what I thought."

She slid her hands behind his neck and pulled him close. "I can't look at you when I say this because I don't want to see your eyes when—when you h-hear it."

He was on his knees now with mud soaking into his jeans, holding her waist, his forehead pressed against hers. "You don't have to do this," he was saying.

But she did, she *did* have to. "You won't—I mean you might not, not l-like me."

"How could you think that? Don't you know that I—"

"Michael, listen please." She pressed her eyes against his shoulder, the one already wet from her tears. "Someone did it right before I got here, in Atlanta." Her fingers were gripping his arms so tightly she must have been bruising him, but she didn't realize it at first and he didn't stop her. "I thought I was pregnant. I thought I was, but I'm not."

He was a python around her waist, pulling her so tightly against him she couldn't take a full breath. "Why didn't you tell me before?" came out in his raspiest voice.

Because I'm in love with you and I'm scared you'll leave me. How could she say that out loud? What he needed to hear was the truth, but somehow it was worse because she couldn't remember it—like it was her fault. Not even the horror of being raped could break through the grip alcohol had on her brain, and that made her feel like...nothing, not even human. A rag doll ripped at the seams and ejaculated on. That's why he had to know. If he knew the truth about her, he could never love her. Maybe no one could.

"I don't know who it was," she sobbed. "I can't remember. And maybe I'm, maybe I'm infected. I don't know. The HIV test was negative, but..."

"I thought you were thinking that about me," he said, his words weakening his grip. "That I was infected, because of the needles. I never shared them, though. Are you scared of being with me?"

"No," she released with her breath. "I'm scared of *not* being with you."

Suddenly his warm lips were on hers and his silky breath was in her mouth. She inhaled it, trying to breathe him inside her. If she could just do that, she could be whole again and safe. She could forget everything that came before, all the things that made her stop feeling and now made her feel like a vase with a huge crack running through its center, threatening to split her in half. Soon Michael's wet eyelashes on her skin were the only reminder of the conversation. The taste of salty tears subsided to the blackberries and sugar flavor of his mouth, and the painful throb in her chest gave way to the warmest, tingliest sensation that seemed to be pumping from her heart into the rest of her, up and down her spine, and even into her fingertips. *Nirvana,* she thought and the word pulsated through her brain with all the new sensations Michael was creating inside her. If she could fashion it herself this is what it would be like, her Nirvana. She thought of her first conversation with Brian. She'd have to remember to tell him that she'd found it.

"You won't be without me," he was saying, "If you're sure it's what you want—"

"I am." Her lips brushed against his and tickled her skin. "I am sure." She'd known that she wanted to stay with him since nearly the very beginning, since that first morning at breakfast when she found him waiting for her in the dining room, his eyes still heavy with sleep and his hair wet from the shower.

His lips skimmed across her face like a stone across a pool of water. "I love you," he exhaled into her ear with his warm breath, the fingers of one hand tangled in her hair. *Only Michael...only Michael could still love someone like her even when he knew how damaged she was.* Maybe his body was tainted by the meth, but his heart was as pure as an angel's.

"Come with me to Jacksonville when you get out," he pleaded. "I'll drive up and get you. My parents won't mind if you stay with us until we find our own place. I don't want you going back there." *Back there...to Massachusetts.* To Michael it was the place she was raped, the place she hid bottles in her toy box, the place she'd learned to hate herself. Could she even imagine herself going back there? The thought put a lump of fear in her throat. But how could she stay away from everything she'd ever known?

It was right about then, in the midst of the chaos swirling around her mind, that Brian showed up to drag them back. According to the sentinel nurse, it was 5:48 and they had overstayed by ten minutes. "Was she watching us?" Stevie asked him.

"Listen, y'all," he continued without answering her. "I've got news." Stevie and Michael exchanged a worried glance. "Liz left AMA."

"What's that mean?" Stevie asked.

"It means she signed herself out and left against medical advice," Michael explained. "I did it once. That's why they got the court order this time."

"But why would Liz do that?"

Brian heaved a sigh. "Because she wanted to drink."

"No," Stevie argued. "No, I don't believe that, not with her little girls at home."

"This is the fourth time she's done the exact same thing. It's not 'cause she doesn't love 'em. It's 'cause she can't stop drinking."

"But there's something wrong with her liver—"

"And her pancreas," Brian added. "It's dangerous for her to drink."

The horrified look on Stevie's face must have prompted him to comfort her. He gave her a big hug. "I'm sorry," he said, swaying back and forth with her in his arms like he was rocking a baby. "I know you were good friends." *Were* good friends; Stevie's hands started to shake. It was almost like Liz had died. Would she ever see her again or even talk to her? Then she remembered what Ellen had said about her rehab group, how she'd always think of them as her friends even though she might never see them again.

"But you were her closest friend, Brian."

"Mm hm, and she didn't even tell me good-bye." The loneliness of his words made her belly ache. She looked over at Michael's ebony eyes. They were turbulent, like storm clouds. What would she do if he walked out like Liz did? As if he knew what she was thinking, he responded.

"That won't happen to us. Come on now. We've got to get back." He took her hands and pulled her to her feet. The three of them were half way back to the building when he repeated himself. "It won't," he said close to her ear.

But Stevie couldn't stop wondering what Liz's eyes looked like when she walked out. Was her new warmth and radiance still visible, or was she a husk again?

The whole group was troubled by Liz's decision. It was a fat reality slap to all of them and it was one less wolf in their pack. The rest were waiting in the den and they all exchanged hugs when Stevie returned with Michael and Brian. Even Michael and David sort of embraced in that "touching but not touching" way that guys do it. It felt almost like someone had died and they were all in the first horrendous stages of grief.

It was dinnertime and on the rehab wing Sunday dinner was an event. The cooks worked all day to make the meal and desserts extra special, there were candles on all the tables with the chandeliers dimmed, and everyone held hands at their own tables while one person said grace for the whole room. Sometimes it was a nurse or one of the cooks. Seldom was it a counselor as most of them spent Sundays at home, and even more seldom was it a patient. This week, surprisingly, Brian volunteered. Stevie held Michael's hand on one side and then had to reach over Liz's empty seat to hold Allison's.

It was the Serenity Prayer adopted by Alcoholics Anonymous that Brian chose to lead them in. He bowed his head humbly and the rest of the room followed suit. *God, grant me the Serenity to accept the things I cannot change. Courage to change the things I can and Wisdom to know the difference.* There was a long pause and Stevie lifted her head to see that Brian was trying not to cry. Everyone in the dining room said "amen" and sat down. It was the first time Stevie realized the significance of the words of the prayer even though she had recited them every day at the end of women's group.

"You're the next one to go, Marcus," Brian noted when he rejoined them.

"Yup, Thursday," Marcus replied.

"Back on the chain gang," David sort of sang.

The group was awkwardly quiet at first, waiting for Marcus' reaction. He snorted out a chuckle and everyone else laughed along, more from relief than the joke. David still had a way of getting underneath people's skin. This was especially true with Marcus who had never quite gotten over his skirmish with Michael.

"I'm leaving a week from today," Michael threw out. "My parents are coming early in the morning, John said. Hey, know what else? He said there's a dance at the AA hall in Valdosta Saturday night for the sober house residents, but we might get to go."

"Doubt it," Marcus said, "but whatever, I won't be here anyway."

"If John can make it work, he will," Michael asserted. "Jake, you've been here almost sixty days. Know where you're going yet?" Jake shook his head and tossed his long blonde hair off his face. Then he shoved a spoonful of stuffing in his mouth. Apparently he wasn't overly concerned about it. "I'll give you my address before I go," Michael added, "so you can write to me." Jake grinned and nodded eagerly.

"It'll be like Purgatory again," David added to the mix. "Just me and the girls."

"I'm moving into the sober house in Valdosta," Allison suddenly said. They all exchanged perplexed glances. "My parents won't let me come home. Since I'm under eighteen, there's nothing I can do about it."

"How 'bout you, Stevie?" Brian asked. "Will you be a Georgia girl, too?"

"I'm hoping she'll be a Florida girl," Michael interjected, looking up from his plate of turkey with his signature grin.

"Holy shit!" Allison exclaimed. "Are you serious? Stevie, that's great. You won't be so far away. We can still see each other!"

"That's funny, I was going to say 'holy shit', too," David remarked flatly.

"What? What David—" Michael started, but was quickly interrupted by Brian.

"Don't start any bullshit, David. I thought you guys were friends now."

"We are friends and I'm not starting anything. I just want to say one thing: I saw you in detox, Michael. Okay? Enough said."

Michael threw his fork down on his plate. "What the fuck's that supposed to mean?"

David ignored him and ate his food. Michael's angry energy didn't seem to touch him. Finally he sighed out the same two words: "Enough said."

The silence that followed made Stevie's insides feel like a rubber band being stretched and waiting to snap. It was like sitting at the dinner table back home the day after she got arrested or did some other stupid thing, like the time she crashed her mother's car when she wasn't even supposed to be using it. Back then she used to listen to the ticking of the grandfather clock in the dining room and wonder exactly how many ticks it would take for the blood to run out of her body if she slashed her wrists with her steak knife.

"Know what I'm thinkin'?" Marcus asked. No one answered. "I'm thinkin' we haven't played poker in a long time and Tom's the night narc."

"Awww man, I love playing with Tom. He's so easy to beat," Jake said. "I'm in."

"Michael?" Marcus asked. "Are you in?"

He shrugged his shoulders and picked up his fork. "What are we playing for?"

"I got some ideas. We'll talk after dinner." Marcus winked at him in his notorious "honor amongst thieves" manner.

"Poor Tom," Michael sighed, shaking his head. "He's just not equipped for this."

"Poor Tom" was right. He had no idea when he was being taken for a ride.

He was not at all like Frank, the other night supervisor who spent the entire shift leering at the female patients over his cans of Pringles. Tom was a big, sluggish guy who always looked like he was about to cry. All the rehab employees were supposed to be recovering addicts, but Stevie had her doubts about Tom. He looked so out of place, like he was scared of the patients. She found it funny to imagine him doctoring up his resume to get the job: *six years downing vodka, three years snorting cocaine—no wait—better make it four*. She also noticed that Tom always flinched whenever Michael walked too close to him, like he was scared Michael would beat him up. But he only thought that, Stevie supposed, because he didn't know Michael like she did. Or then again, maybe he was sensing the now submissive bad dog, like a cat.

Now as she approached the guys in the recreation room with Allison, she saw that he was sitting by Michael's side, studying the cards in his hand like he belonged there, like he was one of them. Michael's backward baseball cap was a sign that they were engaged in a game of poker. Stevie and Allison could hear their conversation as they drew closer.

"We could play for stuff," Marcus suggested, "like jewelry."

"No," Michael snapped. "You're not winning my ring in a poker game."

"I'll throw my chain in," Marcus offered.

"Only 'cause you know you won't lose it," Brian argued. It was common knowledge that Marcus was a shark. Brian had learned the hard way. He'd lost a gold crucifix his wife gave him, but fussed so much about it that Marcus gave it back.

As Stevie and Allison reached the table, Michael was talking. "My mom gave me this ring when I turned eighteen. It's sacred." He turned his eyes to Stevie and winked at her.

"Hey," she said softly, assessing the situation. Marcus had a tremendous pile of cigarettes in front of him. Michael trailed behind with about thirty cigarettes and the other guys were completely out, except for Jake who had the one and only still tucked behind his ear. Obviously they had been playing poker for cigarettes, and they were figuring out new stakes, but still it seemed like there was more to it. Marcus was avoiding her eyes, Jake was grinning impishly and Michael had a guilty expression on his face. The only two who looked remotely innocent were Tom, who was obviously oblivious, and David, a born bull shitter.

"You can't play. We already started," Marcus stated flatly, still not looking at them.

"You can sit with me if you want," Michael offered and Marcus shot him a dirty look.

"What?" Michael asked. "They can stay."

"No they can't," David argued. "It's guys' poker night. Sorry girls."

"Well, screw you," Allison hurled at him. She seemed overly injured by the fact that they were being excluded, but Stevie thought she knew why. She had started to suspect that Allison and David had a "thing" or at least Allison did. Recently she'd been asking Stevie lots of repetitive questions about him, not for answers but for reassurances: *Don't you think he's cute? He's sweet, don't you think?* etc. "Let's go, Stevie," she urged this time, but Stevie didn't budge. She was watching Michael. With the hat keeping his hair off his face, she could see every small line. He was worried about something.

"Why don't you girls pick out a movie and we'll all watch it with you in a little while," Marcus suggested diplomatically.

"Go get Melanie," Jake threw in, combing his fingers through his thick hair. "And make popcorn." He reached for a cigarette from Michael's pile and lit it.

"I'm not your waitress Jake. And we're not watching *Pirates of the Caribbean* again, Marcus, not any of them," Allison protested.

"No, that's not what I meant. We'll watch whatever you girls want."

"Yeah, sure you will," Allison whined and looked around at the guys' faces. They were all nodding in agreement. "What if it's a love story, like *The Notebook*?"

David grinned sweetly at her. "The man said anything you want," he said gently. Marcus visibly cringed and Allison visibly softened. Marcus and David watching *The Notebook*? It was too much for Stevie to believe. She narrowed her eyes.

"Okay," rolled out of Allison in a giggle and she exchanged a flirtatious look with David. With the plan in place, the girls turned to walk away.

"Wait, hold up," Michael suddenly said. "One second." He took Stevie's hand and led her to the back of the lounge. "What's the matter?" he asked with his provocative voice, one hand on her hip. It was ridiculous, she thought, how the feel of his fingers on her body or the smell of his skin could throw off her whole game plan, but it did. She wanted to act pissed off at him for doing whatever it was he was doing—keeping her in the dark—but it was impossible. Her anger vanished like vapors in his presence.

"You're making me nervous," she complained with not the slightest antagonism in it.

"Okay, listen." He looked around the room like he was about to tell her an enormous secret and didn't want anyone else to hear. His tongue apprehensively wet his lips. "This is something for us, but you need to trust me. Can you do that?"

She tore her eyes off his intoxicating mouth and sighed. "I guess so."

Michael laughed at her response. "You never give it up without a fight, do you?"

"No, never," she agreed and he laughed again, but she noticed that this time he purposefully covered his teeth with his lips. He had the cutest way of grinning without showing them. *Hot fucking damn* Allison said every time she witnessed it. But Stevie didn't understand his motivation, other than that it was some form of insecurity. "Why do you do that?" she asked.

"Do what?"

"Hide your teeth when you smile."

Michael snorted, a hybrid between laughing and scoffing. "You ever seen a meth addict's teeth?" he asked.

"Yeah," Stevie answered. He raised a disbelieving eyebrow. "Well, yours."

"They rot right out of their mouths," Michael said and his face flushed.

"But yours aren't like that," Stevie argued. "Michael, they're *not*. I've seen them."

He shrugged. "They're uneven from grinding them. It's…a meth thing."

"So what? You shouldn't hide them. I like your smile."

"Yeah?" he ventured. When she nodded, he lifted her chin and gave her a quick, but no less electrifying kiss. "Don't worry," he quickly added. "Tom knows about us."

The possibility of Tom watching them hadn't even crossed her mind. Her brain was too busy wondering whether or not Michael had any idea how much power he held over her emotions. It was something she'd never experienced, going from anger to ecstasy in three seconds flat, like the speedometer on a race car. What would it be like to sleep with him? For a split second she visualized it—the weight of his body on hers, their limbs tangled perfectly together. The picture of him in her bed pushed the air out of her lungs in almost a groan. She smiled sheepishly and turned to leave, her face a glowing pink.

Allison was waiting impatiently near the door...as if they had somewhere to go.

"So we're cool?" he asked.

"Yeah, but...be careful, okay? Whatever it is you're up to, be careful." She thought about it for a second then kissed his scruffy cheek and watched the expression on his face relax. There was nothing about Michael that wasn't completely adorable to her, even his ears that poked out the sides of his baseball cap. She willed herself to turn away from him and had almost reached Allison, her heart still pumping blood through her body like a marathon runner, when she heard him say something behind her.

"*Tristan and Isolde.*" She turned back to face him. "It's the name of a movie— *Tristan and Isolde.* There's lots of blood and guts, but it's really a love story."

Just right for us, she thought and finally walked away from him.

CHAPTER SIXTEEN:

COURAGE TO CHANGE THE THINGS I CAN...

With the guys approaching discharge, the pressure increased for all of them. Early the next morning Ellen knocked on Stevie's door. She was so sound asleep that she didn't hear it. Ellen let herself in and sat on the end of her bed until, gradually, Stevie felt her presence and awakened. "What are you doing?" she grumbled. The room was still dark. She thought it was the middle of the night before she remembered it was three a.m. when she finally made it to bed. She'd had the best conversation with Michael after the movie ended. The Irish legend that inspired the movie had served as an impetus to a conversation about Irish poets. They'd pieced together lines from Yeats' *The Stolen Child* as if they were playing the t.v. game show *Don't Forget the Lyrics!*

"Late night?" Ellen asked.

Stevie propped up on her elbows and glanced at the clock. It was after eight already and John had planned a special discharge meeting at ten that they were all required to attend. Leave it to Ellen to sandwich a session in between. "Mm hm," she murmured and reached for a cigarette. Ellen wouldn't mind. Smoking wasn't only tolerated by the staff, it was almost encouraged, Stevie thought, probably because it was a lesser evil and it allowed patients to occupy the space usually filled by their drugs of choice. It was a fairly accurate hypothesis—if she was at home, she'd be reaching under the bed for the vodka bottle instead of the Marlboro pack.

"*Tristan and Isolde*, huh?" Ellen threw out. Stevie didn't answer. She was thinking about the source of Ellen's information. Michael seemed to trust Tom. Maybe it was one of the nurses who reported back to her in the morning about the patients' nighttime activities. "Did you like it?"

"Yeah, I liked it," Stevie told her. "I liked it a lot until Tristan died. It was a sucky ending. Why couldn't the writer have let them be together, you know? After everything they went through..."

"I think the filmmakers tried to stay true to reality."

"Yeah, well, reality sucks. When I write a novel, I'm going to come up with a better reality."

"Throw a little my way, would you?" Ellen joked. "Because mine isn't always that great either."

Stevie smiled. It was a cool idea. Write your own reality: the beginning, middle and end of your own story. Maybe life *could* be that way. "Are we doing our session here?"

Ellen shrugged. "It doesn't matter to me either way."

"I need coffee. Can you give me a minute to use the bathroom?" She was already out of bed and heading in that direction when Ellen nodded.

While brushing her teeth, her reflection in the mirror indicated she should at least brush her hair and shed the pajamas, but she didn't bother. Everyone in the place was used to seeing her the way she really looked in the morning, with her wild hair sticking out in all directions and wearing her fuzzy slippers. She pulled her fingers through her curls to loosen the tangles and checked one more time in the mirror. The water weight was gone, her skin was completely clear, and her cheeks and lips had a healthy flush to them. She smiled at her own reflection before she rejoined Ellen and walked with her to her office, stopping only long enough to fill up the biggest coffee mug she could find.

"So what's this about?" she asked, once seated. "I thought I had today off."

"We need to start making arrangements at a sober house, unless, of course, there's something else you need to talk about."

Stevie froze. Going to Jacksonville. Is that what Ellen was inferring? Maybe she could plead the 5th amendment. She wasn't ready to discuss this with Ellen and why should she? Unless Michael had already told John...

"Is there?"

Stevie shrugged. "Like what?"

Ellen's grin looked permanently stuck on her face, like a wooden puppet with the mouth painted on it. "Okay. Do you want to go to a sober house?"

Stevie hesitated. "I don't know. I don't know what I should do yet."

"Why? What other options do you have?"

"I could..." After about thirty seconds it was clear she wasn't going to finish the sentence.

"Stay with Michael?" Ellen suggested.

Stevie met her eyes. So, she did know. Or it was an educated guess. "Why not?" she challenged. "We could help each other stay sober."

"Or the opposite." Ellen was rocking casually back and forth in her chair behind the big mahogany desk, as if what she'd said was not a knife in Stevie's chest. "What do you think would happen to Michael if you picked up a drink? Do you think he'd be strong enough not to?"

"Well, no," Stevie admitted. "I don't think he'd be strong enough, but—"

"What if Michael started using meth again? Do you think you could handle that?"

"No," she gasped, thinking of the Addictionary game. No matter how she tried to erase the image of him snorting drugs up his nose, she couldn't. And when she saw the powder going up his nose, she saw the blood coming out of it...ever since he told her the story about doing lines in the band room at a club and then going back on stage without realizing the bleeding had started. When he began singing, he blew the blood out all over the stage and the audience, and no one even seemed to mind. He bent over with laughter when he told her the story, but she was horrified by it. "I couldn't watch him do that to himself. But who says he's going to? You're assuming the worst because you don't know him like I do. You don't know how smart he is or how, how...stubborn."

Ellen got a good laugh out of that one. (It sounded more like a cackle.) "Unfortunately neither intelligence nor stubbornness can keep us sober. Too bad, though, because you'd be all set if it did."

Stevie squinted her eyes menacingly and tried to think of a comeback.

"I'm kidding, well, sort of," Ellen continued. "But actually I know a few things that might surprise you about Michael and just how smart he is."

"Like what?" she asked and gulped the coffee without shifting her gaze.

"Let's see." Ellen used her foot now planted on the desk to swivel the chair. "He graduated first in his high school class and was accepted to every college he applied to, including Stanford and M.I.T.—with a scholarship. I'd say that's pretty smart."

Stevie stared blankly, feeling like she was the puppet now—the green iris of her eyes painted in oversized black lines shaped like almonds. He'd never told her that. Never had he even breathed a word about his grades or scholarships. *First rank in his class?* She'd thought he was accepted to M.I.T. because his dad helped him, like her dad got her into a college that she wasn't really qualified for.

Ellen must not have noticed that she was struck mute because she kept right on talking. "He plays piano and guitar oh—and writes his own music. Stuff like that, you know that his parents are proud about."

"Michael thinks...they're not." It was painful to think about it. How many times had he said that to her, that his parents thought he was a disappointment? All this time she thought he was exactly like her, but he wasn't. He had a great life once but took a wrong turn. Hers was never really good, even before she started drinking alcoholically. Her very first memory was from when she was four or five years old, sitting on her dad's lap during football games and sipping beer from his can. And she remembered it because he was proud of her for it. Proud. He used to brag about it to his friends.

"He thinks they're not what?" Ellen asked.

"Proud." Stevie dropped her chin to her chest and stared down at her fuzzy slippers that used to be as soft as newborn kittens, but now looked like something their mature counterparts would drag home for dinner.

"Well, they are. They think he's the greatest thing on Earth."

Stevie slowly lifted her face. "So do I. Ellen, do you know them at all—the James'?"

"Only from talking to them on the phone. They call here every single day. Either John or I talk to them, and give them an update." Stevie absorbed the information. Her mother had started to call, too, twice in the last week. But still, after more than six weeks, her father hadn't called once. Big surprise; he was too busy suing people.

"They really love him, right?" she asked.

"There's no doubt about that."

"But I mean, they're not messed up are they, like my parents? They'll help him?"

Ellen took her feet off the desk and leaned forward. "They're good people, Stevie. They'll do whatever they can. His mom's a teacher. She said she was thinking of taking a leave of absence this fall to be with him. I told her I didn't think that was necessary."

The truth was churning the acid in her stomach. That stupid voice inside her head would not shut up—the one that always recognized and reiterated the truth even when she didn't want to hear it. "And Matt?" she asked cautiously.

Ellen sighed. "He moved back home to be there with Michael."

That was the final painful piece. What Michael needed was more than she could give, but it wasn't more than what his family was capable of and more than willing to provide. "Okay," she conceded. "I'll talk to you about going to a sober house, but not today. I need to talk to Michael about it first." Ellen nodded her understanding. "I know you and John talk, and I understand why you do it, but I'm asking you this time not to. It's important." This was a trust issue, and to Michael nothing ranked higher than trust.

It was the first time in her life she'd made a decision that was based more on someone else's welfare than her own. And that euphoric feeling people often describe when doing something motivated by love? Not so euphoric, after all. To her it felt cold and barren, like someone had drawn the shades on her life so no sunshine could eek in.

Showing up at the discharge meeting with a head full of new plans and looking into Michael's trusting eyes was brutal. How was she going to tell him she wasn't going home with him? Not yet, she told herself.

Not yet. Ever since they first talked about it, he'd been walking around like he was "high on crack" as Marcus had pointed out.

"How'd it go?" he asked when she slid into the seat beside him, still wearing her pajamas. "Allison said you were in Ellen's office. Is everything okay?"

"Yeah," she answered, "just a session."

"I thought you had today off."

"So did I, but you know how Ellen is. She was in my bedroom when I woke up."

"Damn," Michael exclaimed and grimaced. "D'you tell her we were up 'til three?"

"I didn't have to. She knows everything we do."

"Not everything," he whispered and winked at her slyly like he was harboring a secret. Before she could ask him what it was John made his grand entrance.

"All right, folks, listen up. We've got a handful of people leaving here in the next few days. That means it's a good time to hammer home a few points." He awkwardly took the last open seat and nearly knocked the desk over, a cartoon bull in a china shop. His near catastrophe didn't interrupt his lecture. "If you want sobriety, you have to work for it— remember that. No one can do it for you. We do the best we can to teach you about your disease and how to treat it, so that you've got a shot at making it on your own. But that's the thing, you see, you *are* on your own. No one will be looking over your shoulder anymore telling you when you're doing the right things or the wrong things. All you'll have are the tools we've tried to give you. I hope you've been listening…"

John had a way of getting a crowd's attention. Some frightened glances were exchanged. Moving into the next sentence, he slowed his speech down for dramatic punch, leaving a long, fat pause between each word. The man was an expert at delivery.

"Don't kid yourself. Addiction is a terminal disease, like cancer. It will kill you. Have no doubt in your minds, if your addiction runs rampant, it will eventually kill you."

Stevie didn't need John to tell her that. There were no doubts remaining about the seriousness of her disease, no doubts she would die if she couldn't stop drinking. It was the numbers that concerned her now. She looked around the circle at the faces of all the people she'd come to love: Michael with his serious eyes and pensive face, listening so carefully to every word John uttered; Jake, who needed someone—anyone— to love him first before he could even understand the need for treatment; Brian, carrying the weight of the world on his shoulders; David, who was finally learning how to relate to the rest of humanity; Marcus, who would have to fight his addiction in the crime and drug ridden community that was his home; and Allison, who still had no idea what she was fighting.

Alcoholism and drug addiction breed duplicitous characters. Stevie could look at all her new friends and see both sides—the good dog and the bad dog in each of them. It didn't make her love them any less, only worry about them more.

John continued his lecture/tirade. "By now you all know the basics. I've said this to you a hundred times already, and here we go again." He used his fingers to count off the important points. "Go to meetings, join a group, get a sponsor, get down on your knees every day of your life and ask your Higher Power to keep you away from a drink or a drug. Learn how to live a spiritual life through the Twelve Steps of recovery. If you're willing to do those things, you've got a bright future ahead of you. If you're not willing, well, maybe we'll see you here again. And maybe we won't. You've been given one chance at recovery. That doesn't mean you'll get two."

John paused and looked around the room, assessing the reaction to his words. He must have been satisfied because both his voice and his attitude softened.

"You all know this stuff and you're all capable of doing it. Now, how many of you are going to?" People weren't sure if the question was real or rhetorical. Some timidly raised a tentative hand, but most didn't. "How many?" John shouted and his voice resonated with the deep boom of a shotgun. Michael's hand shot up with just about everyone else's. John grinned and fixed his glasses on his nose so he could zoom in on him sitting all the way across the circle from him. "Is that Michael James over there with his hand up?" he asked Jake, sitting right beside him.

"Uh huh," Jake muttered, his mouth hanging open enough to show his teeth.

"You sure about that 'cause it's hard to believe and I can't see him very well." John was teasing, which everyone in the circle understood except for Jake. Michael broke into a smile. Amused by John's antics his tongue playfully shot out from behind his teeth.

"No, really, it is, John," Jake answered emphatically.

"Well, well." John sighed and added a "tch, tch" before he took his glasses off and wiped the thick lenses on his football jersey. "You're sure, right?" he asked again before he put the glasses back on and Jake nodded his head fervently. "The same Michael James that used to fall asleep during my step meetings?"

The light finally flashed on inside Jake's brain. Now he was enjoying the game, too. "And threw the desk that time," he offered and Michael outright laughed.

"You're right. He did do that, didn't he?"

"Uh huh."

"So, what do you say about that, Michael James?"

Michael's face could barely contain his grin. He used his fingers to count off the important points, like John had done. "That I'll go to meetings, join a group, get a sponsor, get down on my knees every day and ask God for help. I'll learn how to live a spiritual life through the Twelve Steps of recovery. Didn't think I was listening, huh?"

"Oh, I knew you were listening," John countered. "I know you better than that, my friend. Now tell me this, what are *you personally* willing to do to stay clean?"

All intimation of playfulness disappeared from Michael's face, as if his dimples and the laugh lines around his eyes had never existed. "Whatever it takes," he said quietly.

"*Anything?*"

"Anything."

"You and I are reading off the same page, aren't we, Michael?"

Michael absorbed his words, and Stevie did, too. "Yes, sir," he said.

On Thursday morning, Stevie awoke early. Was it anxiety or guilt that disturbed her sleep? A combination of both, she concluded. Only seventy-two hours were left until Michael's release. The thought alone brought tears to her eyes. Maybe if she got out of bed she could hang at the coffee bar and wait for one of the guys to get up. Usually Brian was up early. And she could ask him to wake up Michael. The clock read 6:42 when her feet hit the floor—not a chance he'd be awake on his own at that hour. It was only four hours prior that he walked Stevie to the women's hallway after their three hour conversation about her going to the sober house in Massachusetts.

He hadn't taken it very well.

Her body was so exhausted that she barely lifted her ratty slippers off the floor as she shuffled down the hallway toward the coffee bar.

She had almost reached it before it dawned on her that someone was sitting there already. It was Marcus. At 6:42 in the morning? She blinked her eyes. Maybe she was still dreaming.

"What are you doing up?" she asked, her voice hoarse from sleep. Through her caffeine deficient eyes, he somehow looked different—very clean and no whiskers…his hair was brushed…and wearing a button down shirt?

"I'm going home," he told her, "waiting for my wife."

"Oh," Stevie sighed. She was so preoccupied with her own problem that she had forgotten Marcus was leaving. "Why so early? Everyone will want to say good bye."

He fidgeted in his seat. "I'm not so good at goodbyes."

"Oh," she said again and poured herself a cup of coffee. She always forgot how sensitive he was. His eyes followed her as she sat down on the bar stool next to his.

"So here's the real question. What are *you* doing up so early?"

Stevie stared into the black liquid in the mug her hand was so tightly wrapped around. She had forgotten to put cream in it. It took a minute to realize what she'd actually done, prepared it as if it were for Michael, with no cream and exactly three teaspoons of sugar. "I don't think I can do this, Marcus," she admitted without looking up.

"Don't think you can do what?"

"Any of it, all of it, be clean and sober…live a normal life. It doesn't seem possible anymore. The last time I was sober, I was eleven years old."

"Yes, you can. It's only one day at time, remember? The day you get out of here, right? You think you can stay away from a drink for that whole day, just that day?"

She thought about it before she answered him. "Yeah, I think I can do that."

"See? That's how it works. The next mornin' when you get up out of bed, ask yourself the same question. Just that day, see? Years go by a day at a time."

Stevie smiled at him. Maybe she could stay sober if she looked at it that way. But for her that would require a whole new way of thinking, learning to simplify her perspective. Already she was worried about holiday parties, graduations, weddings—events that weren't even on the radar yet, but every one sure to be overflowing with alcohol.

"You and Michael work everything out?"

"Not really, no. We talked all night, but I'm going back to Massachusetts to live in a sober house and he doesn't want me to."

"Why you doin' that?" he asked, not in a challenging way, but like he needed more information.

She blew all the air out of her lungs so hard it pushed her bottom lip into a pout. And she let it stay that way. "Because I love him," she finally acknowledged. It was the first time she'd ever said it out loud. It wasn't as hard as she thought it would be and Marcus didn't laugh at her. He was very thoughtfully watching her expression.

"Mm hm. So, you're what, tryin' to protect him?"

"Yeah. If I could I'd go with him, but it wouldn't be right. He needs to get better first. He has everything he needs at home—he has a good family. And I'm scared I'll pick up. You know what that would do to him."

Marcus nodded his head. "Mm hm, I do," he said. "Can I say som'in?"

"Go ahead."

By now Stevie had learned a few things about Marcus, things that weren't obvious by his rough exterior. For one, he had great insight. Sometimes in the middle of a card game or Addictionary some pearl of wisdom would drop from his mouth and the rest of them would crack up laughing, not because it wasn't true, but because it was and because Marcus was the one pointing it out. Michael liked to call those truths "Marcusisms". They all had a few Marcusisms they'd be carrying home with them. She could use another one or two before he left.

"Here's the way I see it. Michael got here thinkin' he was nothin' more than a street junkie. He was on his way out. But he's a smart dude, and now, well, now he remembers that and he's itchin' to use it. That 'bout right?"

Stevie nodded. True to character, Marcus had him nailed.

"But it don't matter how smart you are when you're usin'. He gotta stay clean first, both of yous. Or you'll end up with nothin'. Even if you stay alive, you get what I got—a fucked up life in and out of rehab, doin' jail time." He sucked more smoke into his body with one drag than Stevie could inhale with a whole cigarette. She imagined his face turning a sickly green like a cartoon character's. "Not bein' the right person," he added reflectively.

It was almost like a confession, the way he said it. He was cuing her in on where he went wrong so she didn't have to. "First things first," she said, quoting an AA slogan. "Is that what you're saying? Get clean first and the rest will come in time?"

"Stay clean and you'll have a whole lifetime." Marcus winked at her and gulped down the rest of his coffee. "That's what you're lookin' for, ain't it?"

"Yeah," she admitted. "That is what I want, a whole lifetime with Michael."

"Back before he knew you, he was diff'rent, you know. He didn't give a fuck 'bout nothin'. He was lookin' to get his hands on speed, and he would've. There're ways, even when you're locked up. Michael, he never wanted any of this." He swept his arm around the room. "This place was a big ol' cage. But now his eyes don't see it that way, do they? You hearin' me? That's 'cause of you. You helped him see it diff'rent."

As Marcus' comforting words washed over her, she remembered how she had suggested to Michael on the first day they met that Marcus might not be suitable for them to hang out with. Her face turned red at the realization of her own arrogance. How wrong she had been about him. The track marks on his arms meant nothing to her now. They were nothing more than an outward sign of his illness. Marcus was her friend. That was what mattered. And he was Michael's friend. Even in the beginning before she knew him, Marcus was his friend, even then when no one else was. And that mattered to her even more. *How blind we are sometimes*, she thought. *Looking out at humanity through our own eyes, we see its vastness, and we feel like we're separate from it. Heroin addicts and prisoners aren't connected to us, they're just people that we think don't matter. Until we meet them face to face and get to know them…and their irreplaceable value. And then, and only then, do they matter very much.*

"You ought to know that, Stevie," Marcus continued. "N'matter what happens down the road, remember that, that you helped him."

"Thank you, Marcus," she said, wiping away tears with the heel of her hand. "You've been a good friend to me, and to Michael. Thank you for that."

"My pleasure," he stated as if he were an English gentleman and it made Stevie giggle. She tasted the coffee. It was sweet and delicious, even without the cream. And she still had three days left with Michael to talk things through. Three days of merely being in his presence was a lot to look forward to. Thanks to Marcus' perspective, things were looking brighter and clearer.

"Som'in goes wrong", he added, and blew a monstrous cloud of gray smoke from his body, "if you need help or Michael needs help, you can call me you know."

"Yeah, I do know that Marcus." She had his phone number in her jeans pocket. He had scribbled it on a napkin at the dinner table the night before.

Just then Julie entered from the women's hallway. "You're wife's here," she announced. Marcus received the news with a beaming nearly toothless grin before he turned his world-weary gray eyes back to Stevie.

"Want me to get him up before I go?"

So he had known all along that's why she was up so early, that as usual she was trying to find her way back to Michael. What else had he known that she'd thought she'd hidden so well? "No, that's okay. He could use the sleep." She stood up to bid him farewell. "I'll always remember you, Marcus," she told him.

"I'll remember you, too, Stevie Gates from Boston, Massachusetts." He extended his hand to her. She threw her arms around him instead, and it was hard to let go. "Take care of yourself," she whispered as he walked away.

CHAPTER SEVENTEEN:

...AND WISDOM TO KNOW THE DIFFERENCE

"I'm coming to Boston. I already told John."

Michael came up behind her in line and made the announcement right as one of the cooks plopped a pile of grits on her plate. Stevie almost dropped her tray when he said it. After all the soul-searching and the planning—Michael's entire aftercare plan had been worked out with a day treatment facility in Jacksonville—he was changing the course.

"You're kidding, right?"

"No, I'm not kidding. I thought about it. If you feel better about going to Boston, why can't I go with you? I can apply to M.I.T. again next fall. And the music—"

"No," she said emphatically, cutting him off. "You're not coming to Boston."

They were walking now toward the table where Brian and David were already seated, but Stevie's response stopped Michael in his tracks. "Why not? I thought you'd be happy about it. I thought the whole idea was for us to be together."

She kept walking and he followed along behind her. "It is, but how can we be together when I'm living in an all female sober house? How is that going to work?"

"I don't know. I don't have all the answers, but we can figure this out."

"We already figured it out, Michael."

"Yeah, but you were supposed to be in Jacksonville, too, remember? I didn't agree to the day treatment program until after you said you'd be there. And now I want to change it because I don't want to live a thousand miles away from you."

"Do you really think that's what I want?" The frustration was more than she knew how to cope with. She dropped her tray so abrasively on the table that her orange juice glass tipped over, spilled into the grits and saturated her biscuits.

A moment of stunned silence passed at the table before Michael picked up her tray and walked away with it.

"What're you so pissed about?" Brian asked as soon as he was out of earshot.

"I'm not pissed!" she screeched and fell into her chair. Okay, so maybe she was. Her face was flushed an unnatural shade of red and her eyes were gleaming with anger. "Do you have any idea how hard it was for me to tell him no the first time? It took me days. Now I have to go through it all over again—"

"Wait, are we talking about sex?" David asked.

"No. That would be so much easier."

David lifted a seductive eyebrow. "Because you wouldn't say no?"

"To Michael," Stevie snapped and David went back to his scrambled eggs and bacon.

"Whatever it is, you can talk it through," Brian advised. "Try to calm down."

"A couple Valium ought to do it."

Brian glared at her. "Why do you always make jokes about picking up?" he asked.

Stevie shrugged. *Maybe because I have no idea how to live without being fucked up?* passed through her brain. "Quaaludes?" she threw out.

"It's not funny," Brian scolded in father-like fashion. "Here he comes. Now try to be nice. He spent the last hour getting crap from John. And he didn't sleep last night."

So Brian did know what it was about. He knew more about this than she did. Michael put the new tray in front of her and sat down beside her. He had brought her a plate of chocolate chip pancakes—her favorite. The cooks must have recently started making them because they weren't being offered when she went through the line. Michael didn't mention it. He was carefully preparing his omelet that was probably cold by now anyway, cutting it into a dozen uniform pieces.

"Thank you," she said to him and he flashed an automatic pilot smile at her, not his characteristic easy-going grin that lit up his whole face. It was one of those strained polite smiles that made her feel distant and alone, like she wasn't his girlfriend, just a girl who happened to be sitting next to him at the breakfast table, some girl that he somehow discovered had a chocolate monster living inside her. She slid a hand onto his lap and squeezed his thigh. He barely glanced over at her.

"Got a new letter from the wife," Brian said. This was big news. Brian always read them out loud and they were invariably hot and steamy. The guys went nuts over writing back to her, venting all their pent up sexual energies into the letters. The poor woman, Stevie thought, she actually thought it was her husband writing to her. She'd probably be horrified to know that most of the words—the eloquent ones at least—were dictated by Michael. The thought made her feel sick. Soon he'd be writing letters to her.

"So, let's hear it," David pushed. "Come on, don't hold out on us."

"Aren't you getting tired of living vicariously?" Michael threw at him.

David rolled his scrambled eggs around on his tongue. "Meaning…?"

"Never mind," Michael barked and pushed his chair away from the table.

"Where are you going?" Stevie asked.

"I've got to talk to John, right? Before he cancels everything?"

"What's vicarious mean?" David asked, and Michael walked away before Stevie could answer either one of them.

It was a brutal thirteen hours later when they finally reached an agreement they could both live with. Michael was in a bearish mood the entire day, which made him difficult to talk to. And the day was extraordinarily busy. In addition to meetings, Dr. Jim performed Michael's weekly EKG, and John and Ellen both called impromptu sessions. Finally, when the night meeting ended after ten o'clock, they found time to be alone.

"I know where no one will bother us," Michael informed her as they headed into the recreation room. "I'll be right back." He approached Tom, the night supervisor, who was holed up with his books in a corner. Stevie watched them converse and saw Tom nod his approval. *Good dog or bad dog?* she wondered. Michael offered his hand and Tom slapped it before he returned to her side, fighting a grin. "Okay, we're all set."

Stevie squinted her eyes while she mulled over his actions. "What'd you just do?"

"Worked it out with my friend, Tom," he replied. "Don't worry about it." He led her to the back of the lounge where he took hold of a large high-back couch and turned it around so it was facing the back wall. It was Marcus' old trick. He used to nap there during the day because he couldn't sleep in the silence of his bedroom. He said he was too used to hearing his five kids raise hell in the small apartment they shared. Once he slept through a meeting and the staff frantically searched the grounds for him until Marcus woke up and wandered past them, oblivious that they thought he was missing. From that day forward, it was referred to as "Marcus' couch".

"Now it's our couch," Michael announced as they curled up together on it.

Stevie felt like she'd been holding her breath since breakfast and could finally exhale. A string of words spilled out with the breath: "I'm sorry. I should have listened to you this morning." She snuggled her face against his chest and his arms wrapped tightly around her. She felt his lips press against the top of her head—Michael's way of saying *it's okay, all is forgiven*—and slid a hand under his shirt to feel his soft skin. This was it, the place she loved most in the entire world. In Michael's arms she was untouchable, immortal and happy beyond words. Her fingers caressed the soft hair on his belly. "I love you, Michael James," she finally told him and nestled her face into the space between his neck and his shoulder so she didn't have to see his reaction.

He pulled her onto his lap with her face close to his. "I love you," he answered and looked into her eyes for the longest time it seemed before he kissed her. When he drew his mouth away from hers, he stayed so close she felt his eyelashes brush against her cheek. "You're the only one...ever," he told her and broke eye contact for a second, shyly, until his eyelashes moved like fluttering butterflies again and he grinned at her.

The pulsating of her heart was mimicking the movement of his eyelashes, but was loud inside her ears as it pushed warm blood to her face. "Me, too," she mumbled.

191

This time there was a desperation to the way his mouth took hers in, a release perhaps of all the frustration they'd both felt the entire day, or the entire seven weeks since they met. His hands were so well behaved, holding her face carefully, but hers were out of control, with a mind of their own it seemed. She unbuttoned the first two buttons of his shirt, enough to get her hands on his chest, to touch his nipples with her fingertips and the soft stretch of skin where she knew without looking that the tattoo was imprinted on him. For some reason, it drove her mind to distraction, knowing those words were there under his shirt like a silent invitation.

It was brutal, knowing they had to stop because any second a nurse could barge in on them, and there she'd be practically undressing him. But what were the odds of being found right at that moment? And even if they were caught, what was the worst thing that could happen? They only had hours left together anyway. His soft lips and his tongue and the warmth of his body were all worth the risk. *What wouldn't she do for this man?* she pondered as his hands pressed against the small of her back, pulling her against him. *Absolutely nothing.* So, why did she feel like she was denying him?

Every time she pulled away, she was drawn back in by her own lack of resistance. It was impossible to stop. "I wish we could—"

"Me to," he said breathily, finishing her thought, and she laughed.

His head fell back on the couch and he closed his eyes, but his hands were still under her shirt, barely touching her skin like it was something breakable. "You're killing me," she admitted and this time he laughed. He moved his fingers to her belly and watched her eyes as he repeated a rhythmic circular motion around her belly button. If she moved one leg over, she'd be straddling him she realized and gasped out loud at the image.

"We should stop," she suggested and he languidly moved his head in agreement. Their friends were close enough that Stevie and Michael could hear their comments about the card game, but not close enough that the group could hear their whispers. And for some reason, Tom was being extremely accommodating, his face hidden behind a magazine.

"Okay," she said, coaching herself, and reluctantly crawled off his lap. "You want to play cards?"

"No. I want you to tell me what you were trying to say this morning."

He exhaled an impatient huff and ran his fingers through his long loose hair. "I already told you. There's nothing left to fight about. I already told John what you said."

"I don't want to fight. I just want to be sure you understand that this is only for a little while."

He shrugged. "To tell you the truth, I don't know if I understand. What's a little while mean?"

She hadn't thought that carefully about it before she said it, the way Michael always did. He seemed to measure every word before it escaped his lips. "Long enough to feel like I can stay sober, and like you're back on your feet."

"So...?"

"So I don't know really. Six months maybe?"

He blinked, his mind carefully calculating. "Six months from the time you leave here or six months of sobriety?" She tried thinking it through quickly. What was he getting at? "Listen," he continued. "You know how your sobriety date is June 25th?"

"Mm hm."

"Well, that means you'll have six months on Christmas Day, right?"

She smiled. My God, his mind was always working. He had the dates all figured out and it had never even crossed her mind. "Yeah, I guess that is right."

"So, can we be together by Christmas? Then I can be there to see you get your six month chip." He was referring to a poker chip given out at AA meetings for various intervals of sobriety, to be carried in an addict's pocket as a reminder: Twenty four hours, thirty days, sixty days, ninety days and six months. After a year a medallion was customarily given to mark the importance of the day.

Following the day of agony, of feeling separate from him in a way she worried she could never fix, it was exhilarating to unexpectedly feel like everything could be resolved. Christmas with Michael and both of them with six months of sobriety; what could possibly be better than that? She pressed her mouth to his and didn't even try to make herself stop. Kissing Michael was like eating chocolate, she decided. There was no point in fighting the urge. She pushed him down on the couch playfully and his arms pulled her closer so she was lying on top of him, her belly flush against his.

She could feel the soft fuzz on his belly rubbing against her smooth skin. The sensation was maddening. Thousands of tiny waves of energy were rolling from her belly button all the way down to her clitoris. She couldn't have pulled herself off him in that moment if her entire future depended on it, or even if poor under-equipped Tom's terror-stricken face suddenly came into focus, peering at them from behind the couch.

"Is that a yes?" Michael asked when she navigated her lips from his mouth to his neck.

"That's an absolutely," she answered, practically panting in his ear even though she was trying her hardest to sound in control. "But you've got to come visit me before that. I won't make it four months without seeing you."

"If I have to wait four months I will…fucking…explode," he said slowly, painfully before laughter busted out of him. "But seriously, after the surgery, I'll come to Boston." The word "surgery" stole a little bit of her adrenalin buzz. "Hey, and my mom said to invite you down for Thanksgiving."

Stevie finally peeled her lips off of him. "Your mom?" she gasped. For some reason, she'd assumed Michael's parents knew nothing about her, but of course they did—John had probably introduced that subject. *"Your mom invited me for Thanksgiving? What else did she say?" And what would his mother think if she knew what she was imagining doing with her son at that very moment...?*

"We can't sleep together."

Holy shit; it was like he read her mind.

"She's Catholic," he offered as an explanation.

"Oh," she answered, her face flushed pink with guilt. "My parents are Catholic, too. Of course, that doesn't stop my father from sleeping wherever he wants. What else did your mom say?"

"Lots of stuff. I got a letter today. I'll sleep in Matt's room. You can have mine."

Even the idea of sleeping in Michael's bed *without* him was alluring. It would be so intimate to fall asleep in his sheets, on his pillow—wait. What the hell was wrong with her? She was fantasizing like a sex-crazed housewife. She had to snap out of it, stop thinking about his body...and what it could do to hers. "When you write back—"

"I'll see her in two days, remember?"

"Oh yeah. Tell her I'll come for Thanksgiving if the sober house will let me out."

"Yeah, I hear they've got bars on the windows."

"Oh my God, really?"

"No. I'm kidding. So, here's the deal. I'll come to Boston in September, you come to Jacksonville for Thanksgiving, and then by Christmas the whole ordeal's over, right? We make a decision and live one place or the other."

Stevie nodded her head excitedly and it was done.

CHAPTER EIGHTEEN:
THE STRENGTH OF THE PACK

As soon as dinner ended on Saturday night Stevie and Allison scurried back to Stevie's room to get ready for the AA dance. Michael had been right about John—he came through after all and even arranged for a bus to transport all the patients. In actuality, it was a meeting followed by a dance, but to them it was a social event, and a cause for celebration. Approximately seven weeks had passed since they'd left the building at all, except for short walking excursions to the duck pond.

"You have to help me look amazing tonight," Allison implored as she closed the bedroom door behind them.

"I don't know anything about looking amazing. You've got the wrong person."

"Can I wear some of your clothes?"

Okay, now it all made sense. Stevie's mother, even though she didn't bother to write letters, had sent her a huge box of clothes, things Stevie hadn't even worn. It was designer kind of stuff that she rarely bothered with. There were even two pairs of shoes in the box—kitten heels. *Kitten heels.* Stevie laughed for ten minutes straight when she saw them. Kitten heels at a drug rehab; only her mother would have come up with that idea, but still, she recognized the intent of her mother's gesture. It was Jimmy Choo for passing the peace pipe. Now Allison was eyeing a pair of them as if they were a possibility, a viable step toward looking "amazing". Like Ellen would allow it anyway.

"You can wear anything you want," Stevie told her, "but I don't know what I have that will fit you."

It took all of two seconds for Allison to pull a red tank dress out of the closet. She had obviously put thought into this. "Think it'll be too big?" she asked.

"No, because it's a size small, but it will be too long. You can cut it if you want."

"Are you serious? It still has the tags on it."

Stevie shrugged. She had a whole closet full of clothes at home with the tags still on them, and she didn't care about those either. She had overdosed on her mother's clothes obsession somewhere around sixth or seventh grade. The only expensive clothes she navigated toward were jeans and sunglasses. Paired with either a band t-shirt or a vintage bohemian-style blouse, all she needed was flip-flops in the summer and boots in the winter. The variations were as simple as that.

"Cut it. It will look great on you," she suggested and Allison nearly leaped into her arms.

"You're so lucky!" she exclaimed, "to be able to live like that."

Stevie didn't respond and knew it wouldn't matter anyway because Allison would whisk off to her next mission without even realizing she was talking. The shoes—she was zeroing in. The thing is it would have taken time to give an accurate response. Stevie was *privileged*. That she knew very well, but she wasn't convinced that she was *lucky*. They were two entirely different things, but try explaining that to Allison in the five seconds flat that it took her to flit from the dress to the shoes.

Stevie understood that Allison made assumptions about her life because it was entirely different from hers. Allison's father, a truck driver, was often away from home, and her mother's alcoholism was so advanced that she was rarely sober. She would drink to pass out, then wake up and drink again, and on and on in a vicious circle that left Allison alone. She was responsible not only for herself but for her mother, as well as day-to-day necessities like cooking and cleaning. Allison had one sibling, a younger sister who moved away two years prior to live with an aunt. Her voice had an odd, hollow quality to it every time she talked about her sister that Stevie finally concluded was a combination of loneliness and resentment. Her sister had found a way out, but Allison couldn't escape for two reasons: she was the oldest child and therefore expected to take care of her sick mother and, perhaps more crucial, she was swept up in the same disease.

Using the food budget to finance her cocaine habit had grabbed her father's attention. It was a selfless decision on his part, Stevie thought, to place Allison in a residential treatment facility and to arrange for her to live in a sober house. It meant her father had to give up his job. It was no secret that her mother could not be left alone or she would drink herself to death. Maybe sending Allison to the sober house was her father's way of trying to set her free, not only from her own disease, but from her mother's.

"I'll get Julie," Allison chirped and scampered out of the room.

Stevie lay down on her bed to enjoy the moment of silence before the storm the combination of Allison and Julie would create. It was then that it hit her. Maybe she should put some thought into what she was going to wear, too. Michael had called it a date, hadn't he? She wondered what he'd be wearing. Maybe that pale blue shirt he wore to the doctor's appointment that he looked like such an angel in. She sat up and looked at her reflection in the mirror over her dresser. She should at least do something with her wild hair. Thank God Allison would know what to do.

The storm arrived in the form of Allison, Julie and Melanie, formerly known as *the punk girl*, but she didn't look like a punk anymore. What was it exactly? Less piercings maybe? Oh, and she had shed the thick black eyeliner. Her eyes were actually a soft shade of green. Who would have guessed that underneath the sludge and hair product was a pretty girl? But there she was, a very pretty girl, in fact. "Hey," Stevie said to her and smiled. They had something in common now. They were probably the two least likely women in the place to undergo a makeover, but Allison had recruited them both. Maybe it was Allison's way of saving the world, one fashion faux pas at a time.

And she did an astonishing job. By the time they were ready to go, even Julie was stunning. She couldn't join them because she had to stay in Purgatory with the new patients, but still Allison had insisted on fixing her hair and makeup. She sat Julie down as if she were a client at a boutique, unleashed the hair from her messy bun and quickly wrapped it into large curlers. Then she plucked her eyebrows and used some kind of magical makeup to cover the broken blood vessels on Julie's nose and cheeks that were caused by her prior alcohol abuse. Afterward she didn't look fake or overly done up, just like the same old Julie, but more alluring. Stevie entertained herself by imagining the response of her husband when she returned home from work. You were *where* all night?

"What if Michael's not dressed up?" she threw out. Not that she was technically dressed up either, but she was wearing a new emerald green tank top that made her eyes look the same color, and mascara. And Allison had pulled part of her hair into a small ponytail with the rest falling loose. With those simple changes she really did look like a different person than the one who entered her bedroom less than an hour before.

"I'll scope it out," Julie suggested, and strolled toward the lounge on the undercover mission.

"Thank God she's on our side," Allison noted.

Julie was back within two minutes. "The bus is already here. You have to go." She held her hand to her chest as she turned to Stevie. "Wait'll you see him."

Stevie's eyes became as bright and alert as cat-eye marbles. "Do I look all right?"

"You look beautiful," Allison replied and Melanie nodded her agreement.

"Come here," Julie commanded and pulled Stevie toward the dresser, her hands resting encouragingly on her shoulders. "Look at yourself. You're not the same person you were the night I met you. Do you know that? I'm not talking about the makeup."

Stevie turned her eyes toward the mirror. Julie was right; she could look at herself and not turn away in shame. She didn't look sick anymore. Her face had the freshness of a normal twenty year old. The visage that resembled a reflection in a funhouse mirror had finally vanished. She felt a sweep of appreciation for her new life and all the people who had been leading her toward it. "Thank you, Julie," she voiced, trying *again* not to cry, but this time because she was happy. "Thanks for everything." Julie gave her a big hug and then hugged Allison and Melanie, too, before they opened the door to leave.

Michael was stretched out in the infamous lounge chair—the same one they got in trouble over reclining in together—so Stevie could see him as soon as she stepped into the hallway. When he saw her approaching with Allison and Melanie he stood up and her breath caught in her throat. He was dressed in a white button down shirt and jeans, his face was clean-shaven and his dark hair was still wet from the shower.

"*My* knees just gave out," Allison whispered. "And he's not even looking at me."

Melanie slid in between the two of them. "Hey Stevie," she said conspiratorially, "good luck tonight." Then she bolted in Jake's direction before Stevie had a chance to ask her what she needed luck for. Maybe because it was her last night with Michael and she'd have to tell him goodbye. *Don't think about that now*, she told herself to fend off the swell of emotion. What was she thinking wearing mascara tonight of all nights?

The nurse at the nurse's station was obviously enjoying the invisible rein she had on Michael. Every time he took a step toward Stevie, she chided him. He wasn't allowed in the women's hallway, not even one foot. Finally, Stevie was close enough that he could reach her. He held out his hand. "Hey beautiful girl," rolled off his lips. "You ready?"

It was the first time a man had called her beautiful. She nodded and took his hand.

"Wow, look at you two," John said the moment they boarded the bus and passed him and Ellen sitting together in the front seat like the good chaperones that they were, "If your parents could see you now."

"Mine will see me soon enough," Michael answered playfully. "In twelve hours."

"Have a good time tonight, guys," Ellen said over her shoulder.

"Thanks, Ellen," Michael responded and led Stevie toward the back of the bus. "Maybe she likes me now, do you think?" he asked as they slid into a seat.

"She likes you. She thinks you're smart."

"Did you tell her our new plan?"

"No, I figured that could wait until after you're gone. Are you okay with all this?"

"With all what?"

"Going home." Her voice actually cracked on the word "home".

Michael slid an arm around her shoulders and pulled her closer. "Actually, I'd rather stay here with you," he admitted.

His comment made her think about Marcus' observation that Michael used to view the rehab as a cage. Now the door was about to be sprung wide open, but he'd be willing to stay because of her. She *was lucky*, she realized, not only privileged. Somewhere in the past sixty days her luck had dramatically changed.

With her cheek resting on his shoulder, she studied the details of Michael's face, trying to commit them to memory: his bottom lip that was fuller than his top lip that curved at its center like a heart, the way one of his front teeth was a little smaller than the other one from grinding them, and the tiny lines around his eyes that were always more pronounced when he was tired. "Do you still think about it sometimes, how lucky we are that we got here at the same time?" she asked him.

"It wasn't luck—it was *by design*, and yes, it's on my gratitude list," he replied. He meant that he thanked his Higher Power for it at the end of each day, and he looked so happy when he said it that even his eyes smiled. That was the best thing about his face, she decided, his eyes smiling. It made her feel like she was the only person on Earth.

"So, I've got two surprises for you tonight," he told her, his eyes taking on a mischievous glint. "I'll give you one now and one later. You get to pick."

She sat up. "What do you mean 'surprises'? What kind of surprises?"

"Well, one's an object and one's not. One you can hold in your hand and the other is more of a...hm...event."

"Event?"

"No, that's not the right word. That's *definitely* not the right word. Later you'll give me shit for saying that." He laughed at his own mistake.

"Michael, you're not getting us in trouble, are you?"

"No," he said emphatically, and waited about ten seconds before he completed his thought: "Because we won't get caught."

A small gasp caught in her throat. "Get caught doing what?"

He squirmed uncomfortably under her watch. "Give me a little time to get up the nerve." Like she could let it go after *that* comment. She narrowed her eyes some more. "All right, all right," he surrendered. "I'll give you the other one now. How's that?"

"I don't know. Is it dangerous?" What *the hell* was he up to?

"Close your eyes and give me your hands." It took her a few seconds, but she did. "Now don't open them." He took his ring off, the silver band she always played with, and slid it onto her ring finger. "You can open them now." She was so astonished by the gesture that she didn't know what to say. She just stared at it and soaked it in—the way it felt on her finger, so heavy and still warm from his hand. "Don't you like it?" he asked.

"Of course I like it. I love it. I'm just...surprised. I thought you said it was sacred."

"It is. It's sacred *to me*. That's why I gave it to you."

She was still lost for words. "Are you sure?" was all she could come up with.

"Yeah, I'm sure. That way you won't forget about me. See, my initials are right there carved in it." She brought it closer to her eyes, and sure enough, there they were: MTJ. Michael Theodore James.

The ring was huge on her finger, but still it felt so right on her hand. "You'll have to have it fitted when you get home."

"How could I forget you?" she stammered. He was the one person who had impacted her life more than anyone else she'd known in two decades of being alive. He helped her see the world and everything in it through new eyes, even (and maybe especially) herself. Because of him, life would be an adventure from now on, not something to be afraid of. With his encouragement, she had even decided to pursue writing and not law, as her parents expected. And in so deciding her own cage door sprung open.

"I know you won't forget me, but if you're having a bad day or you feel like you're alone, you can look down at your hand, and this'll remind you that you're not."

Yeah. Exactly. "Thank you," she whispered and hugged him. The first surprise was so captivating that the second one didn't even cross her mind, not until much later.

She sat with all her friends in the second row of metal fold-up chairs at the AA hall, but she couldn't keep her eyes looking forward. It was her first real AA meeting and she was fascinated, blown away even. There were close to three hundred people in attendance, all sober—and on a Saturday night. "They've got coffee," Michael quickly observed and darted off to get some. In fact, the aroma was so potent it seemed possible to acquire a caffeine buzz by simply breathing. And there was such an excited murmur of conversation that it felt like being at a concert, only no one was messed up.

"Look over there," Allison said to Stevie, pointing toward a group of young women leaning against the back wall. "They're from the sober house."

"How do you know?"

"I recognize some of them from the meeting. And they're checking out the guys, see?" She was right. Stevie noticed Lee Ann whose words had so profoundly affected her. And a group of guys near the coffee table were obviously aware of the women and vice versa. "Because they're not allowed to date; it makes 'em crazy."

"What do you mean?" Stevie asked.

"It's a sober house rule. No contact with the opposite sex except at meetings." Shit, it was a good thing Michael wasn't coming to Boston. She'd be thrown out of the sober house the first day.

"What'll I do when Michael comes to visit me?"

Allison shrugged her little shoulders. "They let you talk on the phone."

"Don't say that to Michael, okay? Because here he comes—that'll flip him out."

"Hey, do you think any of those girls will end up being my friends?" Allison asked.

In only five more short days, she'd find out. For Allison, watching the women from the sober house was a glimpse of her life for the next six months to a year. "They *all* will be, Allison," Stevie replied. "And they'll be so lucky to have you."

Michael handed Stevie a Styrofoam cup filled with steaming hot coffee and slid into the seat next to her, but he was still looking around at the crowd. "This is a trip, huh?" he observed. "I mean, who would have thought this many people don't drink?"

"In one town," Allison added, wide-eyed.

"I have an idea," Michael said. "Let's get a white chip tonight. All of us."

"I'll do it," Allison quickly answered.

"You *will*?" Stevie spat out.

Three things were circling through her mind at once. First, she hated standing up in front of crowds and this was one huge crowd. Second, a white chip was given out for one day of sobriety. It represented an addict's admission, step one in the twelve steps, and after nearly two months in treatment, Allison still hadn't admitted she was an addict. And third, Michael had exactly sixty days. Why would he want only a white chip?

"I want to get it with you guys," Michael stated as if point number three had actually been vocalized.

"Okay," Stevie agreed. "Pass it down, I guess."

So Allison told David, who told Brian, who told Jake, who told Melanie. It would be a whole throng of them walking up to the podium together and that made Stevie feel a little less afraid. Like John always said, *the strength of the wolf is in the pack and strength of the pack is in the wolf.*

Brian leaned forward to yell over David. "Hey, cool," he said. "Wish Liz was here."

"And Marcus," Stevie added.

The volume of voices died down to a whisper as a teenage girl reached the podium. "She's only about my age," Allison observed. "Maybe she'll go to school with me." It hadn't occurred to Stevie that Allison would have to attend high school while she lived in the sober house. As if it weren't hard enough to make new friends in high school without having to reveal that the move to town was prompted by a cocaine addiction. And how is it possible to have friends over after school when home is a sober house?

The teenage girl's name was Anna Maria and, as it turned out, she was living at the sober house. In fact, all the speakers that night were from the women's sober house because they were hosting the meeting. Anna Maria read from a book she called the "big book" which was written by the founders of Alcoholics Anonymous. Then she gave out the poker chips. When she said the words "twenty four hours of sobriety", Stevie and the rest of the group stood up and approached the podium together. Everyone in the place cheered for them and Ellen and John gave them a standing ovation from the front row.

When the meeting ended, some guys from the men's sober house set up a sound system on the stage. There was no missing Michael's fascination with the process. "Too bad the acoustics suck," he observed, tapping the fingers of his right hand rhythmically on his leg as if it were a bongo.

"Does it make you miss playing?" Stevie asked him. He nodded his head casually like it wasn't a big deal to him, even though it so obviously was. Leaving the band was a grueling decision. Michael had been playing in bands since he was thirteen years old when his father taught him how to play guitar. But nightclubs were no place for a newly clean meth addict. Even Michael couldn't argue against that. And his old roommate, Rob, his dealer, was still the drummer. The front man/guitarist who was covering gigs for the summer would soon be told that he could keep the position for a year—that is, once Michael gave Matt the okay to do so. For someone who had already made the decision, he was holding onto that last piece pretty tightly, Stevie thought.

Sometimes L.A, ICE, the band, felt as menacing to her as L.A. ICE, the drug.

Most of the chairs had been cleared away to make room for dancing so they were leaning against the wall when the band kicked off. The punk song the band opened with gave way to a soft, melodic rock tune so Michael gave up the head banging from the sidelines and led Stevie onto the dance floor. When he found a clear spot he stopped walking and leaned in toward her. Her arms hugged him so close she could feel his heart beating against her chest.

Over his shoulder Stevie saw Allison approaching with David and they were holding hands. She watched Allison's pixie face light up as David pulled her into an embrace, and it made her feel both happy and sad simultaneously. It was like looking in a mirror—at two addicts barely hanging on to life who had found someone else to hold onto. Beautiful and tragic like a fairytale, the odds against them were overwhelming. Stevie tucked a long lock of Michael's hair behind his ear before she whispered in it the words that had been occupying her mind the entire night. "I'll miss you so much."

He squeezed her so tight he lifted her feet off the ground. "I'll miss you, too," he acknowledged, "but it won't be for long. I won't let it be." When his strong arms placed her back on the floor, he pressed his forehead against hers and touched her face in a way that only Michael had ever done, with the tips of his fingers barely making contact with her skin. It always reminded her of how she'd handled the wings of captured butterflies when she was a little girl, knowing that if she weren't careful she'd knock the powder off and damage them irreparably. "Everything will be okay," he added and then repeated it like a mantra, his fingers threading through her hair.

"Michael..." She sighed. "You are going to leave the band, aren't you?"

He hesitated far too long for her to be confident about his answer, no matter how confidently he spoke it. "Yeah," he said. "I told you I would."

But he hadn't yet. What was stopping him from giving Matt the word? She wanted to dig deeper, but Michael had already put up a wall. She could see it in the way he shifted his eyes away from hers. So she turned her attention to her next concern. "And you'll see the cardiologist, right?"

This time he threw his head back and laughed as if the subject of her question was not nearly as serious as she'd made it sound. "Why are you so worried tonight?" he asked.

"Well, there's a lot to worry *about*, isn't there?"

"Nah," he breathed out and flashed his dimples at her. "Nothing's going to hurt us."

She nestled her face closer to his neck, trying to memorize the smell of his skin as the band shifted into a new song. It was *Everlong* by the Foo Fighters, not slow by any standard but she didn't want to let go of him. And Michael was singing along with the vocalist, exhaling his warm breath into her ear. Even though it was one of her favorite songs, hearing the words come from Michael's lips was torturous now. She swallowed and choked back tears. On any other night of her life she would have absorbed each and every word with great deference not only because they were beautiful and poignant, but because Michael's voice was breathing life into them, but this was no ordinary night.

"Please don't sing," she pleaded.

"What's wrong?"

"I'm having a hard time with it, you leaving."

"Listen, I—I have to tell you something," he suddenly spit out. "What if..." He took a step backward and his hands moved behind his head where his intertwined fingers served as a prop while he stared at the ceiling. Stevie watched apprehensively as his tongue moved nervously over his bottom lip. Maybe he'd changed the plan again.

"What, Michael?" she pushed. "Just say it."

His dark eyes returned to her face. "Okay, but don't be mad," he asserted.

Don't be mad. What other three words could have caused her more anxiety? The possibilities raced through her brain: He had withdrawn from the day treatment program in Jacksonville...he had already applied to M.I.T. for *this* term…he had decided *not* to leave the band… he was moving back into the apartment with Rob…

"I figured out a way I can spend tonight with you," burst out of him, "in your room." He exhaled, finally. "I mean…if you want me to." It was the last thing she had expected him to say. And it was a good thing, not a bad thing at all, like she had been so sure it was. She started laughing and couldn't stop. Maybe it was the stress finding a way out of her body. Whatever it was, it was cathartic, even though Michael was still watching her with a sort of lopsided grin like he wasn't sure if he should be relieved or scared.

"Okay," she muttered when she regained control. "You better tell me the story." The band was already belting out an Offspring song when she took his hand and led him toward a quasi-private area near the back of the hall.

"So, you're not mad?" Michael asked as soon they were far enough away from the band that Stevie could hear him. But the front man's words were still getting through, penetrating her brain and mixing together with her anxieties. The lyrics were about someone who had died, but to Stevie they spoke of separation from a lover and seemed to have been written and performed specifically for Michael and her. Songs always seemed to fit whatever was transpiring in her life, as if the universe had its own music producer.

"I'm not mad," she told him and dragged him by his hand until they were standing near the rest rooms in the hallway by the exit, the quietest spot in the building, which explained the mostly elderly people who had gathered in the same area. "So, you said you figured it out. What's that mean?"

"Well, there are two pieces to this," he explained, "because we have to get past the night narc—it turns out they take notes on everything we do and what time we do it—and I'd have to get past the nurse at the desk by the women's hallway."

"Wait, let me guess. Your new best friend, Tom, is the night narc tonight?"

Michael smirked. "Well, yeah. I mean we're not really best friends, but he won't turn us in. He'll write it in his notebook that we were watching a movie or something."

"And why would Tom do that?"

Michael visibly squirmed. "Are you sure you want to know?" he finally asked.

"*Michael James*," she scolded.

"All right, all right," he said as if she were beating it out of him with a stick. "I won the favor in a card game."

Stevie let it soak in. So that's what the guys were up to that night when they wouldn't let her and Allison play cards with them. Then she took the thought process one step further—Michael had won the opportunity to sleep in her bed in a card game. Wasn't that what he said? So, why wasn't she mad?

"Actually, I won two favors from Tom," he quickly added, "but I already cashed one in the other night. Remember, the couch thing?"

The couch thing. Oh yeah. How could she forget the couch thing? And they were still on piece one of the plan. "I'm almost scared to ask, but how are you planning to get past the night nurse?" Surely he hadn't cut a deal with her, too.

"Jake's got asthma," he said as if it were a reasonable response. She pinched her eyebrows together, a habit she had picked up from him. "If I'd known I wouldn't have been giving him cigarettes for the past two months."

"Yeah," she ventured. "So?"

"So, he'll have a coughing fit and tell the nurse he needs his inhaler. It's locked up with all the medications in the exam room. She'll have to leave her desk to get it."

"Uh *huh*," Stevie said. She could picture all the guys planning and scheming. They were such con artists, all of them, except maybe Brian. What was Tom thinking betting against them? The poor guy; he really was under equipped for his job. How many other patients had taken advantage of him? Hadn't he figured it out yet that addicts were masters of bullshit? Now Stevie knew for sure—he'd definitely fudged his resume.

Michael waved to John across the hall. Apparently John's eyes had been searching the room for him. "It's not like we have to have sex…I mean if you want to wait. I'm not trying to push you." If only John could hear the words coming from Michael at the very moment he was waving so amiably to him, innocence dripping from his angelic mouth. "Is that what you think?" he asked, turning his serious eyes back to Stevie.

"I wasn't thinking that, but I don't want to get caught." As if her father wasn't pissed enough about her being in rehab, imagine what he'd say if she got *tossed out* of rehab because she got caught with another addict in her bed?

"We won't," he said. "Let's go back in before Ellen has a stroke." She was straining her neck to keep an eye on them. Maybe she thought they planned to bolt out the exit? "Just so you know," Michael shouted over the music. "I only have one condom."

Stevie stopped in her tracks. She hadn't even thought of that yet. But now that he'd mentioned it she realized there was no way to get condoms in the rehab. Even if he had one in his wallet when he arrived, that wouldn't have helped because wallets were confiscated on admission with all other personal property. That's why he had such a hard time buying her the chocolates in Savannah. He had borrowed the money from John.

"Should I ask where you got it?" she asked.

"Uh, no. Please don't," Michael answered and laughed again.

CHAPTER NINETEEN:
JUST ONCE

The plan was executed perfectly like a play in their mini football game that Sunday afternoon when they had practiced their "working as a team" chops. Stevie was already in her bedroom and Tom had noted her departure. "You can't put anything too early or they won't believe it," Michael had instructed, "especially on my last night." So Tom had written 1:30 instead of 11:30 in his notebook, a reasonable time by rehab standards. Then he wrote it next to Michael's name, too. They always went to bed at the same time.

The night nurse was so absorbed by her romance novel (that ironically sported a cover with a man scaling a castle wall to get to his voluptuous lover) that she didn't know Jake was on the radar screen until he started to cough. It started as a small tickle that only minimally disturbed her enjoyment of the lovers' tryst. Her eyes peered over the book at Jake lazing about in the den and she huffed loudly, hinting that's Jake's bodily function was an annoyance beyond words. He smiled cherubically and instantly burst into a full-fledged cough. That was Michael's cue to start his trek down the men's hallway.

No sooner had the nurse brought the paperback closer to her face than Jake fell into a hacking fit that tossed his skinny little body dramatically off of the couch. The nurse threw the book down on her desk. The deflowering of Angelica would have to wait.

"What's the matter with you?" she demanded.

Jake said one simple word: "Asthma" and the nurse gasped. She worked her chubby legs like an aerobics instructor to reach his side and helped him back onto the couch.

"Try to calm down," she coached, then helped him into a sitting position and checked his fingernails to make sure they weren't blue.

Michael peeked around the corner of the men's hallway at Jake's performance. He was an expert, working the nurse with everything he had. A squeaky sound eked from his lungs like a wheeze and his eyes rolled back a little bit in his head. Even Michael almost believed it was real. "Stay right here," the nurse commanded and he lethargically nodded his little boy head like he was about to pass out. The nurse scurried toward the exam room door and once her large body disappeared behind it, Michael emerged from the men's hallway and moved quickly through the den.

"You're awesome at this," he whispered to Jake. "You should be an actor."

Jake grinned ear to ear. There are no sweeter words to a con artist than the compliments of another con. He hand motioned Michael to hurry. The nurse's cumbersome movements behind the door were audible now. She was approaching. Michael ran into the women's hallway and nearly mowed down Melanie, who was running in the other direction. "Oops, sorry," she whispered and burst into giggles. She ran past him into the den and then into the men's hallway.

The reality of what transpired halted Michael momentarily. Melanie was on her way to Jake's room. Jake had used the plan to his own advantage, mapped it out eagerly with Michael not so much to get Michael into Stevie's room, but to get Melanie into his. There were two condoms left in his sock drawer that apparently wouldn't be going to waste. Michael looked back at Jake, still playing the sick kid on the couch.

"You played me?" he mouthed.

Jake raised an eyebrow and pursed his lips in his very best *what do you take me for?* manner. "Hurry," he hissed, and Michael did. He ran straight to Stevie's room and turned the doorknob.

In one swift movement, Michael was inside her room with the door closed behind him, bent over with a belly laugh rolling out of him at the realization of what Jake had done. Stevie had been waiting for him, sitting on the bed and staring at the doorknob, but still she gasped when she saw him standing there. "Shhh," she frantically warned. He bit his bottom lip to stop his laughter and left his shoes by the door before he approached her and sat down next to her on the bed. "I'm scared," she whispered into his neck.

"Don't be," he told her. "It'll be okay." He started kissing her, but immediately stopped. His mind was still turning. "Where's Allison?" he asked.

Stevie shrugged her shoulders. "I haven't seen her in awhile. Why?"

"Yeah, that's what I'm worried about. I haven't seen David either."

"You mean—"

"Yeah. The whole place has gone crazy. Melanie's in Jake's room."

It took a minute to sink in. "But Jake's only thirteen."

"Trust me; the kid knows his way around."

"So, you're worried about him?"

Michael sighed. "I'm more worried about David. He's the one that's supposed to get me back out of here in the morning."

"Oh." Duh. Why hadn't she thought about how he was getting back *out*? "What's he supposed to do?"

"I don't know exactly," Michael intimated. "Distract the nurse somehow and get her away from the desk at exactly five o'clock."

"He will. You trust him, don't you?"

Michael thought about it for a minute and Stevie wondered what was crossing his mind. *The guy that tormented me for weeks, christened me 'meth head'...the guy I pummeled the shit out of...*"Yeah, I do trust him," Michael answered. "We're friends."

"Okay then. Let's forget about him for now." She started unbuttoning his shirt. He grinned and kissed her with all his attention this time. *An entire night*, passed through her mind, *an entire night of this*, as his tongue gently pushed her lips apart. The last button...she undid it and stole a glimpse of his bare chest and belly. *You're the most beautiful man I've ever seen*, she thought, but didn't dare breathe it out loud. She slid his shirt off and let her hands discover every muscle in his chest and arms.

"Can I?" he asked, his hands slipping underneath her shirt and caressing her belly, soft and whispery on her skin. She understood that he was asking so she wouldn't feel like he was taking something from her. She nodded and lifted her arms so he could remove her tank top. His eyes moving over her nearly bare breasts were somehow even more intimate than his hands. She shivered. "Want to go under the blankets?" he asked.

"Wait," she said and turned her back to him so he could unfasten her bra. When she turned to face him, she was too shy to meet his eyes. She ran her hands over his warm belly while he carefully took the bra off her arms and dropped it on the floor. Other guys she'd known would have taken that moment to grab her breasts, like they'd been waiting all night for the chance. But Michael didn't. He barely touched them—the same way he did with her face—with his fingertips, and then with his lips and his tongue. Her hands followed her eyes to his crotch and a whimper escaped her throat. "Okay, now," she said urgently, and pulled the blankets back. He silently slipped out of his jeans before he crawled into the bed beside her.

It took less than a minute for him to remove her jeans and panties and drop them onto the floor. His hand moved up the inside of her thigh and his fingers slid inside her, then again and again as his thumb found her clitoris and pressed against it in a circular motion. It was the rhythm that made her lose control. Her lower back was lifting off the bed, her hips moving in rhythm with his hand. "Michael, I—"

"Sh," he reminded her. "They might hear." He pressed his mouth to hers just in time, right before she exploded and moaned into his mouth. It was something she had never experienced before. Never had she trusted anyone enough to allow it.

"I'm in love with you, Michael James," she whispered when the waves had stopped moving so intensely through her body and kissed his neck, then his ear, his jaw, his lips.

He laughed softly. "I'm in love with you, too," he answered and moved on top of her. She could feel his muscles tighten under her hands as he pushed himself inside her. Then his sounds were in her mouth, mixing together with hers.

And she had an epiphany: It would be impossible to do this just once.

It was 4:50 a.m. when she finally decided to wake him. He looked like a little boy asleep in her arms with his ringlets still wet from the shower they took the last time they made love. The wilting water lily was still on the bathroom counter, its petals almost entirely brown, and had drawn Michael's attention. *I could get you another one*, he'd offered. She shook her head. It didn't matter how many water lilies were floating in the duck pond. It didn't matter to her how beautiful they were or how far they rested beyond her grasp. They held no allure. *I want this one* she'd replied and he had laughed.

"Michael," she whispered, her heart starting to palpitate. In ten more minutes he'd be gone. "Michael, you have to wake up."

"Mm," he groaned and his thick eyelashes quivered until his eyes were peering at her. "I don't want to," he said. "I don't want to go."

Then please don't, she thought, in near panic. She'd give anything, absolute anything for another twenty-four hours with him. This is how deals with the devil are cut, she imagined, at moments of utter weakness and lack of control. The thought of him walking out and closing the door behind him made her voice tremble. "I'm scared, Michael," she breathed.

"What are you scared about?" His eyes glanced at the clock—4:53—before his fingers combed through her damp hair.

"You leaving me," she answered and immediately regretted how it sounded, like a whiny little girl.

He shifted his body onto his side with his head resting in his hand. "I'm not leaving you," he said, his eyebrows pulled so tightly together the wrinkle stood out on his brow.

"Are you sure?" she forced out. She had to say it. It was the only way she knew how to get relief from the nausea in her stomach and her flip-flopping heart that felt like a fish caught in her ribcage.

"Yeah," he answered without hesitation. "I am sure."

She kissed his warm mouth. His face was still flushed from sleeping. "I love you so much. You just...don't know."

"What do you mean I don't know? This is just as hard for me. Don't you know that?"

She did know that. At least part of her did, the more rational and intellectual part, her brain. But it wasn't her brain that was causing her trouble, for once. It was her *emotions*. They were running rampant, like preschoolers at a carnival. "You've got to get dressed," she told him.

He didn't move. He was worried—she could see it in the way he squinted his eyes and pushed his lips into a pout. "Don't start doubting me, Stevie. It's too late for that."

The clock read 4:57. "David will be out there in three minutes, Michael."

He held her face in his hands, carefully, barely—the way he always did it, but there was something new, a solemnity to his voice. "If you want to come with me, call me next week when you get out, and I'll drive up. We can still change this."

She felt bad now. It was her plan they were following, not his. But in the anxiety of the moment it was impossible to stay on course, to let go of him without at least expressing her longing to be with him always, for every single second of her life. That's what her heart was saying. It was her brain that made the inane decision to go back to Massachusetts. She nodded confidently. "I'll be okay," she assured him, a total lie. She'd fall apart the second he walked out the door, but she could fake it for now. She pulled herself free from his arms and got out of bed.

4:58: She handed him his jeans from the floor. He wriggled his lithe body out of the sheets and slid them on, then the white shirt without bothering to button it. Stevie stood there, still naked, watching him; her emotions turned to ice.

Michael's hands pulled her against him and her mind took a picture. It wasn't a visual picture like a photograph, but a sensation—his fingers pressed against the skin on the small of her back. She'd carry that moment with her forever. It was encrypted in her memory. "I will love you *always*," he said in her ear. "Do you understand?" She nodded again, her face nestled against his neck. She couldn't look in his eyes. That would be asking too much of her temporarily nonexistent emotions.

5:00: "Do you?" he asked again and his lips barely skimmed her forehead.

"Yes," she replied and he kissed her mouth, almost roughly this time. Then he let go of her and picked up his shoes. Five seconds later he was gone.

220

He was still in the shower in his own room when his parents and Matt arrived at 6:50 a.m. to bring him back home. Brian and David were awake and waiting to tell him goodbye. John and Ellen came in to see him off, too, even though it was a Sunday. So his parents' first glimpse of the new Michael came through the eyes of his friends and counselors as they ate breakfast together and talked comfortably about the past two months.

It was close to seven thirty when Michael rounded the corner and stopped short in the entrance to the dining room, faced suddenly with the reality of his impending release. Freedom is a double-edged sword, a mustang running recklessly on the beach, mane flowing like the wind, but also the motorcycle rider flying above a deep ravine, his arms spread like Jesus Christ. Both sides exist concurrently; of this fact Michael was fully aware.

He was clean-shaven and his wet hair was combed back off his face. In two months he'd gained twelve pounds. To the James' it must have been the exact opposite of seeing a ghost. It was more akin to traveling back in time to visit the Michael that used to be their son—alive and well again. They were momentarily too stunned to move, but Matt wasn't. He shouted something inarticulate, scrambled out of his chair and rushed over to Michael. And he hugged him so hard he picked him up off the floor. By the time he let go, Michael's parents were waiting their turns, his mom trying unsuccessfully to blot away her tears as quickly as they leaked from her eyes.

"It's all right, Mom," Michael assured her. "I'm all right now." He held her in his arms while his dad shook his head in disbelief. Finally, Michael walked arm in arm with his dad, who still hadn't been able to muster any words, back to the table.

"So, you all know each other?" Michael asked, appearing uncomfortable by all the attention. "This is my brother I told you about," he said to David and Brian.

"Come sit down, Michael. I'll get you some breakfast," his mom suggested.

"I can get it," he said but smiled at the offer. She looked so disappointed that he added, "Come with me." So they went together through the buffet line, Michael's arm around her shoulders, even though she had already eaten.

"So do we get to meet your new girl friend?" his mom asked as she loaded his plate with various forms of fattening food: Danish, muffins, biscuits with butter...everything she could find that might add some more bulk to his body. The fact that he was actually eating breakfast now must have been a startling discovery.

Michael twisted his mouth into a petulant frown. "Girl friend? Don't you mean girlfriend?"

"I mean Stephanie."

He shook his head. "She's not coming. I won't eat all that."

"No? Why can't we meet her?"

"It would be too hard for us to say good bye in front of everyone. She's coming for Thanksgiving. You can meet her then."

Perhaps it was the first time it occurred to his mother that it might be difficult for Michael to leave Georgia. Maybe she thought he had been counting down the days on the calendar like she had, not an irrational thought given the fact that they had to sedate him to get him there. "You're not sad about coming home, are you?" she asked.

He pondered it. "I'm not sad about coming home. I'm sad about leaving her."

One of the cooks was preparing eggs and while waiting for his to be done, Michael sighed at the puzzled expression on his mother's face. The cook, an old guy who worked the breakfast shift every morning and had served Michael dozens of meals, slid a spatula under the cheese omelet and delivered it gently onto his plate. "Good luck, kid," he said and winked at him in a conspiratorial manner.

"Thanks," Michael answered and shook his hand before he walked away.

His mom still looked affected by his comment about going home. "You sounded so serious, what you said about Stephanie," she finally expressed as they reached the table.

"It's Stevie. She doesn't like to be called Stephanie. I told you that in the letter."

"Okay, Stevie. So, is she like…a real girlfriend?"

"No," Michael quickly replied and watched the expression on his mother's face transform from mild perplexity to pure confusion. "She's a lot more than that."

CHAPTER TWENTY:
THE STRENGTH OF THE WOLF

She was having a dream. They were riding a horse on the most beautiful beach. Holding tightly onto Michael's waist, she could see the mustang's brown legs and its hooves stirring up the white sand that fell in geometric patterns like shapes in a kaleidoscope. The air was cool and warm all at once as she inhaled it, and when she breathed out the air was exhaled, not only by her lungs, but by every pore in her body. It was cleansing her. Michael's bare back was warm on her cheek and the sky was turning colors from pale pink to yellow to vermilion. The more vibrant the colors became, the more she and Michael and the mustang became a part of it, merged with the sky and the specks of white sand, swirling into the purple sea…

I will love you *always*. I will love you *always*. I will love you *always*.

She inhaled sharply and woke herself up. Michael wasn't in her arms. And her hand, the one with the ring, was clenched in a fist. She must have been afraid of losing it even in her sleep. Her tongue licked at her dry lips. Blackberries and sugar. Michael.

"Are you all right?" Allison asked. She was perched on the end of Stevie's bed, drinking a can of Coke and nursing a cigarette. She looked rough, like she hadn't slept. She was still wearing Stevie's red tank dress that she wore to the dance, but she had pulled a pair of pajama bottoms under it and her eyeliner and mascara were smudged underneath her eyes. She bore a disturbing resemblance to Courtney Love.

Stevie sat up against the headboard. She wanted to stretch and crack her bones, but then she'd have to drop the blanket that was covering her bare breasts. The words were already in her mouth as if they had arrived before her brain was even awake enough to think them up, but still they were nearly impossible to push off her tongue: "Is he gone?"

Mercifully, Allison only nodded her little head like a porcelain doll in the window of a toyshop. Stevie ignored the pain the gesture created in her chest and focused her eyes on Allison's face that portrayed the contrasting reality of a teenage drug addict. Her new, unwrinkled skin was set against ancient eyes and her small baby-like mouth had an old and tainted expression.

"What's the matter?" Stevie asked her. "He didn't get caught, did he?"

"No."

Allison lit another cigarette and handed it to Stevie, who inhaled the smoke deeply, needing the nicotine more than she'd want to admit. One hand tried to comb through her tangled mane. It reminded her of Michael, his fingers in her hair just a little while before. She didn't want to think about it, how long she'd have to wait to feel his hands on her again. She turned her burning eyes onto Allison. They were swollen and bloodshot from crying herself to sleep, like a little girl mad at the world.

"So, what is it then?"

"Two things—one's public knowledge, one's not. Okay?"

"Yeah," Stevie answered. She understood. That was Allison's way of saying it was a secret. She always said it that way.

225

"Okay. Public knowledge, Melanie got caught in Jake's bed. They're gone—both of them."

"Gone where?"

"Melanie's fucked up father came for her. He does shit to her, you know, perverted shit."

Stevie didn't know. It was the first she'd heard of it, but Allison was closer to her age and closer to her in other ways. And family incest was never really revealed in women's group. That was the kind of information that leaked out after hours with friends, on the veranda when everybody confessed the worst thing that had ever happened to them. Stevie had been part of many of those conversations, but never with Melanie present. Sometimes the admissions were less taboo, but still mortifying, like peeing the bed at a friend's house after too many drinks (a "to remain anonymous" girl), or getting a blowjob from another guy (a "to remain anonymous" guy). It was a mad circle that went like this: a horrendous thing happens while using. The pain of the event is too much to bear, even the image of it causes shame, so the addict drinks or drugs as much as necessary to blot out the unthinkable and something even more horrendous happens. And so on...

Stevie had often thought *if those Georgia stars could talk, the gruesome stories they could tell.*

So Melanie was another soul like her blackened by sexual abuse. She wouldn't have guessed it, but Jake probably had, just like he had with her. He had known somehow, even though Stevie had never uttered a word about it. It was sad to think about, a thirteen year old so in tune to abuse that he could read it like trial lawyers read potential jurors. She thought about how much Melanie had changed since she arrived and realized that Jake must have played a role in that transformation. It made her feel as short-sighted as Ellen, like she had underestimated their relationship. But what would happen to the two of them now? Melanie was being thrown back into the lion's pit. And Jake...

"What happened to Jake?" she asked Allison. She had a lump in her throat thinking about him being sent off to some foster home, to two more people who probably wouldn't love him, either.

"He's on his way to a group home. John was so pissed. I can't believe you didn't wake up from him screaming."

Stevie sucked harder on her cigarette....more nicotine and more. When she finished it, she'd light another one. She wished she could smoke two at once. Something needed to stop her mind from racing, from regurgitating every word he'd said. *Don't start doubting me, Stevie.* "How'd they get caught?" *It's too late for that.*

"They were sleeping. I guess Michael woke Jake up around seven, but they fell back asleep."

"Michael told him good-bye?" Of course he did. He would never leave Jake without saying goodbye. If there was one person on earth who did love Jake, it was Michael.

"Yeah and gave him some shit, some CDs and clothes. John thought Jake stole 'em."

"Oh my God, poor Jake," Stevie gasped. "He said he wanted to be a musician, like Michael. That's why Michael gave him his CDs."

"Fat chance in fucking Hell of that ever happening." Angry tears shot out of Allison's eyes. She turned them onto her perfect fingernails. "He said to tell you good bye."

Stevie smashed her cigarette out and lit another one. She used to think about how hard it would be to hug Jake goodbye, to send him off into the world knowing better than he did what awaited him. But now she'd never get the chance.

"Toss me a shirt, will you?" she asked. She was feeling trapped in the bed. She needed to get up and move and move and never stop moving. Maybe then her brain would be too busy to keep repeating Michael's words. *I'm not leaving you.*

Allison handed her the Foo Fighters t-shirt off her dresser, ironically Stevie thought. It was the same t-shirt Michael had smudged with David's blood (What was it he called *Tristan & Isolde?* A love story with lots of blood and guts), and the same band whose song he sang to her the night before. The Foo Fighters lyrics still echoed in her mind, but it wasn't Dave Grohl's sweet sultry voice she heard now. It was Michael's scruffy whispers singing in her ear. Her eyes fell on her clothes from the night before still lying haphazardly on the floor where Michael had dropped them when he undressed her. She let go of her modesty before the blanket and tugged the t-shirt on over her head.

"Let's get coffee," she pleaded urgently.

"I need to tell you the other thing...in here."

"Oh," Stevie replied and pulled the jeans from the floor onto her long legs. Her frazzled brain had completely forgotten the other *confidential* thing. "What is it?"

"David isn't going to the sober house in town like I thought because he has to go to trial next month."

"What do you mean?" Stevie's brain spilled out, but she knew the answer the second the words escaped her lips. He had almost killed someone with his car; he'd told her that when they were still in detox... so long ago it seemed. He was like a different person now. She hadn't even thought about that confession he'd made since he'd started acting like a normal human being. She wished she could say to the jury, "*This* David would never run someone down with his car. That was the *other* David."

"'Cause of the car accident. He said he told you."

"Yeah."

"He's probably going to prison."

Now *that* he hadn't told her. It seemed so unfair to think of David who was finally recovering, finally dealing with his illness, being locked up in a jail cell. What good would it serve? But what about the person he hit? How fair was it to him? The guy almost died in a hospital bed because he crossed the street at the wrong moment, not knowing that a wasted twenty year old was headed in his direction and was unable to stop. *Unable to stop.* The phrase triggered other painful thoughts: Liz leaving AMA because she was *unable to stop*; Michael almost having a stroke or a heart attack because he was *unable to stop*; Allison trading sex for cocaine because she was *unable to stop*; Herself alienating everyone in her life because she was *unable to stop*.

"His lawyer tried to get it postponed so he could live at the sober house for six months. The judge said no," Allison told her. "He found out on Friday."

For sixty days they'd all been given a reprieve. For sixty days they'd had nothing but each other. But now the world was reaching its fingers inside the doors, seeking payback for their mistakes, for every stupid thing they'd ever done because they were messed up. Brian's wife. David's court case. They all had something waiting for them. "I've got to get out of here. Let's go," she spit out, and Allison followed at her heels like a puppy.

The guys were waiting for them at the coffee bar. Stevie headed straight for Brian's arms and he hugged her and rocked her like he did the day Liz left. When she broke free from him, she hugged David. Her body was heavy, like she was carrying around an extra hundred pounds of dead weight. It felt like David was holding her up. Maybe if he let go of her, she'd fall into a messy heap on the floor. She rested her face on his shoulder and felt loved and protected. "I made a fresh pot of coffee," he told her in the softest voice she'd ever heard pass out of him and squeezed her waist with his arms.

Stevie kissed his cheek. She wanted to tell him how sorry she was about everything he still had to go through, but she couldn't. That would be breaking confidence with Allison. "Thanks for helping Michael this morning," she said instead.

"No problem. Michael's a good guy."

His words made her eyes fill with tears. They were outward evidence of how far they had all come. Back on detox they were the very words Julie had spoken about Michael before Stevie even met him, and David had fiercely protested. *He's a filthy meth addict* he had said. Of all the words in the English language to describe Michael, filthy wasn't even on the list. But how could she point her finger at anyone else for thinking that way when she had been guilty of it, too? She had judged Marcus by his tattoos and missing teeth, just like David had judged Michael by the track marks on his arm. She nodded at David, but couldn't seem to pull any words out of her cramped up throat.

Brian handed her coffee in her favorite mug. "So, we met Michael's parents this morning," he offered and Stevie almost choked on the coffee she was already gulping.

"You got up with him?" she sputtered.

"To tell him good bye," David said as if it was a given. But it wasn't at all what Stevie had expected. To her it was thoughtful beyond words that Brian and David woke up so early on a Sunday morning to see Michael off. If only the outside world could see beyond their exteriors and get a privileged glimpse, like she'd been given, of what lay on the inside—two men she would trust with her life.

"They're real nice, Stevie," Brian said comfortingly and David nodded his agreement. "His dad looks a lot like him."

"Freakishly like him," David added.

Michael's dad: probably exactly what Michael would look like some day; the thought forced a smile to her lips, the first one of the day. *Michael as a grown man in his thirties or forties, Michael as a father…*

"Matt was here, too," Brian added.

"Really? That's so nice. What's he like?" The subject of Matt, Michael's quasi-brother was an intriguing one to her. "Is he anything like Michael?"

"No!" Brian answered forcefully and David laughed out loud.

"More like John," he suggested.

"*John?*"

"Well, kind of," David rallied. "He's a jock."

"He's a *jock?*" Stevie gasped. "Michael used to ride dirt bikes with him. Is he big like John?"

"No one's big like John," David pointed out. "But he's big, bigger than Michael."

"Is he hot like Michael?" Allison asked.

The guys exchanged bewildered looks. "I have no idea," Brian admitted.

"I'd say so," David stated confidently. "Blue-eyed blonde, good build."

"Sounds like my type," Allison remarked, which caused David's head to spin like the little girl from *The Exorcist.* "I'm kidding," she added with a satisfied smile.

"So, what happened with you two last night?" Stevie interjected. "Did you stay in Allison's room?"

"Me?" David asked.

"Yeah you. Who else would I be talking to, Brian?" As soon as it was out, she regretted it. "I didn't mean that," she quickly added. Brian waved his hand around like it wasn't a big deal, but the last thing she'd want to do was make Brian feel any worse about his marital transgression. He already wore his guilt in the lines of his face and in his shoulders that were always slumped. Michael commented once that Brian was like that guy in Greek mythology whose punishment was to eternally push a boulder up a mountain, then watch it roll back down again. But Brian's punishment was self-induced.

"No, I didn't stay in Allison's room. Where'd you get that?"

Stevie shrugged. "We didn't know where you were. We just thought..."

"You two got sex on the brain," David contended.

"Must have been a full moon last night," Brian threw into the mix. "Jake and Melanie, can you believe that? I don't think I knew what sex was when I was thirteen."

No one got the chance to respond because Ellen came into view, walking toward them from the dining room. "What are you doing here on a Sunday?" Stevie's voice croaked. She didn't notice the envelope in Ellen's hand. She was too busy worrying that she knew about Michael sleeping in her room. Maybe Jake had confessed it under duress.

"I came to meet Michael's parents, and to wish him luck."

Stevie smiled at her, a little bit at least. It was a nice thing to do.

"I'd like to talk to you before I go," Ellen continued. "No rush, though."

"Why?" she whined and her bottom lip actually quivered. She knew something. Why else would she want to talk to her on a Sunday morning? Maybe she was only pretending everything was okay so she could catch her off guard then toss her out on her ass.

"Your mom called. She wants to make your plane reservation. We need to call her back. You can talk to her if you'd like."

"Why would I want to talk to her? She hasn't even written to me once."

Ellen unceremoniously handed her the envelope. Stevie glanced down at it and saw her mother's familiar handwriting. "It came yesterday," Ellen explained. "Maybe you should hear me out first and read the letter, then decide whether or not you want to talk to your mother. Besides, you're going all the way back to Massachusetts to live in a sober house there. If you don't want a relationship with her, you could stay here."

Stevie's face flushed hot with anger. It was true. She had known it all along and Michael had known it, but at least he'd had the decency not to say it. Her yearning to win her parents' approval was something she couldn't deny, but she never spoke about it out loud. It was too humiliating. Why should she care about her relationship with them after everything they'd done to her? She didn't know the answer. She only knew that for whatever demented and twisted reason, she did care.

"Why don't you stay here?" Allison suggested. She was bubbling over with excitement at the idea. "Maybe we could be roommates. Could we, Ellen?"

"No," Stevie said without even looking at her and Allison deflated like someone had popped her. Stevie stared coldly at Ellen. Why did she always make it so easy to hate her? As if this morning weren't bad enough without Ellen here to harass her about her dysfunctional family. "Let's talk about it in your office then seeing how it's *personal*."

"You're the one who asked," Ellen replied and walked away toward her office.

The big news Ellen had to inform her of was that her father had moved out. Actually, he had moved out of the family home and into his twenty seven year old girlfriend's apartment six weeks prior, but her mother had only now gotten around to spreading the word down south. "She didn't want it to get in the way of your recovery," Ellen stated.

"Since when does my mother even know the word 'recovery'?" Stevie snapped.

Ellen snorted. "I'm just telling you what she said."

"Over her glass of Chardonnay?"

"You are going to talk to her someday, aren't you?" Ellen probed.

"Sure. She'll probably be there at the airport when I get off the plane, acting like she's my real mother or something."

"Well, isn't she?"

"No," Stevie hissed. "She's not. If she were a real mother she would have let me come home from the hospital instead of acting like I was already in a body bag."

"And what do you think would have happened to you if she did that?"

"I would have gone through life thinking my parents cared about me maybe?" It was an outright lie. Even if they had welcomed her home, she wouldn't have thought that.

"And you'd be drinking. Did you ever think of that?"

She'd be drinking and she wouldn't have met Michael. Of course she'd thought of both those things...a million times. Still, it didn't seem right to give them credit. They didn't let her come home because they were too absorbed with their own problems to deal with hers. But as it turned out, they really did have problems, much deeper than she had imagined. "They probably think they can stick me in another college to study pre-law," she fumed. "I'll barely be in the car and she'll start slobbering about B.C. or B.U."

"Your mother hasn't mentioned school to me."

"Yeah, because my dad hasn't been there telling her what to say. He's like the master puppeteer in the family, pulling everyone's strings. Scott's starting law school. Did my mother mention that, or that he's only going because my father expects him to?"

Ellen rocked in her chair, her fingers propped like a steeple in front of her face.

"My father's ashamed of me," Stevie continued. "Did she tell you that?"

"Listen, I don't know your mother or your father, but I do know you—"

"No, you *don't*, Ellen. My friends out there—" Her thumb pointed at the door. "They know me. Michael, he knows me. Even Marcus and Jake know me. But you don't. No matter how many times you say it, it's just not true."

The words didn't have quite the impact on Ellen that Stevie expected. But they did make her feel a whole lot better, like she was tugging around an extra sixty pounds of dead weight instead of a hundred. She was angry. She was *fucking rip shit*. And she didn't even know why but her heart felt like it was pumping molten lava instead of blood. Who did her father think he was looking down his nose at her while he was banging some girl barely older than her? And where the hell was her mother all summer, shopping at the boutiques in their snotty little town? Why couldn't they just give a shit about her like Michael's parents did and actually make an effort to *talk* to her?

"You're full of fucking shit, Ellen," she belted out. "You're full of shit if you think those two self absorbed people care anything about helping me. Haven't you figured it out yet? They left me in Georgia so no one in their town will find out that I'm an alcoholic. So no one important will know that I spent the entire summer in a drug rehab. Because God knows once that gets out they won't even admit that I'm their daughter."

Ellen stayed unexpectedly calm throughout the whole tirade, as if she had people telling her she was full of shit every day of her life. She took a nice long sip of her coffee before she tested the waters. "So, is that why you're going back there, out of spite?"

"I don't know why I'm going back there!" Stevie screamed with every ounce of pent up animosity she could summon without rupturing a blood vessel. "Because I'm an idiot, I guess. Because I'm so God damn fixated on getting some response from them that makes me think they at least *like* me." The last line—the admission—was the final straw. She started crying again, but angrily this time. They didn't deserve her tears. Michael did, but they didn't. To cry over his departure was an honest expression of her emotions, but to cry over her parents' apathy was nothing more than pathetic.

"I don't want to talk to her, not today," she stated more sedately. "She probably wants me to feel sorry for her about my dad. And for the record, I told her years ago he was cheating on her. I saw him with someone else. She didn't do anything about it, only acted like she was pissed at me for saying it, like I made up the whole story to hurt her."

"You don't have to talk to her. But you do have to decide if you're going back there. I need to confirm with the sober house in Quincy."

"The sober house is in *Quincy*?" Stevie hiccupped and then busted out laughing. "My mother wouldn't set foot in Quincy if it were to buy the last Chanel suit on the planet."

Ellen didn't laugh. "You mean it's a bad area?" she inquired seriously.

"No!" Stevie replied as if the question were ridiculous. "By anyone else's standards it's a perfectly lovely city. By my mother's it's a hellhole…because it's not Cohasset."

"Maybe that's because Cohasset is the one place she feels safe," Ellen suggested. "Let's not lose track of the fact that she has a lot on her plate."

The solemnity of her tone took Stevie aback. "Like what?" she ventured.

"Like separation after a long-term marriage, likely a divorce, another woman in her place. Her son's moving out, her daughter's in a drug rehab and moving into a sober house instead of back home. I'd call that a lot."

It was enough to make Stevie stare down at her lap. It wasn't often that she thought of her mother as a sympathetic creature. She was usually too in control to merit any pity. Even her alcoholism she somehow managed to keep hidden from public view. There was one incident, however that the tone of Ellen's voice seemed to call out of her memory bank. Stevie had come home one afternoon when she was a sophomore or junior in high school and found her mother passed out on her bed. The actual event wasn't that unusual. What was memorable, what was somehow scratched into Stevie's brain, was her mother's appearance. She was half-way undressed. Her blouse was unbuttoned but not removed and her legs were lying in a vulgar position with a shoe on only one foot. Something about that one shoe had struck Stevie as repulsive…and lonely. It was the loneliness of the image that had carved a place in Stevie's recollection.

Now her mother would be all alone with her wine bottles in that five thousand square foot home. "What are you suggesting?" she asked.

"That you keep an open mind and try to remember that you're not the only person in your family with problems."

Alcoholism is a disease of extreme self-centeredness. Until Ellen laid it right out on the table like that, Stevie had never once thought of it that way. It took her stubborn brain a minute to accept it, but she finally nodded her assent.

CHAPTER TWENTY ONE:

A POWER GREATER THAN HERSELF

That night Brian lay in Michael's spot next to Stevie on the veranda so she wouldn't feel his absence so much when she looked up at the Georgia stars. It didn't work, but she didn't tell Brian that. Not even for one nightly ritual could anyone take Michael's place. His presence was unlike anyone else's. Her brain tried to analyze it with Brian by her side, but all it came up with was this: He was *Michael* and there was only one of him.

"I miss him," Stevie said, exhaling her words with the smoke like Michael always did.

"Mm hm."

"Why do you think it is that it hurts in my chest like that? You know what I mean?"

Brian rolled onto his side to face her and rested his head in his hand. "Guess that's why they call it heartache," he suggested.

"But why? I mean, why would loving someone make your heart ache? It doesn't make sense. The heart is there to pump blood through the body, right? So why does it hurt when we miss someone, because the blood somehow pumps differently?"

"Shit. (It sounded like shee-it.) That's the kind of thing you ought to ask Michael, not me 'cause he's smart enough to know the answer. I never even thought about it."

"What do you think he's doing right now?"

"Prob'ly wondering what we're doing. I hope he's sleeping, though. He looked like he didn't get any sleep last night." Stevie's face instantly took on a guilty expression. Brian shook his head at her playfully and whistled. "All night?" he asked.

"Until he fell asleep around four," she answered with a laugh.

Brian laughed along with her and rolled onto his back to look at the stars again. "That's two months worth of waitin', I guess," he said simply.

He was such a good friend. Who else could she have told that she spent the entire night making love with Michael and felt comfortable with it? No one. Brian understood it for what it was. He wouldn't try to turn it into something dirty. "Remember the first time we met?" she asked him.

"You and me? Sure, I remember it. You called me a hick."

"No, I called you 'farm boy'."

Brian chuckled. "Oh yeah, farm boy. You did say that, didn't you?"

"And you told me about Michael."

"Mm hm. That seem as long ago to you as it does to me?"

"A lifetime. Brian, I wish we could stay friends. I'll really miss you."

He turned his eyes away from the amazing light show overhead and onto Stevie's face. "I'll miss you, too, darlin', but you can't really run with a pack when you're married with kids, you know? I wish it weren't true. I'm scared of being lonely again."

She had worried over the very same thing. How could her life go on without all these people she loved and trusted? Finally, *finally* after twenty years of living, she had learned how to trust. But it was a remarkable group of people she had been brought together with. That's how she saw it, as a conscious effort by her Higher Power to bring the people she needed into her life so she could learn how to live. And she had helped them. It was like they were each pieces of a huge puzzle that could only be completed if they were together. Like Step Two in the program said, she came to believe in a Power greater than herself, and in so doing, she came to believe in the people that the Higher Power was working through...even Ellen. She sat up so she could see Brian better. "But you don't think you'll go back to drinking, do you?"

He lit another cigarette with an old-fashioned silver Zippo lighter and measured his words a long time to produce only three of them. "I hope not," he said.

She rolled into a sitting position and hugged her knees to her chin. She needed a good view of Brian's face before she asked the next question. "Do you think Michael will?"

The silence was painful. Brian sat up next to her. "Darlin'..." It seemed like another whole minute passed. He put an arm around her back as if his physical strength could shelter her from the words he was about to offer. "I just don't know."

Stevie rested her head on Brian's shoulder like she used to do with Michael and looked up at the stars, so clear against the ink-black sky that even the five points were visible. Why couldn't everything in life be that clear? Why couldn't Brian say 'no, of course Michael won't use again'? Because he didn't want to lie to her and the answer wasn't obvious. Trying to discern an addict's future was like trying to find stars on a foggy night. It was temporarily submerged in murkiness like diamonds in a mud puddle.

"I don't think he will," she asserted.

"That's good. 'Cause he's counting on that, you having faith in him."

"I do have faith in him," she quickly replied. And that was what it came down to wasn't it, faith? It came down to trusting what you believe in. And she believed in Michael, above all else. "I know he'll do his best, Brian. I know he'll try. But sometimes I get scared because of how sick he used to be."

"He's still sick, Stevie," Brian softly voiced and passed her his cigarette like they were smoking a blunt. He started to say something else until he noticed her scowl and back peddled—or so she thought. "Did he tell you about when we met?" he asked. She took a strong drag, playing along with the getting high game and handed it back.

"No. He never talks about detox."

"That's because it was ugly over there. I'll tell you, but you sure you want to hear it?"

"No, I'm not sure. Brian? I read the letter…from my mother."

"What'd she say?"

"I don't know…not that much, what she's been doing—playing tennis and stuff like that. But then she said she was sorry that I was here. It made me feel like crying; I don't even know why, if it was because she finally apologized for something or because I felt bad for her that she didn't understand."

"I'm sure she doesn't."

"She feels bad for me because I can't drink. She'll spend her entire life handcuffed to a glass of wine, and you know what? She thinks I'm the one that's locked up."

"She might surprise you. Sometimes we surprise ourselves, right? Have a little faith."

"In my mother?"

Brian chuckled at the shocked tone of her voice, but his comment about people surprising themselves made Stevie think about her own situation. When she arrived at the rehab, it certainly wasn't because she was chasing sobriety. It was because she had nowhere else to go, and the rehab was a safe place. Had someone asked her then if she could imagine herself living a clean and sober life, she would have laughed in their face. But still, her mother obtaining sobriety was a little more than Stevie could fathom. She didn't have Brian's good Baptist boy faith in the human race.

"Maybe you should tell me about when you met Michael in detox," she suggested and settled her head back on his shoulder. If they talked about something other than her mother, she could breathe a little easier.

So Brian told her. "I didn't see him the day I got here because he was passed out in his room from all the drugs they gave him. My second day, I was in that little lounge in the detox when I first saw him. Marcus was there, too, but he didn't talk to me back then. He had a hard time coming off the alcohol."

"I thought he detoxed from heroin," Stevie asserted.

"Not this time. Julie told me once that you're more apt to die detoxing from alcohol."

Scary shit, Stevie thought. And alcohol was the legal drug. "Hm," she said out loud.

"It was late—close to midnight, I think, when Michael came to. All of a sudden, there was this big ol' crash. I thought maybe someone hit the building with a car it was so loud. We ran to the door and there was Michael screwing out of his room into the hallway like a maniac. I found out later he threw the blood pressure machine against a wall. He had all kinds of wires stuck on him and two nurses were trying to hold him. One of 'em, the big one that's always near the women's hallway, she pulled an alarm."

"The one Michael snuck past last night," Stevie added when Brian took a breath.

"Yeah her. Anyway, John was there and tried to wrestle him onto the floor, but Michael was out of control, and he's strong. He was trying to break out, and John couldn't handle him. The nurse went and got Tom. When Tom laid a hand on Michael, Marcus jumped in to help him. That's how they got to be friends. Marcus said later that he couldn't stand an unfair fight. Poor Tom got the shit kicked out of him. And John, man, he was hurting, too, by the time he hobbled out of here to go home. That's how Marcus got that black eye. Remember it?"

"Yeah, it was there when I met him," Stevie said, but she was thinking of poor scared Tom. No wonder he was terrified of Michael.

"That fat nurse, she shot Michael in the ass with something and he passed out. They kept him sedated after that and strapped him in his bed when John wasn't right with him. You know, he'd drag him to men's group. I used to try not to look at him back then. I figured he was like one of those wild dogs that'll attack if you look it in the eye."

Stevie let his words sink in. They made the little hairs on her arms stand up straight.

"At a meeting one time he was having a mental fit because he left his cigarettes in his room and John wouldn't let him go back. I threw one at him like he was an animal in a cage. I feel bad about it now. I didn't know what he was really like, you know?"

"So how'd you get to be friends with him then?"

"Well, after that, I guess he liked me 'cause he used to nod his head at me, like a hello. Then one night John took the straps off. Michael walked into the lounge where we were playing cards. Marcus asked him to play. He didn't talk much at first. I couldn't believe it when I found out how smart he was, and funny. Really, I just...couldn't believe it."

Stevie hadn't asked Brian to stop, but she had considered it. It was painful to think about Michael before they met and to visualize what the drugs had done to him. "I was a mess, too, when I detoxed," she admitted. "I couldn't even feed myself at the hospital. And when I got here, that's how I saw myself, like that person who couldn't do anything, even take care of myself. I never thought someone like Michael would ever look at me."

"But how come? You're a pretty girl."

Until Michael, she hadn't thought of herself as pretty in a very long time. Why exactly was it that she'd been unable to see anything good or beautiful in herself? "You know how when you're messed up, things go wrong, or you do something stupid?"

"Mm, yeah," Brian answered.

"And then afterward, when you wake up, you feel bad because what you did was only because you were wasted?"

"Yeah. You know I got that going."

"Right. Only after a while, it's not recovering from a mistake anymore. It's your life. Do you know what I mean? It's going from one buzz into the next without a break. Life becomes one big mistake. At the end, I wasn't even sober when I got up. Every night before I passed out I made sure I had enough for the morning. Because if I didn't I'd go into DTs. That happened to me once."

"What, you went into DTs?"

She nodded sullenly. *Delerium tremens*; was that really her life only two months ago? "I woke up because the bed was shaking and making the headboard hit the wall. There was blood on my pillow from my nose and my clothes and hair were wet from sweat. It wasn't the first time I woke up like that, and I knew I needed a drink so I reached under my bed for the bottle. It was gone. My parents must have found it and poured it out."

"How old were you?"

"Eighteen. It was the summer after I graduated from high school."

"Holy shit, Stevie."

"I know. I know, and it gets worse. I went downstairs to find a drink, but my parents had locked it up. My mother came down when she heard me trying to get into the liquor cabinet. I told her I'd die if I didn't drink something. She said to go back to bed and sleep it off. After awhile I called 911 from my room. When they showed up, they said I was in DTs and I could have died. They said it right in front of my parents, but they still didn't forgive me for calling the ambulance. Because of the neighbors, you know?"

When she finished the story, she lifted her head off his shoulder so she could see his expression, and she noticed, like she did on the day they met, that his eyes twinkled with kindness. "I'm just like him, Brian. I'm just like Michael...smart and everything but down deep just a really fucked up—"

"Addict," he said softly, barely—like Michael. "You're an addict."

It wasn't the word she was planning to use but she nodded her agreement anyway. His was better—it was the *truth*. "Know what he said to me once? He said we're so much alike because we're both crawling out of the grave. I guess it kind of scared me so I tried to make it into a joke. I told him maybe we were pulling each other out."

"Mm hm," Brian chimed in with a small laugh.

"And then, and then he said..." She didn't intend to break off the sentence midway, but her throat choked up. She took a breath. "He said, 'I won't let go if you don't'."

The recollection of his words made her cry. She wanted to finish what she was saying about her parents and the night she went into DTs, but it was taking awhile for the knot in her throat to dissolve. It reminded her of watching an Alka-Seltzer tablet in a glass of water.

The more you pay attention to it, the longer it takes to disappear. She almost, not quite, but almost made herself laugh by coming up with that silly analogy because it was focused on what her brother Scott always called her "neurotic stomach problems".

Brian still wasn't rushing her. That was one of the things she discovered about him on the day they met and that she now loved about him the most—he was a great listener.

When she was ready to finish her thought, he was still listening, not only hearing her, but processing the words. "What I was trying to say before is that all the stuff that happens from drinking and the way people look at you, after awhile it becomes who you are."

For some reason, the words hit Brian like a heat-seeking missile. "Hold on," he said and quickly scooted over so that he was facing her. "I want you to listen to me for a second. Are you listenin'?" His expression was somber, the way he looked when he told her how he'd cheated on his wife. Not a trace of his carefree personality shone through.

She looked straight into his blue eyes. "Yeah," she assured him. "I am."

"Okay. Did Liz ever tell you what brought her here this time?" Stevie shook her head. She knew some of the story, but she had a feeling that what Brian had in mind was something she hadn't heard. "Okay then," Brian continued, "I'm saying this because I don't think she'd mind and it might help you. The last night she drank, she got so loaded she didn't remember anything about the night, not even her husband coming home from work or where her daughters were. She woke up on the kitchen floor. Check this out—this is what woke her up. In the morning her littlest girl, she's three or four I think, she came around the corner and fell on her. She slipped on her puke and fell."

Stevie gasped. She understood immediately. This was about shame.

"Thing is, Liz couldn't let go of it. She thought all the things she did because of her alcoholism, that those things made her who she was. She thought she was a bad mother and a bad person. She couldn't separate it. See? That's why she went back to drinking. You can't look at yourself that way. Don't you see? You don't have to anymore."

Before her time in Georgia Stevie couldn't have imagined having such a conversation with anyone on Earth, let alone a *guy* friend who had no interest in sleeping with her. She grinned to think of it—Brian actually cared about her and how she saw herself. "I don't always now," she softly voiced, "but that's because of you guys, because of the way you see me. It's been sort of…contagious."

"You helped me, too," Brian admitted. "If I didn't have all of you to talk to, I'd go back out again. I know I would. But I've got a chance now."

Now they all had a chance, she realized which was a lot more than any of them had when they arrived.

When Brian left, it felt like the pack had officially disbanded. Now Stevie had only the company of Allison and David, who were mostly interested in being with each other. It must have been how Allison felt, Stevie realized, when she first came over from detox and she was with Michael all the time. It was lonely. And it accentuated the fact that Michael wasn't there. More than anything she wished she could talk to him. He called to check on her when he first arrived home, but John got on the phone and told him he wasn't allowed to give out any information on her because he wasn't a family member.

So after that he sent letters, and John, respectfully, didn't screen them. He was doing fine, he'd written, "no worries", hanging out with Matt and getting along well with his parents. His mother doted on him and cooked him all his favorite foods. He was sure Stevie wouldn't recognize him by the time he made it to Boston because he would gain another twelve pounds. By day he participated in counseling at a day treatment facility and by night went to AA or NA (Narcotics Anonymous) meetings with Matt.

Michael was writing prolifically, hoping to record a new CD once he returned to music. He hadn't technically given up L.A. ICE—the band— but he had met with the front man who was covering the gigs and told him he could have the job for one year, and then pending a conversation with John about Michael's readiness to reclaim the position, he would let him know about the next year. He kept one condition in place. If for any reason, the guy couldn't make a gig, he was to call Michael first. Michael didn't want him to sub it out to "someone lame" that would make the band look bad. It was probably as close as he was going to get to letting go of music for an entire year, Stevie intuited, so she didn't argue against it. After all, he was making progress.

All in all, the good dog was prevailing. It was hard to imagine, though, Michael living in his own world separate from her: driving around Jacksonville in his vintage black Mustang, walking down to the beach at night after the meetings ended so he could look at the stars when she did, and playing basketball in the driveway with Matt and his dad, like he told her in his letters. She could see him in her mind's eye sitting on his bed with his acoustic guitar strapped on, writing a new song, his eyebrows pinched so seriously together. It made her heart ache to think of it. She wished she could go back to the beginning and do it all over again so she could have that time with him—hit the rewind button back to the scene when he first walked into the step meeting and smiled at her. If she'd known then what she knew now she would have smiled back at him.

She ended up spending a lot more time with Ellen than she ever would have anticipated. And, surprisingly, she was actually okay with it. The outburst in her office the day Michael left for home was food for seemingly endless self-analysis. And Ellen was the one who led her through it, day after day of rehashing painful episodes with her parents. The more she disclosed, the more she remembered. And the anger came out. Ellen was okay with that. She advised her to scream into her pillow and punch her mattress. So Stevie screamed and punched and talked and cried, and after awhile, she actually did feel better...freer. And that was what she wanted, to be free.

To get from point A (zero trust) to point B (complete confidence) Ellen had built a bridge formed out of five simple words: "My husband's a junkie, too." Why hadn't she told her earlier? Stevie wondered. Maybe she thought it would undermine her position as Stevie's counselor. Ellen confided in her the struggle she had lived through due to her own addiction and her husband's. He had relapsed twice, but was clean now. To Stevie, it was a monumental disclosure. Ellen really had been protecting her, and Michael. So that wall she had so carefully constructed came crashing down into a pile of junk.

Ellen helped her to realize something crucial to her new life: She was a grown woman who could make her own decisions. As obvious as that would be to most people, to Stevie, after spending her entire life under the reign of her parents—the wielders of power—the idea was mind blowing and astonishingly liberating. Now she understood that she actually had a right to choose the sober house and wasn't responsible for her parents' reaction to that decision ("That's *their* problem," Ellen pointed out). And she had the right to choose Michael, even though they were likely to reject him.

She also made Stevie promise to think about something else that hadn't occurred to her. If her parents were alcoholics, then they were sick from their diseases, too. Ellen didn't try to beat it into her brain. Instead she offered the thought like dropping a seed in a garden with the hope that it would germinate. And she shared a piece of wisdom that she had discovered with her own family: a little forgiveness goes a long way.

Once she stepped out of the rehab and back into the world dealing with her family would be challenging, but not nearly as difficult as her first and foremost objective: to steer clear of alcohol. In the safety of the rehab alcohol was not an option and there was an endless supply of friends to turn to whenever she felt the compulsion to drink. But once she was discharged the opposite would be true. Her friends would scatter in different directions and liquor stores would dot the highways of every town, as prevalent as gas stations and super markets. Every time she visualized herself trying desperately to maneuver past opportunities to drink like a character in a video game, she would remember Marcus' words. *Break it down*, she would tell herself. *It's only for today.*

On Friday morning, the day before Stevie flew back to Boston, Ellen approached her with a request. Eleven new patients had been admitted during the previous ten days; seven of them were under the age of twenty-one. A meeting was to be held that afternoon in the small lounge where the women from the sober house had spoken weeks before. The intent was to help the new young patients identify with addicts a few steps ahead of them. It was a way of marking the path, Ellen said, and she wanted Stevie to be one of the speakers. Initially Stevie denied the request until she recalled Lee Ann who had been strong enough to share her experience, and Michael who had seen the same strength lying dormant in her. And so she apprehensively agreed.

She was scared. People call them "butterflies", but to Stevie it felt more like a herd of elephants marching through her stomach. Ellen called on her first, Stevie was sure, so she didn't have a chance to run.

She took a deep breath and asked her Higher Power for help to remember why she was doing this—it was about *them*, not about *her*, and to guide her words so she could accomplish that.

It was an odd feeling to be standing behind the podium and taking in the faces of the newcomers. The only patient still there from the beginning was Barbara, the elderly woman who was walking laps around the nurses' station on Stevie's first day and remarkably she actually did look like someone's grandmother now. Her hair was done in the way that old ladies do it, puffed up with lots of hairspray (Julie's doing) and she was wearing a pretty white dress with yellow daffodils on it, as if it were April and life was starting all over again. She wasn't in constant motion the way she used to be. In fact, she was sitting very still in the front row with her ankles crossed and her hands gently folded on her lap, like she was posing for an elementary school class photograph. Even her insurgent eye seemed to have stopped twitching. And she looked *happy*. Stevie smiled at her from the podium, and she smiled back in a very grandmotherly fashion.

Above the rows of patients, thumb tacked onto a wooden beam, was a small sign with a familiar slogan, *But for the Grace of God*. From where Stevie was standing, it appeared as if the words were hovering above Barbara's head like a balloon in a comic strip, as if they were the words her smiling lips were silently uttering. And she had a startling revelation. It was the grace of God that brought on the remarkable changes in Barbara...and in all of them.

Miracles occurred inside these walls.

And it was the miracle *workers* who changed an old bag lady into a grandmother, a falling down drunk into a faithful husband, a junkie into the son he used to be and a heap of spoiled mush into a strong young woman. She looked out at the miracle workers who had not only saved her life, but had reminded her of how precious that life was. There was

Louise, who gave her the strength to begin and Ellen who tenaciously stayed by her side and forced her to find her own strength. Her eyes fell on John, who scared her in the beginning and saved Michael in the end with his compassion, and on Julie who helped restore her self-esteem and had kept hers and Michael's secret.

Then she looked again at the terrified newcomers who were watching her so expectantly and she remembered when she had felt just like them—like she was hanging on by her broken fingernails to her bruised and battered life. What could she possibly say that could help any of them? All she had was her own story. And so she told them— the whole demoralizing tale, and then she told them about the people who had saved her, not only the counselors, doctors and nurses, but her friends, the ones who had listened and loved her with no conditions. She thought she saw sparks of recognition in the eyes of a few of the addicts and one girl, who was about seventeen, managed to smile at her. And Stevie hoped she had gotten through. It was all she had to give.

CHAPTER TWENTY-TWO:
THE PICTURE OF SOBRIETY

By the time the plane hit the runway in Boston, Stevie felt as old and world-weary as Barbara appeared on the first day she laid eyes on her. Saying goodbye to John, Ellen, Julie and Louise had been every bit as hard as she had anticipated and walking out the door of the facility to the parking lot where her ride was waiting to escort her to the airport was agonizing. Butterflies turned quickly to nausea. By the time she boarded the plane she had consumed two of the chocolate candy bars and a can of cola from the stash Louise had prepared. Plenty of sugar was within reach so she could use it to combat the urge to drink. After two months of not being anywhere in alcohol's presence, once she was on the plane it would be offered to her. And simple as that, she could stay on course or watch two months of reflection and work unravel before her eyes.

Logan Airport in Boston was nothing short of culture shock when returning from a place as slow paced and graceful as the Deep South. At some unidentifiable time during the last eight weeks she had fallen in love with the slower, more thoughtful speech and the respectful mannerisms that her southern friends exhibited. The rushed northern chatter hit her ears abrasively as she made her way to the baggage claim trying to avoid being run down by other travelers. Was it due to the number of people or was it a cultural difference that made personal space seem less important than it was in Georgia?

Her breath was coming quicker than it should, a familiar sign of anxiety's arrival. What if no one from her family showed up? In that moment of apprehension, it didn't seem like such a terrible option to tuck her tail between her legs and get on the next plane back to Georgia. *No*, she told herself. There was a room waiting for her at the sober house and she would arrive there by evening, like she had promised Ellen. It won't be long, she thought, until I'm boarding a different plane headed for Jacksonville. The image of Michael waiting for her at the airport made her heart race. There was so much to look forward to: walks on the beach at night and meeting Matt and Michael's parents, sitting down for Thanksgiving dinner with Michael by her side...

Someone touched her back and disturbed her reverie. She slowly turned around and found her brother, Scott, beaming at her. "I almost didn't recognize you," he blurted out. "You look like a different person." *On the outside, at least*, Stevie mused *I'm the picture of sobriety* and grinned to think of it. Two months prior she had been the poster child for teenage alcoholism. Scott had an armful of roses but he held them out of the way so he could embrace her. The feeling of him in her arms and the smell of his aftershave were so familiar that it made her emotions race recklessly through her body like a wind storm, bringing her back to the past. Once upon a time, back before her disease took over her life, he had been her closest ally. Silent, hot tears poured down her face onto his shoulder. "I'm sorry, Scott," she whispered "for everything—"

"Whoa," he interrupted. "I'm just glad you're home." He held her chin in one hand and kissed her. "I wanted to talk to you while you were down there. I called a couple times. Some guy named John wouldn't put you on the phone. What a hard ass."

His assessment of John, the colossal teddy bear, made her laugh. "I love you, Scott," she told him for the first time in at least three years and watched only the right side of his mouth respond, like he'd done since he was a child, as if only half of his mouth was responsible for exhibiting emotion. Every grammar school portrait that crawled up the wall beside the spiral staircase in the foyer of their home portrayed the exact same smile.

"I love you, too, and you are incredibly beautiful," he proclaimed. "I honestly didn't recognize you at first. Wait until mom and dad get a look at you."

"I lost ten pounds. They said people usually gain ten, but I had so much water weight." Her eyes were still not at rest. Her parents' absence hadn't escaped her attention. "So...where are they?" she asked and braced herself for disappointment.

"Mom's right out front in the car." His thumb pointed toward the window, and sure enough, there was her mother's ivory Mercedes parked next to the curb. She blinked her eyes quickly to battle a new onslaught of tears. "Oh—these are for you," Scott added and handed her the fuchsia roses ceremoniously as if she were Miss America. "We thought you'd be hungry. We could stop at the North End before we take you to Quincy."

She wanted to ask what he thought about her decision to reside in the sober house, but it was too big a topic to initiate in the middle of an airport. And she wanted to ask him his feelings about law school, starting in only a few days, and mostly she wanted to tell him about Michael. But everything seemed too immense, as if she'd been away for years instead of weeks. Absolutely everything had changed. She had changed, and at least on some level, Scott already knew that. She could tell by the way he was looking at her. The annoying alarm that sounded like a bus backing up reverberated, signaling that the luggage was being spit out onto the revolving belt.

"Let's get my stuff," she suggested. "Mom's waiting."

Like most cities, Quincy, Massachusetts has commercial areas as well as residential neighborhoods with varying degrees of affluence. The sober house was a weathered gray duplex with shingles falling off in a neighborhood where the houses were so close together the shades had to be down to maintain anything even remotely close to privacy. The second Stevie saw the house she knew she couldn't let her mother walk her inside. "I'll call you tomorrow," she said nervously as she opened the door of the Mercedes.

"I'm not going to leave you here until I know it's the right place," her mother argued.

"It's the right place," Stevie countered. "I have the address."

"This is a bad area," her mother noted, looking around.

"I know it looks rough, but it'll be all right."

Scott had already stepped out of the back seat onto the cracked asphalt driveway. "We'll watch from here to make sure you get inside," he offered and locked her in an embrace. She didn't want to let go of him even though she could still smell the beer on his breath from lunch. It was shocking to realize how familiar the smell was, that she actually identified her family members by it. Beer+expensive aftershave=Scott; Scotch+Cuban cigars=her dad; Chardonnay+Chanel No. 5=her mom. "Hey, what's the guy's name again that you were telling us about, the one you're going out with?"

Their mother leaned over into the passenger seat and spoke through the open door. "She's not *going out* with him, Scott. He's someone she met at a hospital."

What kind of logic was that? Stevie thought of five or six immediate comebacks, but quashed them. She would express herself as patiently as she could and then walk away from it. She wasn't responsible for her mother's reaction. "It was a drug rehab, Mom, not a hospital and I *am* going out with him. His name's Michael, Michael James."

Scott offered her his crooked grin and Stevie wanted to curl up in his arms again. In all her anger, she had forgotten how comforting his presence was…her big brother.

When she was a little girl, he was the conqueror of the universe that was their neighborhood, the one person whose opinion mattered to her. To this day she was called Stevie instead of Stephanie largely because *he* was so impressed by the nickname the boys gave her. "That's cool," he'd said and it had meant everything to her. Now he said something else that meant everything to her: "Tell Michael he can stay at my place when he comes up. I can show him around Boston and M.I.T. It's right down the street."

She kissed him. It was the perfect solution. Michael couldn't stay at the sober house and she didn't want him to stay in a hotel. The family home was definitely *out*. The only problem was the drinking. She'd bet money that Scott's new apartment would soon be like a remake of *Animal House*, but maybe if she talked to him about it he'd slow things down for a few days. "Thank you, Scott," she said.

"Hey and the Middle East—we'll check out the bands there. Tell him." *Not this trip*, Stevie thought, but smiled at the suggestion. Michael would love the music scene in Cambridge. "Call me tonight, okay?" Scott added, beaming from her reaction.

"Okay," she agreed, pulling away from him, but feeling like she had an ally again. "Bye, Mom," she said into the car. She started to leave it at that, but had a second thought. She leaned into the car and kissed her mother's cheek. "Thank you," she whispered and her mother smiled at her…sincerely.

When Stevie rang the doorbell and heard footsteps approaching she waved to her mother and Scott. She faked it, looking in their direction but not in their faces. She was scared and she didn't want them to see it in her eyes. And even more importantly, she didn't want to start crying. What a horrible introduction that would be, sobbing in the doorway like a spoiled child with her mom and brother looking on from the driveway.

The door creaked morosely when it was opened, like something from a horror flick. In stark contrast, a fresh-faced young woman in her mid-twenties was standing in the open doorway. "Are you Stevie?" she asked excitedly.

"Yeah," Stevie exhaled, relieved by the young woman's obvious warmth and welcoming energy. She actually waved to Stevie's mom and Scott like she knew them before she closed the door behind them.

"You drink coffee?" More relief. She could use a cup, a strong one, espresso-style. Stevie nodded gratefully. "I'm Chris, your roommate," she said. "I just made a pot."

Stevie dropped her bags in the living room area inside the door and followed Chris to the kitchen table where she had been drinking coffee and reading a *Glamour* magazine. Stevie looked around at her new home. The kitchen was old, like it had been built in the 1950s, but it was clean. It reminded her of old sitcoms like *I Love Lucy*. And the acrid smell of coffee was strong, likely a permanent fixture. This could be home, she thought. She was lonesome for her old home, not the oceanfront estate, but the rehab and everyone in it. She had called Michael twice already, once on route to the airport in Georgia and then again from the restaurant in the North End, Boston's Italian neighborhood. And she had promised to take him there next month.

She watched Chris retrieve half and half from the mustard colored refrigerator. Something about her reminded her of Allison. She was tall, like Stevie, but had a pretty, impish face like Allison with a small mouth that seemed most comfortable bearing a smile. By now Allison was a few days into her new home experience. She'd call her as soon as she was alone. She missed her voice already. "Where is everyone?" she asked. Ellen had told her that twelve women shared the house, six on each side of the duplex.

"At a meeting. There's a Saturday afternoon group we sometimes go to on Hancock Street. I thought I'd wait for you and we could go to the Norwell meeting tonight. I got us a ride. Are you up for that?"

"Sure," Stevie answered. Hancock Street. That's where her interview was on Monday, at a bookstore. Ellen had lined it up for her. *If you want to be a writer, you might as well spend time around books*, she'd said, and Stevie appreciated it, not only the job, but the fact that Ellen took her ambition seriously. And rent at the sober house was seventy-five dollars per week, plus food, so she needed money. It would be her very first job, but she had no intention of letting any of the other women in the house know that. She didn't want to admit that her father had paid her way through life, right down to her expensive sunglasses. *Never again*, she promised herself.

She was starting to understand that because her father supported her financially, he believed he had the right to choose her life's path. Once she understood his mindset, it was easy to fix it. She wouldn't let him buy her anymore. Her first mission was to pay him back for the airfare to Georgia. To her it felt wrong for him to have paid for the most significant event of her life, one he did not remotely understand.

"We have to go to at least one meeting a day," Chris continued. "It's a house rule. After ninety days, if you're working enough hours, you can get away with five a week. But you might want to go to seven, anyway." She shrugged. "It's part of our social life."

Stevie stirred sugar and cream into the oversized ceramic cup Chris handed her and sipped the coffee. It was good and strong, exactly the way she liked it. "How long have you been here?" she asked.

"Almost three weeks. I'm the newest one, other than you. We can stay here for up to a year, if we're doing what we're supposed to. So..." She sat beside her at the table and her hands cupped her face that had suddenly taken on a mischievous expression. "Was that your boyfriend that dropped you off?"

"No. That was my brother, Scott." She grinned, knowing what was coming next.

"Cute," bubbled out of Chris, "very cute."

Stevie laughed. Every friend she'd ever made had said the exact same thing. With a head full of unkempt dirty blonde hair and keen blue eyes, he *was* adorable...and smart and charming. He was all those things, and an alcoholic. "Yeah."

"Next time tell him to come in."

"I didn't think he could. Where I came from in Georgia, guys weren't allowed in the women's sober house."

"They can come here, thank God, as long as they stay downstairs. We have guy friends over to watch movies or whatever all the time. Sunday mornings we usually cook a big breakfast and some of the guys from our group come over. All the bedrooms are upstairs. If you get caught with someone in your room, you're out."

"Hm," Stevie mumbled, processing the information.

"But there's no one in my life to get caught with so that's not a problem. How about you?"

"He's in Florida," Stevie told her and felt the familiar pang in her heart. *A thousand miles away.* It might as well have been a different world.

They could hear the languid sound of the surf lapping against the sand from where they were sitting on the deck out back, both of them stretched out in lounge chairs. From their clothes alone, an observer could fairly accurately decode the distinct personalities of the two men, Matt barefoot, but still wearing a dress shirt and slacks, and Michael, in only a pair of denim cutoff shorts and aviator sunglasses, his hair falling loose on his shoulders.

People who didn't know Michael and Matt very well probably wondered why the two of them were together all the time. They were as different as they could possibly be, Diego Rivera versus Ansel Adams, Brandon Boyd versus Justin Timberlake, punk versus pop. But they were childhood friends. And in childhood bonds are created that can never be broken, not by differences, not by separation and not even by adulthood. Michael and Matt were connected intricately in ways an outsider could never hope to understand. They were like opposite sides of an hourglass sifting sand back and forth, Michael grinding away at the rougher "stones" in his personality and Matt constantly striving to be something less than perfectly smooth, to be more like Michael.

The smell of garlic wafted onto the deck, and through the screen door they could see Mrs. James preparing dinner. "Do you need help, Mom?" Michael yelled in.

She walked over to the screen door to answer him. "You can set the table, but you don't have to get up yet. Dinner won't be ready for another half hour. You boys want something to drink?"

You boys. It made Michael grin. "Espresso?" he suggested.

"Espresso? It's 6:30 at night." The Florida sunshine enveloped his mother, making her dirty blonde hair look three shades lighter as she stepped out onto the deck.

"I could have asked for a vodka and tonic," Michael teased.

"Michael Theodore James," she scolded, though there wasn't the slightest bit of acrimony in her voice. "Why do you say things like that to your mother?"

He took her hand and pulled it until she sat down on his chair with him. "I'm sorry," came out of him in a laugh and he hugged her with his muscular arms until she turned to emotional mush.

"All right, all right," she sighed. "I'll make espresso. Matt?"

"No." Matt shook his head as if it were a preposterous suggestion. "I'd be up all night."

Michael smiled at his friend's response without revealing his analysis of the comment. Matt's life, he thought, wasn't nearly as fun as it could have been if he would just once in awhile allow himself to stray beyond the lines he had so carefully drawn. "So? You can keep me company," Michael said out loud. "I'm not used to going to bed at 10:30."

"Well, you better *get* used to it," Mrs. James said, standing up. "The new job starts tomorrow." She brushed Michael's long hair behind one ear and kissed the top of his head before she left them alone.

"It's not like snorting lines, you know," Michael suggested playfully and waited for Matt's familiar response: evasion. He shrugged his shoulders and looked out to sea, a boat on the horizon suddenly captivating his eyes. Michael knew him well enough to know when to let go. It wasn't worth the turmoil it caused in Matt's tightly coiled brain. Besides it wasn't like Matt *wanted* to be rigid. It was just the way he was made. Even when they were little, he was the only kid Michael knew who didn't like to take his shoes off at the beach because he didn't like the feeling of the sand stuck to his feet. Michael suspected that particular personality glitch was due to the early years with his mother who had created enough chaos to make anyone crave order and control. *Fucking Dexi* Michael thought for about the millionth time in his life.

"You got anything I can wear to work?" he asked Matt. "Somehow I don't think my clothes will cut it."

"We'll find something," Matt answered with a confident nod. He was already part of the Jacksonville business scene, working as an Operations Manager for a small computer company.

"Hey, you know what? You should take a picture of me that I can send to Stevie, you know like a before and after. We'll send her one now and another one in the morning wearing a suit jacket. I'll be the picture of sobriety." He chuckled at the thought.

"On the outside at least," Matt teased. "Give me your cell phone."

Michael tossed it to him before he pushed his aviators up and rested them on top of his head so his eyes were showing.

"Ready?" Matt asked.

"Hang on. One, two..." He pulled out his famous grin...even his slightly uneven teeth were confidently revealed. "Now," he signaled and Matt took the picture.

CHAPTER TWENTY-THREE:
FALLING DOWN

The photograph of Michael was displayed front and center on the mustard-colored refrigerator at the sober house. All the women, including Gail, the "housemaster" who served as the supervisor for the six women on Stevie's side of the duplex, were used to waking up to Michael's face by now and liked to tease Stevie about it. *"No wonder you're not into the guys in our group,"* etc. His endearing grin seemed to have won them all over. He was the poster child so to speak for how good life could be in sobriety.

As much as she hated being separated from him, Stevie was adjusting to life at the sober house. Five weeks had passed and the women she shared a home with, all eleven of them, had become her friends. They usually traveled in a pack to meetings and in smaller groups to places like the grocery store. There was only space in the driveway for three cars. The housemasters on each side of the duplex, the only ones with more than one year of sobriety, were able to bring their own cars. The third slot went to the person with the most sobriety, at the moment a thirty two year old waitress named Hannah with eleven months. Once she hit the one-year mark, she would move out and the next woman in line would have the privilege of bringing her car over. And so on.

According to Stevie's calculations, her little red jeep would remain parked at her mother's house for quite some time. The subway was within walking distance, though. It could be utilized to reach other parts of Quincy for meetings or to get into Boston. She'd taken a couple of trips with Chris to visit her brother at his apartment in Cambridge, but after that Scott and Chris hit it off so much that he often drove down to visit them or pick them up. He became part of the Sunday morning group that cooked breakfast together, but he never accompanied them to the meeting they always attended afterward. Being an alcoholic, Stevie surmised, he could only take so much AA talk. Besides, even though he wasn't working, Scott's schedule was more demanding than hers due to the seven classes he was required to take as a first year law student.

Stevie was hired by the bookshop at a rate of fifty cents over minimum wage and was working thirty hours per week. To her, it was a good deal. Her expenses were so minimal that she didn't need much money to get by. She enjoyed having time to read during off hours while she was working and also liked having time to herself outside of work so that she could write. She hadn't started working on the novel that she had promised Michael she would tackle because she hadn't yet figured out what was close enough to her heart to write passionately about, but she had written poems and had emailed one to Michael, the one about him that she started when they were together in Georgia. Although he was writing prolifically, Stevie hadn't read any of his songs. He insisted on bringing them with him to Boston and handing her the hard copies himself.

In five more days Michael was due to arrive. Twice he had changed travel plans because his surgery was postponed, the first time because of a conflict in the surgeon's schedule and the second time because he had a cold and the anesthesiologist advised against it. But now at last it was over and he was recovering. It was Saturday and all she could think about was how the *next* Saturday Michael would be in town and going to the Norwell meeting with her at night. He was arriving early Thursday morning and was staying for five days...*five whole days*. It was like a dream. And it would come true on Thursday morning at 7:10 when his plane landed at Logan Airport on his twenty-second birthday. There was something she couldn't wait to tell him, something of such significance she couldn't justify doing it by phone, a kind of birthday present.

She hadn't spoken to him since the morning and was anxious to hear his voice. His father was taking him to meet a client in Ponte Vedra and he wasn't sure how long he'd be gone, but he was always good about staying in touch. Some days, however, were harder than others—being so far away from him and living what felt like completely separate lives, and today had been one of those difficult days. Inside the sober house at dinnertime was a frenzied environment. Between dressing for the nightly meeting and preparing food, the energy of all the women in the house was like a hurricane. Stevie couldn't find a peaceful spot. Through the kitchen window, she saw Chris in the backyard manning the grill and threw on a faded denim jacket.

Her old army boots kicked at dead leaves as she made her way toward Chris, a small carton of orange juice in hand. "Hey," she murmured when she reached her.

"Hey. What's the matter?"

"Oh, nothing," Stevie answered nonchalantly and sat down on a brick red picnic table next to the grill. Her gaze fell on a neighbor's yard, only twenty feet or so away, where a couple of toddlers, a brother and sister it seemed, were dressed in winter coats already and playing in a sand box. The little boy had an intense look on his face for someone so tiny. He was scowling as he dug so seriously in the sand with his little pink hand that he had removed his mitten from. But the little girl's face was as placid as a lake. She was gathering fall leaves and dropping them over her head, watching to see where they would land. Stevie wondered what it was that made her so content.

"Want me to throw something on the grill for you?" Chris asked.

"No, thanks. I don't feel like eating."

"That's what you said at lunch," Chris remarked. "Do you feel all right?" Stevie shrugged and sipped her juice. "Don't forget H.A.L.T.," Chris added as she sat down next to her. The acronym stood for the words hungry, angry, lonely and tired, four conditions addicts are taught to avoid because they could cause relapse.

"You can feed me," Stevie replied, "but that won't cure the 'lonely' part."

"He'll be here in another week," Chris reminded her.

Stevie lay back on the table to look at the sky overhead. Tree branches extended over where she was lying and she noticed the leaves that had yet to fall, a few red and yellow stragglers holding on for dear life, and she actually identified with them. Barely holding on, that's how she felt today. "Five days," she mumbled.

Chris laughed. "Right, five days, on Michael's birthday. So, are we having a party?"

Stevie sat up and rubbed her stomach. The orange juice was upsetting it. She felt like puking again. "*We* are, as in Michael and me. Don't expect to meet him Thursday. I'm not sharing him with anyone, not even you."

Laughter flowed out of Chris like musical notes. Everything about her was pretty, even the sound of her voice. "It must be nice to be so in love," she mused.

"I still don't believe it sometimes," Stevie admitted. "I wake up scared because I think it was only a dream. It's like the reverse of a drunk dream, know what I mean? When you dream you're drinking and wake up thinking that your life's still like that?"

"I've had a few of those," Chris admitted. Then her face took on a distant, glassy-eyed expression. "There's something I've wanted to tell you. It's about Scott and me."

"My Scott?" Stevie asked, and belched loudly. "Sorry. My stomach's weird today."

"What other Scott is there?"

Stevie sighed. She knew exactly what was about to come out of Chris' pretty mouth. Every single close friend she'd ever had had fallen in love with Scott, and every single one had regretted it afterward. And for Chris the stakes were so much higher. Scott was an active alcoholic. A long walk off a short cliff, that's what it looked like to her. "I don't know, but I really wish it was a different Scott," she replied, "a sober one."

Chris looked outright pissed. She stood up and slapped slices of cheese on the burgers. "Why is it such a big deal?" she spat out, spinning to face Stevie again.

"Because it is. He's an alcoholic. Don't you know that?" And he's a *player* she wanted to add, but held her tongue. He'd been in law school for less than two months and he'd already slept with two different women he met there. He had told her. And now, she was sure by Chris' reaction, he was sleeping with her, too. He was exactly like her father, she suddenly realized, and that made her feel even sicker. If she didn't break away from the conversation soon, she'd vomit all over the picnic table.

"I'm not sure he is. He never drinks around me," Chris protested, her voice as weak as her argument.

Oh please. This was pathetic. The *only* place he didn't drink was at the *sober* house. "So where is he tonight?"

Chris shrugged. "He said he might see a movie at Harvard Square, an indie flick."

"Yeah okay, Chris. He's trying to impress you. Ask him tomorrow where he ended up going. He'll give you a string of bars. Better yet, take a good look at him. Every Sunday morning he's been here, he's been hung over. Can't you smell it on him?"

"I think you're too hard on him. Honestly, I do. And he loves you so much."

What was that supposed to mean, she was a horrible sister because she told the truth about him? Why was everyone always hiding the ball? "I love him, too, but I don't think that means I have to pretend he's not sick when he is," she hissed and abruptly walked away, but she could still feel Chris' angry energy nipping at her back.

She felt disgusting, and wasn't sure which was making her more ill, the orange juice or Chris' naiveté. If she could miss a meeting and get away with it, tonight would be the night. She wished that for once the women and all their problems would leave the house in a big noisy exodus, and leave her alone for a little while. She wanted nothing more than to lay in her bed in the silence and wait for Michael to get home and call her. What she needed so badly was for him to *understand*. Some days he was the only one that did.

She walked around to the front of the house and sat down by herself on the cold cement steps that led to the front door. Looking out at the busy city street, she felt overwhelmingly lonely. Why was it, she wondered, that loneliness seemed to abound in all the places that overflowed with people? The least lonely place she'd ever been in her life was under the vast Georgia sky with only Michael by her side. A flicker of sunlight drew her attention to her ring—Michael's ring—where he had placed it on her left hand like a wedding band. *I'm not alone* she reminded herself. She hit the number two on her phone to speed dial his cell. It rang and rang, and went to voicemail.

He was in the middle of an argument with Matt when the phone was ringing. That's why he didn't pick it up. Right after Michael returned from Ponte Vedra, Tommy, the band's temporary front man, had called to say he was too sick to cover the gig that night, and furthermore the club manager had leaked to him that an A&R guy from Los Angeles was supposed to be in the audience. Michael told him not to cancel the gig. *He* would cover it. Matt went ballistic when he overheard the conversation and threatened to call Stevie. And as if on cue the cell phone rang, but Michael snatched it off the table before Matt could get a hold of it. "I'll call her from the club," he quickly said.

"If you're not doing anything wrong, why can't you tell her now?"

"Because she'll worry. I can do this, Matt, and it's important. We could get signed."

"You know what I think?" Matt argued. "I think you're taking a big risk for nothing."

Michael immediately became agitated. He started moving quickly, packing his guitar in the case and then wrapping cords and packing them in the guitar case, too. "It's not nothing to me, Matt. Can't you understand that?" he snapped. He stopped moving and watched Matt's face intently for his response. "The band isn't *nothing* to me."

"I know," Matt breathed angrily. "I know all about it, you and the God damned band. You can keep it, Michael. You can have it because I'm out. I don't want anything to do with it anymore." He plopped down on the sofa, looking depleted. They were in the main area of the James' house, the living room, but Mr. and Mrs. James had gone out to dinner so Matt was left to battle Michael alone. "Maybe call your sponsor or John. Have you thought about that?"

Michael walked past him with an amplifier in his hand, and exited the house. He came back briefly to get his guitar. When he got to the door the second time, the guitar slung over his shoulder, he turned back and glared at Matt. "Are you in for tonight or not? You need to tell me if you're not so I can get a sub."

Matt's head dropped back on the couch; he closed his eyes and took a couple of deep breaths. When he opened his eyes again, they stood out like the aquamarine gem that was his birthstone against his angry red complexion. Michael was still standing in the doorway, scowling. "Are you ever going to stop?" he asked him, his voice strained.

"What, the band?" Michael asked tentatively.

"Being a pain in my ass."

Michael turned and walked out. Matt shouted obscenities at the empty room for about ten seconds then picked up his bass and followed Michael out the door.

They had just pulled into the parking lot of the Norwell meeting when Stevie checked her cell phone. *Three missed calls*, it said. "What the hell?" she whined.

"What's wrong?" Chris asked. She was squeezed into the front seat between Stevie and Gail, who was driving. Three other women were in the back seat.

"How did I miss his calls? I didn't even hear it ring."

"It's probably the reception. Check voicemail."

The rest of the women piled out of the car, but Stevie and Chris waited behind. The reception was likely better outside than in the church hall where the meeting was held. Besides, she'd have to silence her cell phone once the meeting started. She pushed the number one to speed dial her voicemail. Michael's scruffy voice was waiting there. Something unexpected had come up, he said and he might not get to call her again until later that night. The last thing he said was "I love you and don't worry."

As soon as she heard "don't worry", she did. She sent him a text: *Where R U?*

The club was packed. Word had gotten out that Michael was fronting the band and all his loyal followers showed up. It was a local club that he had played at dozens of times, but still nothing was familiar. He was clean and that changed the entire dynamic. When sound check was complete, he tried to reach Stevie one more time. It went straight to voicemail. And how could he text her that he was at a club? The clock on his phone said 9:28. If she was at a meeting, it wouldn't end until 10:00, and by then he'd be on stage.

He was alone and pacing in the band room when Rob, his ex room-mate, approached.

"What've you been avoiding me?" Rob asked him, his thin lips curled into a sneer. Michael knew exactly what he was talking about. Rob had called his cell phone and the house numerous times since he got back from Georgia. Michael hadn't returned his calls, and during sound check, he'd barely acknowledged him.

"Yeah, actually," Michael said flatly.

"What the fuck?" Rob snapped. "We've been friends since we were what twelve?"

"It's not you I'm staying away from, Rob, it's the speed, the speed you've probably got in your pocket right now."

Rob laughed obnoxiously and offered up a sardonic grin. "What'd you do let 'em brainwash you?" he taunted.

He was using Michael's old line against him. After he signed him-self out of the first rehab, the one in Jacksonville, he used to say that his parents sent him off to be brainwashed. Before he could reply Matt entered with two cans of soda.

"Oh, so you don't drink anymore either?" Rob spit out and nearly busted a gut laughing. "That's sweet, Michael, really sweet." He turned to leave, shaking his head at Michael as if he were an embarrassment. He stopped briefly before he walked out the door to glance at his watch. "We're on in four minutes. Hope you can pull this off." Then unexpectedly his face became animated by a smile as if everything he had said was a joke amongst friends. "Let me know if you need anything." With the last comment he patted his shirt pocket with his fingertips.

Michael grabbed a can from Matt's hand and slugged down its contents. "I don't know if I can do this, Matt," he said, his voice conspicuously trembling. "I don't think I can do it." He tried to sit but shot out of the chair after only a few seconds. He didn't seem to be talking to Matt anymore but to some invisible force that was making him move like a small part of an elaborate machine, not human at all. "I can taste it," he mumbled, "in my throat." He suddenly spun so that he was facing Matt head on, making intense eye contact. "I've never done this clean. Did you know that?"

"When we were in high school you used to play—"

"No, Matt," Michael interrupted. "That was before we had this band. I was just the guitarist back then. Remember? That was before."

Matt handed Michael his soda and watched him pour it down his throat like he was putting out a fire. "I think we should leave," he softly suggested. "It's just a gig."

"But it's not," Michael railed. "It's not just a gig. Don't you see?" He was grinding his teeth and moving maniacally in front of Matt's nervous eyes. "It's a second chance. And if I can't do this now, I won't ever be able to."

"That's stupid, Michael. Why put that much pressure on yourself?"

"It's not stupid." The volume of his voice kept increasing, and with it, Matt's agitation. "What's going to change? If I can't do it clean, I can't do it clean, right?"

"I...don't know," Matt stammered. "All I know is you're not even supposed to be here. John said maybe after a year. You don't even have four months yet."

"But I am here, and the A&R guy's here. I have to figure this out. Just help me, Matt, please." He sounded desperate and was sweating so much his hair was wet through as if he'd already performed. His hand was clutching his cell phone and he was checking it compulsively.

"How? I don't know what to do," Matt answered, looking like he was about to cry. Michael in this mode was beyond his control. "What'd Stevie say?"

"I can't reach her. I don't know where she is." In his frustration Michael slammed the cell phone onto the floor and it broke into pieces. "Where the fuck is she?" came out in almost a cry. He was tugging on his wet hair now with his restless fingers.

"You mean you didn't tell her?"

Before Michael could answer, the voice of the club manager boomed through the speakers. He was on stage, right beyond the band room, speaking into the microphone. His words were so amplified that they were fuzzy and echoey, nearly inarticulate, but two words were clearly discernible: "L.A. ICE."

CHAPTER TWENTY-FOUR:

ASHES! ASHES!

When she awoke the next morning, she was still gripping her cell phone. It vibrated a split second before the ring and startled her. Sometime after midnight she must have fallen asleep. "Michael?" Stevie said into the phone as relief spread through her chest. *Finally* he called. Last night he had sent her text messages in response to hers: *MUSM* (Miss you so much) and *CMPLZ* (Call me please), but he didn't answer her question. She tried to call, but he didn't pick up. Then a little later, during the meeting when the ringer was turned off, her cell phone had received five more missed calls from his, but after the meeting when she tried to call him back, it went right to voicemail every time.

"Hi Stevie," she heard. It was a man's voice, but not Michael's. She quickly sat up and clutched her stomach. She was sick again. "It's Matt," the voice said.

"Matt? Oh my God, I've been so worried. Where's Michael?" The long pause that followed made her heave. If she had any food in her stomach it would have come up. "Is he okay?" hiccupped out of her.

"N-no," Matt uttered. Even more frightening than the reply was the pain in his voice. He sounded like he'd been crying. There was a nasally, mucous-like quality to the word.

"Wait," she said and put the phone down on her bed so he couldn't hear her trying to catch her breath. She gripped onto the comforter with both hands and closed her eyes. *Please God, please God, please undo this. Whatever happened, please undo it.* The sound of joyous laughter from the kitchen floated up the stairs sounding twisted and perverse in contrast to what was happening in her bedroom. And music was filtering in from next door, in Gail's bedroom, Pearl Jam. With a shaky hand, Stevie brought the phone back to her ear. "Matt," she forced out, "Did he pick up?"

"Yeah," he answered with what sounded like a breathy sob.

"Okay," she said more to herself than to him. He'd picked up. But it could still be okay. He'd go back to detox willingly this time, she was sure of it. They'd get it right this time. He just needed more treatment. That's the way it is for meth addicts—the odds are stacked against them. In the midst of her musings she suddenly became aware of Scott's voice downstairs. Scott was in the kitchen. If she could just breathe, she could yell to him to come up the stairs to help her. Breathe, *breathe*, she told herself. The air was stuck exactly like...like the first time she met Michael.

"He—he had a heart attack," Matt suddenly said.

"What?" somehow escaped her. She was still sleeping. She had to be sleeping. It was a bad dream because she was worried about him, that's all. It couldn't be true. How could Michael, *her* Michael, have had a heart attack?

"You know how he had that arrhythmia," Matt continued as if she hadn't spoken. "The emergency room doctor said that's how it probably happened. I'm so sorry, Stevie. I—I never should have left him alone."

"But Matt," she argued. "He'll be okay. It couldn't have been a bad heart attack because he's only...he's only twenty-two." Not even, she realized, not until Thursday.

Matt heaved a sigh into the receiver. She could feel the dread of what he was about to say. "He didn't make it, Stevie. He...he passed away."

Her fingers hung up the phone before her brain could think. She started retching, spilling some kind of brown fluid out of her stomach and onto the scratched wooden floor. Breath suddenly escaped her lungs like air from a punctured balloon.

"Scott!" she wailed and heard the sudden silence it wreaked downstairs, followed by a man's voice telling Scott not to go upstairs, he wasn't allowed. Then she heard his footsteps running up the stairs anyway like Prince Charming coming to bring Sleeping Beauty back to life. But no magic kiss could do that for her.

Her mind was closing out the world, moving quickly from bright colors to a dull shade of gray. Eddie Vedder bellowed his sinuous love song through the thin walls. *No*, she thought right before the lens closed and everything went black. There were different words beginning their chant in her brain. *Ring a-round the roses, a pocket full of posies.* That was it, the nursery rhyme. *Ashes! Ashes! We all fall down!*

CHAPTER TWENTY-FIVE:
STILL TANGLED

She knew who he was the second she entered the hotel lobby and saw him sitting there on the formal old-fashioned velvet sofa. He was identical to Michael in some unidentifiable way, though he looked nothing like him. With his short blonde hair and blue eyes, he was much more boy-next-doorish than Michael. Yet something in the way he held his head and the expression around his eyes made it unmistakable. He was Matt.

He was intuitive like Michael, too. He looked up at her a second after she spotted him. His eyes were swollen and red from crying, but he was dressed nicely to meet her, in a pinstriped dress shirt and gray slacks. Matt smiled half-heartedly as she approached him, followed close behind by Ellen and John who had driven down from Georgia to Jacksonville to meet her at the airport. Without greeting, she flung her arms around him and for a brief moment she felt like she was holding

Michael again. What was it? And then she knew. The scent of his skin; it was just like Michael's.

She hadn't cried the entire plane ride down, only sat flat line in her seat like a zombie. The flight crew and the other passengers seemed blurry and surreal. She wasn't sure if it was a result of the shock or the medication her primary care doctor had prescribed after consulting with Dr. Jim. When she stood up to leave the airplane, she realized that she could barely feel her limbs, but somehow she was still able to walk. At the baggage claim, her emotions caught up all at once when she laid eyes on Ellen and John. And that's what was happening now, with Matt. Tears were gushing out of her like blood from a deep wound. But now, unlike that time with Julie, she understood what instigated the onslaught. It was because she felt safe, the safest she'd felt since Michael died.

"I'll stay with you if you want me to," he offered. She understood that he meant at the hotel where her room would be adjoined to Ellen's. Ellen had orchestrated everything, remarkably with the assistance of Stevie's mother, who had stayed with Stevie from the moment Scott informed her of Michael's death until she left her at the security gate at the airport. During that twenty-four hour period, Stevie hadn't once seen her take a drink. It was almost like being with a stranger, but a kind stranger. Ellen and Stevie's mother had booked the flight and the room and spoken to Michael's parents about the arrangements. Although the James' offered for Stevie to stay at their house, Ellen thought it would be too emotional for Stevie to stay in a place where Michael's presence so strongly resided. They also worked out the medication she was taking, some kind of sedative, and how and when it was to be disbursed to her. She was not to have possession of it.

Through the unfamiliar haze the pills gave birth to in her brain, it seemed like they were more concerned about her committing suicide than picking up a drink. She thought she might have a breakdown, like she did before she got sober, but she had no intention of drinking or otherwise hurting herself. She tried to tell Ellen and her mother not to worry, that the last thing she would do is drink at Michael's funeral, but they just looked at her with untrusting eyes, as if anything she said had to be taken with a grain of salt. To her, it would be disloyalty to Michael to pick up a drink. And although there was very little in her life that she was sure about now, there was one thing she was absolutely certain of. She never had been and never would be disloyal to Michael.

Stevie unconsciously played with the silver band on her finger as she nodded her head at Matt, accepting his invitation. She needed him to stay. She needed him to explain to her what had happened to Michael and so dramatically altered the course of their lives. No one had told her the story yet about his death, only that he died at home in his bed after using meth. Matt knew everything, not only about what preceded his death, but about Michael, and there was so much she needed him to tell her. There were a few things she wanted to share with him, too. It took all of five seconds in his presence to understand that she could trust him with anything.

Ellen and John exchanged introductions with Matt. It was more than she could bear to witness John, the goliath, crying, so she took Matt's seat on the sofa and listened without watching them as they traded comments about how they felt like they already knew each other because of everything Michael had said. Then Matt said something unexpected. He thanked John for helping Michael, for making it possible to have him back, even if for only a short time. He'd lived four years without him, he said, and it meant a lot to him that they had the last six weeks together with Michael as his old self. The comment spun in Stevie's muddled brain.

What if Michael's parents and Matt hadn't brought him to Georgia? She wouldn't have met him, and never would have believed it was possible to love someone the way she loved Michael. She wished she could be as mature as Matt and take a moment—just one—to be grateful for that, but there was too much pain getting in the way. She was too angry to be grateful. She had thanked God for Michael every night from the day they met until the night he died. And she hadn't uttered a word to God since.

Her mind seemed to be getting farther away from the rest of her body, as if all her thinking was being done on the other side of a tunnel and was slowly transported back, like freight in a Mack truck. She shook her head a little bit to try to clear the blockage. John and Matt walked over to the front desk to check them in, and Ellen sat next to Stevie on the sofa. "Are you hungry?" she asked. It should have been an easy question to answer, but it wasn't. She could barely feel her stomach. Her whole body was tingly and heavy all at once. She shrugged.

"What if we get you settled in your room and then find some food," Ellen suggested. "Matt can stay here with you."

"Yeah," Stevie agreed. "I want to talk to him."

Ellen's face reflected her concern. "You don't need to hear everything at once, do you?" *Do you, do you, do you?* echoed through Stevie's brain.

"Why, is there something I don't know?"

"No, that's not what I meant. I want you to take your time with this, that's all. It's a lot to absorb."

You think? Stevie formulated, but snapped her mouth shut before the words escaped. It was a mean thing to say and Ellen had been so kind to her. She saw Ellen's pained expression and suddenly thought maybe the words had gotten loose. She couldn't remember what had transpired. "I'm sorry. I'm sorry Ellen, it's just the, the…never mind."

She couldn't remember mid-thought what she was intending to say. The *what*?

"It's okay." Ellen patted her knee and walked away to talk to the guys.

Stevie pulled a half-empty pack of Marlboros from her bag and lit one, her attention focused on how uncharacteristically stable her hands were and consequently how easy it was to light the cigarette. She stared at her hand and intermittently turned the wheel on the lighter to recreate the flame that looked like yellow liquid devouring itself. How could her hands be so still at such a moment as this? And why was it she never noticed how the fire disappeared into itself?

A male voice grumbled to get Stevie's attention, but she didn't look up. The sound was somewhere in the farthest reaches of her reality, like background music. "Excuse me, miss. There's no smoking in the lobby." Stevie turned the wheel again. She wasn't being rebellious. She didn't respond because his words weren't important enough to matter. "You'll have to put it out," he loudly commanded.

"All right," she heard Matt say and noticed he had the guy by the arm. "Now leave her alone." He let go of the man, but gave him a threatening look before he sat next to her. "Are you okay?" he asked, his voice soft, comforting.

"No. I want to lie down." The lighter fell from her hand as if it had never mattered.

Matt's clear blue eyes reminded her of a porcelain doll in her bedroom at home, at what used to be home. The place she used to live near the ocean…"I'll take you to your room. I won't leave you," he assured her.

"I know that," she answered. His hand reached for the cigarette as tentatively as Michael had reached for her face the first time he kissed her. "Oh," she added, understanding. Somehow the words of the hotel manager didn't seem to be aimed at her until Matt made the gesture. She handed the cigarette to him like a little girl offering a gift and he dropped it in a paper cup half-filled with water. The cup looked familiar, like she'd used it. Maybe she had washed a pill down, but she couldn't remember doing that. "Did I take more medicine?" she asked Matt, wide-eyed.

Matt looked up at Ellen and John standing nearby, taking all this in. "At the airport," Ellen offered cautiously. She checked her watch. "She can't take anymore until six o'clock." She must have trusted Matt instinctively, too, because she handed the bottle of sedatives to him. "Maybe she can sleep."

"We'll be back with food," John announced and handed Matt the room key.

The room key was one of those plastic cards that slide into a slot to unlock the door. Apparently Matt had never used one because it took him a minute to figure it out. That made sense to Stevie because based on everything Michael had said Matt wasn't a one-night stand kind of guy. The thought tripped off another one. She was entering a hotel room with Michael's best friend—whom she just met. She had never even done that with Michael. She thought she was laughing at that realization, but then heard herself crying. And she was sitting on the floor although she didn't remember doing that, either.

Matt stooped down in front of her. "It's okay," he whispered and pulled her to her feet. The room door was wide open already. He brought her over to one of the beds and sat her down before he pulled back the covers on the other one. "Do you have to go to the bathroom before you lie down?" he asked.

If her body were capable of laughing she would have, but that ability seemed to have been depressed by the sedative. "You'd make a good father," she said instead. She got up by herself this time, moved over to the bed he had prepared and crawled under the sheets. "Matt..." He was sitting on the other bed with his head drooped forward as if it were too heavy for his shoulders to carry. "He was my Michael, you know."

Matt waited a long time to answer, at least it seemed that way. "I know," he finally responded and his mouth became distorted like he was trying not to cry. "I'm sorry. Listen, I know Michael hadn't told you this yet, but he found a house—I feel like he'd want me to tell you that. A guy at his dad's firm has a second house he rents out and the tenant's leaving. He was looking for a new tenant for December first."

"For us? You mean January first?"

A small, ironic laugh escaped him. "No. I mean December first. The guy was holding it until Michael could talk to you about it in person. He was going to ask you on Friday when he got to Boston if you'd stay when you came for Thanksgiving."

And she would have said yes. The separation was too much, more than she had bargained for. Besides, after she told Michael what she had been planning to tell him on Friday, he would have insisted on it. She closed her eyes and thought about a comment he made when they were talking about finding a good place for them to live together, something about orange trees. "Did you see it, Matt, the house?"

"Three times," he replied and shrugged his shoulders. "You know Michael."

"Were there orange trees?" After he nodded she thought maybe she should rest for a while so she closed her eyes again. *Orange trees in the backyard.* There was so much information to process. It soon became clear that her brain wasn't going to sleep until it understood more. So she asked what happened on the night Michael died.

Matt told her about the phone call and the A&R guy. He told her that Michael had tried to reach her and how he started melting down before he went on stage. Then he told her how the club manager announced the band and Michael thought he had to go on even though he was afraid to. Even if he hadn't said another word, she understood now. This was about the band...L.A. ICE. To her, the name had always felt premonitory, like it was a foretelling of Michael's future. He couldn't let it go. *It's tattooed on my chest, close to my heart* he had told her once. What was he referring to, the band or the drug?

The image of a fire-breathing dragon stomped through her drug-hazed mind and made her gasp. *The dragon's not dead, but it's sleeping.* The monster had awakened and swallowed her love, swallowed him whole. What happened when his skin and bones were devoured? Did his spirit slip out unscathed, finally free?

"He...he sort of flipped out when he got onstage. I've never seen him scared like that. He was kind of like stooped down, like he was about to pass out. He—he kept missing the vocal entrance. We played it over and over but he just couldn't do it, you know?" Matt sighed and looked like he was hoping that was all he had to say. No such luck.

"What happened?"

"Can I ask you something?" he abruptly threw out and waited patiently for her belated nod. "Have you ever been in a situation with Michael where there was something he wanted to do and you thought it was a bad idea?"

"Yeah."

"It's not easy, right?"

"Right," Stevie agreed and sat half way up so she was leaning on her elbows. She suddenly realized something. Matt thought Michael's death was his fault. And she thought it was hers. "You think you should have stopped him?" she asked.

"I know I should have, I mean, I know that now. It was stupid of me. I did try to stop him, but I could have done more. I should have called his father or you."

Stevie shook her head. There was no stopping Michael once he had something in his mind that he was determined to do. "And I should have come here with him in August, or let him come to Boston like he wanted. Got any idea how many times I've told myself that in the last two days?"

"I've got a pretty good guess," Matt answered and hung his head again.

"Just tell me how he died, Matt. I need to know that, but afterward I want you to tell me other things about him, good things, the kind of things that only you know."

Matt grinned a little bit. "I've got a lot of Michael stories. It would take years."

"I've got nothing else to do," she replied. "Can I smoke in here?"

"I think so. Do you want me to get your purse?"

"You can take them out."

Matt opened her bag. There were only three things in it besides her wallet: the pack of Marlboro reds, a Foo Fighters CD and a stack of pictures held together by an elastic band. All she had of Michael. "He wrote you some songs," Matt told her as he handed her a cigarette and lit it for her. She noticed he put the lighter back in his pocket, a safe place. She tried to make smoke rings like Michael had taught her, but she still couldn't do it. *Watch my mouth* he'd said with his soothing laughter rolling out of him like a melody, and she had. That's why she couldn't concentrate on what he was telling her.

"He told me. Someday I'll read them," she answered pensively, "but not today. Today I'm not going to drink and that's about it. Tell me what happened, Matt, and then I'll tell you my Michael story. You'll like it."

He cocked his head to the side curiously, perhaps wondering what she could add to his vast knowledge of his best friend/brother, and smiled at her, not quite like Michael, but not that far off either. Their facial expressions were strangely similar. Then he told her the story. When Michael was stooped down on stage, someone in the crowd had handed him a shot of whiskey, and Michael had taken it from his hand and thrown it back. According to Matt, it was as if he didn't even think about it. Then another person and another person did the same thing. The crowd cheered him on while he did the shots and the alcohol made it possible for him to stand up and be the front man, the infamous front man of L.A. ICE. And he was...the old Michael for the span of one set.

Then between sets Matt found him in the band room snorting lines. "I dragged him out of the club, but it was too late—he'd already done the meth, and when we got in Michael's Mustang, his nose was bleeding like it used to."

"The surgeon said that would happen," Stevie interjected and lay back down on the bed. Michael had sworn to her up and down that he would never use a needle again because he knew how much it scared her. So he had snorted it. Would the result have been different if she hadn't made him promise? The walls were starting to breathe.

"I made him hold his t-shirt on his nose until it stopped bleeding. I—I couldn't bring him home like that. I couldn't let his mother see him. I probably should have, but I didn't. I didn't bring him inside until the lights were out."

"And he went to bed?"

"Well, he—he said he was okay, but he was sweating a lot. He was sitting on his bed, leaning against the wall with his phone in his hand. I think it was still broken because he threw it earlier. That's...that's how I left him." His china blue eyes were wet now.

And that's how they found him in the morning. He didn't need to say it. She understood. "Did he know I was trying to reach him?"

Matt moved over to her bed and sat down, and suddenly she could smell him. "Wait," she whispered. "Wait a minute Matt." She closed her eyes and took a deep breath through her nose. Michael. It was exactly how her sheets smelled in the rehab after they spent the night together. "Can we finish this later?" she asked without opening her eyes.

"Do you want to take a nap?"

She nodded. "Would you...would you sit there for a few minutes, until I fall asleep?"

"Sure," he agreed and pulled the bedspread over her shoulders. He was as harmless as a teddy bear, Matt, one out of a handful of men left on Earth who she would feel safe sleeping in the same room with. *Okay, drift back*, she coached herself. She could be there if she could only see it. *Drift back to that morning.* She fell asleep with Michael still asleep in her arms, his damp ringlets falling around his face.

When she awoke it was dark already. The first thing her vision caught was the glowing white sliver of a moon outside the window. This time she remembered the truth before she actually came to, that Michael had died, which was better than waking up and feeling like he was still alive—and then remembering. She wondered, as her eyes took in the beautiful moon, if Michael could see it from wherever he was now. He always liked it when it was sculpted like that. "Matt?" she called out. The room was dark and silent.

"I'm right here," he answered from the floor. He was sitting at the end of her bed watching an old black and white movie on the television with the sound turned off. "That was Ellen that called a couple of minutes ago. Did it wake you?"

No. It was a dream that awakened her. Michael was prompting her. She could see his beautiful dark eyes looking into hers and he was grinning in that little boy way of his, sitting on the bed next to her. And his voice. *Come away, o human child. With a faery hand in hand.* The Yeats poem, that's what he was saying. *For the world's more full of weeping than you can understand.* Even though she was awake now, she could still feel the physical sensations of being in Michael's presence—like her heart was trying to escape her ribcage. She sat up and tugged her fingers through her tangled hair. Her mouth was as sticky as cobwebs. "I didn't hear it. Are Michael's parents here?"

"They're with Ellen and John next door. They'll be here any minute with dinner."

Dinner? The moon was up already. They must have been waiting a long time for her to wake up. "Okay, but there's something I want to tell you before they get here. I was just dreaming about it." She turned on the bedside light and squinted from the glare.

Matt sat on the bed next to her and she noticed he looked tired and disheveled, as if while she was sleeping he had walked to Hell and back again. Ironically, he threw the question at her: "Are you okay?" She must have looked as bad as he did.

"Are you?"

He sort of chuckled, but didn't answer the question. "Want a ginger ale?" he asked.

"Fuck yeah," spilled out of her before it occurred to her that this wasn't Michael, and she probably shouldn't be dropping "F bombs" near someone she didn't even really know. "Sorry," she added and made an apologetic face, "I'm just…really thirsty."

This time he genuinely laughed and shook his head like he couldn't believe such a vulgar word had found its way out of her mouth. He was so different from Michael in some ways, she noted, refined and mild mannered. He poured the ginger ale over ice in a plastic cup and Stevie nearly snatched it from his hand. She couldn't remember a liquid ever looking so appealing. "So, what is it?" he asked her, "your Michael story?"

She gulped the entire glass then made eye contact with him and nodded her head slowly. "But it's a secret, Matt. You'll have to promise it'll stay between you and me."

Matt looked scared out of his wits, as if she was about to reveal some fiendish tale. "I don't know," he stammered. "They'll be here any second. Maybe tomorrow..."

"No. I need you to know today, before they get here. I don't want to be the only one that does, and if Michael were here, *he'd tell you.*" No doubt Matt would conclude that she had lost her grip on reality if she revealed that Michael had said so in her dream. "It's nothing illegal, Matt. It has to do with the last night we were together in Georgia—"

He immediately interrupted her. "Oh, wait," he said, waving his hands around to stop her. His face was slowly turning crimson, starting at the neck and working its way toward his forehead. She knew before he said another word what he thought, that this was about sex. "You don't need to tell me. Michael told me about that night."

"Matt," she said patiently. "He didn't tell you this."

"How do you know?" he asked, pinching his eyebrows in a perfect Michael imitation.

"Because he didn't know it yet."

EPILOGUE:
THE CIRCLE CLOSES

The New England sun was shining brightly and the seagulls were soaring noisily overhead as Stevie tossed the last piece of luggage into her red jeep. The soft summer breeze caught hold of her billowy skirt as she cupped her hand across her brow to block the sun from her eyes that were looking upward at the circling sea birds. They were waiting for her to leave so they could swoop down on the goldfish crackers tossed onto the driveway by other hands for exactly that purpose.

Almost three years had passed since Michael's death. And Stevie was on her way to Jacksonville…to live this time.

The click clack of her heels sent musical notes soaring into the wide open space as she stepped into the massive foyer of her mother's house and passed by the formal living room with its Chippendale style furniture and grand piano. The spiral staircase was still adorned with the childhood pictures of Scott and her. With each step upward she passed another grade level, with each step passed her untamed locks and Scott's familiar lopsided grin. A clatter of dishes in the kitchen drifted up the stairway behind her. It was her mother, she knew, preparing food for the trip.

She opened the door to her bedroom, still clutching the egg-shaped doorknob in her sweaty palm. She was nervous about leaving. This time it was really for good. The house had been sold in accordance with her parents' divorce decree and her mother would be passing papers next month on a smaller home in Jacksonville. Stevie would stay with the James' until she arrived. She admired her mother's decision to move away from a community she had lived in for twenty-five years to start a new life. And there was much more she admired about her now. Two years prior, her mother had attended her first AA meeting and had not taken a drink since. Stevie had never expected that kind of turnaround from her mother, but like John had always said *drunks are unpredictable creatures. There's no telling when they're about to hit bottom and swim back up for air.* She had even started her own Twelve-Step group. As it turned out, she wasn't the only woman in their sleepy coastal town who needed it. Her mother's sobriety combined with her father's absence had made home a safe place, and Stevie had moved back in.

The collection of porcelain dolls in silk frocks perched on a built in bookshelf seemed to whisper to her as she passed on route to the nightstand, where framed pictures portrayed Michael's smiling visage. The first was the photo on the deck that Matt took with his cell phone. When his beautiful face had changed from the sobriety poster child to a reminder of how quickly it could all be lost, Stevie had taken it off of the sober house refrigerator and kept it for herself. In the second photograph, he is barely smiling, focused too much on the acoustic guitar on his lap. He didn't look up at his mother when she pushed the button, not realizing it was a moment of immortality, a picture Stevie and his family would cherish forever. Stevie reached for them, Michael's silver band still gleaming on her finger, and placed both pictures gently in her shoulder bag.

Yet a third photograph was waiting for her on the mahogany dresser that used to house her clothes. This one captured both Michael and Matt on the beach with their surfboards, wearing only shorts. She picked it up and ran the tip of her forefinger across Michael's face and slender body. "I will love you *always*," she whispered before a small voice across the hallway caught her attention. She quickly placed the framed picture in her bag with the others and reached for a thick pile of papers, the last object on the dresser. A wistful smile shaped her lips as her eyes took it in, *L.A. ICE, a novel by Stephanie Gates*. She stuffed it in the bag with her other treasures and took one last look around at her childhood room before leaving and closing the door behind her.

When she opened the door of the room across from hers, a symphony of giggles poured out of the little boy beaming at her from his crib. Michael Theodore James, II, known by his family as Teddy, had dimples, enormous brown eyes, and dark ringlets just like his father. And also like his father, he was nearly impossible to say no to. He was two years old as of May, a result of the one and only night his parents spent together.

To Stevie, he was an angel, Michael incarnate.

"Come here you," she said and he threw his hands up so she would scoop him up in her arms, the very thing he had been fussing for. He immediately threw his head back and blew a raspberry with his lips, his pink tongue darting from his mouth like a baby snake's. It was a familiar invitation. She felt his body fold into a fit of giggles as she blew raspberries all over his neck. "It's time to go now," she told him.

"Berries!" he insisted and watched for her reaction with his intelligent eyes. When it was apparent that she wasn't playing anymore, his thumb went to his mouth and he laid his chubby cheek on her shoulder.

"Don't you want to ride on the airplane?" she coaxed, and kissed the top of his head that was still warm and damp from sleep.

He gasped at the word, then repeated it all the way down the stairs until they reached Stevie's mother in the kitchen. She was baking chocolate chip cookies for the journey, the smell of which delighted Teddy even more than the promise of an airplane ride. He wriggled out of

Stevie's arms and quickly scrambled into a kid-sized chair next to a miniature table where a plate with two cookies was waiting for him.

"Gokey," he said more to himself than anyone else as he grasped onto one, but it was more than enough to call his grandmother to his side. She carefully placed her adult-sized body onto the other miniature plastic chair and smiled proudly at him.

"*C*," she said and Teddy crossed his eyebrows sternly in response. "*Cookie.*"

On the marble countertop next to where they were sitting there was an array of essentials Stevie's mother had acquired for Teddy's use: a dozen Sippy cups and their tops, freshly scrubbed, several match box cars that had needed the mud rinsed off, a yellow box of Nilla Wafers, and a bunch of bananas—Teddy's favorites—all small things with small price tags but every one of them valuable to Stevie because they represented what was now important to her mother. Once, not all that long ago, that very same countertop had been used as a mini bar. All the bottles so tastefully chosen—Johnny Walker Blue, Carpe Diem, Grey Goose and Tanqueray—had been replaced by Motts, Welch's and Juicy Juice. It made Stevie grin appreciatively to think of it.

"You're sure you don't want to wait for me?" her mother asked.

"I'm sure, Mom. We'll be okay."

"But I'll miss you so much. And how can I live a whole month without my baby?"

"We'll call you every day; I promise," Stevie answered and hugged her. "Come on Teddy, you can take the cookies in the car." There was a Sippy cup in his other hand, smeared with chocolate. "Take the milk, too," Stevie added and stuffed some napkins in her shoulder bag before heading to the front door, Teddy toddling behind her. His grandmother handed him a Ziploc bag filled with goldfish crackers.

He immediately unfastened the strip on the plastic bag and dug his chocolaty fingers inside.

Stevie opened the door and her eyes were assaulted by a flock of seagulls surrounding her car. She spotted the bag in his hand, but not before it was too late. He tossed fistfuls onto the front steps. To Teddy's wonderment, the birds swooped down aggressively to claim the orange crackers. He chased them while Stevie hugged her mother good bye. Leaving her was harder than she had imagined it would be. They'd come a long way in three year's time. Stevie and her mother were allies now, with a common love and purpose. Not all their history had been wiped clean, nor would it be. Deep wounds take time to heal, but at least alcohol was no longer being recklessly tossed upon them to set them ablaze. Teddy had brought them together and Stevie suspected his entrance into their lives had played a role in her mother's sobriety, as well.

"I'm proud of you, Stevie," her mother told her. "You're doing a fine job with Teddy."

"Thank you," she answered and tried not to let on that her eyes were filling with tears. "I'm proud of you, too, Mom. I'll call you when we get to Jacksonville." She turned to see her son with his "wings" spread, "flying" across the front lawn. "Teddy!" Stevie shouted. "Come give Grandma kisses." He flew up to the steps, laughing wildly the whole way, and leaped into his grandmother's arms.

Teddy was standing tip-toed on the airplane seat trying to be tall enough to see over the seats in front of them. Only his big brown eyes showed over the worn gray upholstery.

"You have to sit, Teddy," Stevie scolded.

"Juice!" he exclaimed, jumping up and down now and pointing down the aisle with his chubby forefinger. Sure enough, the flight attendant was bumping the oversized cart up the aisle.

"I see that, but you have to sit down if you want her to stop here." Her words had the desired effect. He plopped onto his bottom and leaned across Stevie's lap to watch the flight attendant's approach. "Juice, Mama," he repeated when he spotted the small cans stored on the bottom shelf of the cart. She grinned at his keen observation. Like his father, very little missed his attention.

The flight attendant pushed the cart closer. "Can I get you a cocktail?" she asked.

"No, thank you. Just apple juice—two of them, please."

The flight attendant got one look at Teddy's imploring eyes and reached into the depths of the cart, pulled out a package of oyster crackers and offered them to him. His response was more than she could have bargained for. He let loose a shriek of delight as his fingers took hold of the crinkly package and he flashed his dimples at her.

"What do you say, Teddy?" Stevie coached.

"Thank you!" he shouted with all his breath and the flight attendant laughed like it was the sweetest thing she'd ever heard.

"How old are you?" she elicited, bending down to get a closer look. He revealed his dimples again, demurely this time, and proudly held up two fingers before he stuck them into the cup of ice she had placed on Stevie's tray. "Well, he is just precious," she sighed and pushed the cart past them.

"You have no idea," Stevie answered under her breath.

Teddy's little tongue poked in and out of his mouth again, creating a swishy wet sound. His mother raspberried his neck. "I love you," she told him for the forty or fiftieth time that day. He replied with a sloppy kiss on her nose.

Her life was good. Perfect? Not quite. If only Michael were still there to share it with her, then it would have been. Having a soul mate was the best anyone could hope for. But having a best friend, well, that was good, too. And Matt was Stevie's best friend now. He had faithfully kept the secret of her pregnancy that she shared with him in the hotel room until she felt sure that she'd be able to carry the baby to term. Matt was so excited about the baby's arrival that he flew to Boston twice to accompany her to ultrasounds, the first of which revealed that the baby was a boy. "Michael junior," he said when they found out, and it had stuck. "Teddy" evolved out of Stevie's desire to lessen the confusion between the two Michaels, because even though one was no longer in the physical world his name was tossed around routinely, almost as if he was.

Matt was with her the morning Teddy was born and even held him before Stevie did. The doctor assumed he was the father and immediately placed the baby in his hands.

And on that day, he took on the role of protector. He called every single night to check on them. Stevie knew that Matt thought of them as his family and he made every effort to keep them safe, in much the same way that he used to with Michael. Like Michael's parents, he had come to Boston many times since then to visit and would have moved there if Stevie hadn't planned to move to Florida. She and Teddy both loved Matt and Michael's parents, and once her mother, who had become vitally important to both her and Teddy's lives, agreed to come along, that sealed the deal.

Michael would have been proud of Matt's loyalty, but not the least bit surprised by it. In many ways, Matt was the antithesis of Michael. He was level headed and practical, calm and patient, a planner. Stevie speculated that he likely started his first savings account when he was six years old and she would not be surprised to learn that it still existed in some form. He would carefully plan his future and all his ducks would remain in a row. His retirement account was fat already. His life was a straight line.

Michael had been everything that Matt was not, spontaneous and impulsive, reckless and wild. It was a meandering path that he had walked, much like hers. And he'd attacked life with the same passion and intensity that she saw in herself. It was this shared character trait that kept them awake all night in Georgia talking about music and novels and poetry. It was passion that pushed Michael to write a stack of songs for her (that was still by his bedside waiting for her), and to cover the show on the night he died.

Despite their differences, Michael and Matt had been brothers in the truest sense of the word. Michael had helped Matt to take more chances, to be less afraid, to be a musician, to laugh more. In return, Matt had stood by Michael's side through his addiction, protected him as much as he could, and would have, Stevie knew, laid down his life for him. Stevie and Matt had found a similar balance. Matt was the voice of reason in her life, and she was his impetus to see life from a more creative angle.

In the almost three years that had passed, life had changed for everyone around her.

Scott graduated from Harvard Law School the same weekend Teddy turned two years old. Stevie and Teddy sat together with her mother and cheered for him when he received his diploma. Her father was there, too, but he sat a dozen rows away with his new wife. Stevie brought Teddy to visit his grandfather and his wife numerous times in their upscale Wellesley home, but they rarely reciprocated the gesture. Scott, however, visited frequently. The mere glimpse of his car pulling into the driveway made Teddy burst into manic hysteria. Scott did things in a grand way, like his father. He'd show up with a massive teddy bear or take him for ice cream and buy him the biggest sundae on the menu. He was always pulling surprises out of his hat, and Teddy adored him for it.

Chris and Scott were no longer together. Chris was asked to leave the sober house shortly after Michael's death when Gail discovered Scott in her bedroom. She moved into Scott's apartment in Cambridge but after only a few weeks started drinking again. Chris stayed in touch with Stevie at first, and came to meet Teddy when he was born. But in the last thirteen months since his first birthday, she had only called twice, and both times admitted that she was still drinking. Stevie prayed for her every night.

It had taken some time, but she did open up to having a relationship with her Higher Power again. She eventually accepted the fact that methamphetamine was responsible for Michael's death, not her Higher Power or his but the drug he'd become addicted to after using it only a few times. Most people, Stevie understood, have a picture in their minds of what a meth addict looks like, similar to the picture she carried in her head (prior to knowing Marcus) of a heroin addict beyond redemption. That picture, she knew, didn't look like Michael James. It didn't look like a good kid who took a wrong turn that turned out to be deadly. *How many other kids*, she sometimes wondered, *had fallen into the same trap? How many faceless addicts had been written off as someone who doesn't matter?*

"Addiction is a terminal disease," John had warned when they were still in treatment. Remembering that fact—carrying it around beneath her skin on a daily basis—was one of the most effective tools she had to prevent a relapse.

Her relationship with Michael had forever altered the course of her life. Like he had expressed on that important night on the veranda, she believed that their meeting in Georgia was no coincidence, and it was now on her gratitude list, like it used to be on his. The Forces that Be had wisely guided them toward each other. On some spiritual level that she didn't completely understand, Michael had saved her. His vision of her had altered the way she saw herself and had given her the strength and the courage to face the world without killing herself in the process. It was Michael that she had dreamed of when she was a little girl, the brown-eyed man who helped her find her way back home. Like their meeting in Georgia, her childhood dreams she now believed, were *by design*, a glimpse of her future. She still dreamed about him, but not like before, when she was a lost soul in a foreign land. Now they were always walking side by side, holding hands, and they weren't lost at all. They were both perfectly content.

But addiction still had its claws dug deeply into most of the people she loved. Of all the "wolf pack" members, Stevie and Brian were the only ones who had stayed sober. Allison left the sober house in Valdosta on her eighteenth birthday, and had been using cocaine since shortly thereafter. Although Stevie had called David a dozen times, he never called her back and, finally, his phone was disconnected. No one knew if he was free or in jail, using or not using, dead or alive. He was on Stevie's prayer list, too.

Just before Teddy was born, Ellen told Stevie in a phone conversation that she had seen Marcus on the news for robbing a convenience store. Presumably by now he was back in prison. Although Stevie was not particularly surprised to hear the news, she was saddened by it. She knew a side of Marcus that all the thousands of television viewers would never know existed. He had taught her to stay away from a drink for one day at a time. Even in the early surreal days after Michael's death she had resisted the urge to put out the grief burning like a wildfire in her belly with a glass of vodka by reminding herself of that principle. And all those days had miraculously added up to three whole years, just like Marcus had said they would. But for him there was a different outcome. Marcus had nearly relinquished himself to his disease by the time Stevie met him. There had been very little chance, if any, of the good dog coming out on top.

Stevie thought about Jake nearly every day. She learned through Ellen that he was still using drugs and had left a trail of foster homes behind him. He'd come close to being adopted once by an upper middle class family in Atlanta, but that fell through after he was arrested for selling Ecstasy in school. At fifteen he did another tour of duty at the Georgia rehab. According to Ellen he didn't latch onto or look up to anyone. He didn't smile or laugh, or even talk much. He was harder, angrier, more like Marcus and less like Michael. Jake, too, would likely be on the news someday, if he lived long enough.

Jake's heartbreaking life made Stevie look at the life of her own son differently. What could she do to protect him from such a dismal fate? When he was old enough, would she let him ride a dirt bike? Probably. Play in a band? Absolutely. Drink alcohol? She couldn't say. Someday he would have to make that decision for himself. No one, she now understood, can live another person's life for them, not even when it appears to be for good reason. Maybe, she surmised, all anyone can do to influence the life of another is to offer the truth of his or her own experience. Like an old guy in AA once told her, smart people learn from their own mistakes, but wise people learn from the mistakes of others. And so, if she had one wish for Teddy, it would be the gift of wisdom. Maybe he could learn from the mistakes of his parents. Maybe.

Addiction is a complicated disease. Like Allison said so long ago, only God knows how to fix it. All the mere mortals, try as they might, still didn't understand its complexities. Did Teddy have genes floating through his body that would predetermine him an alcoholic? Did she when she was four years old and taking sips from her father's beer can? Or Michael, the first time he raised a glass to his lips? She didn't know. No one did. All she knew for sure was that she didn't have to die from her addiction. She had her own story to arm herself, and perhaps, God willing, arm someone else.

And so she told it.

Note to Reader:

*F*irst, thank you for taking precious time out of your life to read my book. It is a little slice of my soul that I feel privileged to share. Second, I feel the need to say (because you have, after all, taken this ride with me) that as much as my heart tugged me in the direction of creating a happily ever after for Michael James, my conscience could not allow it. Too many people have lost their children and other loved ones to methamphetamine abuse for me to pretty up this story. Consider the following:

Methamphetamine is the most abused hard drug on earth, and the world's 26 million meth addicts equals the combined number for cocaine and heroin users. America alone has 1.4 million users [1]

From 1997 to 2007, the number of admissions to treatment in which methamphetamine was the primary drug of abuse increased from 53,694 in 1997 to 137,154 in 2007 [2]

In addition to over-the-counter cold and asthma medications containing ephedrine or pseudoephedrine, the following ingredients are commonly used in "cooking" meth: drain cleaner, battery acid, lye, lantern fuel, and antifreeze [3]

The average life expectancy of a hard core meth addict is only five to seven years [4]

These are methamphetamine statistics alone. In the U.S., over 22 million individuals have a substance dependence or abuse problem, and the majority never recovers. Alcohol contributes to 100,000 deaths annually, making it the third leading cause of preventable death in this country [5]. I wrote this novel to raise awareness about alcohol and drug addiction and to (hopefully) break some common stereotypes about addicts. My objective is to bring light to a few people whose lives have been darkened by this disease, both addicts and those who love them. So if you know someone who could benefit by reading **L.A. ICE**, please pass it on. It is intended as a message of hope. As Stevie said, "there is a way out of the Hellhole called addiction."

With love and a heart full of gratitude for accompanying me on this journey,

Kathleen

"Like" me on Facebook (Kathleen-Ready-Dayan-Author) and be notified on the publication of my second novel, In a Garden White. A contemporary take on Wuthering Heights, this supernatural love story about reincarnation and spirit communication is due out in 2012.

READING GROUPS AND BOOK CLUBS: If your group is reading L.A. ICE, you live in Massachusetts, and would like me to visit for the discussion, please email me through my Facebook page. I will make every effort to attend.

Acknowledgements:

*F*irst and foremost I must thank my family: Edan, Jillian and Ayala for graciously sharing me with my fictitious friends and for having faith in me when my own is wavering. I owe a debt of gratitude to Allison Mulvey, my editorial assistant. I could not have accomplished this novel confidently without you. I would also like to thank my sisters: Christine Ives, Mary Pennie (even though no longer in the physical world, you *so* played a role in this), Julie Mulvey and Martha Murphy for your encouragement and for passing around some early copies of **L.A. ICE** for feedback. Thank you also to the women who took time out of their lives to read the book in its various stages and make suggestions: Althea Lachicotte, Kim Bradford Miller, Kelly Pennie, Lauren Shields, Cathy Hanley, Donna Dean, Meg Flanagan and Kim Robinson Range to name a few. Your comments and positive energy pushed this book forward. To Ryan Jones, the exquisitely gifted cover artist and illustrator: thank you for creating stunning images for my story that until I knew you existed only in my head. Meeting you and having the opportunity to work together has taught me that not only does my Higher Power work in mysterious ways, but apparently even through Facebook. And finally, for the past twenty two years of sobriety and a caliber of life that I could scarcely imagine in 1989, I am thankful on a daily basis to the Great Spirit of Life, my Higher Power.

ENDNOTES

(1) United Nations Office on Drugs and Crime. <u>World Drug Report 2006</u>. Vienna, 2007.

(2) Substance Abuse and Mental Health Services Administration (SAMSHA), Office of Applied Studies (OAS). <u>Treatment Episode Data Set (TEDS) Highlights—2007</u>, 2009.

(3) <u>KCI the Anti-Meth Site, Methamphetamine FAQ. 1999-2011</u>. July 24, 2011.
http://www.kci.org/meth_info/faq_meth.htm

(4) Wells, Matthew. "Fighting the meth epidemic in rural US." BBC News. October 31, 2005. June 1, 2011.
http://news.bbc.co.uk/2/hi/americas/4335026.stm

(5) <u>Alcoholism-statistics.com, Alcoholism in the Population</u>. 2009. June 1, 2011.
http://www.alcoholism-statistics.com/facts.php